MURDER
AT THE RACES

Also edited by Peter Haining

The Television Detectives' Omnibus: Great Tales of Crime and
   Detection
The Television Late Night Horror Omnibus
The Television Crimebusters' Omnibus
The Frankenstein Omnibus
The Vampire Omnibus

MURDER
AT THE RACES

edited by
PETER HAINING

ARTUS

Copyright © 1995 edited by Peter Haining

The right of Peter Haining to be identified as the author of this
work has been asserted by him in accordance with the
Copyright, Designs and Patents Act 1988.

First published in Great Britain in 1995 by Orion

This edition published by Artus Books,
an imprint of Orion Books Ltd
Orion House, 5 Upper St Martin's Lane, London WC2H 9EA

A CIP catalogue record for this book is available
from the British Library

ISBN 1 898799 46 6

Typeset by Deltatype Ltd, Ellesmere Port, Cheshire
Printed in Great Britain by Clays Ltd, St Ives plc

For
BOB TANNER
– a good judge of horseflesh
and fiction!

'The chicanery of the Turf is boundless.'

LOUIS HENRY CURZON

Contents

3 FIXED ODDS: *Crime and the Gamblers*

Introduction

'You do not watch a race, you read it.'
BERYL MARKHAM

Perhaps the most unforgettable and certainly the most unusual sight in Newmarket is a skeleton. Not a human skeleton, but that of the great racehorse, Eclipse, from whose birth in 1764, 'English racing may be dated', according to the historian Nimrod. It stands in the National Horseracing Museum in the centre of the town like a monument to the high drama which has always been an integral part of the world of the Turf. In fact, the slightly unnerving appearance of these bones also seems to exemplify the town itself – a place where the glamour of racing mixes with the rigorous demands of training, the sweat of animals and men and even a little of the shady side of the 'Sport of Kings'. Newmarket has not been described as a potent combination of horseflesh and money without good reason.

Wherever there is racing there is also ambition and greed, crime and death, and Newmarket – known far and wide as the 'Headquarters' of racing – has seen more than its share of these during the three hundred years of its existence as one of the focal points of the sport. As long ago as 1677 when racing was still in its infancy, a plot was only just foiled to assassinate Charles II and the Duke of York while they were visiting Newmarket. Last year there was no such good fortune for a well-known local trainer Alex Scott when he was brutally murdered at his home, the story of his killing making headlines all over the world.

For a long period in the seventeenth century desperate trainers and ruined gamblers fought duels in the shadow of Warren Hill (now famous for its gallop), while highwaymen plagued the roads leading into the town intent on emptying the pockets of racegoers even before they reached the course on Newmarket Heath.

Charles II had another brush with crime at Newmarket which

was more amusing than life-threatening, though it does throw further light on how the Newmarket legend has grown. The eighteenth-century antiquarian William Stukeley was responsible for preserving the details of the events for posterity:

During one meeting the king is said to have seen a pickpocket take a snuff-box out of Lord Arlington's pocket. The rogue, catching the king's eye upon him, had the impudence to put his finger up to his nose and make a sign, with a wink, to say nothing. The king, with like presence of mind, took the hint, and enjoyed the earl's feeling about soon after in one pocket and another, and looking all around him; and then calling to him, said, 'You need not give yourself any more trouble about it, your box is gone, and I own myself an accomplice; I could not help it, I was made a confidant!'

Even when the dangerous 'gentlemen of the road', with their swift horses and willingness to shoot reluctant victims, had been driven away from Newmarket, disgraceful scenes still continued to occur as a report from the *Morning Post* of 19 April 1773 relates:

To the no small mortification of the black-legged family, Hell is broken up at Newmarket, more on account of the general scarcity of cash, than any inclination to suppress gambling. Mother N—ls—n and four fillies kicked up an uncommon riot on account of some indignity offered to her wards. The affray first opened with female execrations, and the brandishing of a pair of tongs, fire-shovel, and poker; at last the attack was general, when jockeys, bawds, whores, noblemen and gentlemen, aided in the deadful engagement.

Ever since the voluptuous Nell Gwynn – Charles II's famous mistress – first came to the Newmarket races (and is now commemorated in the Stakes which bear her name run each April) sex has been another element of local racing life. As J. P. Hore wrote of Nell in his classic study *The History of Newmarket* (1886), 'During the race meeting at the Head-Quarters of the Turf, she usually occupied the house which was her property, adjoining the royal seat, where the king and courtiers paid her frequent visits. Like many other distinguished females of the period she loved to wager on a horse-race.' (Mr Hore also records an intriguing mystery about a local story that there was a subterranean passage running between the king's residence and Nell's house in the direction of the Rutland Arms.)

Two hundred years after Nell had entertained Newmarket, a leading jockey was allegedly enticed into losing a race in which he was riding the favourite in return for enjoying the favours of a rival owner's beautiful, unscrupulous wife. Little has changed today, according to a report by Jamie Reid in the *Independent on Sunday* in November 1994, in which he chronicled the sexual proclivities of certain members of the racing fraternity: 'Then there was the trainer who had to sack his jockey not only because he was selling information to a bookmaker, but because he was having an affair with his wife, too. As it happens, the trainer's wife was also having an affair with another employee, but the trainer took longer to work that one out.'

Bookmakers, too, have come in vast numbers and in all shades of honesty and villainy to the races, giving rise to the conviction of writer John Gully that without them there would have been no Newmarket.

The term 'fixing the favourite' might almost have been invented here. According to J. P. Hore, the running of horses was being interfered with as early as the reign of James I, necessitating the introduction of tougher laws. 'The sheriff was called upon to officiate as starter of all the races,' Mr Hore writes by way of example, 'and if any rider committed foul play during the race he was to be committed to prison and the horse disqualified in case it won.'

In 1809 the town was the centre of a horse-poisoning scandal, during which the *Racing Calendar* offered a reward of 100 guineas for 'the discovery and conviction of the person or persons who poisoned the water in a trough belonging to J. Stevens, stable keeper, from which the horses drank'. Despite the fact two horses died and there was widespread suspicion in the racing community, the reward failed to unmask the culprits. Then in 1811 another similar offence occurred at the stables of trainer Richard Prince, with four horses dying and several others becoming seriously ill. Now the Jockey Club stepped in and, discovering that the water had been treated with arsenic, offered a much increased reward of 500 guineas.

This time the lure worked and the subsequent events have been recorded by the anonymous author of *Horse Racing: Its History & Great Races* (1863):

On 15 August, 1811, a low touter of the name Daniel Dawson was apprehended at Brighton and was tried at the Cambridge Assizes in 1812 for the offence. At this trial, his accomplice, Cecil Bishop, turned king's evidence, and from his disclosures it appeared that in 1809, Dawson had poisoned some horses at Doncaster by putting corrosive sublimate into a trough there. At Dawson's instigation, Bishop went to Newmarket and put the arsenic into Mr Prince's trough by means of a crooked syringe.

Despite Bishop's confession of administering the fatal dose, at the end of the trial Dawson was the one found guilty and sentenced to death. He was hanged at Cambridge on 8 August 1812.

There are some grim memorials to be seen in the Newmarket cemetery right opposite the racecourse: a number marking the last resting place of well-known trainers and jockeys lying cheek by jowl with several notorious contemporaries. There are even some horses buried in the grounds, including the celebrated Brigadier Gerard. A dark, massive marble cross nearby looms over the tomb of the great Fred Archer with a small notice hanging on the surrounding railings giving details of the triumphs of this prodigious but ultimately tragic son of Newmarket: 2,748 winners, 21 classics and five Derby triumphs.

That other favourite son of the town, Lester Piggott, has also, of course, had his brush with the law over his finances. Lester's widely quoted statement that his only bank account was with the local NatWest branch still causes the odd, wry smile on the faces of local people as they pass the bank's premises in the High Street.

Even the names of some of the winning horses that have run on the Rowley Mile, Beacon and July courses in years gone by smack of its colourful and shady tradition: Patch Buttocks, Louse, Tickle-me-Quickly, Jenny-Come-Tie-Me and, most bizarre of all, Kill-'em-and-eat-'em!

But although Newmarket has certainly had its fair share of crimes and mysteries, it is by no means the only racing centre to have earned notoriety. Other hot-beds of the turf, such as Ascot, Brighton and Epsom, though more stylish in appearance, still nurse their own dark secrets. I have merely chosen the town as an example of the sort of environment from which many of the stories in this collection have sprung. Plus the fact that Newmarket is not far from where I live and is a place I like to visit and watch the horses and their riders at the gallops early in the morning, or else mingle with the stable lads, assistant trainers and junior managers who crowd the pubs, restaurants and two night clubs in the evening. With its sixty stables and over 2,000 racehorses, it is a microcosm of all the different elements to be found in the world of racing – and where enough drama occurs to inspire any writer. The town's sombre clock tower and sprinkling of Gothic-style stables give an added air of mystery to the locality on dark nights and winter mornings.

Novels and stories about the turf have, in fact, been appearing for close on a century and a half – even more prolifically of late with the success of Dick Francis, John Francome, Mark Daniel and their ilk. But years before them, Nat Gould, Edgar Wallace, Bat Masters and others were similarly drawing on the glamour of the sport, the excitement of gambling and the thrill of the race to create stories unlike any others in fiction. Amongst these have been a considerable number devoted specifically to crime and murder on the turf and it is the best of these which I have brought together in these pages.

One day whilst researching the book I unexpectedly came across a remark by the Irish novelist Patrick Boyle in which he attempted to define the qualities of a writer. It was a typically colourful quote from a member of that great nation of storytellers who also happen to be among the most passionate racegoers.

'A writer,' Boyle explained, 'is someone with the morals of a tom-cat, the tenderness of Jack the Ripper, and the respect for private property of a racecource pickpocket.'

Now, while I would not specifically label any of *my* contributors with these qualities, immorality, murder and crime are very evident in the stories they tell.

Another remark which I chanced across by the anonymous author of the old volume *Horse Racing* that I mentioned earlier also seemed very apt and perfectly summarized the intent of this book.

'Evils often spring out of the most harmless occupations and amusements,' the Victorian scribe wrote, 'and in many cases even grave and serious matters are perverted to bad purposes by those of bad principles and evil inclinations. It is certain to my mind that the Turf scandals of the present age are not more disgraceful in their nature than they were in the past.'

It is a remark with which I now heartily agree – and it only leaves me to add that my stable of contributors await your selection and, I trust, your enjoyment.

PETER HAINING
Boxford, Suffolk

Under Starter's Orders

JOHN MASEFIELD

(From *Right Royal*, 1920)

Now you need no telling of Compton Course.
It's a dangerous course at the best of times,
But on days like this some jumps are crimes;
With a field like this, nigh forty starting,
After one time round it'll need re-charting.

Now think it a hunt, the first time round;
Don't think too much about losing ground,
Lie out of your ground, for sure as trumps
There'll be people killed in the first three jumps.
The second time round, pipe hands for boarding,
You can see what's doing and act according.

Now your horse is a slug and a sulker too,
Your way with the horse I leave to you;
But, sir, you watch for these jokers' tricks
And watch that devil on number six;
There's nothing he likes like playing it low,
What a horse mayn't like or a man mayn't know,
And what they love when they race a toff
Is to flurry his horse at taking off.
The ways of the crook are hard to learn.

Now watch that fence at the outer turn;
It looks so slight but it's highly like
That it's killed more men than the Dyers' Dyke.
It's down in a dip and you turn to take it,

And men in a bunch, just there, mistake it.
But well to the right, it's firmer ground,
And the quick way there is the long way round.
In Cannibal's year, in just this weather,
There were five came down at that fence together.
I called it murder, not riding races.

I

SPORT OF KILLERS

Mystery on the Course

'I do not say that all those who go racing
are rogues and vagabonds, but I do say
that all rogues and vagabonds go racing.'

SIR ABE BAILEY

The Protection Racket

DICK FRANCIS

Several of the most dramatic moments in any murder story occur on Brighton Racecourse in Graham Greene's classic crime novel, *Brighton Rock*, the seedy tale of Pinky, the psychotic leader of a gang working the racetracks who manipulates both the punters and his fellow crooks. The novel has been called Greene's finest work and this, combined with John Boulting's exceptional 1947 film version starring Richard Attenborough as the young killer, has given the course a kind of notoriety in popular folklore that is unique.

Brighton is also the location of this first story by Dick Francis, in which he draws on his own intimate knowledge of racing as well as the well-documented reports of the protection rackets that once plagued British courses. These mostly occurred in the years between the two world wars when warfare broke out between rival gangs of criminals who were determined to cash in on the new-found prosperity of punters and bookies. According to Roger Mortimer in his history of *The Jockey Club* (1958), 'The enforcement of the "protection" racket and the corruption over bookmakers' pitches were just two lines that brought rich rewards to the perpetrators, especially as clients who displayed any reluctance to comply were not infrequently subjected to extreme physical violence. In fact so bold did some of these desperadoes become that they did not hesitate to set about their victims, in broad daylight and in full public view, on the racecourse . . .'

There are, indeed, numerous accounts of pitched battles between gangs from London and Birmingham, fighting over their 'territory', using razors, knives, bottles and even firearms, and this state of affairs was not brought under control until 1923, when the Jockey Club at last set up their own body of men to supervise security at racecourses and employed a number of highly experienced former police officers to carry out the job. Even so, there were still sporadic outbursts of warfare between the racketeers until just before the outbreak of the Second World War, the last of these occurring at Lewes, not far from Brighton, where, thanks to a tipoff, the police were able to swoop on a number of brawling criminals and haul them off to trial at the Sussex Assizes where all were given punitive prison sentences.

Dick Francis (1920–) is one of the world's best-selling crime writers, and certainly the greatest contemporary author of mysteries about the racing world. A former amateur and professional National Hunt jockey, he won numerous awards on the turf before becoming even more successful as a writer – though he did not actually publish his first book until he was nearly forty. Born in Tenby, Dick served in the RAF 1940–45 and then became a steeplechase jockey. After crowning his career by becoming National Hunt Champion 1953–4, he worked as the *Sunday Express* racing correspondent for over a decade before writing the first of his best-selling novels, *Dead Cert*, in 1962. This was later filmed, and his books have also inspired two TV series, *The Racing Game* and the *Dick Francis Mysteries*.

During his career in the saddle, Dick became used to taking hard knocks – perhaps the hardest of all the sensational collapse of the Queen Mother's horse Devon Lock when he seemed certain to win the 1956 Grand National – and this is something that his fictional characters invariably have to face, too. It was, in fact, that bizarre accident at Aintree which prompted him to begin writing his gripping thrillers and, like that other great lover of the turf, Agatha Christie, he has since produced a new book every year for his huge circle of admirers. Though Dick says he finds writing 'just as tiring as riding in a race', it is a task he relishes. Even today, he still considers himself 'just a jockey who has a story to tell' – and in the following pages combines both of these talents in recounting the drama of a steeplechaser who has fallen foul of a protection gang and literally has to ride for his life . . .

*

All the drivers climbed out of the Marconicar taxis and stood in a dark group on the road beside the racecourse car park. I sat on Admiral halfway up the opposite field, watching them. They seemed to be in no hurry, but having seen their armoury of bicycle chains, knives, and assorted knuckledusters, I had no doubt what would happen if I let them catch me.

The only weapon I carried myself was a paper-wrapped roll of pennies knotted into a sock, a home-made cosh in my trouser pocket. Useless against so many and such pitiless opponents. The bruises on my body from a previous brush with them had barely faded. The scar on my cheek would last for ever.

The Protection racket they ran in Brighton had left a trail of smashed and terrorized little businesses. Their leader, who was to me only a husky voice on the telephone, had warned me often enough to leave his organization alone, and I had dug away at it and paid no heed, and they knew if I escaped them now they all had long-term cells to look forward to. The weeks I had spent investigating them had borne fruit. I had started on their trail after they killed a good friend of mine, an amateur steeplechase jockey like myself; and it looked as if at last I had split the whole hornets' nest wide open.

Just in time I spotted the ambush they had laid for me in the car park of the West Sussex course at the end of the afternoon. If Admiral had not been there walking round to cool off after the race we had just won together, my future would have been a matter of half an hour at the most. It took them by surprise, my sudden dash for the horse, and I was off the racecourse, across the road, and over the fence into the opposite field before they had collected their wits.

Although my hasty escape had meant taking Admiral as he was – bridled, but wearing only a rug, no saddle – I was in a fairly good position. The men could not drive the taxis up the field because there was no gate into it from the road, nor could they hope to reach me on foot. But two things quickly happened to change the picture. First, they began looking and pointing towards the side of the field I was in. Turning my head to the right I saw a car driving downhill on the farther side of the hedge, and realised that there was a road there. Twisting round, I now took note for the first time that a large house with out-buildings and gardens spread extensively across the skyline.

Three of the Marconicars detached themselves from the line and drove round into the road on my right, stopping at intervals along it. I now had the enemy to the right and ahead and the big house at my back, but I was still not unduly dismayed.

Then yet another Marconicar came dashing up and stopped with a jerk. A stocky man swung open the door and raised himself out of the driver's seat. He strode across the road to the hedge, and stood there pointing up at me with his arm extended. I was still wondering why when I heard the low whine of a bullet passing at the level of my feet. There was no sound of a shot.

As I turned Admiral to gallop off across the field, a bullet hit the ground with a phut in front of me. Either the range was too far for accurate shooting with a gun fitted with a silencer, or . . . I began to sweat . . . the marksman was aiming deliberately low, not at me but at Admiral.

It was only an eight- or ten-acre field, nothing like big enough for safety. I used precious moments to pull the horse up and take a look at the ragged sprawling hedge on the far side of the field. It was threaded half-way up with barbed wire. Over my shoulder I could see the man with the gun running along the road parallel to the course I had just taken. He would soon be within range again.

I took Admiral back a little way, faced him towards the hedge and urged him to jump. He cleared the whole thing, wire and all, without bending so much as a twig. We landed in another field, this time occupied by a herd of cows but again small and much too open to the road. Also, I discovered, trotting along the top boundary, that barbed wire had been laid lavishly in three strong strands all round it. All pastures have a gate, however, and I came to it in the farthest corner. I opened it, guided Admiral through into the next field, and shut it behind me.

This field was fenced with posts and wire only, and it was the extent of the barbed wire which decided me then to put as much space as I could between me and my pursuers in the shortest possible time. If I let the taxi drivers follow me slowly from field to field I might find myself in a corner that even Admiral could not jump out of.

I was glad the sun was shining, for at least I could tell in which direction I was going. Since I was already headed towards the east, and because it seemed sensible to have a definite destination to aim for, I decided to take Admiral back to his own stable in the yard where he was trained.

I reckoned I had about twelve miles to cover, and I racked my brains to remember what the country was like in between. I knew the patchwork farmland which I was then grappling with gave way at some point ahead to Forestry Commission plantations. Then there would be a short distance of bare downland before I reached the hollow and the small village where the training stables lay. Of the roads which crossed this area I had but the vaguest idea, and on any of them I could be spotted by a cruising Marconicar.

With this thought uncomfortably in mind, I found another by-road ahead. I let myself out on to it through a gate, and was trotting down it, looking for an opening in the neglected growth on the other side, when a squat black car swept round a distant bend and sped uphill towards me. Without giving Admiral a good chance to sight himself I turned him sharply towards the overgrown hedge and kicked his ribs.

It was too high for him, and too unexpected, but he did his best. He leaped straight into the tangle of sagging wire and beech saplings, crashed his way heavily through, and scrambled up almost from his knees on to the higher ground of the next field. It had been ploughed and planted with mangolds and made heavy going, but I urged him into a canter, hearing behind me the screech of brakes forcefully applied. A glance showed me the driver thrusting through the hole Admiral had made, but he did not try to chase me and I realized thankfully that he was not the man with the gun.

All the same, he had his radio. My whereabouts would be known to all the Marconicars within a minute.

I put another field between us and the taxi before pulling up and dismounting to see what damage Admiral had done himself. To my relief there were only a few scratches and one jagged cut on his stifle from which a thread of blood was trickling. I left it to congeal.

Patting his neck and marvelling at how he retained his calm sensible nature in very upsetting circumstances, I grasped the leather roller he wore round his middle, and sprang up again on to his back. The rug he was wearing now gaped in a right-angled tear on one side, but I decided not to take it off as it gave more purchase for my legs than riding him completely bareback.

Three or four fields farther on the arable land began to give way to bracken, and ahead lay the large enclosures of the Forestry Commission.

The trees, mostly conifers, were being grown in large orderly expanses with rough tracks between each section. These acted both as convenient roadways for the foresters and as breaks in case of fire. They occurred about one in each half-mile, and were crossed at intervals by tracks leading in the opposite direction.

I wanted to set a course towards the south-east, but by consulting my watch and the sun in conjunction, found that the tracks ran from almost due north to south, and from east to west. Fretting at the extra mileage this was going to cost me, I steered Admiral into an eastbound track, took the next turning right to the south, then the next left to the east, and so on, crabwise across the forest.

The sections of trees were of varying ages and stages of growth, and turning again to the south, I found the area on my left was planted with trees only two feet high. This did not specially alarm me until I saw, a hundred yards to my left, a red and white motor coach speeding along apparently through the middle of the plantation.

I pulled Admiral up. Looking carefully I could see the posts and the high wire fence which formed the boundary between the little trees and the road beyond. If I turned east at the next track according to schedule, I would be facing straight down to the road.

The far side of the road looked similar to the section I was in: regular rows of conifers, put there by careful design.

At some point, I knew, I would have to cross a road of some

sort. If I retreated back into the part of the forest I had crossed and took no risks, I would have to stay there all night. All the same, I thought, as I cantered Admiral along the southbound track and turned into the east one, I could have wished for more cover just at that moment.

Ahead of me the wire gates to the road were open, but before going through them I stopped and took a look at the other side of the road. Not all the plantations were surrounded by high mesh wire like the one I was in, and opposite only three strands of plain wire threaded through concrete posts barred the way.

The road had to be crossed quickly because where I was I felt as sheltered as a cock pheasant on a snow field. The heads in all the passing cars turned curiously towards me. But I saw nothing which looked like a Marconicar, and waiting only for a gap in the traffic, I clicked my tongue and set Admiral towards the wire fence opposite. His hooves clattered loudly on the tarmac, drummed on the firm verge, and he lifted into the air like a bird. There was no track straight ahead, only some fairly sparsely growing tall pines, and as Admiral landed I reined him in to a gentle trot before beginning to thread a way through them.

Coming eventually to another track I checked again with my watch and the sun to make sure it was still running from east to west, which it was, and set off along it at a good pace. The going underfoot was perfect, dry and springy with loam and pine needles, and Admiral, though he had completed a three-mile race and covered several miles of an unorthodox cross-country course, showed no signs of flagging.

We made two more turns and the sky began to cloud over, dulling the brilliant spring afternoon; but it was not the fading of beauty which bothered me so much as the fact that you cannot use a wrist watch as a compass unless the sun is shining. I would have to be careful not to get lost.

Just ahead, to my right, a small grass-grown hill rose sharply to its little rounded summit, the conifer forest flowing round its edges like sea round a rock. I had now left the bigger trees and was cantering through sections of young feathery pines only slightly taller than the top of my head, and I could see the hill quite clearly.

A man, a black distant silhouetted man, was standing on the top, waving his arms.

I did not connect him with myself at all because I thought I had slipped my pursuers, so that what happened next had the full shock of a totally unexpected disaster.

From a track to the right, which I had not yet reached and could not see, a sleek black shape rolled out across my path and stopped, blocking the whole width of the track.

The young pines on each side of me were too thick and low-growing to be penetrated. I flung a look over my shoulder. Another squat black Marconicar was bumping up the track behind me.

I was so close to the car ahead that I could see one of the men looking out of the rear window with a gloating grin on his face, and I decided then that even if I broke Admiral's neck and my own in trying to escape, it would be a great deal better than tamely giving in.

There was scarcely a pause between the arrival of the taxi and my legs squeezing tight into Admiral's sides.

I had no reason to suppose he would do it. A horse can dare just so much and no more. He had had a hard day already. He might be the best hunter-'chaser in England, but . . . The thoughts flickered through my brain in a second and were gone. I concentrated wholly, desperately, on getting Admiral to jump.

He scarcely faltered. He put in a short stride and a long one, gathered the immense power of his hindquarters beneath him, and thrust himself into the air. Undeterred even by the opening doors and the threatening shouts of the men scrambling out, he jumped clear over the gleaming black bonnet. He did not even scratch the paint.

I nearly came off when we landed. Admiral stumbled, and I slipped off the rug round on to his shoulder, clinging literally for dear life to the leather roller with one hand and Admiral's plaited mane with the other. The reins hung down, swaying perilously near his galloping feet, and I was afraid he would put his foot through them and trip. I still had one leg half across his rump, and, bumping heavily against his side, I hauled myself inch by inch on to his back. A warning twinge in my shoulder told me my recently broken, newly-mended collar-bone could not be relied upon for too much of this, but leaning along his neck and holding on with all my strength, I reached the reins, gathered them up, and finally succeeded in reducing Admiral to a less headlong pace.

When I got my breath back I looked to see if the taxi was following, but it was so far behind that I was not sure whether it was moving or not. I could not spare time to stop and find out.

I realized that I had underestimated the Marconicars, and that it was only thanks to Admiral's splendid courage that I was still free. They had had an advantage in knowing the lie of the land, and had used the little hill as a spotting point. I suspected that its summit commanded quite a large area, and that as soon as I had entered the younger pines I had been seen.

I was forced to admit that they had guessed which direction I would take and had circled round in front of me. And that being so, they probably knew I had been making for the stable. If I went on I should find them in my way again, with perhaps as little warning and less chance of escape.

I had left the hill behind me, and turned right again on the next track, seeing in the distance a section of taller trees. The horse cantered along tirelessly, but he could not keep it up for ever. I had to reach shelter as quickly as I could, out of sight of the man still standing on the hill-top, and out of the danger of being ambushed on another of the straight and suddenly uninviting tracks. Once we were hidden in the big trees, I promised Admiral, he should have a rest.

The light was dim under the tall pines. They had been allowed to grow close together to encourage their bare trunks to height, and the crowns of foliage far above were matted together like a roof, shutting out most of the daylight. I was glad for the obscurity. I slowed Admiral to a walk and dismounted as we entered the trees, and we went quietly and deeply into them. It was like walking through a forest of telegraph poles. Which of course, I thought fleetingly, perhaps they were destined to be.

The forest felt like home, even though it was different from those I was schooled in as a child in Rhodesia. It was very quiet, very dark. No birds at all. No animals. The horse and I went steadily on, silent on the thick pine needles, relying on instinct to keep us on a straight course.

I did not find our situation particularly encouraging. Whichever way I went in this extensive plantation I would have to come to a road in the end, and within three or four square miles the Marconicars knew exactly where I was. They had only to stand round the forest like hounds waiting for the fox to break cover, then it would be view tally-ho over the radio intercoms and the hunt would be on again.

There was a track ahead. A narrow one. I tied the reins round a tree and went forward alone. Standing still on the edge of the track and giving, I hoped, a good imitation of a tree trunk in my tweed suit, I slowly turned my head both ways. The daylight was much stronger on the track owing to the gap in the trees overhead, and I could see quite clearly for several hundred yards. There was no one in sight.

I went back for Admiral, made a final check, and led him across the track. There was no alarm. We walked steadily on. Admiral had begun to sweat long ago and had worked up a lather, damping large patches of the rug. Now that he was cooling down it was not good for him to keep it on, but I hadn't a dry one to give him. I decided that a damp rug was better than no rug, and trudged on.

Eventually I began to hear the hum of traffic and the occasional toot of a horn, and as soon as I could see the road in the distance I tied Admiral to a tree and went on alone again.

The end of the plantation was marked by a fence made of only two strands of stout wire, looking as if it were designed mainly to prevent picnickers driving their cars farther in than the verge. I chose a tree as near to the fence as I could get, dropped down on to my belly behind it, and wriggled forward until I could look along the road. There was only sporadic traffic on it.

On the far side of the road there were no plantations, and no fence either. It was unorganized woodland, a mixture of trees, rhododendrons, and briars. Perfect cover, if I could reach it.

A heavy lorry ground past five feet from my nose, emitting a choking cloud of diesel fumes. I put my face down into the pine needles and coughed. Two saloon cars sped by in the other direction, one trying to pass the other, followed by a single-decker country bus full of carefree people taking home their Tuesday afternoon's shopping. A pair of schoolgirls in green uniform cycled past without noticing me, and when their high twittering voices had faded into the distance and the road was empty, I put my hands under my chest to heave myself up and go back for Admiral.

At that moment two Marconicars came into sight round a bend. I dropped my face down again and lay absolutely still. They drove past my head slowly, and though I did not look at them, I guessed they must be staring keenly into the forest. I hoped wholeheartedly that I had left Admiral far enough back to be invisible, and that he would not make a noise.

The Marconicars swerved across the road and pulled up on the opposite verge barely twenty-five yards away. The drivers got out of the taxis and slammed the doors. I risked a glance at them. They were lighting cigarettes, leaning casually against the taxis, and chatting. I could hear the mumble of their voices, but not what they were saying.

They had not seen me, or Admiral. Yet. But they seemed to be in no hurry to move on. I glanced at my watch. It was six o'clock. An hour and a half since I had jumped off the racecourse. More important, there was only one hour of full daylight left. When it grew dark my mobility on Admiral would end and we should have to spend the night in the forest, as I could not get him to jump a fence if he could not see it.

There was a sudden clattering noise from one of the taxis. A driver put his hand through the window and brought out a hand microphone attached to a cord. He spoke into it distinctly, and this time I could make out what he said.

'Yeah, we got the road covered. No, he ain't crossed it yet.' There was some more clattering on the taxi radio, and the driver answered. 'Yeah, I'm sure. I'll let you know the second we see him.' He put the microphone back in the taxi.

I began to get the glimmerings of an idea of how to use the manhunt I had caused.

But first things first, I thought; and slowly I started to slither backwards through the trees, pressing close to the ground and keeping my face down. I had left Admiral a good way inside the forest, and I was now certain that the taxi drivers could not see him. It was uncomfortable travelling on my stomach, but I knew if I stood up the drivers would see me moving among the bare tree trunks. When finally I got to my feet my suit was a filthy peat brown, clogged with prickling pine needles. I brushed off the dirt as best I could, went over to Admiral and untied his reins.

Out in the daylight on the road I could still catch glimpses, ·between the tree trunks, of the two taxis and their drivers, but knowing that they could not see me, I set off towards the west, keeping parallel with the road and at some distance from it. It was, I judged, a little more than a quarter of a mile before I saw another Marconicar parked at the side of the road. I turned back and, as I went along, began to collect an armful of small dead branches. About half way between the parked taxis, where they were all out of my sight, I took Admiral right up to the wire fence to give him a look at it. Although extremely simple in construction, it was difficult to see in the shade of the trees. I set the dead branches up on end in a row to make it appear more solid; then jumped on to Admiral's back, and taking him back a few paces, faced him towards the fence and waited for a heavy vehicle to come along. In still air the sound of hooves on tarmacadam would carry clearly, and I did not want the taxi drivers round the nearby bends to hear me crossing the road. The longer they believed I was still in the pine forest, the better. But how long the taxis would *remain* parked I did not know, and the palms of my hands grew damp with tension.

A motor bike sped past, and I stayed still with an effort; but then, obligingly, a big van loaded with empty milk bottles came rattling round the bend on my right. It could not have been better. As it went past me I trotted Admiral forward. He made nothing of the dead-wood patch of fence, popped over on to the grass verge, took three loping strides over the tarmac, and in an instant was safely in the scrub on the far side. The milk lorry rattled out of sight.

I pulled up behind the first big rhododendron, dismounted, and peered round it.

I had not been a second too soon. One of the Marconicars was rolling slowly along in the wake of the milk lorry, and the driver's head was turned towards the forest I had left.

If one driver believed me still there, they all did. I walked Admiral away from the road until it was safe to mount, then jumped onto his back and broke him into a slow trot. The ground now was unevenly moulded into little hillocks and hollows and overgrown with brambles, small conifers, and the brown remains of last year's bracken, so I let the horse pick his own footing to a great extent while I worked out what I was going to do. After a little way he slowed to a walk and I left him to it, because if his limbs felt as heavy and tired as mine he was entitled to crawl.

As nearly as I could judge I travelled west, back the way I had come. If there is one thing you can be sure of in England, it is that a straight line in any direction will bring you to a road without much delay, and I had covered perhaps a mile when I came to the next one. Without going too close I followed it to the north.

I was hunting a prey myself, now. A taxi, detached from the herd.

Admiral was picking his way silently across a bare patch of leaf-moulded earth when I suddenly heard the now familiar clatter of a Marconicar radio, and the answering voice of its driver. I pulled up in two strides, dismounted, and tied Admiral to a nearby young tree. Then I climbed up into the branches.

Some way ahead I saw a white four-fingered signpost, and beside it stood a Marconicar, of which only the roof and the top half of the windows were visible. The rest was hidden from me by the rhododendrons, trees, and undergrowth which crowded the ground ahead. My old friend the pine forest rose in a dark green blur away to the right.

I climbed down from the tree and felt in my pocket for the roll of pennies. I also found two lumps of sugar, which I fed to Admiral. He blew down his nostrils and nuzzled my hand, and I patted his neck gently and blessed the day I got him.

With so much good cover it was easy enough to approach the cross-roads without being seen, but when, from the inside of an old rhododendron, I at length had a clear view of the taxi, the driver was not in it. He was a youngish sallow-faced man in a bright blue suit, and he was standing bareheaded in the middle of the cross-roads with his feet well apart, jingling some coins in his pocket. He inspected all four directions, saw nothing, and yawned.

The radio clattered again, but the driver took no notice. I had intended to creep up to his taxi and knock him out before he could broadcast that I was there; but now I waited, and cursed him, and he stood still and blew his nose.

Suddenly he began to walk purposefully in my direction.

For an instant I thought he had seen me, but he had not. He wheeled round a large patch of brambles close in front of me, turned his back towards my hiding place, and began to relieve himself. It seemed hardly fair to attack a man at such a moment, and I know I was smiling as I stepped out of the rhododendron, but it was an opportunity not to be missed. I took three quick steps and swung, and the sock-wrapped roll of pennies connected solidly with the back of his head. He collapsed without a sound.

I put my wrists under his shoulders and dragged him back to where I had left Admiral. Working as quickly as I could I ripped all the brown binding off the edge of the horse rug and tested it for strength. It seemed strong enough. Fishing my penknife out of my trouser pocket I cut the binding into four pieces and tied together the driver's ankles and knees with two of them. Then I dragged him closer to the tree and tied his wrists behind him. The fourth piece of binding knotted him securely to the trunk.

I patted his pockets. His only weapon was a spiked metal knuckleduster, which I transferred to my own jacket. He began to wake up. His gaze wandered fuzzily from me to Admiral and back again, and then his mouth opened with a gasp as he realized who I was.

He was not a big man in stature, nor, I now discovered, in courage. The sight of the horse looming so close above him seemed to worry him more than his trussed condition or the bump on the head.

'He'll tread on me,' he yelled, fright drawing back his lips to show a nicotine-stained set of cheap artificial teeth.

'He's very particular what he walks on,' I said.

'Take him away. Take him away,' he shouted. Admiral began to move restlessly at the noise.

'Be quiet and he won't harm you,' I said sharply to the driver, but he took no notice and shouted again. I stuffed my handkerchief unceremoniously into his mouth until his eyes bulged.

'Now shut up,' I said. 'If you keep quiet he won't harm you. If you screech you'll frighten him and he might lash out at you. Do you understand?'

He nodded. I took out the handkerchief, and he began to swear vindictively, but fairly quietly.

I soothed Admiral and lengthened his tether so that he could get his head down to a patch of grass. He began munching peacefully.

'What is your name?' I asked the taxi driver.

He spat and said nothing.

I asked him again, and he said, 'What the ruddy hell has it got to do with you?'

I needed particularly to know his name and I was in a hurry.

With no feelings of compunction I took hold of Admiral's reins and turned him round so that the driver had a good close view of a massive pair of hindquarters. My captive's new-found truculence vanished in a flash. He opened his mouth to yell.

'Don't,' I said. 'Remember he'll kick you if you make a noise. Now, what is your name?'

'John Smith.'

'Try again,' I said, backing Admiral a pace nearer.

The taxi driver gave in completely, his mouth trembling and sweat breaking out on his forehead.

'Blake.' He stumbled on the word.

'First name?'

'Corny. It's a nickname, sort of.' His eyes flickered fearfully between me and Admiral's hind legs.

I asked him several questions about the working of the radio, keeping the horse handy. When I had learned all I wanted I untied the reins from the tree and fastened them to a sapling a few feet away, so that when it grew dark the horse would not accidentally tread on the taxi driver.

Before leaving them I gave Blake a final warning. 'Don't start yelling for help. For one thing there's no one to hear you, and for another, you'll upset the horse. He's a thoroughbred, which means nervous, from your point of view. If you frighten him by yelling he's strong enough to break his reins and lash out at you. Shut up and he'll stay tied up. Get it?' I knew if Admiral broke his reins he would not stop to attack the man, but luckily, Blake did not. He nodded, his body sagging with fear and frustration.

'I won't forget you're here,' I said. 'You won't have to stay here all night. Not that I care about you, but the horse needs to be in a stable.'

Admiral had his head down to the grass. I gave his rump a pat, made sure the knots were still tight on the demoralized driver, and picked my way quickly through the bushes to the taxi.

The signpost was important, for I would have to come back and find it in the dark in miles of haphazard woodland. I wrote down all the names and mileages on all of its four arms, just to make sure. Then I got into the taxi and sat in the driver's seat.

Inside the taxi one could hear the radio as a voice and not as a clatter. The receiver was permanently tuned in so that each driver could hear all messages and replies going from taxis to base and base to taxis.

A man was saying, 'Sid, here. No sign of him. I've got a good mile and a half of the road in view from up here, nearly the whole side of the wood he's in. I'll swear he hasn't got across here. The traffic's too thick for him to do it quickly. I'm sure to see him if he tries it.' Sid's voice came out of the radio small and tinny, like a voice on the telephone, and he spoke casually, as if he were looking for a lost dog.

While he spoke I started the engine, sorted out the gears, and drove off along the road going south. The daylight was just beginning to fade. Half an hour of twilight, I calculated, and perhaps another ten minutes of dusk. I put my foot down on the accelerator.

There was a short silence on the radio. Then someone said, 'He has got to be found before dark.'

Even though I had been half-hoping, half-expecting it, the husky timbre-less whisper made me jerk in my seat. I gripped the steering wheel tightly and the muscles round my eyes contracted. The voice was so close it seemed suddenly as if the danger it spelled for me were close as well, and I had to reassure myself by looking out sideways at the deserted heathland, and backwards in the driving mirror at the empty road astern.

'We're doing our best, sir,' said a quiet voice, respectfully. 'I've been driving up and down this ruddy road for nearly an hour. Two miles up and two miles back. All the parked cars in my section are still in position.'

'How many of you have guns?' said the whisper.

'Four altogether, sir. We could do with more, to be sure of him.'

There was a pause. Then the husky voice said, 'I have one here, but you haven't time to come for it. You'll have to manage with what you've got.'

'Yes, sir.'

'Pay attention, all drivers. Aim for the horse. Shoot the horse. The man is not to be found with bullets in him. Do you understand?'

There was a chorus of assent.

'Get the horse and you've got the man . . . And you must get him. If he lives it will be the end for all of us, remember that. He knows too much . . . Tear him to pieces if you like, but no bullets. Bullets make it a hanging matter . . .'

I found it weird to eavesdrop on a man-hunt of which I was myself the quarry. All the way to Brighton I listened to the husky voice grow both more urgent and more violent as the drivers continued to turn in their negative reports.

'Blake,' he said. 'Anything your end?'

I licked my lips and swallowed, and clicked over the switch on the microphone. 'No,' I said, in as bored and nasal a tone as I could muster. He made no comment, but passed on to the next driver, and I thanked heaven that I had not had to impersonate Blake's voice for more than one second, for any attempt at conversation would have found me out.

It was with some relief that I drove into the outskirts of Brighton and made my way to the main police station, circling it until I found a quiet side turning a hundred yards away. There I stopped, close to the kerb. I turned on the side lights and shut the windows. The radio was still chattering, and the man with the husky voice could no longer keep his fury in control. For a last moment I listened to him conceding, now that time was running out, to the drivers' pleas that they should be allowed to shoot me on sight. Then with a grimace I got out of the taxi, shut the door, and walked away.

From a telephone box farther on I rang up the police and told them where to find the taxi, and to listen carefully to the murderous voices speaking on the radio. That should settle the Marconicars once and for all, I thought. But before the police followed the trail to the taxis' main office I had a private reckoning to make there myself.

Swiftly, with quickening pulse, I walked towards it along a darkening deserted street.

Nobbling the Favourite

NAT GOULD

Royal Ascot, which takes place every June, is undoubtedly the high point of the Flat Racing season. The presence of the Queen, a multitude of people from all walks of life, and some of the finest horses, all combine to make the three days of racing a glamorous and exciting event that is famous all over the world. The week has been featured in many novels – and not just those with a racing background – but probably cropped up more frequently than anywhere else in the colourful thrillers of Nat Gould, an author as popular in his day as Dick Francis and of whom the *Morning Post* once wrote, 'He is the most widely read of all modern story-tellers, and a genius in his down-right way.' On the lurid covers of Gould's paperback editions he was described as 'The Prince of Sporting Novelists' and in the year that Dick Francis was born (1920), Gould's publishers, John Long, boasted that he had sold over 30 million books worldwide. Philip Brownrigg, a literary critic and fan of Gould's novels, wrote in the *Strand Magazine* in 1948, 'I first read his racing stories at school – I remember doing it a bit furtively, as if it were one of the major term-time crimes like smoking, using a crib, or going to the cinema unaccompanied by at least one parent or guardian.'

Although the first Nat Gould novel, *The Double Event*, was published in 1890, it was not until the turn of the century that he became a phenomenon, of whom the *Nation* would write, 'In the way of sales, his books surpass all others – and we have heard that a newspaper purchasing the serials rights of one of his stories could promise itself an increased circulation of 100,000 a day, no matter what its politics or principals.' Many of his 150 racing novels remained in paperback until the late thirties, but since then their ephemeral nature has made them scarce and much sought after by collectors. Yet despite all his success, Gould left only £7,797 in his will: a fact which gave added emphasis to what was suspected of the author – though never admitted by him – that he bet heavily on the sport which had given him wealth and fame.

Nathaniel Gould (1857–1919) was born in Newark on Trent in Lincolnshire and began riding while working on a farm. Dissatisfied with the long hours, however, he was employed briefly in the tea trade before getting a job as a reporter on the *Newark Advertiser*. Six years later he decided to try his luck in Australia and was a reporter on the *Brisbane Daily Telegraph* for several years before moving to another paper in Sydney, where he discovered his aptitude for writing about the turf. In 1890 Nat wrote *The Double Event*, but when the sales did not live up to his expectations he returned to England and there began the voluminous output which would later earn the commendation of the Publishers' Circular that, 'One has to go back to Shakespeare or the Bible to find a rival best seller.'

Although Gould wrote all his books in longhand, he could still finish a book in under a fortnight, thanks no doubt to the speed he had learned during his time as a reporter. And of his themes, he admitted, 'I never trouble about any particular plot – I just write away till I bring the tale to its proper end.' Unlike Dick Francis who has no recurring hero, Nat Gould wrote a whole string of books about an owner named Barry Bromley, his valiant horse, Suspense, and beautiful girlfriend, Hazel Sainton. Two of the Bromley stories, *A Great Coup* and *A Fortune At Stake*, were filmed, while some of the most popular titles, such as *One of the Mob*, *A Bit of a Rogue* and *A Fortune at Stake*, sold more than half a million copies in hardback alone. 'Nobbling The Favourite' is a story of one of Barry's attempts to win the Ascot Royal Hunt Cup, justly famous as the biggest betting race of the Royal Meeting. Curiously, in the very year that Nat Gould died a financier and gambler named James White backed his horse, Irish Elegance, to win £100,000 in the Royal Hunt Cup, but when he was unable to gain entrance to the Royal Enclosure angrily left the track. Irish Elegance won with ease . . .

*

1 *RIVALS*

Hazel Sainton had been thinking a good deal about Barry Bromley of late; they were the best of friends, but she had not made up her mind to marry him.

About a fortnight after his horse Suspense won the Jubilee at Kempton Park he asked her to be his wife, and her answer was neither yes nor no. It gave him hope, but he would have preferred certainty; however, he made up his mind to wait. Hazel's aunt, Betsy Sainton, advised her to have nothing to do with Barry; he was a spendthrift, gambler, and many other things of which she did not approve. Wayland Lawton was a much better man; why did she not consider him?

To this Hazel had a quick reply. Wayland Lawton was a sharper – she was very much surprised at her aunt considering such a man as a prospective husband for her. She related how Barry had been insulted by the man at Kempton when he would have thrashed him had she not advised Barry to let him alone.

Her aunt did not believe this, although she was aware that there had been a scene between the two men on Jubilee Day. She defended Lawton and spoke highly of him; she said he was always attentive to her and a perfect gentleman; in addition to which he was a good-looking man and had money.

Hazel smiled as she answered:

'I am afraid you over-estimate him; be careful, aunt, you are still a good-looking woman with money, and Wayland Lawton may prove a danger to your peace of mind. There is no comparison between the two men, as you will ultimately discover.'

At this Betsy became indignant. It was monstrous of her niece to say such things. At the same time she was not ill-pleased to hear the opinion that she was still a good-looking woman, capable of attracting the opposite sex.

Hazel had taken a small house for Ascot and thither she and her aunt went the week before the races. Barry Bromley had his quarters at an hotel where his horse Suspense was stabled; at the same house Danny Grant, the famous jockey, stayed, and many well-known racing men, including two or three big book-makers.

The day after their arrival at The Hollies, Barry called to see Hazel. The Hollies was a charming retreat, away from the bustle of the town and the course, with pleasant gardens, and stabling where Hazel had a couple of racehorses, Sprint and Dandyman, entered in three or four races at the meeting. These horses had been bought for her by Barry, and she was well pleased with them.

She was glad to see him; there were one or two things which she wished to speak about, and she had faith in him and his judgment.

'I suppose you know Wayland Lawton is at Ascot? He has called here twice,' she said.

'Confounded impudence!' replied Barry angrily.

She laughed as she said:

'I think he has given up thinking about me. I keep out of his way.'

'Then why does he call?' asked Barry.

'You will be amused when I tell you. I rather fancy he's paying his attentions to Aunt Betsy,' she returned.

'Nonsense! What a joke!' exclaimed Barry.

'You had better not let her hear you say so; it will not be a joke for her in the end,' declared Hazel seriously.

'I thought she encouraged him in paying attentions to you,' said Barry.

'So did I; she pretends it is so, but I think she does it as a cloak to hide her real feelings. She is flattered by his attentions, I am sure. Barry, we must not allow her to become this man's victim; we must save her from him,' she said.

'We'll try, but it's a delicate matter. She's—'

'Of age,' laughed Hazel.

He joined in her merriment as he replied:

'That is not what I meant. She's prejudiced against me and I don't see what I can do; however, if you suggest anything I'll do my best to carry it through.'

She thanked him and began to talk about the races and the chances of Suspense in the Royal Hunt Cup. He was favourite for the race, his win in the Jubilee having proved him a rattling good horse; he was top weight, nine stone, which was a crushing burden, but the public loved a good horse and would not be 'stalled off'. Barry was certain that he would run well and probably win; his trainer, Mike Burton, and Danny Grant were of the same opinion.

Hazel thought Barry did not speak quite so confidently about the horse's chance today. She said so, and asked the reason.

'I've a presentiment that something will happen to him,' confessed Barry.

'Have you had a bad dream about him?' she asked, smiling.

'No, but every time I go and look at him in the box I fancy there's a change in him,' he replied.

'What sort of a change?' she asked.

'I can't define it, but it's there, although Mike and Danny can't see it,' he answered.

'I will walk over with you and see him,' suggested Hazel.

'Capital! You know the old fellow and you are a good judge. Come along,' he said.

She went inside to put on her things and, coming from her room, met Betsy on the landing.

'Where are you going?' asked her aunt.

'To see Mr Bromley's horse, Suspense,' replied Hazel.

'With him?'

'Yes, of course; he's here,' answered Hazel.

Betsy shrugged her shoulders.

'You'll be sorry for encouraging him some day. Don't forget I warned you,' she said.

Hazel laughed merrily as she replied:

'I will not forget. It will be my fault if I make a mistake.'

II *INSIDE INFORMATION*

They walked along the quiet lane until they came to the town; already there were many people in the place, and there was every sign of the big meeting approaching. Ascot during race week is very different from what it is at normal times.

They arrived at the hotel and went at once to the stables where they found Suspense just returned from afternoon exercise. As usual, he had been watched entering the yard by a crowd of more or less interested spectators.

At first sight the horse appeared quite well, and Hazel noticed no difference in him; yet, in some unaccountable way, she seemed to know that there was something wrong; what it was it would have been difficult to state.

It was some minutes before she spoke, looking him carefully over, and running her hand along his coat; it felt soft and healthy, silky to her touch.

Barry watched her anxiously; was she of his opinion that there was something wrong?

'There's a change in him,' she admitted, 'but what it is I cannot say. He looks all right; perhaps it is presentiment, like yours.'

'I hope so,' he returned. 'I thought you'd notice it. What's to be done?'

'How do you mean – in what way?' she asked.

'If there's anything wrong, somebody is trying to, or has already nobbled him; that's the correct expression,' returned Barry.

'And nobbling the favourite is a serious matter,' said Hazel. 'Is he well watched day and night?'

'Yes, Billy Cope sleeps in his box.'

'And is Billy reliable?'

'I'm sure he is; at least, he's been found so up to now.'

'There are many people about here, in and out of the yard, in the daytime,' reminded Hazel.

'But I do not think anything could be done then. It must be at night,' replied Barry. 'I'll be on the look-out until the race is over.'

She looked at him anxiously. Had he seen her expression it would have made his pulses beat more quickly, but he was looking at Suspense and did not notice it. She knew that if an attempt were made, desperate men would be engaged in it, who would stick at nothing, and if Barry interfered he might be injured, perhaps seriously.

She had tea with him at the hotel, and he then walked with her to The Hollies.

As he was leaving she said:

'Be careful! There must be danger to anybody who interferes with their plans.'

'Then you really think the horse is in danger?' he queried.

'I was not thinking of the horse, but of you. Take care of yourself,' replied Hazel.

'You are anxious about me – you do not wish me to run into danger?' he asked quickly.

'Naturally. Are you not one of my best friends?' she answered.

'Not the best, only one of them?' he countered.

'The best if you wish,' she said, giving him a bright smile.

As Hazel was about to go upstairs she heard voices in her aunt's sitting-room. Betsy always insisted on having one such room to herself no matter where they were. It was a man's voice which she heard. It could only be Wayland Lawton; what was he doing here? He had called in the morning – why did he come again in the afternoon? Something prompted her to listen, which she had never done before. She went quietly to the door and heard her aunt say:

'Well, if you think so, Mr Lawton, I will act on your advice and give you the money to invest for me.'

She heard Lawton reply:

'I am quite certain Suspense cannot win with nine stone; more than that, I don't mind telling you that I do not think he will run. Please do not mention it to anybody.'

'It is very good of you,' returned Betsy. 'I am not a gambler, but I think when a friend tells me what you have told me, I ought to follow the advice; wait a moment and I will give you the money.'

'Oh, that's of no consequence! Any time will do,' said Wayland.

'I'd much rather give it to you now,' answered Betsy.

Hazel had just time to run quickly to the back door leading into the garden, when her aunt came out of the room and hurried upstairs. Hazel was about to go into the garden when she heard footsteps; it must be Lawton coming out of the room. She saw him look up the stairs and hesitate a moment; there was that in his face which made her shudder. She would not have been at all surprised had he followed her aunt, on robbery bent – the man at this moment looked capable of anything. He changed his mind and went into the room again.

Hazel breathed more freely; she had no doubt that his intention for the moment had been dangerous, but evidently he had thought better of it. Betsy came down, went into the room, and a few minutes later she let Lawton out at the front door. He said, as he shook hands:

'I will call on Sunday afternoon if I may?'

'Of course you may! I shall be delighted to see you,' she replied.

Hazel came into the room with her hat on.

'I did not hear you come in,' said Betsy.

'I waited until he left,' she replied. 'I have no desire to meet him again.'

'Well, you saw Suspense?' asked Betsy.

'Yes, he's in good condition – I mean, as far as training goes – but there's something wrong with him. Barry thinks so, and I agree with him. I have no doubt the horse had been nobbled,' said Hazel.

'Nobbled? What do you mean?' asked Betsy.

'Somebody has been doctoring him in order to prevent his winning the Hunt Cup,' explained Hazel, looking at her aunt questioningly.

III *THE MOVING SPIRIT*

Betsy was uneasy under the scrutiny. She wondered if Hazel had overheard Lawton's words about the horse not being able to run. It was hardly likely, yet she had a suspicion that she might have heard.

'You must be mistaken; who would do such a wicked thing?' said Betsy indignantly.

'I wonder! If it is brought home to him it will be serious; it is a criminal offence, I believe,' replied Hazel. 'What had Wayland Lawton to say? He was here this morning. Anything particular about the races? But you take very little interest in them.'

'He was good enough to tell me what he thought would win the Hunt Cup.'

'It was not Suspense, I am sure,' laughed Hazel.

'No; but why are you sure?'

'I have my reasons. What does he fancy?'

'Brocade. I have told him to put me a hundred pounds on her,' intimated Betsy.

Hazel laughed as she said:

'You had better be careful! That is a large amount. I thought you did not bet?'

'I have never had more than five pounds on before, but he is so confident about it that I thought I would risk the hundred,' explained Betsy.

Hazel thought Brocade was about the last horse to win; evidently Wayland Lawton intended pocketing her aunt's hundred – that was quite in his line.

'If Suspense does not win I hope Brocade will, but she has no chance with Suspense if he is well,' said Hazel.

'Suspense will not—' began Betsy, then suddenly stopped as she remembered that Lawton had asked her not to mention it.

'Will not what?' asked Hazel.

'Oh, nothing, my dear – I mean will not win!' replied Betsy.

'I think you intended to say Suspense will not run,' answered Hazel.

'How do you know?' asked her aunt, surprised.

'Perhaps he told you; if he did he must have some good reason,' replied Hazel.

'You will not mention it if I tell you?'

'Please yourself whether you tell me or not. I am quite sure that Wayland Lawton knows all about it.'

'About what?'

'Suspense and the cause of whatever is the matter with him,' said Hazel.

'You surely do not mean to suggest that he has had a hand in the nobbling, as you called it?'

'That is precisely what I mean. He's bad enough for anything,' answered Hazel.

Betsy fired up. She was very indignant; she proclaimed Wayland Lawton a gentleman; he would not condescend to have anything to do with such dastardly proceedings; Hazel was always unjust to him – her infatuation for Barry Bromley was responsible.

Hazel smiled at 'infatuation'; if anybody was infatuated it was her aunt with Lawton.

'Take care, aunt! You were foolish to give him money which he will put in his pocket, for Brocade has no earthly chance of winning,' she warned, at which Betsy was so annoyed that she left the room.

The same evening Hazel called at the hotel and requested to see Barry; he was out, but she determined to wait, and to pass the time away, went to the stables. She saw a man come out of Suspense's box whom she did not remember having seen before.

'Who is that man?' she asked Billy Cope.

'Think his name's Horless; he's often about the stables; he has something to do with the team in those boxes,' and he pointed across the yard.

'Did he ask to see Suspense?'

'No, he just came into the box and spoke to me; he asked what sort of a chance he had on Wednesday. We fellows in the yard often talk over the races,' replied Billy.

'I don't think you ought to allow anybody into the box,' said Hazel. 'What do you think of Suspense?'

'He's all right, as fit as can be. He ought just about to win,' replied Billy.

Hazel walked on, Billy's eyes following her.

'Now, I wonder what's brought her round here? Seems a bit suspicious,' he muttered. 'I don't see what women want wandering about stable yards, it's not the place for 'em; they'll want to be "doing the horses" next.'

Hazel saw Barry go into the hotel and went after him. He was surprised to see her. She asked for a few minutes' private conversation.

'We shall be safe from interruption here,' he said, as he opened the door of a room and they went in.

'When I returned to The Hollies this afternoon Wayland Lawton was with my aunt. They did not see me come in, and I was about to go upstairs when I heard his voice. I stopped to listen – I felt justified in doing so.'

She then went on to tell him what she had overheard, and also the conversation with her aunt later on.

'You are a brick to tell me!' exclaimed Barry.

'I thought you ought to know, so I came at once. I have no doubt Wayland Lawton is the instigator of the trouble with Suspense,' she said and then mentioned Horless coming out of the box and her remonstrance with Cope.

'I must try and clear the matter up,' returned Barry. 'It seems to me strange that neither Mike nor Danny can see anything wrong with him; it is very good of you to help me, Hazel.'

He looked at her in a way that she understood. She had no doubt about his love for her; it was strange that she could not make up her mind.

'I would help anybody in a case of this kind. It is monstrous that a horse, the favourite for a big race, should be tampered with. Wayland Lawton knows all about it, or he would not have told aunt that Suspense would not run,' she declared.

'He'll run,' said Barry. 'It's not as bad as that, but it may be detrimental to his chance of winning.'

IV *BIRDS OF A FEATHER*

Wayland Lawton and Lake Horless were closeted together in a room in a house in the main street of Ascot at the same time that Barry and Hazel were in the hotel.

Wayland Lawton was in a good humour, for his schemes were prospering, and Lake Horless had reported that everything was well with them. Wayland was hand-and-glove with Moses Renter, a book-maker of substance, whose character was not above reproach. Renter did shady things; making money was his object and he cared little how it was made. He had an enormous ready-money business in the ring, also an agency in London, and his turnover on a big handicap amounted to thousands.

Wayland did not think that it was necessary to confide in Horless, although he found him useful and a clever tool when well paid for his work.

'You are certain you have made no mistake?' asked Wayland.

'It doesn't pay to make mistakes,' was the reply.

'Not with me,' agreed Wayland. 'How did you manage it?'

'That's my affair; the less said about it the better. I can assure you Suspense won't be fit to run; even if he did, he'd collapse,' declared Horless.

'Did you dose him?' persisted Wayland.

'I'd rather not say. You ought to be satisfied with results,' replied Horless.

'When I see them,' corrected Wayland.

'You'll have ample proof by Monday at latest; there'll be a knocking out at the clubs that night. Can you let me have a tenner?'

Wayland knew his man; a clever scoundrel who seldom bungled, Horless had been suspected of doctoring horses before now, but was too cute to be detected. Lawton handed him a ten-pound note, one of the number received from Betsy Sainton; she would not have considered him a perfect gentleman had she been aware of that fact.

Soon after Lake Horless left, Moses Renter came into the room. He was a big, burly, coarse man, with a bloated face, small, ferret-like eyes, a close-cropped head of hair, and was dressed in a big, grey-check suit; a huge gold chain hung over his extended waistcoat. His voice sounded like thunder, his language was more forcible than polite; he was one of those men who bring discredit on the ring, and all the better-class book-makers fought shy of him.

'How goes it, Lawton?' he greeted loudly. 'I saw that crawler, Lake Horless, leave just before I came in. What had he to say?'

'Don't bawl here! You're not in the ring,' remonstrated Wayland.

'I'm not afraid of being overheard,' answered Moses, in a subdued voice, clearly showing he was. 'How goes it?'

'Suspense will not run,' declared Wayland, leaning on the table, facing him.

'The trick's been done,' said Moses, with a chuckle like a rusty file at work. 'I've laid him and overlaid him; it means thousands to me if he wins.'

'Don't I tell you he will not run?'

Moses rubbed his thick fat hands together.

'I am glad to hear that; you know how you stand?'

'Yes; it's not much.'

'Two thousand. It's a heap of money – it takes some making,' objected Moses.

'You can easily make it. You're not particular,' said Wayland.

His tone irritated the book-maker.

'Don't you talk to me like that! I've never come across a hotter member than you. Lord love me, you're a beauty to sneer at the likes o' me!' snapped Moses.

Lawton laughed as he answered:

'I don't suppose there's much difference between us; let us settle it by saying we're birds of a feather.'

Moses growled like an angry bear.

'I think my work is clean compared to some of yours,' he said. 'The main thing is, can I safely lay Suspense? If he's as bad as you say why doesn't Bromley scratch him? It's not fair to the public to keep him in till the last moment,' he added, with a grin.

'You can lay him as much as you like; he's as dead as a door-nail,' replied Lawton.

v FOUL PLAY

The same night Barry was restless, dozing in snatches, finally falling into a restless sleep about one o'clock. He was roused by a troubled dream in which he fancied that he was struggling with a man in Suspense's box. So vividly was this sight before him when he awoke that he sprang out of bed and hurriedly put on his dressing-gown. He went quietly downstairs, crossed the yard, and went to the horse's box. He tried the door and found it unlocked; this was strange, for Billy Cope slept inside and always turned the key.

Opening the top part of the door he unfastened the bolt of the lower half and went in, speaking to Suspense, who recognized his voice and whinnied softly. Lighting the gas-jet he looked round. In one corner lay Cope; at first he thought the lad was asleep, but as he bent over him he made no movement, and then he noticed a swelling on his temple; he had been stunned.

It was some minutes before he could rouse him. Billy looked

round bewildered, his head in a whirl; then his eyes dilated and he tried to speak. Before he could do so, however, Barry received a violent blow on the back of the head, and fell insensible against Cope, who had again fallen back overcome by the shock.

A man darted swiftly out of the box after a hurried glance at the horse's manger.

'They've had enough of it, so's the horse,' he muttered, as he slipped round the end of the building and vanished in the direction of the town.

When Barry came round his head ached terribly; he tried to stand but found it impossible. He crawled to the door, cried for help, then became insensible once more.

Mike Burton's window overlooked the stable yard; he heard a cry, got out of bed, opened the window, and saw somebody lying half-way out of the open door of Suspense's box.

It did not take him many minutes to pull on his clothes; he knocked at Danny's door, and said:

'Get up! There's something wrong! Suspense's box is open. I'm going down to see what's up.'

'I'll follow you in a minute,' answered Danny.

Mike hurried across the yard. He was greatly alarmed when he found that the insensible man was Barry Bromley; he was kneeling beside him when the jockey came up.

'He's in a bad way. Look here!' exclaimed Mike, as he pointed to the lump on the back of Barry's head.

'I'll call somebody to help us,' said Danny, and ran back to the hotel.

In a few minutes there was a bustling scene, for most of the people were roused by the noise and came trooping into the yard in all sorts of attire.

Meanwhile, as they gathered round, Billy Cope was discovered in the box still insensible; it was quite evident that there had been a desperate attack on the favourite. Mike examined Suspense as Barry was carried to his room in the hotel. The horse appeared all right, but the trainer had no doubt that an attempt had been made to nobble him. Had it succeeded, or had the miscreants fled when Barry was knocked down on discovering them?

Soon after he was placed on the bed Barry recovered consciousness, and almost the first thing he said was:

'Say nothing. I don't want this to get about.'

Naturally there was much excitement among the numerous people in and about the hotel, and consequently the news spread; it was impossible to prevent it.

During the morning Ascot was in a turmoil of excitement, and many people came to see the scene of the assault and the attempt on Suspense. Transmitted from one to another, the accounts became more and more exaggerated.

Hazel Sainton went into the town to make a few purchases, and learnt what had happened; she at once hastened to the hotel. Mike met her, and at her earnest request took her to Barry's room. He lay on the bed, his head bandaged, Danny Grant by his side. The doctor had said that he must be kept quiet or fever might ensue.

Barry recognized Hazel, and made an attempt to hold out his hand, but it dropped limply on the bed. She placed her hand on his arm, bent over him, and said:

'Are you very bad, Barry? I'm so sorry! I suppose they were getting at Suspense? What a dastardly act!'

Barry made a feeble gesture of assent, then seemed to go off into a doze. Hazel watched him, her eyes moist, her heart beating fast; she wondered if he were in any danger.

Mike guessed her thoughts and said:

'He's not so very bad. The doctor says he'll be about in a day or two; I hope we'll be able to lay hands on the scoundrels.'

During Hazel's absence Betsy Sainton had a visitor at The Hollies. It was Wayland Lawton. He put her in possession of the facts from his point of view. He said it was well known in certain quarters that Barry Bromley was hard pressed for money, and had, in league with some book-makers, laid a lot of money against Suspense for the Hunt Cup; that to make sure that Suspense would not run, and that blame should be put on somebody else, he had gone into the box at night to dose the horse. Billy Cope had seen somebody moving about, there had been a struggle, and both of them were badly hurt.

Betsy listened in amazement; she did not doubt what he said. The story seemed plausible to her, whatever it might be to others.

In the town all sorts of rumours were rife about the affair. Lawton circulated a more plausible version of the story which he had told Betsy Sainton, but it was received with incredulity, and few believed that Barry Bromley would be guilty of nobbling his own horse to make sure he did not run.

Sensational stories circulated during the whole of Monday, paragraphs appeared in the papers, and hints were thrown out that it was a case of nobbling the favourite. Suspense had been 'got at' and would not run for the Hunt Cup.

The wildest rumours went round towards evening, some of which reached Hazel Sainton. She was indignant. These vile accusations about Barry must be refuted; he was incapable of fighting his battles at present, so she would do it for him.

She sent Danny Grant out to find the representatives of the leading papers, which he had no difficulty in doing. Six of them came to the hotel and saw Hazel. They were much impressed by what she said, and she thoroughly convinced them that there was not an atom of truth in the ridiculous stories. She assured them that Barry had backed his horse heavily for the Hunt Cup. Apart from this nobody who knew him, as she did, could for a moment entertain such preposterous ideas about him.

Next morning the result of her interview with the pressmen was seen in the papers; one and all denounced the slanders on Barry Bromley, hinted that there had been foul play, adding that the desperate attempt to nobble the favourite had, there was reason to believe, unfortunately succeeded.

On Tuesday racing commenced, and almost the sole topic of conversation during the intervals was the sensational attack on Barry Bromley and his horse. All day Hazel remained with Barry, although he implored her to go to the races.

'I'm going to look after you,' she declared, 'so you must put up with me.'

Barry made a wonderful recovery; the doctor said he would be able to go out on Wednesday, though he would be better away from the excitement of the races if the temptation were not too strong to resist. Barry said he feared it would be.

It was from Danny Grant that Barry heard of the lying rumours about himself, and how Hazel had countered them. He was very grateful for her championship.

Hazel had an angry scene with Betsy, who told her what Wayland Lawton had said about Barry. She indignantly repudiated his assertions, and said she had very little doubt about Lawton being one of the principals in the attack in Suspense's box. So indignant was she that her aunt quailed before her righteous wrath, and said she was very sorry indeed for what had happened. As soon, however, as Hazel had left the room, she was more than half inclined to believe all that Wayland Lawton had told her.

VI NEXT BEST

The first thing that Barry did, after consulting Mike Burton and Danny Grant, was to scratch Suspense for the Hunt Cup. The horse had been dosed in some way, of that there was no doubt, and it would have been fatal to his future career to run him. It was a sore blow for backers; but none of them blamed Barry Bromley; there was much sympathy with him when he appeared in the enclosure on Hunt Cup day, his head bandaged. He was accompanied by Hazel Sainton, who had never looked more radiantly beautiful and happy.

Wayland Lawton took care to avoid Barry; he had no wish for a scene. His nefarious plot had succeeded, Suspense was scratched, and he and those connected with him had reaped a reward which was destined to bring them a long run of bad luck later on. Moses Renter said to him:

'You managed it well, but it was a fool's game to put that rumour in circulation about his nobbling the horse. Nobody believed it.'

Although Suspense was out of the Hunt Cup, Hazel Sainton's horse, Dandyman, was to run in the Visitors' Handicap, the first race of the day, and Barry was almost as much interested in the result as he would have been in the big handicap had his horse run.

Danny Grant rode Dandyman in a field of fifteen, and the finish proved one of the best at the meeting. A horse called Cocoanut was favourite, and looked all over a winner until the last furlong, when Dandyman came with a terrific rush up the hill, overhauling the field, until he finally drew level with the favourite. The excitement was tremendous. The pair came on neck and neck, neither giving way an inch. The effort which Cocoanut had made earlier in the race told in the end, and Danny, putting in one of his best finishes, won on Dandyman by a neck – a great performance which delighted Hazel.

Seeing her horse win was some recompense to Barry, but the excitement proved too much for him in his weak condition, and he had to leave the course. Hazel accompanied him, although he protested; she said that there would be no enjoyment for her in his absence.

A few weeks later, when they met in London, Barry said he had ample proof that Wayland Lawton had had a hand in the nobbling of Suspense and that he intended getting even with him in his own way. Hazel warned him it would be dangerous, but he promised to be careful.

Suspense soon got over his dosing, and Mike Burton said that he would be ready to run again during the season, which was good news to Barry, as he badly wanted a win.

A Racing Swindle

THOMAS GASPEY ('RICHMOND')

For all his fame, Nat Gould was far from being the first best-selling writer to utilize the drama of the turf in mystery stories. Indeed, what has been described as 'probably the first volume of detective stories' – a collection of cases solved by a member of the pioneer detective force known as the Bow Street Runners – contains the tale of a fraud operated at a race course near Lyndhurst in Hampshire in the early 1820s. Although detective fiction is generally stated to have begun in 1841 with the story of 'The Murders in the Rue Morgue' by the American writer Edgar Allan Poe, there were, in fact, several earlier volumes in which crimes were solved and criminals hunted down. Of these, *Richmond; or, Scenes in the Life of a Bow Street Runner*, published anonymously in 1827, is among the most important, being the only work of fiction about the Bow Street Runners and, from the point of view of this collection, the very earliest volume to contain a crime story of the turf.

The Runners were, of course, the predecessors of our modern police force: an organization of committed and brave detectives at war with crime. They got their name from their first headquarters – in Bow Street, Covent Garden – and their reputation from their unswerving devotion to duty and steadfast refusal to succumb to the corruption that was then widespread in society. Interestingly, they owed their foundation to the novelist Henry Fielding, who had taken on the role of a magistrate to supplement his income and assembled a band of men to help him fight the large number of criminals, thieves and highwaymen who then infested London and much of southern England. The Runners were, in fact, successful in solving many crimes, most notably the brutal murder of William Weare by John Thurtell and the infamous Cato Street Conspiracy.

Richmond, the hero of the 1827 book, is a hazy character rather like his creator. He appears to be a member of the foot patrol, but senior enough to have an assistant, Thady, and to be allowed to conduct enquiries on his own initiative. In the course of the book he tackles five very different cases: grave robbing, smuggling, kidnapping, deception and a racing swindle, behind all of which he senses the hand of a master criminal known only as 'Jones'.

Lyndhurst, the setting of the turf story, has for generations been regarded as the 'Capital' of the New Forest – today it is the major tourist centre in the area – and at the time of the events which are described, had been staging horse races since at least the middle of the previous century. These meetings often had an extra attraction for gamblers by the inclusion of races between partly broken colts caught in the forest and race horses. According to William White in his *Gazeteer and Dictionary of Hampshire* (1859), 'At Emery Down, amidst the richest wood-land scenery, races were held before the fairs upon the pictu-resque race course of Lyndhurst. These stirring spectacles between race horses and the forest ponies have frequently formed the subject of pictorial illustration and remained long in the memory of all those who saw them . . .'

It seems possible that the author of 'A Racing Swindle' had attended at least one of these meetings, although the evidence is scant – as it is about the man himself. Indeed, several names have been proposed as the pen behind 'Richmond', but the most likely appears to be Thomas Gaspey (1788–1871), a member of the staff of the *Morning Chronicle*, who was the paper's crime correspondent for some years and later used his knowledge as the background for several works of fiction. Amongst these was *The History of George Godfrey* (1828), the story of a criminal apprehended by clever detective work and then deported to Australia, which has been ascribed to him by the British Museum. This book is similar in style to the tale by Richmond and of all the candidates he seems the most likely creator to me. In 'A Racing Scandal', the Bow Street Runner is on the track of a group of titled gamblers who are preparing to dupe a wealthy West Indian at a meeting in Lyndhurst, and what follows is a unique tale of crime on the turf which I am delighted to be returning to print.

*

I found that it was little less difficult to procure beds at Lyndhurst during the race week, contemptible as I had imagined the sport would be, than at Doncaster or Epsom at a similar period. The landlord of the inn at which I put up, however, had, to increase the number of his rooms, hit upon a contrivance which I have sometimes seen practised in country inns to meet extraordinary demands for accommodation. This was, to divide such rooms as were large enough to be divisible by means of a temporary wooden partition, which slid in grooves, and could be removed when no longer wanted.

Into one of these half or quarter apartments (I am not certain which it was) I obtained admission by paying about thrice the ordinary price of the best room which mine host had; and I was not displeased to find that he had put the titled gamblers into the divisions next mine. These were larger and better furnished; but I suppose they cared not, in the meantime, for accommodation, so that they could succeed in their designs.

Thady returned rather late, with the excuse that he had been having a drop, to make him comfortable at the same time that he got thereby gracious with a brother tippler who was under-groom to Sir Byam, and had found means to pry into more of their schemes than they had any notion of. Many servants, indeed, make this the occasion of extorting considerable sums of money from their profligate masters, when they are knowing enough to give hints which cannot be misunderstood. Some will even go so far as to provoke their masters to quarrel with them and threaten to dismiss them, in order to get a good opportunity for introducing their private knowledge with the more effect and advantage; and when by such conduct they have once got their masters into their power, they take care to put them in frequent remembrance of it, at the expense of their purses.

Whether Jack Dobson, Sir Byam's under-groom, was playing a

game of this sort I cannot tell; but over his glass, Thady found means to get out of him all he knew of the history of his master's expedition to the Lyndhurst races. From Dobson's account, it would appear that the gamblers had picked up a fool of the first water, descended by the father's side from a family of West India planters, and by the mother's from an African princess, whom the chances of negro warfare had consigned to slavery in the British colonies.

This young creole, as I suppose I may call him, was immensely rich, and passionately fond of showing it by spending his money in making himself ridiculous, under the notion that he was an eccentric, and that eccentricity was the best passport to fashion.

Upon one point the gamblers found him not so well adapted for their modes of plunder: he had imbibed the idea that gambling was a stupid common-place amusement, which every booby took to; and that, therefore, no gentleman eccentric would think of touching a card, a cue, or a dice-box. Betting, indeed, he might occasionally be brought into, as it saved him the trouble of thinking and arguing; but he was not inclined to bet upon ordinary matters. It must be something out of the common line to strike his fancy; such, for instance, as – which of two live frogs would leap highest and farthest? or, whether a hedge-hog or a guinea-pig would swim best in a horse-pond? Upon such matters as these, which he looked upon as the essence of high eccentricity and ton, he would as freely sport his thousands as a chimney-sweeper would bet his sixpence upon a game of chuck-farthing.

Such, it appeared, was Mr Ellice Blizzard, who had been persuaded by the gamblers that all the *crack* races, as they are termed, were becoming quite a bore, and only fit for the everyday vulgar; that blood-horses were now stale, and as plenty as blackberries; and that in a few years nobody, who had any pretensions to ton, would patronise the Derby, the Oaks, or the St Leger. But at Lyndhurst, in the New Forest, they continued, there were races really worth patronizing, if any gentleman of influence would be *eccentric* enough to countenance them, and lead the ton where there was so fine an opening.

It was meant, of course, that if Mr Blizzard, who was a gentleman of influence, at least in his own estimation, would go down to Lyndhurst and patronize the forest races, they must soon eclipse all the *crack* blood-horse races in the kingdom, whilst his name would be immortalized as the leader of the fashionable world.

Blizzard, notwithstanding all the tempting baits in this well-laid snare, was not, however, caught till he was told that the race-horses at Lyndhurst were not only real denizens of the forest, but actually wild horses caught on purpose; many of which would fly open-mouthed at the grooms who were mounting them. The notion of a wild horse-race was precisely the thing to tickle Blizzard's fancy, and he decided to go; while Sir Byam, Lord Blank, and their friends, had equally decided to rook Blizzard, before his return, of as many thousands as they could prevail upon him to venture upon what they were pleased to call wild horses.

This, however, was only the first part of their design, the mere opening or prologue of the play which they intended to enact. It was necessary not only to buy forest horses – that they could easily do for twelve, fifteen, or twenty pounds a horse – but to ascertain their comparative mettle and powers of running; otherwise their bets would be mere lottery and dabbling in the dark; and Blizzard, fool though he was, might by chance succeed at such a game as well as any of them.

It was upon such a trial of skill respecting their newly purchased forest racers, that they had been on the race lawn when I first descried them. As soon as this had been ascertained, they would play their cards accordingly, with some certainty of winning.

But the most important information which Thady had picked up was that one Jones had been written to by Sir Byam to procure the horses; and I had hopes that it might turn out to be the delinquent of many crimes whom I was so anxious to secure; for one scoundrel (I beg Sir Byam's pardon) usually finds out another, when there is any scheme of fraud or villainy to execute by proxy; and Jones seemed to have so great an itch for traffic of all kinds, that I verily believe he would not have hesitated to sell his own father provided that the terms offered should satisfy his avarice. The enormity of the crime would be no obstacle to such a wretch.

If it was really this Jones who had been dealing in the forest horses, I have no doubt that he procured them for a mere trifle, such as a few pounds of tea or tobacco, or a skin of brandy, and that he did not part with them again for less than twenty or thirty pounds each on the nail.

Be that as it might, I resolved to make strict inquiry after this forest horse-jockey, in order to prove or disprove my suspicions; while, in the meantime, I should also give a side-look at the proceedings of Sir Byam and his friends. Besides what I had thus learned, I overheard, through the thin boarded partition which divided my apartment from theirs, the following conversation between Sir Byam and Lord Blank.

'I think,' said Sir Byam, 'we have the raff now as tight as a glove. Mum is the word, you know.'

'But has he brought any stuff with him, do you know? Has he "put money in his purse?"'

'*N'importe*; his note of hand will do as well; or I think we may take his word itself when witnesses are by.'

'I sha'n't, for one. For mark ye, Finch, he manages all his concerns, I find, through a rascally pettyfogging attorney; and if he smoke out a debt of honour to the tune of a few thousands, he may tip us something unpleasant, don't you see?'

' 'Gad! you are quite out there. Blizz is too much afraid of losing caste. He would not, I am convinced, shirk his word to save him from beggary.'

'O! you don't know the lawyers. They are deeper than we, a devilish deal; and a raff like Blizz is so easily bammed. A shrewd attorney might readily persuade him to anything, even to the making over all his property to said attorney, and turning hermit.'

'Aye, I grant you he might be gulled into such a whim, but it would be to gain the laurel of eccentricity; a very different affair from cutting the *haut ton* by shirking a debt of honour, and taking advantage of the gambling laws.'

'Well, if we can't make it better, we must rest content, though I prefer the bankers. But what is to be done about the odds on the grey, and saddling him with that stiff-jawed colt?'

'O! Jones will manage that. He undertakes to persuade him that the colt is the better horse – quite *wild* – only caught yesterday – and fit to run down the fleetest buck that ever started; while we carry the grey against the field at any odds we can persuade him to.'

'This Jones seems to be the very devil, I think. You have him in everything – jockeying for you, pimping for you, and now manager in chief for pigeoning a raff. A deuced excellent factotum, to be sure!'

'Ay, and he can do more than all that. He can chip you off any inconvenient rascal who may know more of your concerns than he ought; and when he has done the job, can make a good bargain with the surgeons for the body, so that it may tell no tales. There is a deep one for you! Would *you* venture upon such a *comédie larmoyante?*'

'Zounds! I wonder how the fellow escapes being nabbed.'

'Luck – all luck. He has been pulled up once or twice, but he always finds some loophole to creep out at, and gets off till the storm blow over. And yet he has not much brains, you would say, for anything, – rather a commonplace sort of a fellow, but contrives to get through very ticklish affairs where cleverer men would stick fast in the mud. The only cunning he can boast of has been beat into him by running his head so often against the gallows' post.'

'There he'll stick at last, if the devil is the boy I take him for.'

'I don't know that: he has too many friends in court to have much to fear. There is scarcely a magistrate, for instance, in this county and the next who would back a warrant for his apprehension; or if they did, he would contrive to avoid being committed by some flaw in the evidence, or by means of a keg of brandy, or a snug supply of prime claret to the committing magistrate, or a present of imperial "*gunpowder,*" purporting to come direct from the particular tea-store of the Emperor of China, to the magistrate's lady. Stupid as he is, Jones has pluck enough for all that.'

From this confidential confab of the two titled swindlers (I might have used a stronger term with no injustice), I perceived that I should have more difficulties to encounter than I had foreseen, with regard to the chief object of my journey. I had now no doubt whatever about the identity of this Hampshire Jones with him of Battersea, though I wondered why the fellow had not thought of changing his name into some *alias*, which might have served so far to protect him. The only explanation I could give of this was, that Jones was so very common a name as not to be liable to excite suspicion; and it might be of much advantage to come into court (the fear of which must be ever before his eyes) without the suspicious circumstance of an *alias* in the warrant or indictment.

If I did find the miscreant, I was at a loss what to do with him, seeing he had so many means of eluding justice. But it would be no fault of mine if I got him once clear off my hands. I was not, luckily, responsible for the conduct of magistrates, particularly those who would take bribes of smuggled merchandise to manoeuvre a delinquent out of a trial for his crimes – so, at least, said Sir Byam Finch: I hoped, for the honour of the Hampshire Commission of the Peace, that it was not so; but such things, I know, are certainly done in other parts besides Hampshire.

All that I had to do, however, was, if possible, to secure the desperado: after that they might either hang him, or make a justice of him for aught I cared: I confess I should not have felt much compunction in the event of his receiving the full reward of his numerous delinquencies.

With regard to the plot formed against Blizzard, I at first thought of introducing myself, and opening his eyes to the character of his *friends*; but upon farther consideration I perceived that this would serve very little purpose; for if he did not lose his money to them by betting on forest horses, he would be certain to lose it to the first Jew who could find him out, for some childish bauble pretended to be unique: – a rifle fowling-piece (not made for firing), which would unscrew and go into the waistcoat pocket; or a dish of strawberries, said to have been produced on the summit of Mont Blanc, would beguile him of hundreds.

It was a pity, however, to see good money passing into the purses of such fellows as the gamblers, one of whom had been ruffian enough to propose the murder of the beautiful girl who had fallen a victim to the other titled scoundrel. If any circumstance, therefore, occurred by which I could prevent their designs of plunder, I should take care not to lose the opportunity.

When the day of the races arrived, I repaired to the lawn to take my station. The first object which attracted my notice was a carriage of a most singularly grotesque construction – an odd mixture of the antique and the modern – drawn by no less than ten horses, with five postilions in *outré* liveries.

It is superfluous to say that the whole assemblage of people were set agaze at this strange equipage. The rustics stared, and the gentlemen-farmers swore their biggest oaths at the extravaganza. The forest girls, who had come decked out in their best holiday apparel, were universally of opinion that it was some of the royal princes, if not the King himself, who had come to honour Lyndhurst races in the state coach. The state coach itself of course they had never seen, with all its gilded and gaudy trappings, otherwise they could not have committed such a mistake.

The person who sat in this odd vehicle was no less fantastic in his dress. He wore a high black fur cap, shaped somewhat like a bishop's mitre, and similar to those which I have seen worn by Armenian merchants on the Exchange; but with this difference, that there was a plume of feathers stuck in the front, and supported by a knot of gaudy ribbands of many colours, like the cockade of a recruiting serjeant. The remaining part of his attire I cannot so easily describe, but it appeared to be equally grotesque.

He was withal a young man, and not unhandsome, though his complexion was dark – too dark for that of an Englishman. In a word, it was no less a personage than Mr Ellice Blizzard, the would-be 'gentleman eccentric,' who had considered it indispensable to his success in stamping the Lyndhurst races as a place of fashionable resort, to open his campaign in this mountebank style of tasteless extravagance. He had set his heart upon having a Lapland sledge drawn by reindeer; but this was an equipage which all his wealth could not command. The sledge, indeed, or something called so, he might have procured in the metropolis; but the reindeer were not to be had, and they could not be manufactured, even by London ingenuity, out of any other species of animal that would draw in a carriage. I have since understood, indeed, that one of Mr Blizzard's Hebrew friends did make the attempt to transform a set of galloways into reindeer by decorating their heads with antlers, and other contrivances; but the horses could not be made into passable stags, and the attempt was abandoned, to the great grief of the Jew speculator, and the sad disappointment of Blizzard, who had to content himself with ordinary steeds for his extraordinary carriage.

It was this disappointment about the reindeer, perhaps, which was preying on his mind; for he did not seem to be in spirits on the present occasion, but looked cross and sullen. Independent of the reindeer, indeed, he might well feel dissatisfied if he had expected to see in the forest, so far from the metropolis, a phalanx of splendid carriages lining the race-course, and filled with the chief beauty and fashion of England. He had no doubt exerted his influence and his eloquence in the circle wherein he moved to bring down to the forest as many *crack* people as he could; but though some might promise to make up parties to honour the new place, not one probably ever thought more of the subject, or if they did, it would only be to laugh at the folly of the proposer.

The original projectors of the expedition, Sir Byam and Lord Blank, had the best reasons imaginable for keeping it private, because they could conduct their machinations much more effectually when out of the range of their fashionable connections, who might otherwise wish to participate in the plunder they had marked out. Their only importations from the capital were one or two desperate broken-down gamblers, who were to assume the dress and character of foresters (to be ready to catch Blizzard upon all points), and to share largely in their winnings with the projectors.

From the disappointed looks of Blizzard, however, it seemed a question whether he might not, after all their trouble, give them the slip, and order his postilions to drive for town. To prevent this consummation, they found it necessary to pique his pride by representing that his credit was staked to go through with what he had undertaken, and that if he could make any display at all this year, they might hope for better sport the next.

The horses, *wild* and tame, were at length ready to start, and I could single out the two which I had formerly heard mentioned as the colt and the grey; the latter belonging to Sir Byam, and the former to Blizzard, who had been persuaded to give a hundred and fifty guineas for it, though it was not worth more than ten: Jones might probably have charged them twenty or thirty. This bargain, indeed, was the commencement of their present nefarious system. The colt, though stiff-necked and badly formed, was palmed upon Blizzard as quite wild, newly caught, and able to outstrip the best blood-horse in speed. As this false character of the animal was not given by the profligates themselves, who pretended to know nothing of it though they had made a careful but secret comparative trial, no blame could attach to them from the anticipated defeat.

Blizzard had swallowed all he had been told respecting this extraordinary colt, whose very defects had been made the subject of panegyric, and exhibited as excellencies. The stiff neck was said to be evidence of its uncontaminated breed, all the finest forest horses, and particularly all which had been winners at Lyndhurst, having had that point in perfection.

The praises which had been so lavishly bestowed upon the colt made Blizzard as vain of possessing it as he was of his fantastic carriage, or his Armenian fur cap; and he was quite in the vein for offering any odds in its favour. This opportunity was not to be lost, for Blizzard was too fickle to be depended upon for an hour at any time. Several thousands, accordingly, were soon staked upon the event of the race. I know not the precise amount, as I judged it prudent to keep aloof for fear of being recognized. The sum, however, I understood to be considerable; and though the riders, who were knowing fellows, and partly in the secret, jockeyed the horses admirably to keep up the deception, yet nobody could doubt, from the relative appearance of the animals, which was certain to be winner.

To the terrible chagrin of Blizzard, who was almost ready to stake his life upon the colt, the grey shot ahead, and won the race easily, and with it a round sum of the West Indian's cash.

Blizzard cared little about his money, as he had a great deal more of it than he knew how to spend; but he was palpably annoyed at his *wild* colt having run so scurvily. Both wise men and fools, however, have a mortal dislike to confess themselves mistaken; and the loss of the race, so far from putting Blizzard out of conceit with the colt, made him more determined than ever to look upon it as an extraordinary animal, and he was convinced that the race had been lost wholly in consequence of bad riding. Had he himself been on the colt, he could have won the race, he said, even in the teeth of Eclipse, Highflyer, or any other horse of celebrity.

These particulars I afterwards learned; for, as I have said, I took care not to mingle too closely with those who might have recognized me. Blizzard's casual boast of his own skill in riding was eagerly caught at by the gamblers to tempt him to another trial of the *wild* colt, and they failed not to urge him to undertake the exploit. Here, however, they found an insuperable obstacle in Blizzard's personal fears; for though he scrupled not to talk of his feats and his fortitude, he was a very dastard when there was any serious apprehension of danger; and to mount a *wild* forest colt, he prudently concluded, might bring his neck into peril if it should take a fancy to run off with him to its native woods. He found means, therefore, to decline this adventure; but he was eager to enter the colt for another trial, under the management of a different rider.

My Irish friend Thady had taken as keen an interest in the sport as any of the London party; and when he discovered this new arrangement, he set himself to defeat the scheme. His plan, which he disclosed to me, was truly Irish, though I have since understood that it has sometimes been practised in England. He had seen, he said, a horse that was lame in one foot cured of halting by rendering him lame in another; for which purpose, driving a nail through the hoof into the quick, was the expedient which would run least hazard of immediate detection.

Upon this barbarous principle Thady proposed to render the grey horse, on which the conspirators depended, lame in both the fore feet, so that it might not appear in his walking, but would be certain to prevent his winning the race, even though the colt were less fleet than it was. Thady would find ways and means, he said, to get into the stable ; and the devil was in it if Blizzard did not gain back all he had lost, with something handsome to boot.

I approved of Thady's desire to defeat the gamblers, but did not like the cruelty of the measure which he meant to practise on the poor horse, though it certainly appeared to offer the most effectual means of success.

This indeed was the way it fell out the next day. At the commencement of the race, the grey horse once more shot ahead, but soon faltered and Blizzard's *wild* colt this time was the easy winner. Thady had evidently done his cruel work well.

The restoration of the West Indian's cash with a profit to boot, and the looks upon the faces of the gamblers when they saw their scheme undone, afforded me no small amusement. But having witnessed the frustration of the swindle, I now had my duty to think of and returned once more to the pursuit of Jones . . .

Silver Blaze

SIR ARTHUR CONAN DOYLE

The first famous detective of fiction to venture onto the turf to solve a crime was Sherlock Holmes who in 1890 investigated the murder of a trainer preparing for the Wessex Plate at another of the now lost race courses of Hampshire: Winchester Downs. Although Holmes never claimed a particular knowledge of racing, he always had Watson to fall back on because, as the good Doctor said when asked, in the *Adventure of Shoscombe Old Place*, whether he knew anything of racing, he replied: 'I ought to. I pay for it with about half my wound pension!'

Racing itself had actually begun at Winchester as early as 1676 according to an old document of the period which states: 'The last Wednesday in August will be run for on Winchester Downs a considerable Plate (for which none but Gentlemen are to ride) consisting of three 4-mile heats.' The popularity of this event is evident from another report of September 1684 that reads: 'His Majesty arrived here lately to see the races attended by a splendid train of nobility and they were welcomed by great numbers of all sorts of people.' Today all that remains of the course is a monument which commemorates one of the most famous horses to run there, Beware Chalk Pit, which was owned by Mr Paulet St John and earned his name because he accidentally jumped into a chalk pit in 1733 yet still recovered to win the Hunter's Plate a year later ridden by his owner!

Bad weather was apparently a frequent curse on this event, as one of Winchester's most famous residents, Jane Austen, noted in verse: 'Shift your race as you will, it shall never be dry/ The curse upon Venta is July in showers.' Just before her death in 1817, Austen composed a further stanza which serves almost as an epitaph to the event:

Silver Blaze

When Winchester races first took their beginning
'Tis said that people forgot their old Saint,
That they never applied for the leave of St Swithin,
And that William Wykeham's approval was faint.

Sir Arthur Conan Doyle (1859–1930), like his famous sleuth, was not a racegoer although he loved horses. He did, though, visit Winchester on several occasions, which may well account for his decision to set the story of 'Silver Blaze' on and around the race track.

At the turn of the century when he wrote the mystery, racing was still being vigorously carried out at nearly all the cathedral towns, including York, Hereford, Chester, Salisbury and Worcester, where it still continues today; and at Gloucester, Durham, Lichfield, Oxford and Winchester, where it has subsequently disappeared. The reason for the demise of these meetings and a host of other small country fixtures – Charles Richardson has explained in *The English Turf* (1901) – 'was the enacting of the rule that every race must be of the clear value of £100 to the winner, and the advent of the gate-money enclosure.'

This said, Conan Doyle certainly revives memories of the course and of racing at that time, although as he subsequently admitted he did commit one fatal error in the plot which observant readers among the fans of Sherlock Holmes were not slow to point out. 'I have never been a racing man,' Doyle confessed when taken to task, 'and yet I ventured to write "Silver Blaze" where the mystery depends upon the laws of training and racing. The story is all right, and Holmes may have been at the top of his form, but my ignorance cries aloud to Heaven. I read an excellent and very damaging criticism of the story in some sporting paper, written clearly by a man who *did* know, in which he explained the exact penalties which would have come upon all concerned if they had acted as I described. Half would have been in jail and the other half warned off the turf forever.'

Such an admission, however, should not be allowed to spoil the unravelling of the mystery which Doyle ultimately considered among the best of the great detective's cases. Interestingly, too, the horse Silver Blaze was probably based on a real animal,

Common, one of the progeny of the great Isonomy who is mentioned in the text and won many races, including the Cambridgeshire at Newmarket in 1878 and the Ascot Gold Cup in both 1879 and 1880. Common, despite his uninspired name, then continued in his sire's winning ways by taking the Two Thousand Guinea Stakes in April 1891, followed this with the Derby, the St James Place Stakes at Ascot and finally the St Leger at Doncaster in September, when the odds on him were 5 to 4.

*

'I am afraid, Watson, that I shall have to go,' said Holmes, as we set down together to our breakfast one morning.

'Go! Where to?'

'To Dartmoor – to King's Pyland.'

I was not surprised. Indeed, my only wonder was that he had not already been mixed up in this extraordinary case, which was the one topic of conversation through the length and breadth of England. For a whole day my companion had rambled about the room with his chin upon his chest and his brows knitted, charging and re-charging his pipe with the strongest black tobacco, and absolutely deaf to any of my questions or remarks. Fresh editions of every paper had been sent up by our newsagent only to be glanced over and tossed down into a corner. Yet, silent as he was, I knew perfectly well what it was over which he was brooding. There was but one problem before the public which could challenge his powers of analysis, and that was the singular disappearance of the favourite for the Wessex Cup, and the tragic murder of its trainer. When, therefore, he suddenly announced his intention of setting out for the scene of the drama, it was only what I had both expected and hoped for.

'I should be most happy to go down with you if I should not be in the way,' said I.

'My dear Watson, you would confer a great favour upon me by coming. And I think that your time will not be misspent, for there are points about this case which promise to make it an absolutely unique one. We have, I think, just time to catch our train at Paddington, and I will go further into the matter upon our journey. You would oblige me by bringing with you your very excellent field-glass.'

And so it happened that an hour or so later I found myself in the corner of a first-class carriage, flying along, *en route* for Exeter, while Sherlock Holmes, with his sharp, eager face framed in his earflapped travelling cap, dipped rapidly into the bundle of fresh papers which he had procured at Paddington. We had left Reading far behind us before he thrust the last of them under the seat, and offered me his cigar-case.

'We are going well,' said he, looking out of the window and glancing at his watch. 'Our rate at present is fifty-three and a half miles an hour.'

'I have not observed the quarter-mile posts,' said I.

'Nor have I. But the telegraph posts upon this line are sixty yards apart, and the calculation is a simple one. I presume that you have already looked into this matter of the murder of John Straker and the disappearance of Silver Blaze?'

'I have seen what the *Telegraph* and the *Chronicle* have to say.'

'It is one of those cases where the art of the reasoner should be used rather for the sifting of details than for the acquiring of fresh evidence. The tragedy has been so uncommon, so complete, and of such personal importance to so many people that we are suffering from a plethora of surmise, conjecture, and hypothesis. The difficulty is to detach the framework of fact – of absolute, undeniable fact – from the embellishments of theorists and reporters. Then, having established ourselves upon this sound basis, it is our duty to see what inferences may be drawn, and which are the special points upon which the whole mystery turns. On Tuesday evening I received telegrams, both from Colonel Ross, the owner of the horse, and from Inspector Gregory, who is looking after the case, inviting my co-operation.'

'Tuesday evening!' I exclaimed. 'And this is Thursday morning. Why did you not go down yesterday?'

'Because I made a blunder, my dear Watson – which is, I am afraid, a more common occurrence than anyone would think who only knew me through your memoirs. The fact is that I could not believe it possible that the most remarkable horse in England could long remain concealed, especially in so sparsely inhabited a place as the north of Dartmoor. From hour to hour yesterday I expected to hear that he had been found, and that his abductor was the murderer of John Straker. When, however, another morning had come and I found that, beyond the arrest of young Fitzroy Simpson, nothing had been done, I felt that it was time for me to take action. Yet in some ways I feel that yesterday has not been wasted.'

'You have formed a theory, then?'

'At least I have a grip of the essential facts of the case. I shall enumerate them to you, for nothing clears up a case so much as stating it to another person, and I can hardly expect your co-operation if I do not show you the position from which we start.'

I lay back against the cushions, puffing at my cigar, while Holmes, leaning forward, with his long thin forefinger checking off the points upon the palm of his left hand, gave me a sketch of the events which had led to our journey.

'Silver Blaze,' said he, 'is from the Isonomy stock, and holds as brilliant a record as his famous ancestor. He is now in his fifth year, and has brought in turn each of the prizes of the turf to Colonel Ross, his fortunate owner. Up to the time of the catastrophe he was first favourite for the Wessex Cup, the betting being three to one on. He has always, however, been a prime favourite with the racing public, and has never yet disappointed them, so that even at short odds enormous sums of money have been laid upon him. It is obvious, therefore, that there were many people who had the strongest interest in preventing Silver Blaze from being there at the fall of the flag next Tuesday.

'This fact was, of course, appreciated at King's Pyland, where the Colonel's training stable is situated. Every precaution was taken to guard the favourite. The trainer, John Straker, is a retired jockey, who rode in Colonel Ross's colours before he became too heavy for the weighing chair. He has served the Colonel for five years as jockey, and for seven as trainer, and has always shown himself to be a zealous and honest servant. Under him were three lads, for the establishment was a small one, containing only four horses in all. One of these lads sat up each night in the stable, while the others slept in the loft. All three bore excellent characters. John Straker, who is a married man, lived in a small villa about two hundred yards from the stables. He has no children, keeps one maid-servant, and is comfortably off. The country round is very lonely, but about half a mile to the north there is a small cluster of villas which have been built by a Tavistock contractor for the use of invalids and others who may wish to enjoy the pure Dartmoor air. Tavistock itself lies two miles to the west, while across the moor, also about two miles distant, is the larger training establishment of Capleton, which belongs to Lord Backwater, and is managed by Silas Brown. In every other direction the moor is a complete wilderness, inhabited only by a few roaming gipsies. Such was the general situation last Monday night, when the catastrophe occurred.

'On that evening the horses had been exercised and watered as usual, and the stables were locked up at nine o'clock. Two of the lads walked up to the trainer's house, where they had supper in the kitchen, while the third, Ned Hunter, remained on guard. At a few minutes after nine the maid, Edith Baxter, carried down to the stables his supper, which consisted of a dish of curried mutton. She took no liquid, as there was a water-tap in the stables, and it was the rule that the lad on duty should drink nothing else. The maid carried a lantern with her, as it was very dark, and the path ran across the open moor.

'Edith Baxter was within thirty yards of the stables when a man appeared out of the darkness and called to her to stop. As he stepped into the circle of yellow light thrown by the lantern she saw that he was a person of gentlemanly bearing, dressed in a grey suit of tweed with a cloth cap. He wore gaiters, and carried a heavy stick with a knob to it. She was most impressed, however, by the extreme pallor of his face and by the nervousness of his manner. His age, she thought, would be rather over thirty than under it.

' "Can you tell me where I am?" he asked. "I had almost made up my mind to sleep on the moor, when I saw the light of your lantern."

' "You are close to the King's Pyland training stables," she said.

' "Oh, indeed! What a stroke of luck!" he cried. "I understand that a stable boy sleeps there alone every night. Perhaps that is his supper which you are carrying to him. Now I am sure that you would not be too proud to earn the price of a new dress, would you?" He took a piece of white paper folded up out of his waistcoat pocket. "See that the boy has this tonight, and you shall have the prettiest frock that money can buy."

'She was frightened by the earnestness of his manner, and ran past him to the window through which she was accustomed to hand the meals. It was already open, and Hunter was seated at the small table inside. She had begun to tell him of what had happened, when the stranger came up again.

' "Good evening," said he, looking through the window, "I wanted to have a word with you." The girl has sworn that as he spoke she noticed the corner of the little paper packet protruding from his closed hand.

' "What business have you here?" asked the lad.

' "It's business that may put something into your pocket," said the other. "You've two horses in for the Wessex Cup – Silver Blaze and Bayard. Let me have the straight tip, and you won't be a loser. Is it a fact that at the weights Bayard could give the other a hundred yards in five furlongs, and that the stable have put their money on him?"

' "So you're one of those damned touts," cried the lad. "I'll show you how we serve them in King's Pyland." He sprang up and rushed across the stable to unloose the dog. The girl fled away to the house, but as she ran she looked back, and saw that the stranger was leaning through the window. A minute later, however, when Hunter rushed out with the hound he was gone, and though the lad ran all round the buildings he failed to find any trace of him.'

'One moment!' I asked. 'Did the stable boy, when he ran out with the dog, leave the door unlocked behind him?'

'Excellent, Watson; excellent!' murmured my companion. 'The importance of the point struck me so forcibly, that I sent a special wire to Dartmoor yesterday to clear the matter up. The boy locked the door before he left it. The window, I may add, was not large enough for a man to go through.

'Hunter waited until his fellow grooms had returned, when he sent a message up to the trainer and told him what had occurred. Straker was excited at hearing the account, although he does not seem to have quite realized its true significance. It left him, however, vaguely uneasy, and Mrs Straker, waking at one in the morning, found that he was dressing. In reply to her inquiries, he said that he could not sleep on account of his anxiety about the horses, and that he intended to walk down to the stables to see that all was well. She begged him to remain at home, as she could hear the rain pattering against the windows, but in spite of her entreaties he pulled on his large macintosh and left the house.

'Mrs Straker awoke at seven in the morning, to find that her husband had not yet returned. She dressed herself hastily, called the maid, and set off for the stables. The door was open; inside, huddled together upon a chair, Hunter was sunk in a state of absolute stupor, the favourite's stall was empty, and there were no signs of his trainer.

'The two lads who slept in the chaff-cutting loft above the harness-room were quickly roused. They had heard nothing during the night, for they are both sound sleepers. Hunter was obviously under the influence of some powerful drug; and, as no sense could be got out of him, he was left to sleep it off while the two lads and the two women ran out in search of the absentees. They still had hopes that the trainer had for some reason taken out the horse for early exercise, but on ascending the knoll near the house, from which all the neighbouring moors were visible, they not only could see no signs of the favourite, but they perceived something which warned them that they were in the presence of a tragedy.

'About a quarter of a mile from the stables, John Straker's overcoat was flapping from a furze bush. Immediately beyond there was a bowl-shaped depression in the moor, and at the bottom of this was found the dead body of the unfortunate trainer. His head had been shattered by a savage blow from some heavy weapon, and he was wounded in the thigh, where there was a long, clean cut, inflicted evidently by some very sharp instrument. It was clear, however, that Straker had defended himself vigorously against his assailants, for in his right hand he held a small knife, which was clotted with blood up to the handle, while in his left he grasped a red and black silk cravat, which was recognised by the maid as having been worn on the preceding evening by the stranger who had visited the stables.

'Hunter, on recovering from his stupor, was also quite positive as to the ownership of the cravat. He was equally certain that the same stranger had, while standing at the window, drugged his curried mutton, and so deprived the stables of their watchman.

'As to the missing horse, there were abundant proofs in the mud which lay at the bottom of the fatal hollow that he had been there at the time of the struggle. But from that morning he has disappeared; and although a large reward has been offered, and all the gipsies of Dartmoor are on the alert, no news has come of him. Finally an analysis has shown that the remains of his supper, left by the stable lad, contain an appreciable quantity of powdered opium, while the people of the house partook of the same dish on the same night without any ill-effect.

'Those are the main facts of the case stripped of all surmise and stated as baldly as possible. I shall now recapitulate what the police have done in the matter.

'Inspector Gregory, to whom the case has been committed, is an extremely competent officer. Were he but gifted with imagination he might rise to great heights in his profession. On his arrival he promptly found and arrested the man upon whom suspicion naturally rested. There was little difficulty in finding him, for he was thoroughly well known in the neighbourhood. His name, it appears, was Fitzroy Simpson. He was a man of excellent birth and education, who had squandered a fortune upon the turf, and who lived now by doing a little quiet and genteel book-making in the sporting clubs of London. An examination of his betting-book shows that bets to the amount of five thousand pounds had been registered by him against the favourite.

'On being arrested he volunteered the statement that he had come down to Dartmoor in the hope of getting some information about the King's Pyland horses, and also about Desborough, the second favourite, which was in charge of Silas Brown, at the Capleton stables. He did not attempt to deny that he had acted as described upon the evening before, but declared that he had no sinister designs, and had simply wished to obtain first-hand information. When confronted with the cravat he turned very pale, and was utterly unable to account for its presence in the hand of the murdered man. His wet clothing showed that he had been out in the storm of the night before, and his stick, which was a Penang lawyer, weighted with lead, was just such a weapon as might, by repeated blows, have inflicted the terrible injuries to which the trainer had succumbed.

'On the other hand, there was no wound upon his person, while the state of Straker's knife would show that one, at least, of his assailants must bear his mark upon him. There you have it all in a nutshell, Watson, and if you can give me any light I shall be infinitely obliged to you.'

I had listened with the greatest interest to the statement which Holmes, with characteristic clearness, had laid before me. Though most of the facts were familiar to me, I had not sufficiently appreciated their relative importance, nor their connection with each other.

'Is it not possible,' I suggested, 'that the incised wound upon Straker may have been caused by his own knife in the convulsive struggles which follow any brain injury?'

'It is more than possible; it is probable,' said Holmes. 'In that case, one of the main points in favour of the accused disappears.'

'And yet,' said I, 'even now I fail to understand what the theory of the police can be.'

'I am afraid that whatever theory we state has very grave objections to it,' returned my companion. 'The police imagine, I take it, that this Fitzroy Simpson, having drugged the lad, and having in some way obtained a duplicate key, opened the stable door, and took out the horse, with the intention, apparently, of kidnapping him altogether. His bridle is missing, so that Simpson must have put it on. Then, having left the door open behind him, he was leading the horse away over the moor, when he was either met or overtaken by the trainer. A row naturally ensued, Simpson beat out the trainer's brains with his heavy stick without receiving any injury from the small knife which Straker used in self-defence, and then the thief either led the horse on to some secret hiding-place, or else it may have bolted during the struggle, and be now wandering out on the moors. That is the case as it appears to the police, and improbable as it is, all other explanations are more improbable still. However, I shall very quickly test the matter when I am once upon the spot, and until then I really cannot see how we can get much further than our present position.'

It was evening before we reached the little town of Tavistock, which lies, like the boss of a shield, in the middle of the huge circle of Dartmoor. Two gentlemen were awaiting us at the station; the one a tall fair man with lion-like hair and beard, and curiously penetrating light blue eyes, the other a small alert person, very neat and dapper, in a frock-coat and gaiters, with trim little side-whiskers and an eyeglass. The latter was Colonel Ross, the well-known sportsman, the other Inspector Gregory, a man who was rapidly making his name in the English detective service.

'I am delighted that you have come down, Mr Holmes,' said the Colonel. 'The Inspector here has done all that could possibly be suggested; but I wish to leave no stone unturned in trying to avenge poor Straker, and in recovering my horse.'

'Have there been any fresh developments?' asked Holmes.

'I am sorry to say that we have made very little progress,' said the Inspector. 'We have an open carriage outside, and as you would no doubt like to see the place before the light fails, we might talk it over as we drive.'

A minute later we were all seated in a comfortable landau and were rattling through the quaint old Devonshire town. Inspector Gregory was full of his case, and poured out a stream of remarks, while Holmes threw in an occasional question or interjection. Colonel Ross leaned back with his arms folded and his hat tilted over his eyes, while I listened with interest to the dialogue of the two detectives. Gregory was formulating his theory, which was almost exactly what Holmes had foretold in the train.

'The net is drawn pretty close round Fitzroy Simpson,' he

remarked, 'and I believe myself that he is our man. At the same time, I recognise that the evidence is purely circumstantial, and that some new development may upset it.'

'How about Straker's knife?'

'We have quite come to the conclusion that he wounded himself in his fall.'

'My friend Dr Watson made that suggestion to me as we came down. If so, it would tell against this man Simpson.'

'Undoubtedly. He has neither a knife nor any sign of a wound. The evidence against him is certainly very strong. He had a great interest in the disappearance of the favourite, he lies under the suspicion of having poisoned the stable boy, he was undoubtedly out in the storm, he was armed with a heavy stick, and his cravat was found in the dead man's hand. I really think we have enough to go before a jury.'

Holmes shook his head. 'A clever counsel would tear it all to rags,' said he. 'Why should he take the horse out of the stable? If he wished to injure it, why could he not do it there? Has a duplicate key been found in his possession? What chemist sold him the powdered opium? Above all, where could he, a stranger to the district, hide a horse, and such a horse as this? What is his own explanation as to the paper which he wished the maid to give to the stable boy?'

'He says that it was a ten-pound note. One was found in his purse. But your other difficulties are not so formidable as they seem. He is not a stranger to the district. He has twice lodged at Tavistock in the summer. The opium was probably brought from London. The key, having served its purpose, would be hurled away. The horse may lie at the bottom of one of the pits or old mines upon the moor.'

'What does he say about the cravat?'

'He acknowledges that it is his, and declares that he had lost it. But a new element has been introduced into the case which may account for his leading the horse from the stable.'

Holmes pricked up his ears.

'We have found traces which show that a party of gipsies encamped on Monday night within a mile of the spot where the murder took place. On Tuesday they were gone. Now, presuming that there was some understanding between Simpson and these gipsies, might he not have been leading the horse to them when he was overtaken, and may they not have him now?'

'It is certainly possible.'

'The moor is being scoured for these gipsies. I have also examined every stable and outhouse in Tavistock, and for a radius of ten miles.'

'There is another training stable quite close, I understand?'

'Yes, and that is a factor which we must certainly not neglect. As Desborough, their horse, was second in the betting, they had an interest in the disappearance of the favourite. Silas Brown, the trainer, is known to have had large bets upon the event, and he was no friend to poor Straker. We have, however, examined the stables, and there is nothing to connect him with the affair.'

'And nothing to connect this man Simpson with the interests of the Capleton stable?'

'Nothing at all.'

Holmes leaned back in the carriage and the conversation ceased. A few minutes later our driver pulled up at a neat little red-brick villa with overhanging eaves, which stood by the road. Some distance off, across a paddock, lay a long grey-tiled outbuilding. In every other direction the low curves of the moor, bronze-coloured from the fading ferns, stretched away to the sky-line, broken only by the steeples of Tavistock, and by a cluster of houses away to the westward, which marked the Capleton stables. We all sprang out with the exception of Holmes, who continued to lean back with his eyes fixed upon the sky in front of him; entirely absorbed in his own thoughts. It was only when I touched his arm that he roused himself with a violent start and stepped out of the carriage.

'Excuse me,' said he, turning to Colonel Ross, who had looked at him in some surprise. 'I was day-dreaming.' There was a gleam in his eyes and a suppressed excitement in his manner which convinced me, used as I was to his ways, that his hand was upon a clue, though I could not imagine where he had found it.

'Perhaps you would prefer at once to go on to the scene of the crime, Mr Holmes?' said Gregory.

'I think that I should prefer to stay here a little and go into one or two questions of detail. Straker was brought back here, I presume?'

'Yes, he lies upstairs. The inquest is tomorrow.'

'He has been in your service some years, Colonel Ross?'

'I have always found him an excellent servant.'

'I presume that you made an inventory of what he had in his pockets at the time of his death, Inspector?'

'I have the things themselves in the sitting-room if you would care to see them.'

'I should be very glad.'

We all filed into the front room and sat round the central table, while the Inspector unlocked a square tin box and laid a small heap of things before us. There was a box of vestas, two inches of tallow candle, an A.D.P. briar-root pipe, a pouch of sealskin with half an ounce of long-cut Cavendish, a silver watch with a gold chain, five soverigns in gold, an aluminium pencil-case, a few papers, and an ivory-handled knife with a very delicate inflexible blade marked 'Weiss and Co., London.'

'This is a very singular knife,' said Holmes, lifting it up and examining it minutely. 'I presume, as I see bloodstains upon it, that it is the one which was found in the dead man's grasp. Watson, this knife is surely in your line.'

'It is what we call a cataract knife,' said I.

'I thought so. A very delicate blade devised for very delicate work. A strange thing for a man to carry with him upon a rough expedition, especially as it would not shut in his pocket.'

'The tip was guarded by a disc of cork which we found beside his body,' said the Inspector. 'His wife tells us that the knife had lain for some days upon the dressing-table, and that he had picked it up as he left the room. It was a poor weapon, but perhaps the best that he could lay his hand on at the moment.'

'Very possibly. How about these papers?'

'Three of them are receipted hay-dealers' accounts. One of them is a letter of instructions from Colonel Ross. This other is a milliner's account for thirty-seven pounds fifteen, made out by Madame Lesurier, of Bond Street, to William Darbyshire. Mrs

Straker tells us that Darbyshire was a friend of her husband's, and that occasionally his letters were addressed here.'

'Madame Darbyshire had somewhat expensive tastes,' remarked Holmes, glancing down the account. 'Twenty-two guineas is rather heavy for a single costume. However, there appears to be nothing more to learn, and we may now go down to the scene of the crime.'

As we emerged from the sitting-room a woman who had been waiting in the passage took a step forward and laid her hand upon the Inspector's sleeve. Her face was haggard, and thin, and eager; stamped with the print of a recent horror.

'Have you got them? Have you found them?' she panted.

'No, Mrs Straker; but Mr Holmes, here, has come from London to help us, and we shall do all that is possible.'

'Surely I met you in Plymouth, at a garden party, some little time ago, Mrs Straker,' said Holmes.

'No, sir; you are mistaken.'

'Dear me, why, I could have sworn to it. You wore a costume of dove-coloured silk with ostrich feather trimming.'

'I never had such a dress, sir,' answered the lady.

'Ah; that quite settles it,' said Holmes; and, with an apology, he followed the Inspector outside. A short walk across the moor took us to the hollow in which the body had been found. At the brink of it was the furze bush upon which the coat had been hung.

'There was no wind that night, I understand,' said Holmes.

'None; but very heavy rain.'

'In that case the overcoat was not blown against the furze bushes, but placed there.'

'Yes, it was laid across the bush.'

'You fill me with interest. I perceive that the ground has been trampled up a good deal. No doubt many feet have been there since Monday night.'

'A piece of matting has been laid here at the side, and we have all stood upon that.'

'Excellent.'

'In this bag I have one of the boots which Straker wore, one of Fitzroy Simpson's shoes, and a cast horse-shoe of Silver Blaze.'

'My dear Inspector, you surpass yourself!'

Holmes took the bag, and descending into the hollow he pushed the matting into a more central position. Then stretching himself upon his face and leaning his chin upon his hands he made a careful study of the trampled mud in front of him.

'Halloa!' said he, suddenly, 'what's this?'

It was a wax vesta, half burned, which was so coated with mud that it looked at first like a little chip of wood.

'I cannot think how I came to overlook it,' said the Inspector, with an expression of annoyance.

'It was invisible, buried in the mud. I only saw it because I was looking for it.'

'What! You expected to find it?'

'I thought it not unlikely.' He took the boots from the bag and compared the impressions of each of them with marks upon the ground. Then he clambered up to the rim of the hollow and crawled about among the ferns and bushes.

'I am afraid that there are no more tracks,' said the Inspector. 'I have examined the ground very carefully for a hundred yards in each direction.'

'Indeed!' said Holmes, rising; 'I should not have the impertinence to do it again after what you say. But I should like to take a little walk over the moors before it grows dark, that I may know my ground tomorrow, and I think that I shall put this horse-shoe into my pocket for luck.'

Colonel Ross, who had shown some signs of impatience at my companion's quiet and systematic method of work, glanced at his watch.

'I wish you would come back with me, Inspector,' said he. 'There are several points on which I should like your advice, and especially as to whether we do not owe it to the public to remove our horse's name from the entries for the Cup.'

'Certainly not,' cried Holmes, with decision; 'I should let the name stand.'

The Colonel bowed. 'I am very glad to have had your opinion, sir,' said he. 'You will find us at poor Straker's house when you have finished your walk, and we can drive together into Tavistock.'

He turned back with the Inspector, while Holmes and I walked slowly across the moor. The sun was beginning to sink behind the stables of Capleton, and the long sloping plain in front of us was tinged with gold, deepening into rich, ruddy brown where the faded ferns and brambles caught the evening light. But the glories of the landscape were all wasted upon my companion, who was sunk in the deepest thought.

'It's this way, Watson,' he said at last. 'We may leave the question of who killed John Straker for the instant, and confine ourselves to finding out what has become of the horse. Now, supposing that he broke away during or after the tragedy, where could he have gone to? The horse is a very gregarious creature. If left to himself his instincts would have been either to return to King's Pyland or go over to Capleton. Why should he run wild upon the moor? He would surely have been seen by now. And why should gipsies kidnap him? These people always clear out when they hear of trouble, for they do not wish to be pestered by the police. They could not hope to sell such a horse. They would run a great risk and gain nothing by taking him. Surely that is clear.'

'Where is he, then?'

'I have already said that he must have gone to King's Pyland or Capleton. He is not at King's Pyland, therefore he is at Capleton. Let us take that as a working hypothesis, and see what it leads us to. This part of the moor, as the Inspector remarked, is very hard and dry. But it falls away towards Capleton, and you can see from here that there is a long hollow over yonder, which must have been very wet on Monday night. If our supposition is correct, then the horse must have crossed that, and there is the point where we should look for his tracks.'

We had been walking briskly during this conversation, and a few more minutes brought us to the hollow in question. At Holmes's request I walked down the bank to the right, and he to the left, but I had not taken fifty paces before I heard him give a shout, and saw him waving his hand to me. The track of a horse was plainly outlined in the soft earth in front of him, and the shoe which he took from his pocket exactly fitted the impression.

'See the value of imagination,' said Holmes. 'It is the one

quality which Gregory lacks. We imagined what might have happened, acted upon the supposition, and find ourselves justified. Let us proceed.'

We crossed the marshy bottom and passed over a quarter of a mile of dry, hard turf. Again the ground sloped and again we came on the tracks. Then we lost them for half a mile, but only to pick them up once more quite close to Capleton. It was Holmes who saw them first, and he stood pointing with a look of triumph upon his face. A man's track was visible beside the horse's.

'The horse was alone before,' I cried.

'Quite so. It was alone before. Halloa! what is this?'

The double track turned sharp off and took the direction of King's Pyland. Holmes whistled, and we both followed along after it. His eyes were on the trail, but I happened to look a little to one side, and saw to my surprise the same tracks coming back again in the opposite direction.

'One for you, Watson,' said Holmes, when I pointed it out; 'you have saved us a long walk which would have brought us back on our own traces. Let us follow the return track.'

We had not to go far. It ended at the paving of asphalt which led up to the gates of the Capleton stables. As we approached a groom ran out from them.

'We don't want any loiterers about here,' said he.

'I only wish to ask a question,' said Holmes, with his finger and thumb in his waistcoat pocket. 'Should I be too early to see your master, Mr Silas Brown, if I were to call at five o'clock to-morrow morning?'

'Bless you, sir, if anyone is about he will be, for he is always the first stirring. But here he is, sir, to answer your questions for himself. No, sir, no; it's as much as my place is worth to let him see me touch your money. Afterwards, if you like.'

As Sherlock Holmes replaced the half-crown which he had drawn from his pocket, a fierce-looking elderly man strode out from the gate with a hunting-crop swinging in his hand.

'What's this, Dawson?' he cried. 'No gossiping! Go about your business! And you – what the devil do you want here?'

'Ten minutes' talk with you, my good sir,' said Holmes, in the sweetest of voices.

'I've no time to talk to every gadabout. We want no strangers here. Be off, or you may find a dog at your heels.'

Holmes leaned forward and whispered something in the trainer's ear. He started violently and flushed to the temples.

'It's a lie!' he shouted. 'An infernal lie!'

'Very good! Shall we argue about it here in public, or talk it over in your parlour?'

'Oh, come in if you wish to.'

Holmes smiled. 'I shall not keep you more than a few minutes, Watson,' he said. 'Now, Mr Brown, I am quite at your disposal.'

It was quite twenty minutes, and the reds had all faded into greys before Holmes and the trainer reappeared. Never have I seen such a change as had been brought about in Silas Brown in that short time. His face was ashy pale, beads of perspiration shone upon his brow, and his hands shook until his hunting-crop wagged like a branch in the wind. His bullying, overbearing manner was all gone too, and he cringed along at my companion's side like a dog with its master.

'Your instructions will be done. It shall be done,' said he.

'There must be no mistake,' said Holmes, looking round at him. The other winced as he read the menace in his eyes.

'Oh, no, there shall be no mistake. It shall be there. Should I change it first or not?'

Holmes thought a little and then burst out laughing.

'No, don't,' said he. 'I shall write to you about it. No tricks now or—'

'Oh, you can trust me, you can trust me!'

'You must see to it on the day as if it were your own.'

'You can rely upon me.'

'Yes, I think I can. Well, you shall hear from me tomorrow.' He turned upon his heel, disregarding the trembling hand which the other held out to him, and we set off for King's Pyland.

'A more perfect compound of the bully, coward and sneak than Master Silas Brown I have seldom met with,' remarked Holmes, as we trudged along together.

'He has the horse, then?'

'He tried to bluster out of it, but I described to him so exactly what his actions had been upon that morning, that he is convinced that I was watching him. Of course, you observed the peculiarly square toes in the impressions, and that his own boots exactly corresponded to them. Again, of course, no subordinate would have dared to have done such a thing. I described to him how when, according to his custom, he was the first down, he perceived a strange horse wandering over the moor; how he went out to it, and his astonishment at recognising from the white forehead which has given the favourite its name that chance had put in his power the only horse which could beat the one upon which he had put his money. Then I described how his first impulse had been to lead him back to King's Pyland, and how the devil had shown him how he could hide the horse until the race was over, and how he had led it back and concealed it at Capleton. When I told him every detail he gave it up, and thought only of saving his own skin.'

'But his stables had been searched.'

'Oh, an old horse-faker like him has many a dodge.'

'But are you not afraid to leave the horse in his power now, since he has every interest in injuring it?'

'My dear fellow, he will guard it as the apple of his eye. He knows that his only hope of mercy is to produce it safe.'

'Colonel Ross did not impress me as a man who would be likely to show much mercy in any case.'

'The matter does not rest with Colonel Ross. I follow my own methods, and tell as much or as little as I choose. That is the advantage of being unofficial. I don't know whether you observed it, Watson, but the Colonel's manner has been just a trifle cavalier to me. I am inclined now to have a little amusement at his expense. Say nothing to him about the horse.'

'Certainly not, without your permission.'

'And, of course, this is all quite a minor case compared with the question of who killed John Straker.'

'And you will devote yourself to that?'

'On the contrary, we both go back to London by the night train.'

I was thunderstruck by my friend's words. We had only been a few hours in Devonshire, and that he should give up an investigation which he had begun so brilliantly was quite incomprehensible to me. Not a word more could I draw from him until we were back at the trainer's house. The Colonel and the Inspector were awaiting us in the parlour.

'My friend and I return to town by the midnight express,' said Holmes. 'We have had a charming little breath of your beautiful Dartmoor air.'

The Inspector opened his eyes, and the Colonel's lips curled in a sneer.

'So you despair of arresting the murderer of poor Straker,' said he.

Holmes shrugged his shoulders. 'There are certainly grave difficulties in the way,' said he. 'I have every hope, however, that your horse will start upon Tuesday, and I beg that you will have your jockey in readiness. Might I ask for a photograph of Mr John Straker?'

The Inspector took one from an envelope in his pocket and handed it to him. 'My dear Gregory, you anticipate all my wants. If I might ask you to wait here for an instant, I have a question which I should like to put to the maid.'

'I must say that I am rather disappointed in our London consultant,' said Colonel Ross, bluntly, as my friend left the room. 'I do not see that we are any further than when he came.'

'At least, you have his assurance that your horse will run,' said I.

'Yes, I have his assurance,' said the Colonel, with a shrug of his shoulders. 'I should prefer to have the horse.'

I was about to make some reply in defence of my friend, when he entered the room again.

'Now, gentlemen,' said he, 'I am quite ready for Tavistock.'

As we stepped into the carriage one of the stable lads held the door open for us. A sudden idea seemed to occur to Holmes, for he leaned forward and touched the lad upon the sleeve.

'You have a few sheep in the paddock,' he said. 'Who attends to them?'

'I do, sir.'

'Have you noticed anything amiss with them of late?'

'Well, sir, not of much account; but three of them have gone lame, sir.'

I could see that Holmes was extremely pleased, for he chuckled and rubbed his hands together.

'A long shot, Watson; a very long shot!' said he, pinching my arm. 'Gregory, let me recommend to your attention this singular epidemic among the sheep. Drive on, coachman!'

Colonel Ross still wore an expression which showed the poor opinion which he had formed of my companion's ability, but I saw by the Inspector's face that his attention had been keenly aroused.

'You consider that to be important?' he asked.

'Exceedingly so.'

'Is there any other point to which you would wish to draw my attention?'

'To the curious incident of the dog in the night-time.'

'The dog did nothing in the night-time.'

'That was the curious incident,' remarked Sherlock Holmes.

Four days later Holmes and I were again in the train bound for Winchester, to see the race for the Wessex Cup. Colonel Ross met us, by appointment, outside the station, and we drove in his drag to the course beyond the town. His face was grave and his manner was cold in the extreme.

'I have seen nothing of my horse,' said he.

'I suppose that you would know him when you saw him?' asked Holmes.

The Colonel was very angry. 'I have been on the turf for twenty years, and never was asked such a question as that before,' said he. 'A child would know Silver Blaze with his white forehead and his mottled off fore leg.'

'How is the betting?'

'Well, that is the curious part of it. You could have got fifteen to one yesterday, but the price has become shorter and shorter, until you can hardly get three to one now.'

'Hum!' said Holmes. 'Somebody knows something, that is clear!'

As the drag drew up in the enclosure near the grand stand, I glanced at the card to see the entries. It ran:—

Wessex Plate. 50 sovs. each, h ft, with 1,000 sovs. added, for four and five-year olds. Second £300. Third £200. New course (one mile and five furlongs).

1. Mr Heath Newton's The Negro (red cap, cinnamon jacket).
2. Colonel Wardlaw's Pugilist (pink cap, blue and black jacket).
3. Lord Backwater's Desborough (yellow cap and sleeves).
4. Colonel Ross's Silver Blaze (black cap, red jacket).
5. Duke of Balmoral's Iris (yellow and black stripes).
6. Lord Singleford's Rasper (purple cap, black sleeves).

'We scratched our other one and put all hopes on your word,' said the Colonel. 'Why, what is that? Silver Blaze favourite?'

'Five to four against Silver Blaze!' roared the ring. 'Five to four against Silver Blaze! Fifteen to five against Desborough! Five to four on the field!'

'There are the numbers up,' I cried. 'They are all six there.'

'All six there! Then my horse is running,' cried the Colonel in great agitation. 'But I don't see him. My colours have not passed.'

'Only five have passed. This must be he.'

As I spoke a powerful bay horse swept out from the weighing inclosure and cantered past us, bearing on its back the well-known black and red of the Colonel.

'That's not my horse,' cried the owner. 'That beast has not a white hair upon its body. What is this that you have done, Mr Holmes?'

'Well, well, let us see how he gets on,' said my friend imperturbably. For a few minutes he gazed through my field-glass. 'Capital! An excellent start!' he cried suddenly. 'There they are, coming round the curve!'

From our drag we had a superb view as they came up the straight. The six horses were so close together that a carpet could have covered them, but half-way up the yellow the Capleton stable showed to the front. Before they reached us, however, Desborough's bolt was shot, and the Colonel's horse, coming away with a rush, passed the post a good six lengths before its rival, the Duke of Balmoral's Iris making a bad third.

'It's my race anyhow,' gasped the Colonel, passing his hand over his eyes. 'I confess that I can make neither head nor tail of it. Don't you think that you have kept up your mystery long enough, Mr Holmes?'

'Certainly, Colonel. You shall know everything. Let us all go round and have a look at the horse together. Here he is,' he continued, as we made our way into the weighing inclosure where only owners and their friends find admittance. 'You have only to wash his face and his leg in spirits of wine and you will find that he is the same old Silver Blaze as ever.'

'You take my breath away!'

'I found him in the hands of a faker, and took the liberty of running him just as he was sent over.'

'My dear sir, you have done wonders. The horse looks very fit and well. It never went better in its life. I owe you a thousand apologies for having doubted your ability. You have done me a great service by recovering my horse. You would do me a greater still if you could lay your hands on the murderer of John Straker.'

'I have done so,' said Holmes quietly.

The Colonel and I stared at him in amazement. 'You have got him! Where is he, then?'

'He is here.'

'Here! Where?'

'In my company at the present moment.'

The Colonel flushed angrily. 'I quite recognize that I am under obligations to you, Mr Holmes,' said he, 'but I must regard what you have just said as either a very bad joke or an insult.'

Sherlock Holmes laughed. 'I assure you that I have not associated you with the crime, Colonel,' said he; 'the real murderer is standing immediately behind you!'

He stepped past and laid his hand upon the glossy neck of the thoroughbred.

'The horse!' cried both the Colonel and myself.

'Yes, the horse. And it may lessen his guilt if I say that it was done in self-defence, and that John Straker was a man who was entirely unworthy of your confidence. But there goes the bell; and as I stand to win a little on this next race, I shall defer a more lengthy explanation until a more fitting time.'

We had the corner of a Pullman car to ourselves that evening as we whirled back to London, and I fancy that the journey was a short one to Colonel Ross as well as to myself, as we listened to our companion's narrative of the events which had occurred at the Dartmoor training stables upon that Monday night, and the means by which he had unravelled them.

'I confess,' said he, 'that any theories which I had formed from the newspaper reports were entirely erroneous. And yet there were indications there, had they not been overlaid by other details which concealed their true import. I went to Devonshire with the conviction that Fitzroy Simpson was the true culprit, although, of course, I saw that the evidence against him was by no means complete.

'It was while I was in the carriage, just as we reached the trainer's house, that the immense significance of the curried mutton occurred to me. You may remember that I was distrait, and remained sitting after you had all alighted. I was marvelling in my own mind how I could possibly have overlooked so obvious a clue.'

'I confess,' said the Colonel, 'that even now I cannot see how it helps us.'

'It was the first link in my chain of reasoning. Powdered opium is by no means tasteless. The flavour is not disagreeable, but it is perceptible. Were it mixed with any ordinary dish, the eater would undoubtedly detect it, and would probably eat no more. A curry was exactly the medium which would disguise this taste. By no possible supposition could this stranger, Fitzroy Simpson, have caused curry to be served in the trainer's family that night, and it is surely too monstrous a coincidence to suppose that he happened to come along with powdered opium upon the very night when a dish happened to be served which would disguise the flavour. That is unthinkable. Therefore Simpson becomes eliminated from the case, and our attention centres upon Straker and his wife, the only two people who could have chosen curried mutton for supper that night. The opium was added after the dish was set aside for the stable boy, for the others had the same for supper with no ill effects. Which of them, then, had access to that dish without the maid seeing them?

'Before deciding that question I had grasped the significance of the silence of the dog, for one true inference invariably suggests others. The Simpson incident had shown me that a dog was kept in the stables, and yet, though someone had been in and had fetched out a horse, he had not barked enough to arouse the two lads in the loft. Obviously the midnight visitor was someone whom the dog knew well.

'I was already convinced, or almost convinced, that John Straker went down to the stables in the dead of the night and took out Silver Blaze. For what purpose? For a dishonest one, obviously, or why should he drug his own stable boy? And yet I was at a loss to know why. There have been cases before now where trainers have made sure of great sums of money by laying against their own horses, through agents, and then prevented them from winning by fraud. Sometimes it is a pulling jockey. Sometimes it is some surer and subtler means. What was it here? I hoped that the contents of his pockets might help me to form a conclusion.

'And they did so. You cannot have forgotten the singular knife which was found in the dead man's hand, a knife which certainly no sane man would choose for a weapon. It was, as Dr Watson told us, a form of knife which is used for the most delicate operations known in surgery. And it was to be used for a delicate operation that night. You must know, with your wide experience of turf matters, Colonel Ross, that it is possible to make a slight nick upon the tendons of a horse's ham, and to do it subcutaneously so as to leave absolutely no trace. A horse so treated would develop a slight lameness which would be put down to a strain in exercise or a touch of rheumatism, but never to foul play.'

'Villain! Scoundrel!' cried the Colonel.

'We have here the explanation of why John Straker wished to take the horse out on to the moor. So spirited a creature would have certainly roused the soundest of sleepers when it felt the prick of the knife. It was absolutely necessary to do it in the open air.'

'I have been blind!' cried the Colonel. 'Of course, that was why he needed the candle, and struck the match.'

'Undoubtedly. But in examining his belongings, I was fortunate enough to discover, not only the method of the crime, but even its motives. As a man of the world, Colonel, you know that men do not carry other people's bills about in their pockets. We have most of us quite enough to do to settle our own. I at once concluded that Straker was leading a double life, and keeping a second establishment. The nature of the bill showed that there was a lady in the case, and one who had expensive tastes. Liberal as you are with your servants, one hardly expects that they can buy twenty-guinea walking dresses for their women. I questioned Mrs Straker as to the dress without her knowing it, and having satisfied myself that it had never reached her, I made a note of the milliner's address, and felt that by calling there with Straker's photograph, I could easily dispose of the mythical Darbyshire.

'From that time on all was plain. Straker had led out the horse to a hollow where his light would be invisible. Simpson, in his flight, had dropped his cravat, and Straker had picked it up with some idea, perhaps, that he might use it in securing the horse's leg. Once in the hollow he had got behind the horse, and had struck a light, but the creature, frightened at the sudden glare, and with the strange instinct of animals feeling that some mischief was intended, had lashed out, and the steel shoe had struck Straker full on the forehead. He had already, in spite of the rain, taken off his overcoat in order to do his delicate task, and so, as he fell, his knife gashed his thigh. Do I make it clear?'

'Wonderful!' cried the Colonel. 'Wonderful! You might have been there.'

'My final shot was, I confess, a very long one. It struck me that so astute a man as Straker would not undertake this delicate tendon-nicking without a little practice. What could he practise on? My eyes fell upon the sheep, and I asked a question which, rather to my surprise, showed that my surmise was correct.'

'You have made it perfectly clear, Mr Holmes.'

'When I returned to London I called upon the milliner, who at once recognized Straker as an excellent customer, of the name of Darbyshire, who had a very dashing wife with a strong partiality for expensive dresses. I have no doubt that this woman had plunged him over head and ears in debt, and so led him into this miserable plot.'

'You have explained all but one thing,' cried the Colonel. 'Where was the horse?'

'Ah, it bolted and was cared for by one of your neighbours. We must have an amnesty in that direction, I think. This is Clapham Junction, if I am not mistaken, and we shall be in Victoria in less than ten minutes. If you care to smoke a cigar in our rooms, Colonel, I shall be happy to give you any other details which might interest you.'

Won By A Neck

LESLIE CHARTERIS

Another famous race course which has disappeared to make way for Britain's second largest airport, Gatwick, is the focus of this next story featuring The Saint, the crime fighter whose exploits in print, in films and on television, have made him every bit as familiar as Sherlock Holmes. The difference between the authors of the two stories, however, was that Leslie Charteris was an inveterate follower of racing who for a time owned his own horse and even devised a betting system.

The Horley track at Gatwick, which Charteris frequently visited from his home not far distant at Englefield Green, was for years one of the most attractive meeting places in Southern England – vying in popularity with Lingfield, eight miles away, which, of course, still flourishes today. Writing in 1901, Charles Richardson said of it, 'Gatwick is in many respects a model racecourse. Everything is on so large a scale that there is far less crowding than there is elsewhere and the range of stands is one of the finest in the kingdom. The course, too, is a magnificent one: a furlong short of two miles round and wide everywhere. For long races, Gatwick offers a better course than any other Metropolitan enclosure.'

During its existence the track promoted three principal meetings in May, the end of July and in October, with the Worth Stakes and the Prince's Handicap being the most important events. Although Richardson believed that the paddock at Gatwick was one of the largest and best in the UK and the course had 'a great future', the demands of 'progress' proved too much, as another writer, Basil Cracknell, reported ruefully in his *Portrait of Surrey* (1970): 'Like Lingfield, Horley once had a race course, but when Gatwick Airport was built and enlarged to take the larger aircraft coming into use, the race course was swallowed up and so also the old London to Brighton road.' With its closure went half a century of great racing in one of the most picturesque areas of Surrey.

Leslie Charteris (1907–93) actually spent many years of his life in this county, although the fame of his character Simon Templar, aka The Saint 'the modern Robin Hood', whom he created in 1928, took him all over the world, especially to America where the early films about the handsome enemy of crime were made. The Saint also shared Charteris' love of horses – both were excellent horsemen – and enjoyed gambling. It was the success of the Saint books that enabled Charteris to pursue this love of racing and for a while he owned a horse named, not surprisingly, Simon Templar, which he hoped might win the Derby. W. O. G. Lofts, Charteris' biographer, says that racing was very much the author's main hobby. 'Apart from the horse, he was very interested in racing systems and devised one of his own,' says Lofts. 'It was called "The Windicator" and I handled it for him. Unfortunately, the fees for advertising it in the sporting papers were so high that in the end all it did was break even.'

Charteris had no more luck with his horse. In a letter to Lofts dated 20 January 1968 he says optimistically, 'About the begining of May I'll start making the Bookies unhappy again – and you can look out for a 2-year-old called "Simon Templar" of which Doug Marks is the trainer. Wouldn't it be funny if it won the Derby?'

A letter from Marks, the Lambourn trainer, dated 8 July 1970, reveals how these hopes were dashed: 'After Simon Templar's poor showing at Folkstone yesterday in what was a very poor event we feel it is just a waste of time and money to race him again and consequently we will be sending him to the sales at Ascot on 27 July.'

But Charteris was not a complete loser from these experiences, as the titles of several of the stories he wrote about The Saint bear witness: 'The Noble Sportsman', 'The Mug's Game' and 'Won By A Neck'. The last, which first appeared in the *Empire News* of 11 September 1932, and from which this reprint is taken, specifically features Charteris' local course. And in the light of the author's ambitions the events which occur – subtitled in the newspaper, 'The running of "Hill Billy" in the Owners' Handicap' – make doubly intriguing reading.

*

'The art of crime,' said Simon Templar, carefully mayonnaising a section of *truite à la gelée*, 'is to be versatile. Repetition breeds contempt – and promotion – some fellow from Scotland Yard. I assure you, Pat, I have never felt the slightest urge to be the means of helping any detective on his upward climb. Therefore, we soak bucket-shops one week and bootleggers the next, and poor old Chief Inspector Teal never knows where he is.'

Patricia Holm fingered the stem of her wine-glass with a far-away smile. Perhaps the smile was a trifle wistful. Perhaps it wasn't. You never knew. But she had been the Saint's partner in outlawry long enough to know what any such oratorical opening as that portended; and she smiled.

'It dawns upon me,' said the Saint, 'that our talents have not yet been applied to the crooked angles of the Sport of Kings.'

'I don't know,' said Patricia mildly. 'After picking the winner of the Derby with a pin and the winner of the Oaks with a pack of cards—'

Simon waved away the argument.

'You may think,' he remarked, 'that we came here to celebrate. But we didn't. Not exactly. We came here to feast our eyes on the celebrations of a brace of lads of the village who always tap the champagne here when they've brought off a coup. Let me introduce you. They're sitting at the corner table behind me on your right.'

Two Of The Lads

The girl glanced casually across the restaurant in the direction indicated. She located the two men at once – there were three magnums on the table in front of them, and their appearance was definitely hilarious.

Simon finished his plate and ordered strawberries and cream.

'The fat one with the face like an egg and the diamond tie-pin is Mr Joseph Graner. He wasn't always Graner, but what the hell? He's a very successful bookmaker; and believe it or not, Pat, I've got an account with him.'

'I suppose he doesn't know who you are?'

'That's where you're wrong. He does know – and the idea simply tickles him to death. It's the funniest thing he has to talk about. He lets me run an account, pays me when I win, and gets a cheque on the nail when I lose. And all the time he's splitting his sides, telling all his friends about it, and watching everything I do with an eagle eye – just waiting to catch me trying to put something across him.'

'Who's the thin one?'

'That's Vincent Lesbon. Origin believed to be Levantine. He owns the horses, and the way those horses run is nobody's business. Lesbon wins with 'em when he feels like it, and Graner fields against 'em so generously that the starting price usually goes out to the hundred-to-eight mark. It's an old racket, but they work it well.'

Patricia nodded. She was still waiting for the sequel that was bound to come – the reckless light in the Saint's eyes presaged it like a red sky at morning. But he annihilated his strawberries with innocent deliberation before he leaned back in his chair and groaned at her.

'Let's go racing tomorrow,' he said. 'I want to buy a horse.'

To Beat Most In His Class

They went down to Kempton Park, and arrived when the runners for the second race were going up. The race was a selling plate: with the aid of his faithful pin, Simon selected an outsider that finished third, but the favourite won easily by two lengths.

They went round to the ring after the numbers were posted, and the Saint had to bid up to four hundred guineas before he became the proud owner of Hill Billy.

As the circle of buyers and bystanders broke up, Simon felt a hand on his arm. He looked round, and saw a small thick-set man in check breeches and a bowler hat who had the unmistakable air of an ex-jockey.

'Excuse me, sir – have you arranged with a trainer to take care of your horse? My name's Mart Farrell. If I could do anything for you . . .'

Simon gazed thoughtfully at his new acquisition, which was being held by an expectant groom.

'Why, yes,' he murmured. 'I suppose I can't put the thing in my pocket and take it home. Let's go and have a drink.'

They strolled over to the bar. Simon knew Farrell's name as that of one of the straightest trainers on the turf, and was glad that one of his problems had been solved so easily.

'Think we'll win some more races?' he murmured, as the drinks were set up.

'Hill Billy's a good horse,' said the trainer judiciously: 'I used to have him in my stable when he was a two-year-old. I think he'll beat most things in his class if the handicaps give him a run. By the way, sir, I don't know your name.'

The Owners' Handicap

It occurred to the Saint that his baptismal title was perhaps too notorious for him to be able to hide the nucleus of his racing stud under a bushel, and for once he had no desire to attract undue publicity.

'Hill Billy belongs to the lady,' he said. 'Miss Patricia Holm. I'm just helping her to watch it.'

As far as Simon Templar was concerned, Hill Billy's career had only one object, and that was to run in a race in which one of the Graner-Lesbon stud was also a competitor. The suitability of the fixture was rather more important and more difficult to be sure of, but his luck was in.

Early the next week he learned that Hill Billy was favourably handicapped in the Owners' Plate at Gatwick on the following Saturday, and it so happened that his most serious opponent was a horse named Rickaway, owned by Mr Vincent Lesbon.

Simon drove down to Epsom early the next morning and saw Hill Billy at exercise. Afterwards he had a talk with Farrell.

'Hill Billy could win the first race at Ascot next week if the going's good,' said the trainer. 'I'd like to save him for it – it'd be a nice win for you. He's got the beating of most of the other entries.'

'Couldn't he win the Owners' Handicap on Saturday?' asked the Saint; and Farrell pursed his lips.

'It depends on what they decide to do with Rickaway, Sir. I don't like betting on a race when Mr Lesbon has a runner – if I may say so between ourselves. Lesbon had a filly in my stable last year, and I had to tell him I couldn't keep it. The jockey went up before the stewards after the way it ran one day at Newmarket, and that sort of thing doesn't do a trainer's reputation any good. Rickaway's been running down the course on his last three outings, but the way I work out the Owners' Handicap is that he could win if he wanted to.'

Simon nodded.

'Miss Holm rather wants to run at Gatwick, though,' he said. 'She's got an aunt or something from the North coming down for the weekend, and naturally she's keen to show off her new toy.'

Angel-faced Caller

Farrell shrugged cheerfully.

'Oh, well, sir. I suppose the ladies have got to have their way. I'll run Hill Billy at Gatwick if Miss Holm tells me to, but I couldn't advise her to have much of a bet. I'm afraid Rickaway might do well if he's a trier.'

Simon went back to London jubilantly.

'It's a match between Hill Billy and Rickaway,' he said. 'In other words, Pat, between Saintliness and Sin. Don't you think the angels might do a job for us?'

One angel did a job for them, anyway. It was Mr Vincent Lesbon's first experience of any such exquisite interference with his racing activities; and it may be mentioned that he was a very susceptible man.

This happened on the Gatwick Friday. The Graner-Lesbon

combination was putting in no smart work that day, and Mr Lesbon had whiled away the afternoon at a betting club in Long Acre, where he would sometimes beguile the time with innocuous half-crown punting between sessions at the snooker table. He stayed there until after the result of the last race was through on the tape, and then took a taxi to his flat in Maida Vale to dress for an evening's diversion.

Feminine visitors of the synthetic blonde variety were never rare at his apartment; but they usually came by invitation, and when they were not invited the call generally foreboded unpleasant news. The girl who stood on Mr Lesbon's doorstep this evening, with the air of having waited there for a long time, was an exception. Mr Lesbon's sensitive conscience cleared when he saw her face.

'May I – may I speak to you for a minute?'

The Blonde's Story

Mr Lesbon hesitated fractionally. Then he smiled – which did not make him more beautiful.

'Yes, of course. Come in.'

He fitted his key in the lock and led the way through to his sitting-room. Shedding his hat and gloves, he inspected the girl more closely. She was tall and straight as a sapling, with an easy grace of carriage that was not lost on him. Her face was one of the loveliest he had ever seen; and his practised eye told him that the cornfield gold of her hair owed nothing to artifice.

'What is it, my dear?'

'It's . . . Oh, I don't know how to begin! I've got no right to come and see you, Mr Lesbon, but – there wasn't any other way.'

'Won't you sit down?'

One of Mr Lesbon's few illusions was that women loved him for himself. He was a devotee of the more glutinous productions of the cinema, and prided himself on his polished technique. He offered her a cigarette, and sat on the arm of her chair.

'Tell me what's the trouble, and I'll see what we can do about it.'

'Well – you see – it's my brother . . . I'm afraid he's rather young and – well, silly. He's been backing horses. He's lost a lot of money, ever so much more than he can pay. You must know how easy it is. Putting on more and more to try and make up for his losses, and still losing . . . Well, he works in a bank; and his bookmaker's threatened to write to the manager if he doesn't pay up. Of course, Derek would lose his job at once . . .'

Mr Lesbon sighed.

'Dear me!' he said.

'Oh, I'm not trying to ask for money! Don't think that. I shouldn't be such a fool. But – well, Derek's made a friend of a man who's a trainer. His name's Farrell – I've met him, and I think he's quite straight. He's tried to make Derek give up betting, but it wasn't any good. However, he's got a horse in his stable called Hill Billy – I don't know anything about horses, but apparently Farrell said Hill Billy would be a certainty tomorrow if your horse didn't win. He advised Derek to do something about it – clear his losses and give it up for good.'

The girl twisted her handkerchief nervously.

'He said – please don't think I'm being rude, Mr Lesbon, but I'm just trying to be honest – he said you didn't always want to win – and – and – perhaps if I came and saw you—'

She looked up at Rickaway's owner with liquid eyes, her lower lip trembling a little. Mr Lesbon's breath came a shade faster.

'I know Farrell,' he said, as quietly as he could. 'I had a horse in his stable last year, and he asked me to take it away – just because I didn't always want to win with it. He's changed his principles rather suddenly.'

'I – I'm sure he'd never have done it if it wasn't for Derek, Mr Lesbon. He's really fond of the boy. Derek's awfully nice. He's a bit wild, but . . . Well, you see, I'm four years older than he is, and I simply have to look after him. I'd do anything for him.'

Lesbon cleared his throat.

'Yes, yes, my dear. Naturally.' He patted her hand. 'I see your predicament. So you want me to lose the race. Well, if Farrell's so fond of Derek, why doesn't he scratch Hill Billy and let the boy win on Rickaway?'

Lesbon Names His Price

'Because, oh, I suppose I can't help telling you. He said no one ever knew what your horses were going to do, and perhaps you mightn't be wanting to win with Rickaway tomorrow.'

Lesbon rose and poured himself out a glass of whisky.

'My dear, what a thing it is to have a reputation!' He gestured picturesquely. 'But I suppose we can't all be paragons of virtue . . . Still, that's quite a lot for you to ask me to do. Interfering with horses is a serious offence – a very serious offence. You can be warned off for it. You can be branded, metaphorically. Your whole career' – Mr Lesbon repeated his gesture – 'can be ruined.'

The girl bit her lip.

'Did you know that?' demanded Lesbon.

'I – I suppose I must have realized it. But when you're only thinking about someone you love—'

'Yes, I understand.' Lesbon drained his glass. 'You would do anything to save your brother. Isn't that what you said?'

He sat on the arm of the chair again, searching her face. There was no misreading the significance of his gaze.

The girl avoided his eyes.

'How much do you think you could do, my dear?' he whispered.

'No!' Suddenly she looked at him again, her lovely face pale and tragic. 'You couldn't want that – you couldn't be so—'

'Couldn't I?' The man laughed.

'My dear, you're too innocent!' He went back to the decanter. 'Well, I respect your innocence. I respect it enormously. We won't say any more about – unpleasant things like that. I will be philanthropical. Rickaway will lose. And there are no strings to it. I give way to a charming and courageous lady.'

She sprang up.

'Mr Lesbon! Do you mean that – will you really—'

'My dear, I will,' pronounced Mr Lesbon thickly. 'I will present your courage with the reward that it deserves. Of course,' he added, 'If you feel very grateful – after Rickaway has lost – and if you would like to come to a little supper party – I should be delighted. I should feel honoured. Now if you weren't doing anything after the races on Saturday . . .'

So Happy To Help

'I should love to come,' she said huskily. 'I think you're the kindest man I've ever known. I'll be on the course tomorrow, and if you still think you'd like to see me again—'

'My dear, nothing in the world could please me more!' Lesbon put a hand on her shoulder and pressed her towards the door. 'Now you run along home and forget all about it. I'm only too happy to be able to help such a charming lady.'

Patricia Holm walked round the block in which Mr Lesbon's flat was situated and found Simon Templar waiting patiently at the wheel of his car. She stepped in beside him, and they whirled down into the line of traffic that was crawling towards Marble Arch.

'How d'you like Vincent?' asked the Saint, and Patricia shivered.

'If I'd known what he was like at close quarters I'd never have gone,' she said. 'He's got hot slimy hands, and the way he looks at you . . . But I think I did the job well.'

Simon smiled a little, and flicked the car through a gap between two taxis that gave him half an inch to spare on either wing.

'So that for once we can give the pin a rest,' he said.

Saturday morning dawned clear and fine, which was very nearly a record for the season. What was more, it stayed fine; and Mart Farrell was optimistic.

'The going's just right for Hill Billy,' he said. 'If he's ever going to beat Rickaway he'll have to do it today. Perhaps your aunt might have five shillings on him after all, Miss Holm.'

Patricia's eyebrows lifted vaguely. 'My – er—'

A Fast One Coming

'Miss Holm's aunt got up this morning with a bilious attack,' said the Saint glibly. 'It's all very annoying after we've put on this race for her benefit, but since Hill Billy's here he'd better have the run.'

The Owners' Handicap stood fourth on the card. They lunched on the course, and afterwards the Saint made an excuse to leave Patricia in the Silver Ring and went into Tattersall's with Farrell. Mr Lesbon favoured the more expensive enclosure, and the Saint was not inclined to give him the chance to acquire any premature doubts.

The runners for the three-thirty were being put in the frame, and Farrell went off to give his blessing to a charge of his that was booked to go to the post. Simon strolled down to the rails and faced the expansive smile of Mr Graner.

'You having anything on this one, Mr Templar?' asked the bookie juicily.

'I don't think so,' said the Saint. 'But there's a fast one coming to you in the next race. Look out!'

As he wandered away, he heard Mr Graner chortling over the unparalleled humour of the situation in the ear of his next-door neighbour.

Simon watched the finish of the three-thirty, and went to find Farrell.

'I've got a first-class jockey to ride Hill Billy,' the trainer told him. 'He came to my place this morning and tried him out, and he thinks we've a good chance. Lesbon is putting Penterham up – he's a funny rider. Does a lot of Lesbon's work, so it doesn't tell us anything.'

'We'll soon see what happens,' said the Saint calmly. He stayed to see Hill Billy saddled, and then went back to where the opening odds were being shouted. With his hands in his pockets he sauntered leisurely up and down the line of bawling bookmakers, listening to the fluctuation of the prices.

Hill Billy opened favourite at 2 to 1, with Rickaway a close second at threes – in spite of its owner's dubious reputation. Another horse named Tilbury, which had originally been quoted at 8 to 1, suddenly came in demand at 9 to 2.

The £100 'Plunge'

Simon overheard snatches of the gossip that was flashing along the line, and smiled to himself. The Graner-Lesbon combination was expert at drawing that particular brand of red herring across the trail, and the Saint could guess at the source of the rumour. Hill Billy weakened to five to two, while Tilbury pressed close behind it from fours to threes. Rickaway faded out to five to one.

'There are always mugs who'll go for a horse just because other people are backing it,' Mr Graner muttered to his clerk: and then he saw the Saint coming up. 'Well, Mr Templar, what's this fast one you promised me?'

'Hill Billy's the name,' said the Saint, 'and I guess it's good for a hundred.'

'Two hundred and fifty pounds to one hundred for Mr Templar,' said Graner lusciously, and watched his clerk entering up the bet.

When he looked up the Saint had gone.

Tilbury dropped back to seven to two, and Hill Billy stayed solid at two and a half. Just before the off Mr Graner shouted: 'Six to one Rickaway!' and had the satisfaction of seeing the odds go down before the recorder closed his notebook.

He mopped his brow, and found Mr Lesbon beside him.

'I wired off five hundred pounds to ten different offices,' said Lesbon. 'A little more of this and I'll be moving into Park Lane. When that girl came to see me I nearly fainted. What does that man Templar take us for?'

'I don't know,' said Mr Graner phlegmatically.

Won By A Neck

A general bellow from the crowd announced the off, and Mr Graner mounted his stool and watched the race through his field glasses.

'Tilbury's jumped off in front: Hill Billy's third, and Ricka-way's going well on the outside . . . Rickaway's moving up, and Hill Billy's on a tight rein . . . Hill Billy's gone up to second. The rest of the field's packed behind, but they don't look like springing any surprises . . . Tilbury's finished. He's falling back. Hill Billy leads, Mandrake running second, Rickaway half a length behind with plenty in hand . . . Penterham's using the whip, and Rickaway's picking up. He's level with Mandrake – no, he's got it by a short head. Hill Billy's a length in front, and they're putting everything in for the finish.'

The roar of the crowd grew louder as the field entered the last furlong. Graner raised his voice.

'Mandrake's out of it, and Rickaway's coming up. Hill Billy's flat out with Rickaway's nose at his saddle . . . Hill Billy's making a race of it. It's neck and neck now. Penterham left it a bit late. Rickaway's gaining slowly . . .'

The yelling of the crowd rose to a final crescendo, and suddenly died away.

'Well,' Mr Graner said comfortably, 'that's three thousand pounds to the good.'

The two men shook hands gravely. They did not see Simon Templar's smile as he stood behind them.

After a while the Saint drifted towards them.

'Too bad about Hill Billy, Mr Templar,' remarked Graner succulently. 'Rickaway only did it by a neck, though I won't say he mightn't have done better if he'd started his sprint a bit sooner.'

Simon Templar removed the cigar. 'Oh, I don't know,' he said. 'As a matter of fact, I rather changed my mind about Hill Billy's chance just before the off. I was over at the telegraph office, and I didn't think I'd be able to reach you in time, so I wired another bet to your London office. Only a small one – six hundred pounds, if you want to know. I hope Vincent's winnings will stand it.' He beamed seraphically at Mr Lesbon, whose face had suddenly gone a sickly grey. 'Of course you recognized Miss Holm – she isn't easy to forget, and I saw you noticing her at the Savoy the other night.'

There was an awful silence.

'By the way,' said the Saint, patting Mr Lesbon affably on the shoulder, 'she tells me you've got hot, slimy hands. Apart from that, your technique makes Clark Gable look like something the cat brought in. Just a friendly tip, old dear.'

He waved to the two stupefied men and wandered away; and they stood gaping dumbly at his retreating back.

It was Mr Lesbon who spoke first, after a long and pregnant interval.

'Of course you won't settle, Joe,' he said half-heartedly.

'Won't I?' snarled Mr Graner. 'And let him have me up before Tattersall's Committee for welshing? I've *got* to settle, you fool!'

Mr Graner choked.

Then he cleared his throat. He had a great deal more to say, and he wanted to say it distinctly.

The American Invasion

FRANK JOHNSON

There has never been a threat to the existence of Newmarket, the main setting of this next story and the course where the Flat Racing Season starts each April with the Craven Meeting and the famous Nell Gwyn Stakes. It was at this particular meeting in April 1895 that what subsequently became known as the 'American Invasion' began with the entry of a number of horses from across the Atlantic which proceeded to win race after race all over the country. Forced here by the anti-racing lobby in America, which seemed then on the verge of winning its crusade to extinguish the sport, an army of owners, trainers, jockeys, horses and even gamblers descended onto the English courses and were soon being viewed with open hostility by many of the people involved in racing. The reason for this attitude was not hard to discover, as Wray Vamplew has explained in *The Turf: A Social and Economic History of Horse Racing* (1976): 'Not all the trans-Atlantic visitors came with criminal intent, but some of them had fraud and turf abuse down to a fine art, if not a science.' This verdict was even shared by some of the Americans themselves: John Huggins, the trainer of Volodyovski, the winner of the 1901 Derby, responded to a question as to whether there were many crooks on the American turf with the emphatic remark, 'No, they have all come over here to England!'

The reason for the astonishing success of the Americans soon became evident: horses were doped to enhance their perform-ance, jockeys were bribed, favourites pulled and the whole business of handicapping turned into a farce. The success of these 'slick Yankees' as they were dubbed – in 1905, for instance, five of the leading ten jockeys were from the USA – finally forced the Jockey Club to take action: tightening up the rules of entry and warning off the most blatant offenders.

In order to compete with the newcomers, some English riders began to copy their 'monkey-on-a-stick' style of riding, said to have evolved from the Red Indians. This involved a forward crouching position with short reins and shortened stirrup leathers which was designed to save wind pressure and bring forward the centre of gravity. The American jockeys also took to riding each race from the front rather than waiting in the pack. Within a few years, the US jockeys, owners and even the gamblers had gone – though the memory of their 'invasion' remained a part of popular folklore for years and provided a rich source of material for thriller writers.

Frank Johnston (1900–65) was not born when the 'American Invasion' occurred, but stories about it were still circulating when he became a racing journalist on the *Morning Post*. All the suggestions of doping and foul riding naturally intrigued him and he began to specialize in investigating crime on the turf. Then in the early thirties he started to make use of the information that his paper could not print in novels like *Turf Racketeers* (1933), *The Mystery Tipster* (1934), *Disqualified* (1935) and *Easy Money* (1935) which was subtitled, 'The Amazing Adventures of Tony Denton, The Raffles of the Turf'. But it was not until two years after this that Johnston created the character for whom he is best remembered – Marcus Thaine, the 'Turf Crook'. In the very first story about Thaine, 'The Regent Street Fiasco', Frank explained his antihero's philosophy: 'Because ready money plays such a big part in racing, and because it is one of the few directions in which a man may acquire wealth quickly, the Turf will always be subject to evils. In the same way that the Stock Exchange attracts crook speculators, so will there always be a section in racing out to capture easy money.' Thaine was certainly an ingenious and cunning 'speculator' who made his money either by gambling, as a tipster, running a book or simply fixing races – not always successfully, but invariably just out of the reach of the law.

The popularity of 'The Turf Crook' earned Johnson the reputation of being the 'Modern Nat Gould' and his books continued to sell in large quantities until the late fifties. Though now long out of print, the novels about the shady Marcus Thaine are still avidly collected and command high prices from second-hand book dealers. Here, then, is one of Frank Johnston's stories, written in 1937, which features a battle of wits between England's famous turf crook and a typical group of the 'slick Yankees' who in just a few years were responsible for writing one of the shadiest chapters in the history of British racing.

*

I wonder how many of my readers remember the American invasion of the Turf. It was a very thrilling time for those who were involved and for the racing generation of that day.

Exactly how the Yankees conceived the idea of raiding the British Turf is not known; but it was in the days when doping was not against the regulations, although the practice was frowned upon by the authorities. Later, and as a result of the American habit, it was made illegal to dose a horse before a race.

There are many thrilling episodes in connection with the days of the Yankee invasion, but for the moment I, Marcus Thaine, will relate only a few of those with which I was intimately connected.

I purposely refrain from giving the real names of the people concerned, but the reader will appreciate that, as some of them might still be living, it would not be wise to do so. When the Yankees first came into the game many of us laughed at them – at least, we smiled politely when we heard the boasts that they would take a million out of the ring. Others had evolved similar schemes before and had always ended by asking for parish relief or by paying twopence-halfpenny in the pound.

But, to the general amazement, the American horses brought over here to run in their colours kept on winning. Victory after victory was recorded, and every time they won a packet of money. In fact, it became the custom to mark all their runners with a cross before betting commenced on any afternoon, and after a while none of the leading pencillers would lay a fair price against an 'invader'.

Then the Yanks got wise to it, and ran a few down the course, and someone backed the 'danger' for them with the result that the ring nearly always lost. After an American-owned horse had been well beaten it was often at a better price next time out – at least, until the money went on – and when they had backed it it was any odds on the brute winning.

As I have tried to explain, affairs developed into a battle of wits between the American contingent and the ring, and the invaders most times came through with honours – and the boodle. We were not sure they were trying until they stepped in with the money, and were badly caught on the occasions when they placed the commissions away from the course and landed a coup at long odds at starting price.

I say 'we', but was not actually concerned myself with any firm operating in Tattersalls, although, naturally, I had many friends among the bookmakers. I'll give the Yankees their due, however, for they were most thorough and left little to chance when they had a gamble. Of course, they lost now and again, but on balance they had made deep impressions on the banking accounts of many of the leading lights of the ring, who were finding out – for once in a way – that making a book was not the surest way to build a row of houses.

Matters got to such a pitch that a number of those who had been badly hit – including one prominent professional who had frequently opposed the Yanks – got together and had a private conference. They invited a few of the 'heads', myself included, and we passed a resolution that 'steps must be taken'. It was not put exactly that way, but I cannot here repeat the language, which was extremely forcible. Anyway, we decided that the American 'gentlemen' must be given a shock.

Cunning had to be met with cunning. They employed clever methods – we must retaliate. That was the beginning, and a few of us formed ourselves into a 'committee' to work out a practical plan.

We waited and watched for the slightest sign of a big coup on the part of the 'enemy', and as a result of the most searching inquiries, and plotting, we formed strong suspicions that they would try to win with Dolcis at Newbury.

I should like to say that we were not guessing, for men had been employed to watch day and night the stable and gallops where their horses were trained, and we knew of every exercise spin that had taken place. These watchers had to use the utmost caution, and devised many ways by which they should remain hidden. They climbed high trees, lay under furze bushes, and even moved the bushes during the night to get better positions. We had no chance to plant anyone inside the stable, but did everything else that was possible, and, as I say, we knew every stride of work done by their horses.

We discussed the prospects of Dolcis winning at Newbury. 'It's any odds you like,' I said, 'that they'll dope him.' And the others concurred.

From information which had come into our possession in an indirect way we knew that the Yankees bought the dope – a mixture of cocaine and some other drug, which maddened their horses when it took effect – from a chemist in Paris, and that one of them made periodical trips to get the stuff. It was administered about ten minutes before the race while the horse was being saddled in the enclosed stall, so that the act could not be seen by the public, and an ordinary syringe was employed. The question was, could we stop them doping Dolcis at Newbury?

Then I had one of those brilliant flashes which come only a few times during a man's life. 'Why not let 'em dope it, but tamper with the stuff so that the injection will be harmless?' I suggested.

I was, of course, derided, but I persisted. 'It is not so impossible,' I told them. 'Leave the matter in my hands and I will guarantee that they will think Dolcis has been doped, whereas nothing of the sort will have happened.'

On my swearing that I knew how it could be done, the others agreed to take a chance on my word. As soon as I gave them the 'office' that Dolcis was not doped they would lay against the horse for all they were worth, and the Yankees would lose their money. The horse had only a fair chance even on its best form unless it was doped, and it would be a racing certainty for Clear Tom and Hebrides to beat it if all other things were equal.

I then sought out Jem Murphy. He was, I regret to say, more

often in prison than out, but was just the man for my purpose, being the most expert pickpocket ever known to Scotland Yard. It is said of him that he even took the wallet out of an inspector's pocket while in a cab when he was handcuffed. Anyway, his exploits do not matter now. It remains that I gave him £50 and promised him another hundred if he followed my instructions and was completely successful. All he had to do was to make a short train journey from Dover to London.

In due course Dolcis was saddled for the race at Newbury, and when I gave the word everything was as planned they began to pepper the horse in the market. From 2 to 1 he gradually drifted out to 5's, and all the time the Yankees were betting like mad. They thought the layers had gone nuts, and could not resist the offers. They really ought to have taken the warning, for whenever a horse goes like that in betting it is any odds against it, for the layers do not – as a rule – take a liberty.

I heard one or two of the Yanks in the ring discussing the matter. They were convinced that the layers had lost their senses; but wait and see what happened.

Dolcis was under the whip at half-way and never threatened the least danger, the race being won by Clear Tom with Hebrides second, and the Americans were several thousand pounds poorer as a result.

Then I had to explain exactly how success had been achieved. At an *élite* gathering, when we celebrated the occasion, I told the others just how it had been brought about.

After explaining that I had employed Jem Murphy – at which there was a gasp of surprise – I continued: 'To a man of his ability it was simple in the extreme. He boarded the boat-train at Dover and readily located the man who had been sent to Paris for the dope. I had given him a full description beforehand. I am not sure exactly when he did it, but either on the journey or at the station he relieved the Yank of his dope and substituted an exactly similar bottle of harmless fluid, mostly consisting of water. I found out in Paris exactly how the stuff was supplied, and, in fact, bought some so that I should have the same type of bottle. To Jem Murphy it was child's play, and as a result Dolcis could not be doped, although they thought it had been. Probably they will discover the trick we played them when they examine the rest of the stuff in the bottle, but the chemist in Paris will get the blame for that.'

They marvelled at the ingenuity of the scheme, and were loud in their praise of my plan, which had been completely successful.

The next occasion that we delivered a smashing blow to the Yanks was in connection with the Cesarewitch, which is run at Newmarket. The watchers were still employed to report the gallops done by their horses, and had become so well acquainted with the stable that they knew everything there was to know about the place.

It was entirely due to this service that we formed the plan which was put into operation. They had two horses entered in the Cesarewitch, one of the big gambling races of the autumn, which is run over two miles and a quarter and is probably the most exacting test in the year for handicap horses.

Anyway, we learned that only one of their horses had any real chance, and in due course the other was scratched. The White House was the name of the colt with which they hoped to win, and our touts reported he was making wonderful progress and that on home form he held a magnificent chance.

The White House was, however, a peculiar animal, and, like so many humans, had passionate likes and dislikes. He was devoted to a little terrier in the stables, and would never gallop a yard on the training-ground unless satisfied that his little canine companion was there to see him perform. It had been the same at the meetings when he had run, and the terrier was allowed in the parade ring and would accompany the horse to the post, never causing the slightest annoyance to anyone when walking round with the horse. He would gallop along when The White House cantered to the start, and the only time he barked was at the off, after which he would follow the field and rejoin his equine friend in the unsaddling enclosure. This had evoked comment, but people only smiled, for it touched a soft spot in everybody's heart.

But this was where we proposed to step in. Action was unnecessary until after the Yanks had backed The White House, which they did, and for very substantial amounts, too. In gradually shortening the odds the layers exercised great cunning, for it put the Americans off their guard, and they had no conception of the plot we had prepared for their undoing. Every time they wanted to bet they were accommodated, and I shudder to think how much they would have won if . . . But that is the story.

The most difficult part of the scheme – in fact everything – depended upon our getting hold of that terrier. I took Bill Huggins and Pat O'Neill with me to the American stables near Lambourn two days before the Cesarewitch was to be run, and we consulted with the men who had been spying for us.

From these men we learned the exact routine of the stable, and one of them drew up a plan of the place. Of course, the Yanks were not entirely unprepared for anyone trying to get at The White House, but thanks to our exact knowledge of the topography of the stable it did not prove very hard to get inside.

Firstly we had to get past a watch-dog at the entrance. This was easy, for I threw him a nice piece of steak from a distance and within five minutes he was 'out', the meat having been saturated with a drug. We left him to sleep it off and made straight for the box in which The White House was stabled.

From our information the terrier would be in the box. In fact the little chap never had a kennel, but lived in the stall with the horse. This was where Pat O'Neill came in. In his early days he had tried many things for a living – some of them not exactly respectable, I will admit; nevertheless that was only a fortunate circumstance so far as the present occasion was concerned. Suffice it to say that he dealt with the lock on the door of that stall in less time than it takes to relate, and the way was clear. I remember him pocketing the skeleton-keys with a grin of satisfaction that his hand had lost none of its old cunning. Our luck was dead in that night, for the terrier never barked once. Again I threw a piece of doped meat, and after a suspicious sniff the terrier took a couple of bites. We saw him drop within a few seconds, and I crept into the stall and picked him up. So far we had scarcely made a sound, and while the horse stirred he did not wake, and we were able to lock the door again and steal away with the terrier. Poor little chap – it seemed a shame to play such a trick on him; but then, what were a dog's feelings compared with the immense amount of money at stake?

We heard later that the theft of the terrier caused great alarm at the stable, and the Yanks offered a large reward for his recovery. True enough, the horse was missing his little companion, and when brought out for a canter at Newmarket on the morning of the race moved in the worst possible manner, simply refusing to put any energy into his work. Those of us who saw this were delighted, and as a result the odds against The White House were extended.

Then the time came for the horses to be saddled. We presumed that The White House would be doped, but did not worry about it. The colt was staring all round the parade ring and seemed in a terribly nervous state. His affection for that little terrier was very real. You may think that stealing the dog was not enough to be absolutely certain that the horse would not win. Quite right, but I have yet to come to the real part of the plot. Getting the dog was only the first step.

In due course the horses cantered down towards the starting-post. This is situated out of sight of the stands and is 'behind the Ditch', as it is called at Newmarket. Actually the Ditch is well over a mile from the stands, and in front of it is a huge mound extending for nearly three-quarters of a mile. The first part of the Cesarewitch cannot be seen, only the flash of the colours at the gap – which is about half-way along the 'Ditch' – being visible from the enclosure.

Some time before the horses had been saddled I had made my way down to the starting-post, and waited for the field to come along. The White House was almost the last horse to arrive, and was giving his rider – a very famous jockey, by the way – a tremendous amount of trouble. The colt simply would not raise any sort of gallop, moving sluggishly and displaying the obstinacy of a mule.

The starter had become impatient, and as soon as The White House arrived at the post called the roll very rapidly. It was a bit of luck that the American horse was drawn on the right of the field, as this simplified matters, and I moved to a spot about twenty yards behind the line and immediately to the rear of The White House.

As soon as the horses began to line up I undid my overcoat, under which I had been holding the terrier, and allowed him to see the horses. It required the most exact judgment on my part, for I did not want The White House to observe his little companion until close upon the off.

At last I determined that the time had come for action, and gave the terrier several sharp pinches. Of course, he yelped with pain, but that was only momentarily, and then commenced barking for all he was worth. Just as I expected, the American colt pricked up his ears at the noise and, sensing the familiar yelp, turned his head towards me. At that moment the starter was preparing to let the field go, and the jockey on The White House spurred the colt into line. He had, however, not reckoned with his mount. To make sure of our plan succeeding I gave the terrier several more pinches, and he yelped and howled for a few seconds. That did the trick, for The White House again turned his head, and when the starter dropped his flag the horse stood quite still, and then turned towards where I was standing. Meanwhile the field had gone over a hundred yards, and I released the little terrier.

He simply flew towards The White House, and it was really a joy to see him jumping round the colt. If ever there was real affection between two animals here it was. The horse bent down and nosed the little fellow, and together they went slowly back to the paddock, the jockey having accepted the situation – which was quite hopeless – and allowing the horse to go along at his own pace.

The colt was overjoyed. His step was jaunty, but it must have been an amazing sight to see them coming along the straight course at Turf Headquarters, neither animal having the slightest conception of the ludicrous situation. Of course, the Americans knew how we had tricked them, and that was the beginning of the end, for they soon gave up the game when they found they were being outwitted. On balance they were substantial winners, but the two instances which I have related left a deep hole in their pockets, and my only regret at the latter affair was that I should have to be unkind to the little terrier.

A Derby Horse

MICHAEL INNES

The Derby, first run in 1780, is without doubt the most famous Flat Race in the world, and Derby Day itself on the first Saturday in June is the event that every owner, trainer and jockey most wants to win. For those that do triumph the event means a place in racing history, while for the countless thousands who converge on Epsom Downs it is the highlight of the year, a day which has no equal anywhere else in the world.

The appeal of this great race has understandably caught the imagination of many great writers – the American Henry James, for instance, said that it gave any visitor 'a meaning to the old description of England as merry' – but equally any such gathering at which the allure of money provides such a vital element is bound to have its darker side, too, as Guy Logan observed in his book, *Classic Races of the Turf* (1928): 'The supposed poisoning of the Duke of Westminster's "Orme" was the great Derby sensation of the year 1892 and appealed to the lovers of the romantic and marvellous, suggesting, as it did, a Drury Lane drama or a novel by Nat Gould. The "nobbled favourite" became quite a popular topic and is, no doubt, believed in by many persons to this day.' Small wonder, then, that the Derby has proved such a natural setting for the crime novel and mystery short story. Pre-eminent, in my opinion, among the shorter fiction is this next tale by Michael Innes, whose early novels were heralded as highlights of the Golden Age of detective fiction, while his continuing output of sophisticated, puzzling crime stories have justifiably earned him a unique position in the genre. In his main character, John Appleby, he has also fashioned one of the most erudite detectives in mystery fiction: a man born in the backstreets of a Midland town who has risen from the rank of

Inspector to Commissioner of the Metropolitan Police. Although Appleby has now retired from the force and been knighted for his services, crime still continues to dog his footsteps and demand the attention of his special investigative powers. Sir John's position allows him to move easily among the highest circles of British society – especially at major sporting events – which equips him well for events such as those which unfold in the case of 'A Derby Horse'.

Michael Innes is the pen-name of John Innes Mackintosh Stewart (1906–), the Edinburgh-born academic who served for over a decade as Jury Professor of English at the University of Adelaide in Australia, and has since combined a career writing crime fiction with several highly praised biographies of literary figures, including Rudyard Kipling, Joseph Conrad and Thomas Hardy. Of his forty-five crime novels, over thirty feature the commanding figure of Appleby, who combines a profound knowledge of modern police techniques with an ability to spot obscure Latin and Shakespearean quotations in conversation which frequently hold the key to a crime. There is a little of both these capabilities at work in 'A Derby Horse', which also splendidly captures the excitement felt by all those who fancy a flutter on the race of races.

*

'Such curious names,' Mrs Mutter murmured, and let an eye travel vaguely down her card. 'Gay Time and Postman's Path and Summer Rain. Often *witty*, of course – one sees that when one looks at the names of the dear creatures' fathers and mothers – but inadequately *equine*, if you understand me.'

'Nonsense, m'dear.' Mrs Mutter's husband had tipped back his chair the better to scan through his binoculars the vast carpet of humanity covering the downs. 'You couldn't call a likely colt Dobbin, or a well-bred filly Dapple or Daisy . . . But what a tremendous turn-out there is. Biggest crowd, if you ask me, since 'forty-six – Airborne's race.'

'And the time's creeping on, and the excitement's creeping up.' Lady Appleby had glanced at her watch.

'Anxious about your husband – eh?' Mr Mutter shook his head. 'Exacting, being high up in the police. Hope he hasn't been detained by somebody's pinching the favourite. Or perhaps—'

'Nothing of that sort.' A new voice was heard – that of Sir John Appleby himself as he strolled up to join his party. 'But I did not long ago have to do with a Derby horse that went rather badly missing. Have you ever known, Mutter, a strong colt, closely knit and with the quarters of a sprinter, disappear into thin air? Disconcerting experience.'

'But no doubt instructive.' Mutter dropped his binoculars. 'And you've just got time to tell us about it.'

Appleby sat down. 'It began with a frantic telephone-call from a certain Major Gunton, who trains near Blandford. Pantomime had vanished.'

Mrs Mutter made one of her well-known charming gestures. 'What did I say? Such *curious* names. Who could take seriously a horse called that?'

'Gunton did, and so did the brute's owner. They had entered Pantomime for this very Derby.'

'Hasn't that to be done very young?' Mrs Mutter was eager for knowledge. 'Like Eton boys, and that sort of thing?'

Mutter groaned. 'As yearlings, m'dear. Appleby, go on.'

'Pantomime was being sent from Blandford to Newbury. The journey, which was to be made by road—'

'It would be in one of those horrid little boxes.' Mrs Mutter was expressive. 'Almost like *coffins*, supposing horses to *have* coffins. The poor things can't so much as turn round.'

'It wouldn't be to their advantage to do so.' Appleby took the point seriously. 'Bumpy, you know. But the box was certainly what you describe – a simple, open affair, hitched to the back of an estate-wagon. Gunton had a reliable man called Merry, who saw to getting Pantomime into the thing at about dusk one fine autumn evening. Gunton himself came out and saw that the creature was safely locked in; and then Merry and a stable-lad got into the wagon and drove off. Short of a road accident, Pantomime seemed as safe as houses. And until Salisbury, if Merry could be believed, he *was* safe. After that, it grew dark. And in the dark – again if Merry could be believed – some mysterious violation of the very laws of nature took place. In other words, when the box arrived in Newbury, Pantomime had disappeared.'

Mutter raised his eyebrows. 'Lock tampered with?'

'No. And they hadn't had to pull up during the whole journey.'

'Then Pantomime must have *jumped*.' Mrs Mutter was horrified.

Appleby shook his head. 'Quite impossible. Those boxes give a horse no room for tricks. There seemed only one conceivable explanation: that some Brobdingnagian bird had descended on poor little Pantomime and carried him off in his beak.

'I was working on a case in Oxford when I got the message asking me to take over this queer affair. There wasn't much more information forthcoming than what I've given you, but of course there was a description of the horse: a chestnut with black spots on the hind quarters – like Eclipse and Pantaloon, I was told by a man at the Yard who specialises in the Stud-Book. With this I set out very early on the morning following the disappearance, intending to drive straight to Blandford, and from there retrace Pantomime's last journey if it should be necessary.

'I had got to Newbury, and was wondering whether Andover would be a good place to stop for breakfast, when I ran into fog. It seemed best to press on – and I must confess that probably I pressed on pretty fast. Still, policemen do well always to drive with a bit of extra care; and I was doing nothing that any normal contingency could render dangerous. Nevertheless, I had an accident. At one moment I had been staring into empty air – or fog. The next, there was a solid object plumb in front of my bonnet, and this was followed by a slight but ominous impact before I brought the car to a stop. For a second I wondered whether I'd fallen asleep at the wheel. For what I had *seen* in that moment decidedly suggested a dream. It had been a substantial chestnut mass, diversified with black spots.

'I climbed out and ran back. There, sure enough – and with all the appearance of having been hurled violently into a high hedge – I glimpsed the figure of a chestnut colt. But it was only for a moment; the wretched fog was getting worse, with drifting patches as thick as a horse-blanket. Pantomime was obscured for a couple of seconds – and when the place cleared again he had vanished.

'That was all to the good, since it meant he could scarcely have broken any bones. The road was empty, so I concluded he had forced his way through the hedge. I followed suit – it wasn't a comfortable dive – and there he was. But by *there* I mean a quarter of a mile off. He seemed to have done that in about twenty seconds.'

Mutter chuckled. 'A Derby horse, decidedly. Mahmoud's record for the twelve furlongs—'

'Quite so. Well, off I went in pursuit – and presently the dream had turned to nightmare. It's an odd bit of country – open, undulating, and covered with scattered patches of gorse which seem to have been blown into all sorts of fantastic shapes by the wind. What with the fog thrown in, it was easy to feel oneself hunting the hapless Pantomime amid a sort of menagerie of prehistoric monsters. And Pantomime was – well, illusive. For one thing, he had more than flat-racing in him. At one moment I even had a confused notion that he had cleared a hay-stack. And this was the more surprising, since he did now appear to have injured himself. I was getting no more than peeps at him, but his gait was certainly queer. And if horses get concussion – well, Pantomime was badly concussed.

'The end came quickly. Somewhere near by there was a chap out with a shot-gun after rabbits – a silly employment in those conditions – and he was coming near enough to worry me. Suddenly I rounded a clump of gorse and came upon Pantomime apparently cornered and at bay. I had just time to feel that there was something pretty weirdly wrong when the creature rose in air like a tiger and came sailing down at me. At the same instant I heard a patter of shot at my feet – it was the silly ass with the gun blazing away at goodness knows what – and Pantomime just faded out. I found myself looking down, not at a horse, but at the punctured and deflated remains of a highly ingenious balloon.'

'Not Pantomime but Pegasus.' Mrs Mutter offered this unexpected piece of classical learning with a brilliant smile.

'Quite so. The thieves' object, of course, had been to gain time. They managed to substitute their extraordinary contrivance for the real Pantomime just before Gunton came out in the dusk, locked the horse-box, and told Merry to drive off. The thing was tethered by no more than a nicely-calculated fraying cord, so that eventually it freed itself and simply soared up into the night. Probably it was designed that it should blow out to sea. Poor Merry and his lad were going to look very like the guilty parties – and while the trail was thus hopelessly confused at the start, the real Pantomime could be smuggled abroad.'

'And it was?'

'Certainly. The colt was discovered some months later in France. I believe there may be a good deal of litigation.'

Mutter, who had for some minutes been engaged in applying the friction of a silk handkerchief to his top-hat, paused from this important labour. 'Haven't you told us rather a *tall* story?'

Appleby nodded. 'I'm assured the false Pantomime may have gone up to something like twenty thousand feet. So I suppose it *is* tall.'

'Perhaps you could say something about Pantomime's pedigree?'

This time it was Lady Appleby who spoke. 'By Airborne, without a doubt,' she said. 'And from Chimera.'

'Chimera? I don't believe there was ever any such—'

'No more do I.'

The Horse That Died of Shame

PETER TREMAYNE

The Irish Derby, held at The Curragh in County Kildare in the first week of July, is another red-letter day in the racing calendar as eagerly awaited as its namesake in England. Although the Curragh has been a focus of racing for as long – if not longer – than any other course in the world, the Derby itself was not run until 1866 and did not become a major international event until 1962, thanks to the vision of the great Irish owner and breeder, Joe McGrath. This was perhaps no more than was due to a nation where racing has been an obsession for at least two thousand years and its mythology is full of references to the sport. It was, for example, the favourite pastime of the legendary Finn MacCool and of St Brigid of Kildare; while in the famous folk tale, 'The Destruction of Da Derga's Hostal', it is said that the High King Conaire Mór (AD 1–65) always attended the annual meeting at the Curragh which was known as the *Aenach Life*. The name Curragh in Old Irish means race course and it was originally referred to as the *Cuirrech Life*, or race course of the Liffey. Today all the major Irish classics are held there – the Airlie/Coolmore 1,000 Guineas, Goffs Irish 1,000 Guineas, the Kildangan Irish Oaks, the Irish St Leger and, of course, the Budweiser Derby.

In his story 'The Horse That Died For Shame', leading Irish crime novelist, Peter Tremayne (1943–) has drawn on the Curragh's ancient racing tradition to create a murder mystery quite unlike any other in this collection. Peter, who is also an acknowledged expert on Celtic history and culture, has done extensive research into the history of horse racing in Ireland and come up with some surprising facts. For example, the ancient Irish law system – known as the Brehon Laws, which were first codified in AD 438 – stipulated that race course owners were liable for accidents that resulted in injury or death. If horses and riders collided accidentally, however, the owner was exempted; but if the course had not been maintained properly – if a hole or rut had been left unprotected – then he was liable. Spectators, likewise, had laws to protect them.

According to Tremayne, the origin of the word jockey is also most likely Irish. Among the country's ancient words for horse, he says, is *ech*, from which the modern term *each* derives. Thus an old Irish word for a horse rider was *echaidh* – pronounced y'kee. 'Some people argue that the word jockey first appeared in English in the 17th Century as the name for a dealer in horses or a rider in professional races,' Tremayne has written, 'actually it is far more likely to have been borrowed from the Irish rather than from the Scottish diminutive of Jock or John, as claimed by the Oxford Dictionary.'

It is from this heritage that he has gathered the background information for his latest story about Sister Fidelma of Kildare, 'a 7th Century Irish Perry Mason' as she has been described by reviewers, who is a *dalaigh* or advocate of the Brehon Courts and lives in a community not far from the Curragh. Already she has appeared in several very popular novels, including *Absolution By Murder* (1993) and *Shroud For The Archbishop* (1995), and a number of short stories, but is certainly breaking new ground in the tale of 'The Horse That Died For Shame', which occurs in the year AD 665 and is probably the oldest setting for a horse racing mystery ever used by a thriller writer.

*

'Horse racing,' observed the Abbot Laisran of Durrow, 'is a cure for all the ills of humankind. It is a surrogate for people's aggression and for their greed. We would find the world a harsher place without its institution.'

The abbot was a short, rotund, red-faced man with an almost exuberant sense of humour. In fact, the abbot's features were permanently fixed in a state of jollity for he was born with that rare gift of fun and a sense that the world was there to provide enjoyment to those who inhabited it.

Sister Fidelma of Kildare, walking at his side, answered his philosophical pronouncement with an urchin-like grin which seemed to belie her calling as a member of the religieuse of the community of Kildare.

'I doubt that Archbishop Ultan would agree with you, Laisran,' she responded, raising a hand to her forehead in a vain attempt to push back the rebellious strands of red hair which tumbled from beneath her head-dress.

The abbot's lips quirked in amusement as he gazed at his one-time protégée, for it had been Laisran who had urged Fidelma to study law under the renowned Brehon, Morann of Tara, and, when she had reached the qualification of *Anruth*, one degree below the highest rank of learning, becoming an advocate of the courts of law, he had persuaded her to join the community of Brigid.

'But the Bishop Bressal would agree with me,' he countered. 'He has two horses which he races regularly and he is not averse to placing wagers on them.'

Sister Fidelma knew that Bressal, who was bishop to Fáelán of the Uí Dúnlainge, king of Laighin, was a keen supporter of the sport but, then, there were few to be found in the five kingdoms of Éireann who were not. Even the ancient word for a festival in Eireann, *aenach*, meant 'the contention of horses', when people came together to discuss weighty matters, to race their horses, to place wagers, to feast, to make merry and generally indulge in celebrations. Only recently had Ultan of Armagh, the archbishop and primate, begun to denounce the great fairs as contrary to the Faith for, so he claimed, the fairs were merely an excuse for the people to indulge in idolatry and pagan dissoluteness. Mostly, his denouncements were ignored, even by his own clergy, for the ancient customs were so instilled in the people's lives that it would take more than one man's prejudice to alter or dilute them.

In fact, Ultan's pronouncements were being ignored that very day by Abbot Laisran and Sister Fidelma as they strolled through the crowds gathering for the Aenach Lifé, the great annual fair held on the plain which, since the days of the High King Conaire

Mór, had been called the Curragh Lífé, or 'the race course of the Life', after the name of the broad river flowing close by, twisting under the shadow of Dún Aillin. Indeed, was it not recorded that the saintly Brigid, who had founded Fidelma's own community at nearby Kildare, had raced her own horses on this very plain? The Curragh was now the most celebrated race course in all the five kingdoms and the Aenach Lífé attracted people from all the corners of Éireann. Each year, the King of Laighin himself would come to officially open the proceedings as well as to race his own champion horses there.

Fidelma, with a smile, waved away a youth trying to sell them hot griddle cakes, and glanced at her elderly companion.

'Have you seen Bishop Bressal this morning?'

'I heard that he was here earlier,' Laisran replied, 'but I have not seen him. He is racing his favourite horse, Ochain, today. However, I have seen the bishop's jockey, Murchad, laying heavy wagers on himself to win with Ochain. At least Murchad shares the bishop's faith in himself and his horse.'

Fidelma pursed her lips reflectively.

'Ochain. I have heard of that beast. But why name a horse "moaner"?'

'I understand that Ochain utters a moaning sound as it senses that it is about to win. Horses are intelligent creatures.'

'More intelligent than most men, oftimes,' agreed Fidelma.

'Between ourselves, certainly more intelligent than the good bishop,' chuckled Laisran. 'He is openly boasting that he will win the race today against Fáelán's own horse, which does not please the king. They say the king is in a sour mood at his bishop's bragging.'

'So Fáelán is also racing today?'

'His best horse,' confirmed the abbot. 'And, in truth, there is little doubt of the outcome for the king's champion Illan is in the saddle and with Aonbharr beneath his thighs, no team in Laighin will even come near . . . not even Murchad and Ochain. And, indeed, the fact that Illan is riding the king's horse is doubtless a matter of displeasure for Bishop Bressal.'

'Why so?' Fidelma was interested in Laisran's gossip.

'Because Illan used to train and race Bressal's horses before the king of Laighin offered him more money to train and ride Aonbharr.'

'Aonbharr, eh?' Fidelma had heard of the king's horse. So fleet was it that the king had named it after the fabulous horse of the ancient god of the oceans, Manánnan Mac Lir, a wondrous steed which could fly over land and sea without missing a pace. 'I have seen this horse race at the Curragh last year and no one could best it. This horse of Bressal's better be good or the bishop's boasting will rebound on him.'

Abbot Laisran sniffed cynically.

'You have been away travelling this year, Fidelma. Perhaps you have not heard that there is something of a feud now between the king and his bishop. Four times during the last year Bressal has presented horses at races to run against the king's champion horse and his jockey. Four times now he has been beaten. Bressal is mortified. He has become a man with an obsession. He thinks that he is being made a fool of, especially by his former trainer and jockey. Now he has one aim, to best the king's horse and Illan in particular. The trouble is that his very efforts are making him a laughing stock.'

Abbot Laisran raised an arm and let his hand describe a half circle in the air towards the throng around them.

'I reckon a goodly proportion of these people have come here to see Bressal humiliated yet again when Aonbharr romps pasts the winning post.'

Fidelma shook her head sadly.

'Did I not say that horses had more sense than men, Laisran? Why must a simple pleasure be turned into warfare?'

Laisran suddenly halted and turned his head.

Pushing towards them, and clearly hurrying to make contact with them, was a young man in the livery of the Baoisgne, the king of Laighin's élite warrior guard. There was anxiety on his youthful features. He halted before them awkwardly.

'Forgive me, Abbot Laisran,' he began and then turned directly to Fidelma. 'Are you Sister Fidelma of Kildare?'

Fidelma inclined her head in acknowledgment.

'Then would you come at once, Sister?'

'What is the matter?'

'It is the wish of the king, Fáelán himself.' The young man glanced quickly round before lowering his voice so that he would not be overheard by the surrounding crowds. 'Illan, the king's champion jockey, has been found . . . dead. The King's horse, Aonbharr, is dying. The king's believes that there has been foul play and has caused Bishop Bressal to be arrested.'

Fáelán of the Uí Dúnlainge, king of Laighin, sat scowling in his tent. Fidelma and Laisran had been escorted to the veritable township of tents which had been set up for the king and chieftains and their ladies alongside the course. Often entire families would camp at the Curragh during the nine days of the meeting. Behind the tents of the nobles were the tents of the trainers, riders and owners of lesser status as well as the tents which served as stables for their horses.

Fáelán of the Uí Dúnlainge was a man approaching his fortieth year. His dark features, black hair and bushy eyebrows, made his features saturnine. When he scowled, his face took on the appearance of a malignant spirit which caused many a person to quail in his presence and stand uneasy.

Abbot Laisran, however, who had accompanied Fidelma, stood imperturbably smiling at the king, hands folded in his robes. He was acquainted with Fáelán and knew his grim features disguised a fair and honourable man. At Fáelán's side sat his queen, the beautiful Muadnat of the burnished hair; tall and sensual, the tales of whose amours were legend. She was richly dressed with a jewelled belt and dagger sheath at her waist, such as all noble ladies carried. But, Fidelma noticed curiously, the sheath was empty of its small ceremonial dagger. The queen looked dejected, as if she had been given to a recent fit of weeping.

Behind the king and queen stood the *tánaiste*, the heir-presumptive, a nephew of Fáelán's named Énna; and beside him was his wife, Dagháin. They were both in their mid-twenties. Énna was a handsome, though morose man, while his wife was almost non-descript at first glance, although she was fashionably dressed yet without the same care as her queen for Fidelma noticed that her dress was mud-stained and dishevelled. Even the bejewelled belt and sheath looked scuffed and its ceremonial dagger fitted badly. She seemed ill at ease and impatient.

Fidelma stood before the king, waiting with her hands quietly folded before her.

'I have need of a Brehon, Sister,' began Fáelán. 'Énna, here,' he motioned with his head towards his *tánaiste*, 'Énna told me that you were on the course with the Abbot Laisran.'

Fidelma still waited expectantly.

'Have you heard the news?' Énna interrupted his king who controlled a look of annoyance at the breach of protocol. As Fidelma turned her gaze, Fáelán continued before she could reply to the question.

'My champion jockey has been murdered and an attempt has been made to kill my best horse. The horse doctor tells me that the beast is already dying and will be dead before noon.'

'This much your guard told me,' Fidelma said. 'Also, I am informed, that Bishop Bressal has been arrested.'

'On my orders,' confirmed the king. 'There is no one else who benefits from this outrage but Bressal. You see . . .'

Fidelma staid his explanation with a small impatient gesture of her hand.

'I have heard of your disputes over the matter of horse racing. Why do you send for me? You have your own Brehon?'

Fáelán blinked at her unceremonious address.

'He is not in attendance today,' explained the king. 'And it is only permitted that a Brehon should decide whether there are grounds to hold the bishop so that he may be taken before the law courts. In the case of a bishop, who better qualified to this task than a *dálaigh* who is also a member of the religious?'

'Then let me hear the facts,' Fidelma assented. 'Who discovered the body of your jockey?'

'I did.'

It was Dagháin who spoke. She was, now that Fidelma had time to assess her closely, a rather plain looking girl, blonde of hair and features which seemed without animation. The eyes were grey and cold but they did not shy away from her level gaze.

'Let me hear your story.'

Dagháin glanced towards the king as if seeking permission and, after he had nodded approvingly, she turned to Fidelma.

'It was an hour ago. I had just arrived for the races. I went into Illan's tent. I found Illan's body on the floor. He was dead. So I hurried to find my husband, who was with the king, and told them what I had seen.'

Dagháin's voice was matter of fact, without guile.

Fidelma examined her closely.

'Let us go through this more carefully,' she smiled. 'You arrived – from where?'

It was Énna who answered.

'My wife and I had been staying at Dún Ailinn. I came on here early this morning to meet with Fáelán.'

Fidelma nodded.

'And what made you go directly to Illan's tent instead of coming to find your husband?'

Did Dagháin blush and hesitate a little?

'Why, I went first to see the horse, Aonbharr. He was raised in my husband's stables before he was sold to the king. I saw that he looked unwell and went to tell Illan.'

'And found him dead?'

'Yes. I was shocked. I did not know what to do and so I ran here.'

'Did you fall in your haste?' asked Fidelma.

'Yes, I did,' admitted the girl with a puzzled expression.

'And that would explain the disarray of your dress?' Fidelma's question was more rhetorical, but the woman nodded in hasty relief.

'I see. What was the cause of Illan's death, were you able to see? And how was he lying?'

Dagháin reflected.

'On his back. There was blood on his clothing but I did not see anything else. I was too intent to inform my husband.'

A sob caused Fidelma to glance up quickly to where the king's wife, Muadnat, was sitting, dabbing at her eyes with a piece of lace.

'You will forgive my wife,' interposed Fáelán quickly. 'She has a horror of violence and Illan was one of our household. Perhaps she can withdraw? She has no knowledge of these events and so cannot help your deliberations.'

Fidelma glanced at the woman and nodded. Muadnat forced a small grimace of relief and gratitude, rose and left with her female attendant.

Fidelma then turned to Énna.

'Do you agree with this record thus far?'

'It is as my wife says,' he confirmed. 'She came into our tent, where I was talking with Fáelán, and came in a state of distress telling us exactly what she has now told you.'

'And what did you do?'

Énna shrugged.

'I called some guards and went to the tent of Illan. He lay dead on the floor of the tent as Daghàin has described.'

'He was lying on his back?'

'That is so.'

'Very well. Continue. What then? Did you look for the cause of death?'

'Not closely. But it appeared that he had been stabbed in the lower part of the chest. I left a guard there and went with a second guard to the stable tent and saw Aonbharr. As Daghàin had said, the horse was obviously distressed. Its legs were splayed apart and its head depressed between its shoulders. There was froth around its muzzle. I know enough of horses to know that it was poisoned in some way. I called Cellach, the horse doctor, and told him to do what he could for the beast. Then I came back to report to Fáelán.'

Fidelma now turned to the king.

'And do you, Fáelán of the Uí Dúnlainge, agree that this is an accurate account thus far?'

'Thus far, it is as Daghàin and Énna have related,' confirmed the king.

'What then? At what point did you come to believe that the culprit responsible for these events was your own bishop, Bressal?'

Fáelán gave a loud bark of cynical laughter.

'At the very point I heard the news. This year my bishop has become obsessed with beating my horse, Aonbharr. He has made vain boasts, has wagered heavily and, indeed, is deeply in debt.

He has put forward a horse to race Illan in the main race of today, a horse named Ochain. It is a good horse but it would not have stood a chance against Aonbharr. It became obvious that Bressal could not afford to lose against me. If Illan and Aonbharr did not run, then Ochain would win. It is as simple as that. And Bressal hated Illan, who was once his jockey.'

Fidelma smiled softly.

'It is a well conceived suspicion but there is not enough evidence here to arrest nor charge a man, Fáelán. If it is only this suspicion which has caused your action, then my advice is to free Bressal immediately lest he cite the law against you.'

'There is more,' Énna said quietly, and motioned to the warrior of the Baoisgne who stood at the flap of the tent. The man went out and called to someone. A moment later, a large man with a bushy beard and rough clothes entered and bowed to the king and his *tánaiste*.

'Tell the Brehon your name and station,' Énna ordered.

The big man turned to Fidelma.

'I am Angaire, hostler to Bishop Bressal.'

Fidelma raised an eyebrow but controlled all other expression on her features.

'You are not a member of Bressal's community in Christ,' she observed.

'No, Sister. The bishop employed me because of my expertise with horses. I train his horse Ochain. But I am no religious.'

Angaire was a confident man, smiling and sure of himself.

'Tell Sister Fidelma what you have told us,' prompted Énna.

'Well, Bressal has often boasted how Ochain would best Aonbharr at this race and he has laid heavy wagers upon the outcome.'

'Get to the main point,' pressed Fáelán irritably.

'Well, this morning, I was preparing Ochain . . .'

'You were to ride him in this race?' interrupted Fidelma. 'I thought . . .'

The big man shook his head.

'Bressal's jockey is Murchad. I am only Ochain's trainer.'

Fidelma motioned him to continue.

'Well, I told Bressal that it was my opinion, having seen

Aonbharr in a trial run yesterday, that Ochain would have difficulty in catching the beast on the straight. Bressal went berserk. I have never seen a man so angry. He would not listen to me and so I withdrew. Half-an-hour later I was passing the tent of Illan . . .'

'How did you know it was Illan's tent?' demanded Fidelma.

'Easy enough. Each jockey has a small banner outside showing the emblem of the owner of the horse he rides. The insignia of owners are important at such gatherings as this.'

Fáelán interrupted: 'This is true.'

'As I passed the tent I heard voices raised in anger. I recognized Bressal's voice at once. The other I presumed to be that of Illan.'

'What did you do?'

Angaire shrugged.

'No business of mine. I went on to Murchad's tent to advise him how best to handle the race, though I knew he had little chance against Illan.'

'Then?'

'As I was leaving Murchad's tent I saw . . .'

'How much later was this?' interjected Fidelma again.

Angaire blinked at the interruption.

'Ten minutes probably. I can't recall. Murchad and I did not speak for very long.'

'So what did you see?'

'I saw Bressal hurrying by. There was a red welt on his cheek. His face was suffused with anger. He did not see me. Furthermore, he was carrying something concealed under his cloak.'

'What sort of something?'

'It could have been a long, thin knife.'

Fidelma drew her brows together.

'What makes you say that? Describe what you saw exactly.'

'He held something long and thin in one hand, hidden under his cloth, it was no more than nine inches long but I have no idea of the width.'

'So you cannot take oath that it was a knife?' snapped Fidelma. 'I am not here to listen to surmise and guesses but only facts. What then?'

Angaire looked grieved for a moment and then shrugged.

'I went about my business until I heard a guard telling someone that Illan had been found dead in his tent. I felt it my duty to tell the guard what I knew.'

'That guard came to me,' Énna agreed. 'I later verified Angaire's story with him.'

'And I had Bressal arrested,' confirmed Fáelán as if it ended the matter.

'What has Bressal replied to these charges?' Fidelma asked.

'He has refused to speak until a Brehon was sent for,' the king replied. 'When Énna told me that you were on the course, I sent for you. Now you know as much as we. I think I have the right to hold the bishop for trial. Will you see Bressal now?'

Fidelma surprised them by shaking her head.

'I will see the body of Illan. Has a physician been in attendance?'

'None, since Illan is dead.'

'Then one needs to be sent for. I want Illan's body examined. While that is being done, I shall see the horse, Aonbharr, and this horse doctor . . . what name did you say?'

'Cellach,' the king said. 'He attends all my horses.'

'Very well. Your guard may escort me to the place where the animal is stabled.' She turned to Abbot Laisran, who had remained quiet during the entire proceedings. 'Will you accompany me, Laisran? I have need of your advice.'

Outside as they walked in the direction which the warrior of the Baoisgne conducted them, Fidelma turned to Laisran.

'I wanted to speak to you. I noticed that Queen Muadnat seemed to be very upset by the death of Illan.'

'Your perception is keen, Fidelma,' agreed Laisran. 'For example, I did not even notice the disarray of Dagháin's clothes until you mentioned it. But Muadnat has obviously been weeping. The death of Illan has upset her.'

Fidelma smiled thinly.

'That much I know. You know more of the gossip of the court, however. Why would she be so upset?'

'Muadnat is a handsome woman with, by all accounts, a

voracious appetite in sexual matters. Perhaps I should say no more for Fáelán is a tolerant monarch.'

'You are still speaking in riddles, Laisran,' sighed Fidelma.

'I am sorry. I thought you might have heard of Illan's reputation as a ladies' man. Illan was only one of many lovers who has graced the queen's entourage.'

When Fidelma and Laisran reached the stable tent in which Aonbharr was, the horse was lying on its side, its great breath coming in deep grunting pants. It was clearly nearing the end. A few men were gathered around it and one of these was Cellach, the horse doctor.

He was a thin man with a brown weather-beaten face and regarded the sister with large, sad grey eyes. He was obviously upset by the suffering of the animal.

'Aonbharr is dying,' he replied to Fidelma's question.

'Can you confirm that the horse been poisoned?'

Cellach grimaced angrily.

'It has. A mixture of wolfsbane, ground ivy leaves and mandrake root. That is my diagnosis, Sister.'

Fidelma stared at Cellach in surprise.

The man sniffed as he saw her scepticism.

'No magic in that, Sister.'

He reached toward to the horse's muzzle and gently pried it open. There were flecks of blood and spittle around the discoloured gums. Amidst this mucus Fidelma could see speckles of the remains of feed.

'You can see the remnants of these poisons. Yes, someone fed the horse on a potent mixture.'

'When would such feed have been administered?' she asked.

'Not long,' replied Cellach. 'Within the last hour or so. Such a mixture on this beast would have an almost instantaneous effect.'

Fidelma laid a gentle hand on the big animal's muzzle and stroked it softly.

The great soft brown eyes flickered open, stared at her and then the beast let out a grunting breath.

'Are there no other signs of violence inflicted on it?' she asked.

Cellach shook his head.

'None, Sister.'

'Could Aonbharr have eaten some poisonous plants by accident?' asked Laisran.

Cellach shrugged.

'While tethered in its stable here? Hardly likely, abbot. Even in the wilderness, horses are intelligent and sensitive creatures. They usually have a sense of things that will harm them. Apart from the fact that one would not find mandrake root nor wolfsbane around these parts. And how would it crush ivy leaves? No, this was a deliberate act.'

'Is there no hope for the animal?' asked Fidelma sadly.

Cellach grimaced and shook his head.

'It will be dead by noon,' he replied.

'I will see Illan's body now,' Fidelma said quietly, turning towards the tent of the king's jockey.

'Are you Sister Fidelma?'

As Fidelma entered the tent of Illan she found a religieuse straightening up from the body of the man who lay on its back on the floor. The woman was a big boned woman with large hands and an irritable expression on her broad features. On Fidelma's acknowledgement she went on: 'I am Sister Eblenn, the apothecary from the community of the Blessed Darerca.'

'Have you examined the body of Illan?'

Sister Eblenn made a swift obeisance to Laisran as he entered the tent before answering Fidelma.

'Yes. A fatal stabbing. One wound in the heart.'

Fidelma exchanged a glance with the abbot.

'Is there sign of the knife?'

'The wound was not made by a knife, Sister.' The apothecary was confident.

Fidelma controlled her irritation at the pause.

'Then by what?' she demanded, when there had been a sufficient silence and the religieuse had made no attempt to amplify her statement.

Sister Eblenn pointed to the table. A broken arrow lay on it. It was the front half of the arrow, about nine inches, of the shaft and head. It was splintered where the shaft had been snapped in two.

Fidelma reached forward and took up the section of arrow. She could see that it was covered with blood and it was clear that Sister Eblenn had taken it from the wound.

'Are you telling us that Illan was stabbed in the heart with this arrow?' intervened Abbot Laisran. 'Stabbed, you say, not shot with the arrow?'

Sister Eblenn pursed her lips and regarded him dourly.

'Have I not said so?' she asked petulantly.

Fidelma's voice was brittle.

'No; so far you have not explained matters at all. Tell us what you have discovered and be specific.'

Eblenn blinked. She was obviously unused to people questioning her. She was given to assuming knowledge on the part of others and did not explain herself clearly. She flushed angrily at the rebuke.

'The dead man,' she began slowly, speaking in wooden but distinct tones, like a petulant child explaining the obvious, 'was stabbed in the heart. The instrument was this arrow. Whoever killed him thrust the arrow under the rib cage, avoiding the sternum and thrusting with some force upwards so that it entered the heart. Death was instantaneous. There was little bleeding.'

'Why do you discount the arrow being shot into the body?' insisted Abbot Laisran.

'The angle of incision is of such a degree that it would be impossible unless the archer was standing five feet away and shooting upwards at a forty-five degree angle at least five feet below the target. There is also the fact that the arrow snapped in two. I believe the impact of the blow, the arrow gripped hard in the hand of the attacker, was the cause of its breaking.'

'I presumed that you cut out the arrowhead?'

Eblenn pursed her thin lips and shook her head.

'The head is part of the shaft, simply a carved wooden point. I did not cut the arrow out at all but merely pulled it out. As it went in, so it came out. It was easy enough.'

Fidelma sighed deeply.

'So that when you came to examine the body, the arrow was in two pieces? One in the body, the other ... where was that exactly?'

Sister Eblenn looked suddenly startled and peered around as if seeking the answer.

'I do not know. I presume it is somewhere about.'

Fidelma bit her lip. Extracting information from Sister Eblenn was like fishing for trout. One had to cast about blindly.

For a moment or two she stood looking down at the arrow. She became aware that Sister Eblenn was speaking.

'What?'

'I said, I must return to my apothecary's tent. I have already had one theft this morning and do not want to chance another.'

Fidelma swung round with sudden interest.

'What was taken from your tent.'

'Some herbs, that is all. But herbs cost money.'

'And these herbs – were they mandrake root, wolfsbane and crushed ivy?'

'Ah, you have spoken to the lady Dagháin?'

Fidelma's eyes rounded slightly.

'What has the lady Dagháin to do with this matter?'

'Nothing. She was passing my tent just after I discovered the theft. I asked her to inform her husband as the *tánaiste* has charge of the royal guards.'

'When exactly was this?'

'Just after the breakfast hour. Early this morning. Queen Muadnat had come by requesting a balm for a headache. It was soon after that I noticed the herbs were gone. Then, as I was going to breakfast, I saw the lady Dagháin and told her.'

After Sister Eblenn had left, still showing some bewilderment, Laisran grimaced.

'So now we know where the killer obtained the poison from.'

Fidelma nodded absently. While Laisran watched silently, Fidelma lowered herself to her knees and began to examine the body. Then she motioned Laisran to join her.

'Look at the wound, Laisran,' she said. 'It seems our Sister Eblenn is not as perceptive as she should be.'

Laisran peered closely to where Fidelma indicated.

'No pointed arrowhead made that wound,' he agreed after a moment. 'It is more of a gash, such as a broad bladed knife would have made.'

'Exactly so,' agreed Fidelma.

For a while she searched all around the body in an ever increasing circles to cover the whole floor of the tent. There was nothing on the floor except for a leather *cena*, a medium sized bag, which she placed on a table top. She could not find what she was expecting to discover and climbed back to her feet. She took up the splintered arrow again and stared at it as if perplexed. Then she thrust it into the *marsupium* or purse which she always carried.

She gazed down to study Illan's features for a final time. Laisran was right; he had been a handsome young man. But his face was a little too handsome to attract her. She could imagine the self-satisfaction of his expression while he was in life.

Abbot Laisran coughed, as if to remind her of his presence.

'Do you have any ideas?' he asked.

She smiled at her old mentor.

'None that makes sense at this moment.'

'While you have been examining the corpse, I have examined this *cena* which you found in a corner of the tent. I think that you'd better look in it.'

Frowning, Fidelma did so. There was a mixture of herbs inside. She picked out a handful and sniffed suspiciously. Then she turned to Laisran with wide eyes.

'Are they what I suspect them to be?' she asked.

'Yes,' confirmed Laisran. 'Mandrake root, wolf's bane and ivy leaves. Moreover, there is a small insignia on the *cena* and it is not the same one as I noticed on Sister Eblenn's apothecary's bag.'

Fidelma pursed her lips as though to whistle but did not do so.

'This is a mystery that goes deep, Laisran,' she reflected slowly. 'We must discover the owner of the insignia.'

Énna suddenly entered the tent.

'Ah, there you are, Sister. Have you seen enough here?'

'I have seen all that I can see,' Fidelma replied.

She gestured down at Illan's body. 'A sad end for one who was so young and talented in his profession.'

Énna sniffed deprecatingly.

'Many a husband would not agree with you, Sister.'

'Ah? You mean the queen?' Laisran smiled.

Énna blinked rapidly and looked embarrassed. Many knew of the gossip of Muadnat's affairs but none in the court circle would openly discuss them.

'Doubtless,' he turned to Fidelma, 'you will want to see Bishop Bressal now? He is upset that you have not gone directly to see him.'

Fidelma suppressed a sigh.

'Before we do so, Énna, perhaps you can help. I believe, as *tánaiste*, that you have a knowledge of insignia, don't you?'

Énna made an affirmative gesture.

'What insignia is this?' Fidelma showed him the *cena* Laisran had discovered.

Énna didn't hesitate.

'That is the insignia of Bishop Bressal's household.'

Fidelma's lips thinned while Laisran could not hold back an audible gasp.

'I would not wish to keep the good bishop waiting longer than is necessary,' Fidelma said, with soft irony in her voice. 'We will see him now.'

'Well, Bressal, tell me your story,' invited Fidelma as she seated herself before the agitated portly figure of the king of Laighin's bishop. Bressal was a large, heavily built man, with pale, baby-like features and a balding head. One of the first things she noticed was that Bressal had a red welt on his left cheek.

Bressal frowned at the young religieuse before glancing across to acknowledge Abbot Laisran who had followed her into the tent and taken a stand with folded arms by the tent flap. The only other occupant of the tent was a tall warrior of Bressal's personal household for the bishop's rank and position entitled him to a bodyguard.

'You have seated yourself in my presence without permission, Sister,' Bressal thundered ominously.

Fidelma regarded him calmly.

'I may be seated in the presence of any provincial king without permission,' she informed him icily. 'I am a *dálaigh*, an advocate of the courts, qualified to the level of *Anruth*. Therefore, I can sit even in the presence of the High King, though with his permission. I am . . .'

Bressal waved a hand in annoyance. He was well informed on the rules of the rank and privileges of the Brehons.

'Very well *Anruth*. Why were you not here sooner? The sooner I am heard, the sooner I can be released from this outrageous imprisonment.'

Fidelma eyed the bishop with distaste. Bressal was certainly a haughty man. She could well believe the stories that she had heard about him and this vanity of racing against the king of Laighin's horse.

'If you wish speed and urgency in this matter, it would be better to answer my questions without interpolating any of your own. Now, to this matter . . .'

'Is it not clear?' demanded the bishop with outrage in his voice. 'Fáelán is trying to blame me for something that I have not done. That much is simple. He has probably done this evil deed himself to discredit me, knowing my horse would have beaten his.'

Fidelma sat back with raised eyebrows.

'Counter accusations come better when you can demonstrate your own innocence. Tell me of your movements this morning.'

Bressal bit his lip and was about to argue and then he shrugged and flung himself onto a chair.

'I came to the race track with my personal guard, Sílán,' he gestured to the silent warrior. 'We came straightaway to see Ochain, my horse.'

'Who had brought Ochain here?'

'Why, Angaire, my trainer, and Murchad, my rider.'

'At what time was this? Tell me in relationship to the finding of Illan's body?'

'I do not know when it was discovered but I was here about an hour before that oaf Fáelán had me arrested.'

'And did you see anyone else apart from Angaire and Murchad in that time?'

Bressal sniffed in annoyance.

'There were many people at the track. Many who might well have seen me but who they were I cannot remember.'

'I mean, did you engage with anyone else in conversation; anyone in particular . . . Illan himself, for example?'

Bressal stared back at her and then shook his head. She could see that he was lying by the light of anxiety in his dark eyes.

'So you did not speak to Illan this morning?' pressed Fidelma.

'I have said as much.'

'Think carefully, Bressal. Did you not go to his tent and speak with him?'

Bressal stared at her and a look of guilty resignation spread over his features.

'A man of God should not lie, Bressal,' admonished Laisran from the entrance. 'Least of all, a bishop.'

'I did not kill Illan,' the man said stubbornly.

'How did you obtain that recent scar on your left cheek?' Fidelma demanded abruptly.

Bressal raised his hand automatically.

'I . . .' He suddenly stopped, apparently unable to think of an adequate reply. Suddenly his shoulders slumped and he seemed to grow smaller in his chair, looking like a defeated man.

'Truth is the best refuge in adversity,' Fidelma advised coldly.

'It is true that I went to Illan's tent and argued with him. It is true that he struck me.' Bressal's voice was sullen.

'And did you strike him back?'

'Is it not written in the Gospel of Luke: "Unto him that smiteth thee on the one cheek offer also the other"?' parried Bressal.

'That which is written is not always obeyed. Am I to take it that you, who are obviously a man who is not poor in spirit, did not retaliate when Illan struck you?'

'I left Illan alive,' muttered Bressal.

'But you did strike him?'

'Of course I did,' snapped Bressal. 'The dog dared to strike me, a prince and bishop of Laighin!'

Fidelma sighed deeply.

'And why did he strike you?'

'I . . . roused his anger.'

'Your argument was to do with the fact that he had once been your rider and had left your service to ride for Fáelán?'

Bressal was surprised.

'You seem to know many things, Sister Fidelma.'

'So how did you leave Illan?'

'I hit him on the jaw and he fell unconscious. Our conversation had thus ended and so I left. I did not kill him.'

'How did the argument arise?'

Bressal hung his head shamefully but once having embarked on the path of truth he decided to maintain it to the end.

'I went to his tent to offer him money to stand down from the race and return his allegiance to me.'

'Did anyone else know of your intention to bribe Illan?'

'Yes; Angaire did.'

'Your trainer?' Fidelma thought hard for a moment.

'I told Angaire that I was not happy with the way he was training my horse, Ochain. I told him that if I could persuade Illan to return, then he could look elsewhere for a job. In all my races this year, Angaire has failed to provide me with a winner.'

Fidelma turned to the silent warrior within the tent.

'How much of this story can you confirm, Sílán?'

For a moment the warrior stared at her in surprise. He glanced to Bressal, as if seeking his permission to speak.

'Tell them what happened this morning,' snapped Bressal.

Sílán stood stiffly before Fidelma, his eyes focused in the middle distance and his voice wooden in its recital.

'I came to the Curragh at . . .'

'Have you been personal guard to the bishop for a long time?' interrupted Fidelma. She disliked rehearsed speeches and when she sensed one she liked to interrupt and put the reciter out of stride.

'I have,' replied the surprised guard. 'For one year, Sister.'

'Go on.'

'I came to the Curragh not long after dawn to help set up the bishop's tent.'

'Did you see Illan at this time?'

'Surely. There were many people here already. The bishop, also Angaire, Murchad, Illan, even Fáelán and his queen and the *tánaiste* . . .'

Fidelma was not looking at his face. Her eyes had fastened thoughtfully on the quiver at the guard's side. One arrow seemed shorter than the others. Its feathered flight seemed to be sinking into the quiver among the other arrows.

'Turn out your quiver!' she suddenly ordered.

'What?'

Sílán was gazing at her, clearly amazed at her behaviour. Even Bressal was staring as if she had gone mad.

'Turn out the arrows in your quiver and place them on the table here before me,' instructed Fidelma.

Frowning, the warrior did so with no further hesitation.

Fidelma seized upon a shaft of an arrow. It was snapped off and only some six inches with its tail feathered flight remained. There was no need for Fidelma to look for the other half among the rest of the arrows.

They watched in silent fascination as Fidelma took from her *marsupium* the section of the arrow which had been found by Sister Eblenn in the body of Illan. She carefully brought the two pieces together before their fixed gaze. They fitted almost perfectly.

'You seem to be in a great deal of trouble, Sílán,' Fidelma said slowly. 'The head of your arrow was buried in the wound that killed Illan.'

'I did not do it!' gasped the warrior in horror.

'Is this one of your arrows?' Fidelma asked, holding out the two halves.

'What do you mean?' interrupted Bressal.

Laisran came forward with interest on his features.

'The design on the flights are the same.'

Sílán was nodding.

'Yes, it is obviously one of my arrows. Anyone will tell you that it bears the emblem of the bishop's household.'

Fidelma turned to Laisran.

'Place the *cena* that we found in Illan's tent on the table, Laisran.'

The abbot did as she bid him.

Fidelma pointed to the insignia.

'And this emblem, being the same as on the arrow flight, is also the emblem of Bishop Bressal?'

Bressal shrugged.

'What of it? All the members of my household carry my insignia. Such bags as these are saddle bags, freely available among those who serve my stables.'

'Would it surprise you that this contains the mixture of poisonous herbs used to poison Aonbharr?'

Sílan and Bressal were silent.

'It could be argued that Sílán killed Illan and poisoned Aonbharr on the orders of his master, Bishop Bressal,' suggested Fidelma as if musing with an idea.

'I did not!'

'And I gave him no such order,' cried Bressal, his face turning white in horror.

'If you confessed that you were acting on the orders of Bressal,' Fidelma went on, speaking softly to Sílán, 'little blame would attach to you.'

Sílán shook his head stubbornly.

'I had no such orders and did not do this thing.'

Fidelma turned to Bressal.

'The evidence was circumstantial in the first place, bishop. Yet, circumstantial as it is, it is against you. The evidence of this arrow and the *cena*, containing the poisons, now seem hard to refute.'

Bressal was clearly perturbed. He turned to Sílán.

'Did you slay Illan of your own volition?' he demanded.

The warrior shook his head violently and turned pleading eyes upon Fidelma. She could see the innocence in his face. The guard was clearly shocked at the evidence against him and his bishop.

'I am at a loss to explain this,' he said inadequately.

'Tell me, Sílán, have your carried your quiver of arrows all morning?'

Sílán paused to give thought to the question.

'Not all morning. I left my quiver and bow in the bishop's tent most of the morning while I had errands to run.'

'What kind of errands?'

'To find Murchad, for example. I found him talking with Angaire near Illan's tent at the time we saw the lady Dagháin come out, white faced, and go running to her tent. I remember that Angaire passed some unseemly and lewd remark. I left Angaire and returned here with Murchad.'

'So the quiver of arrows was in this tent while you went to find the bishop's jockey at the bishop's request?' Fidelma summed up. 'The bishop was alone in the tent, then?'

Once more a look of indignation caused Bressal's face to flush.

'If you are saying that I took an arrow and went to kill Illan . . .' he began.

'Yet you were alone in this tent at that time?'

'Some of the time,' admitted Bressal. 'Sílán left his weapons most of the morning and we were constantly in and out of the tent. Also, there were visitors coming and going. Why, even Fáelán and his wife, Muadnat, were here for a moment.'

Fidelma was surprised. 'Why would he come here? You had become bitter rivals.'

'Fáelán merely wanted to boast about Aonbharr.'

'Was that before or after you had your argument with Illan?'

'Before.'

'And Muadnat was with him?'

'Yes. Then Énna came by.'

'What for?'

'To beg me to withdraw Ochain from the race, saying my argument with Fáelán was an embarassment to the kingdom. This is pointless. Angaire and Murchad were here as well . . .'

'Was Énna's wife, the lady Dagháin, one of your visitors?' queried Fidelma.

The bishop shook his head.

'However, if you are looking for an opportunity to take an arrow and kill Illan, why, several people had that opportunity.'

'And what about the *cena* full of poison herbs?'

'All I can say is that it bears my insignia but I have no knowledge of it.'

Fidelma smiled thinly and turned to Laisran. 'Walk with me a moment.'

Bressal stared at her in outrage as she made to leave his tent.

'What do you propose to do?' he demanded.

Fidelma glanced across her shoulder towards him.

'I propose to finish my investigation, Bressal,' she said shortly before stepping through the flap, followed by the bewildered Laisran.

Outside, Fáelán had posted several of his élite guards to keep the bishop a prisoner.

'You do not like the good bishop,' Laisran reflected once they were outside.

Fidelma gave her urchin-like grin.

'The bishop is not a likeable man.'

'And the evidence weighs heavily against him,' went on Laisran, as he fell into step with the religieuse. 'Surely that evidence is now conclusive?'

Fidelma shook her head.

'If Bressal or Sílán had used the arrow to kill Illan then neither would have kept hold of the incriminating half of the arrow so that it could be found so easily.'

'But, it makes sense. Either one of them could have stabbed Illan with the arrow. Then, realizing that the design on the flight would betray them, they broke off the arrow and took the incriminating part away with them . . .'

Fidelma smiled gently. 'Leaving the *cena* with the poison and its insignia conspicuously in Illan's tent? No, my good mentor, if they were that clever then they would have simply destroyed the arrow. There are enough braziers in which to have burnt it. Why place it invitingly back in the quiver where it would easily be discovered? And they would have rid themselves of the *cena*. Also, my friend, in the excitement you have forgotten the very fact that neither Bressal nor Sílán appears to be aware of and which demonstrates their innocence.'

Laisran looked bewildered.

'What fact?'

'The fact that the arrow was placed in the wound after Illan was dead in order to mislead us. The fact that Illan was killed by a dagger thrust and not by stabbing with the arrow.'

Laisran clapped a hand to his head. He had forgotten that very point in the agitation of Fidelma's cross examination of Bressal and Sílán.

'Are you suggesting that there is some plot to make Bressal appear guilty?'

'I am,' confirmed Fidelma.

Laisran looked at her thunderstruck.

'Then who . . . ?' His eyes widened. 'Surely you are not suggesting that the king . . . ? Are you saying that Fáelán might have feared that his horse would not win against Bressal's horse and so he contrived this intricate plot . . . ?'

Fidelma pursed her lips.

'Your hypothesis is good but there is more work to be done before the hypothesis can be used in argument.'

Énna was suddenly blocking their path.

'Have you seen Bressal, Sister?' he greeted and when she nodded he smiled grimly. 'Has he now confessed his guilt?'

Fidelma regarded him for a moment.

'So you believe him to be guilty?'

Énna stood in surprise.

'*Believe?* Surely there is no doubt?'

'Under our laws, one must be proven guilty of the offence unless one confesses that guilt. Bressal does not accept any guilt. My investigation must show proof against him.'

'Then that is not difficult.'

'You think not?' Énna looked uncomfortable at her mocking tone. 'I would have everyone concerned now gather in Fáelán's tent: Bressal, Sílán, Angaire, Murchad, Fáelán and Muadnat, yourself and Dagháin. There I will reveal the result of my investigation.'

As Énna hurried away, Fidelma turned to Laisran.

'Wait for me at Fáelán's tent, I will not be long.' At Laisran's look of interrogation, she added: 'I have to look for something to complete my speculation.'

At Fidelma's request they had all crowded into the tent of Fáelán of the Uí Dúnlainge, king of the Laighin.

'This has been a most perplexing mystery,' she began when the king signalled her to speak. 'What seemed simple at first began to become mysterious and obscure. That was until now.'

Fidelma smiled broadly at them.

'And now?' It was Fáelán who prompted her.

'Now all the pieces of the puzzle fit together. Firstly, the evidence against Bressal is overwhelming.'

There was a gasp of outrage from Bressal.

'It is not true. I am not guilty,' he protested indignatly.

Fidelma raised her hand for silence.

'I did not say that you were. Only that the evidence against you was overwhelming. However, if you had been guilty, or, indeed, if Sílán had carried out the deed for you, then you would have known that Illan had not been stabbed with an arrow but with a dagger. Only the real killer knew this and the person who placed the arrow in the wound. The arrow was a false scent planted in an attempt to lay a path to Bressal. It was obvious, therefore, that someone wanted me to find that evidence and draw the inevitable but wrong conclusion.'

Bressal gave a deep sigh and relaxed for the first time. Sílán, behind him, looked less defensive.

'I first approached this matter from the viewpoint of the motive, which seemed obvious,' went on Fidelma. 'What immediately sprang to all minds was the idea that both Illan and the horse, Aonbharr, had been killed to prevent them taking part in the race today. Who would benefit by this? Well, Bressal, of course, for his horse, Ochain, and Murchad, his jockey, were the only serious contenders in the race other than Illan and Aonbharr. So if Bressal was not guilty, who could it have been? Who would benefit? Was it Murchad, who had laid a large wager on his winning? Laisran had already witnessed Murchad earlier this morning placing heavy wagers on himself to win.'

'No law against that!'

Murchad had flushed angrily but Fidelma ignored him and went on: 'Obviously it was not Murchad for he did not have a motive. He would only have collected his winnings if he had won the race which essentially meant taking part in it. If he had murdered Illan, poisoned Aonbharr and left the trail of false clues of Bressal, then it would be obvious that Bressal would be arrested and his horse and Murchad would be disqualified from racing. That being so, Murchad would have forfeited his wager.'

Murchad nodded slowly in agreement and relief. Fidelma went blithely on.

'If not Murchad, what of Angaire, the trainer? He was not doing well for Bressal and had been told this very morning that Bressal was going to get rid of him. Bressal had made no secret of the fact that he had gone this very morning to see Illan in an attempt to persuade him to return to his stable and ride for him instead of Fáelán. Angaire had a better motive than Murchad.'

Angaire shifted uneasily where he stood. But Fidelma continued.

'You see, sticking to the line of argument about the horse race as the motive, there was only one other person with a motive who might benefit from putting the blame on Bressal.'

She turned towards Fáelán, the king. He stared at her in astonishment which swiftly grew into anger.

'Wait,' she cut his protests short. 'Such a plot was too convoluted. Besides everyone was of the opinion that Aonbharr could out-distance Ochain. There was no challenge there to be worried about. So there was no motive.'

She paused and looked around at their perplexed faces.

'It eventually became clear that the killing of Illan was not caused by rivalries on the race track. There was another motive for that crime. But was it the same motive as that for poisoning Aonbharr?'

They were all silent now, waiting for her to continue.

'The motive for Illan's death was as ageless as time. Unrequited love. Illan was young, handsome and his reputation among women was such that he had many lovers. He picked them up as one might pick up flowers, kept them until the affair withered and them threw them away. Am I not right?'

Fáelán was pale and he glanced surreptitiously at Muadnat.

'That is no crime, Fidelma. In our society, many still take second wives, husbands or lovers.'

'True enough. But one of the flowers which Illan had picked was not ready to be discarded. She went to his tent this morning and argued with him. And when he spurned her, when he said he would have no more to do with her, she, in a fit of rage, stabbed him to death. All it needed was one swift dagger blow under the rib cage.'

'If this is so,' said Énna, quietly, 'why would she go to such lengths to put the blame on Bressal? Why poison Aonbharr? The laws of our society allow leniency to those who perpetrate such crimes of passion.'

Fidelma inclined her head.

'A case could be made that any non fatal injury inflicted by the woman in such circumstances does not incur liability. Our laws recognize the stirring of uncontrollable passion in such circumstances. In the matter of death she would be fined her victim's honour price only. No other punishment would be necessary.'

'Then why, if this were so, did the woman conceal her crime, for the concealment brings forth greater punishment?' repeated Énna.

'Because there were two separate villainies at work here and one fed off the initial deed of the other,' replied Fidelma.

'I don't understand. Who killed Illan?' Fáelán again glanced uneasily at his wife. 'You say it was a woman. By attempting to conceal the crime such a woman, no matter her rank, if found guilty, would be placed into a boat with one paddle and a vessel of gruel and the mercy of God. Sister Fidelma,' his voice suddenly broke with passion, 'is it Muadnat of whom you speak?'

Fáelán's wife sat as if turned to stone.

Fidelma did not reply immediately but drew out of her *marsupium* a belt with a bejewelled ceremonial sheath. There was a small dagger in it. She took out the dagger and handed it to Muadnat.

'Does the dagger belong to you, my lady?'

'It is mine,' Muadnat replied grimly.

Fáelán gasped in horror, as if his worst fears were confirmed. 'Then . . . ?' he began. Fidelma was shaking her head.

'No, Daghháin killed Illan.'

There was a gasp of astonishment from the company and all eyes turned on the flushed face of Énna's wife. Daghháin sat stunned for a moment by the revelation. Then, as if in a dream, she slowly rose to her feet and looked about her, as if searching out someone. 'Liar! Betrayer!' she hissed venomously. Fidelma glanced quickly in the direction the woman was gazing and felt satisfied.

Daghháin now turned towards her and cursed her in a way which left no one in doubt as to her guilt. Énna had simply collapsed into a chair, immobile with shock.

After Daghháin had been removed to a place of confinement,

Fidelma had to raise her hands to quell the questions that were thrown at her.

'Dagháin was seen coming to the Curragh early this morning. The apothecary, Sister Eblenn, saw her soon after she had been robbed which was just after breakfast. Dagháin therefore lied when she said that she had come later in the morning to the course. That lie alerted my suspicions. A suspicion which was increased when I realized that the arrow was not the murder weapon but the wound had been made by a dagger. When I first came before Fáelán, Muadnat had been wearing a ceremonial dagger sheath yet there was no dagger in it.'

'This I don't understand,' Fáelán said. 'Surely this would lay the suspicion on Muadnat?'

'Indeed, I was suspicious for a while, that I admit. But it was obvious to my eye that the dagger in Dagháin's sheath was too small to fit comfortably in it. That I had to work out. Then I realized that she, at some stage, put Muadnat's dagger in her sheath, is that not so?'

Muadnat spoke softly.

'She wanted an apple to calm her nerves and asked me for the loan of my dagger, saying she had mislaid her own. It was only a moment ago that I realized Dagháin had not returned it.'

'Dagháin,' Fidelma went on, 'in her description of the finding of Illan, said that she had run straight to tell Énna. Yet she was seen running from his tent directly to her own tent. I searched her tent a moment ago. Thankfully, she had discarded her ceremonial belt and sheath. I was confirmed in my suspicion that the dagger did not belong to her but was that of Muadnat.'

'Then where was Dagháin's own dagger?' demanded Laisran, intrigued.

'I found it where I suspected it would be, the blade is still covered with Illan's blood. It was in Angaire's saddle bag.'

Angaire, with a cry of rage, made to jump to the tent door but one of the Baoisgne, the king's guards, stayed him with a drawn sword to his chest. Fidelma continued on without taking any notice of the drama.

'While Angaire did not kill Illan, he did poison Aonbharr, and then tried to place the guilt for both deeds on Bressal by planting the arrow and *cena* as evidence. Angaire's actions obscured the real murderer of Illan. You see Angaire knew that he was about to be discarded by Bressal. I have already given you his motive. Bressal had been quite open in his intention to replace Angaire. Indeed, even if Illan had not refused Bressal's offer to return to his stable, Angaire's days as trainer were still numbered.

'Angaire had, I believe, already devised a plan to hurt Bressal. I believe his original intention was to poison Ochain. For that end, he stole some poisonous plants from the tent of Sister Eblenn early this morning. Then the mysteries of Fate itself took over. Angaire overheard Bressal arguing with Illan. But the plot did not occur to him then.

'It was only when he was with Murchad and Sílán a little while later, that he saw Daghain fleeing from Illan's tent. Her dress was dishevelled and the ceremonial dagger missing. She fled to her own tent. He had made a lewd remark, an automatic remark. His companions, Sílán and Murchad, were leaving. Perhaps even before then the thought had struck him that his unthinking remark might be true and what if . . . his mind was thinking about the missing dagger.

'He went to Illan's tent. There was Daghain's knife buried in Illan's chest. His suspicion was right. He took out the knife with the idea was growing in his mind. Here was his chance to get even with Bressal and to secure a future lucrative role for himself in the service of Daghain. He hurried to her tent, showed her the knife, which he kept as a hold over her. He told her to wait a while before she should find her husband and tell him the story which she has subsequently told us. The reason for her to be in Illan's tent was that she had noticed that Aonbharr was ill. This was Angaire's addition providing a perfect excuse and an essential part of his intrigue.

'Then he hurried to Bressal's tent, furtively took an arrow from Sílán's quiver, broke it in two, and left one half in the quiver. The other he took, together with his *cena* full of poisonous herbs, and hurried to his task. He fed Aonbharr the poison. Then went into Illan's tent and thrust the forward section of the broken arrow into the wound. He left the *cena* in plain sight. The false trail was laid.

'Thus two separate villainies were at work, coming together over the one great crime. And who is the greater villain – Dagháin, a pitiful, rejected woman or Angaire, petty and vengeful, whose spite might have led to an even greater crime? I tell you this, Fáelán, when the time comes for Dagháin to be tried before the courts, I would like to be retained as her advocate.'

'But what made you connect Dagháin with Illan?' demanded Fáelán.

'Énna himself indicated that his wife had had an affair with Illan by a chance remark. You knew of the affair, didn't you, Énna?'

Énna glanced up from his chair, red eyed with emotional exhaustion. He nodded slowly.

'I knew. I did not know that she was so besotted with Illan that she would resort to such means to keep him when he finally rejected her,' he whispered. 'Fáelán, I will stand down as your *tánaiste*. I am not worthy now.'

The king of the Laighin grimaced.

'We will talk of this, Énna,' he said, with considerable discomfit, studiously ignoring his wife, Muadnat. 'I am not without sympathy for your situation. There are doubtless several victims in this terrible drama. Yet I still do not understand why Dagháin would do this thing. She was the wife of a *tánaiste*, heir-presumptive to the throne of the Laighin, while Illan was merely a jockey. How could she behave thus simply because Illan rejected her for a new lover?'

The question was aimed at Fidelma.

'There is no simplicity about the complexity of human emotions, Fáelán,' replied Fidelma.'But if we are to seek the real victim then it is the poor beast Aonbharr. Truly, Aonbharr was a horse that died in an attempt to conceal the shame of others.'

A trumpet was sounding outside.

Fáelán bit his lip and sighed.

'That is the signal for me to open the afternoon's race . . . my heart is not in it.'

He rose and automatically held out his arm to Muadnat, his wife. She hesitated before taking it, not looking at her husband.

There would be much to mend in that relationship, thought Fidelma. Then Fáelán turned and called to his bishop:

'Bressal, will you come with us? Stand alongside me while I open the proceedings so that the people will clearly see that we are together and are not enemies? As neither of our horses can now enter this race let us show unity to our people for this day at least.'

Bressal hesitated before nodding his reluctant agreement.

'I'll send your fee to Kildare, Fidelma,' Fáelán called over his shoulder. 'I thank God we have Brehons as wise as you.'

After they had left the tent, Énna slowly rose. He stared at Fidelma and Laisran with sad eyes for a moment.

'I knew she was having an affair. I would have stood by her, even resign my office for her as I will now. I would not have divorced nor rejected her had she come to me with the truth. I will continue to stand by her now.'

Fidelma and Laisran silently watched him leave the tent.

'Sad,' remarked Fidelma. 'It is, indeed, a sad world.'

They left the tent and began walking through the shouting, carefree masses, milling towards the race course. Fidelma smiled thinly at Laisran.

'As you were saying, Laisran, horse racing is a cure for all the ills of humankind. It is a surrogate for people's aggression and for their greed.'

Laisran grimaced wryly but was wisely silent before the cynical gaze of his protégée.

Murder on the Race Course

JULIAN SYMONS

The Grand National is the most famous National Hunt Race in the world, an unrivalled event that generates superlatives every year. Widely referred to as the 'People's Race', it is said to attract a worldwide TV audience of close to 850 million, generate more than £60 million in bets, and provide the kind of high drama and agonizing heartbreak that can be seen nowhere else. The names of the jumps such as The Chair, Becher's Brook (called after the first man to fall there in the opening Grand National, Captain Martin Becher) and the Canal Turn are household words; while the triumphs of horses like Golden Miller, Aldaniti (ridden by Bob Champion after recovering from cancer) and Red Rum (the only horse to ever win the event three times) are matched in the public imagination only by the fatal falls of Brown Trix and Seeandem, and Dick Francis' heart-stopping collapse on Devon Lock. Every year since it was first run in 1838, the Grand National has drawn vast crowds to Aintree and never failed to provide the dashing of many expectations and the fulfilment of a host of dreams. As many as sixty-six horses have started the race which, like the Derby, has provided enough material from its four and half mile duration over thirty obstacles that take about ten minutes to complete by the winning jockey and his mount, to inspire all kinds of writers of fact and fiction. It has, with every justification, been called the race in which absolutely anything not only can happen, but often *does*.

It is perhaps very appropriate that this unique race should be featured here in a murder story by one of the best modern crime writers, Julian Symons (1912–94), whose death sadly occurred while I was working on this book and whose help and suggestions with it had been invaluable. *The Times*, in its obituary, described

Symons as being 'among the most distinguished authors and expositors of the postwar British crime novel' which was no mean achievement for the son of poor Russian-Jewish immigrants who had come to London at the turn of the century.

Symons' interest in the world of racing was early formed by his flamboyant father, who overcame poverty by running an auction room and dealing in racehorses. He discovered crime fiction as a teenager through reading the adventures of Sherlock Holmes and Father Brown, and these were to inspire his own literary endeavours, which would embrace poetry, journalism, reviewing, historical biographies, radio and TV plays, and crime fiction, his first novel, *The Immaterial Murder Case*, being published in 1945. His literary career thereafter brought him innumerable awards, the presidency of the Detection Club (succeeding that other racing lover, Dame Agatha Christie) and the Cartier Diamond Dagger Award for a lifetime's achievement in the field of crime fiction. Symons retained an interest in horse racing all his life, attended the Grand National a few times, but went more regularly to meetings in Southern England near his home at Deal, Kent. The story 'Murder on the Race Course' features his debonair private eye, Francis Quarles, about whom he wrote a dozen cases for *Ellery Queen's Mystery Magazine*. It is a fitting reminder of a great mystery story writer and has a climax every bit as exciting as the great race which inspired it.

*

'With my son up he can do it,' Sir Reginald Bartley said emphatically. 'There's no better amateur in the country than Harry. I tell you I'm not sorry Baker can't ride him.'

There was something challenging in his tone. Trainer Norman Johnson, wooden-faced, bowlegged, said noncommitally, 'He can ride, your son, I'm not denying it.'

'And Lucky Charm's a fine horse.'

'Ay, there's nothing against the horse,' Johnson said.

'Then what's the matter with you, man? A few days ago you were keen as mustard, telling me I had a chance of leading in my first Grand National winner. Today you're as enthusiastic as the cat who started lapping a saucer of cream and found it was sour milk.'

'I wouldn't want to raise false hopes, Sir Reginald, that's all. Here comes Lucky Charm.'

'And here comes Harry.'

Private detective Francis Quarles stood with them in the paddock at Aintree and listened to this conversation with interest. Horse racing was one of the few subjects about which he had no specialized knowledge, and he was here only because he had been tracking down the man who later became known as the Liverpool Forger.

Quarles had once cleared up a troublesome series of robberies committed in the chain of department stores owned by Sir Reginald, and when they met again at the Adelphi Hotel the business magnate had invited the private detective to be his guest at Aintree.

In the hotel that morning Quarles had learned that Lucky Charm was a 40-to-1 outsider in this year's Grand National, that his jockey Baker had fallen and thrown out his shoulder on the previous day, and that Lucky Charm would now be ridden by Sir Reginald's son, Harry.

Now he looked at the big-shouldered powerful-looking black horse, with the number 8 on his saddle cloth, being led round by a stable boy. Then he looked at the young man who walked up to them wearing a jacket of distinctive cerise and gold hoops.

'How is it, Harry? All set?' asked Sir Reginald.

'Why not?' Harry Bartley had the kind of dark, arrogant good looks that Quarles distrusted.

'We're all ready to lead him in,' Sir Reginald said, with what seemed to Quarles almost fatuous complacency. 'We know we've got the horse and the jockey too, Harry my boy.'

Johnson said nothing. Harry Bartley pulled a handkerchief out of his breast pocket and blew his nose.

'Got your lucky charm?' the owner persisted.

'Of course.' Harry's voice was slightly blurred, as though he had just had a tooth out. From the same pocket he produced a rabbit's foot, kissed it, and put it back carefully.

'There's Mountain Pride,' said Sir Reginald a little wistfully.

Mountain Pride, Quarles knew, was the favourite, a bay gelding with a white star on his forehead.

'Time to go.' Harry Bartley gave them a casual nod and turned away, walking a little erratically across the paddock to the place where the stable boy stood, holding Lucky Charm. Had he been drinking, Quarles wondered?

'Good luck,' his father called. 'Better be getting along to the stand.' Sir Reginald was a choleric little man, and now his face was purple as he turned to the trainer. 'You may not like the boy, but you could have wished him luck.'

Johnson's wooden expression did not change. 'You know I wish Lucky Charm all the luck there is, Sir Reginald.'

'Trouble with Johnson is, he's sulking,' Sir Reginald said when they were in the stand. 'Insisted Baker should ride the horse when I wanted Harry. I gave way – after all, Baker's a professional jockey. Then, when Baker was injured, he wanted to have some stable boy and I put my foot down.'

'What has he got against your son?'

Sir Reginald looked at Quarles out of the corner of one slightly bloodshot eye. 'The boy's a bit wild, y'know. Nothing wrong with him, but – a bit wild. There they go.'

The horses had paraded in front of the stand and now they were going down to the starting post. Bright March sunlight illuminated the course and even Francis Quarles, who was not particularly susceptible to such things, found something delightful in the scene. The men and women in the stands and the crowd chattering along the rails, the men with their raglans and mackintoshes and the patches of color in women's coats and hats, the ballet-like grace of the horses and the vivid yet melting green of the Aintree background . . .

Quarles pulled himself up on the edge of sentiment. His companion said sharply, 'Harry's having trouble.'

The horses were at the starting post. Quarles raised his glasses. After a moment he picked out Lucky Charm. The black horse was refusing to get into line with the rest. Three times Harry Bartley brought him up and he turned away.

Sir Reginald tapped his stick on the ground. 'Come on now,

Harry, show him who's master. Never known Lucky Charm to act like this before.'

'Is he used to your son?'

The question was not well received. 'Harry can ride any horse,' Bartley snapped. Then he drew in his breath and his voice joined with thousands of others in the cry, 'They're off!'

Now in the stand a mass of binoculars was raised to follow the progress of some thirty horses over some of the most testing fences in the world. Now bookmakers looked anxious, punters let cigars go out, women twisted race cards in gloved hands. Everything depended now on the jumping skill and staying power of horses that had been trained for months in preparation for this day, and on the adeptness of the jockeys in nursing their charges and then urging them forward to moments of supreme endeavor.

The horses came up in a bunch to the first fence, rose to it, cleared it. Thousands of throats exhaled and articulated sighingly the words: 'They're over.'

They were not all over, Quarles saw. A jockey lay on the ground, a jockey wearing red jacket and white cap. A riderless horse ran on.

On to the second jump and the third, a six-foot ditch with a four-foot-nine fence on the other side of it. Now there was a cry: 'O'Grady's down. Double or Quits is down. Bonny Dundee's down.'

There were more riderless horses, more jockeys on the ground who stumbled to their feet and ran to the rails when all the horses had passed.

Past Becher's they came and round the Canal Turn and then over Valentine's, the field beginning to string out.

'There's Mountain Pride in front,' Sir Reginald cried. 'And Johnny Come Lately and Lost Horizon. And Lucky Charm's with them.' Almost under his breath he muttered, 'But I don't like the way the boy's handling him.'

The horses came round toward the stand. Quarles watched the cerise and gold jacket take the fourteenth fence, and it seemed to him that Harry Bartley was not so much riding as desperately clinging to the horse.

They came to the fifteenth fence, the Chair, which is one of the most awkward at Aintree – a six-foot ditch and then a fence five-foot-two in height which rises roughly in a chair's shape.

Mountain Pride soared over, and so did the two horses that followed. Then came the cerise and gold jacket. Lucky Charm rose to the fence and went over beautifully, but as he landed the jockey seemed simply to slip off and lay prone on the turf.

Lucky Charm ran on, the rest of the field thundered by.

Sir Reginald lowered his glasses slowly. 'That's that. Not my Grand National, I'm afraid.'

Quarles waited for the figure on the turf to get up, but it did not move. Ambulance men beside the jump ran onto the course with a stretcher and bent over the jockey. Still he did not move as they lifted him onto the stretcher.

They watched in stupefaction as the ambulance men carried him away. Then Sir Reginald, his usually ruddy face white as milk, said, 'Come on, man, come on.'

'What about the race?'

'To hell with the race,' Sir Reginald cried. 'I want to know what's happened to my son.'

The limp body of Harry Bartley was carried round to the course hospital, in the administrative block. Doctor Ferguson, the local doctor, had just begun his examination when the door of the ward was pushed open and a handsome gray-haired man, with a pair of binoculars slung round his neck, came in.

'Ferguson? My name's Ramsay, I'm Harry's doctor. We've met before, up here last year. Is the boy badly hurt?'

'As far as I can see he's received no injury at all. There's something very wrong though – his pulse is feeble and irregular. Was he subject to any kind of fits, do you know?'

'Harry? Not to my knowledge.' Ferguson made way as Doctor Ramsay approached the body and bent over it. He straightened up with a puzzled frown. 'Have you smelled round the nose and mouth?'

'No, I haven't. I'd only begun to examine him.' Ferguson bent over too and caught the odor of bitter almonds. 'My God, he's taken poison!'

'Taken it – or it's been administered to him.' Ramsay's face was grave. 'The question is what, and how? It's not cyanide, obviously, or he wouldn't be alive now.'

'I must telephone—' Doctor Ferguson broke off as Sir Reginald and Francis Quarles, followed by trainer Norman Johnson, came into the room. Ramsay went over to Sir Reginald and placed a hand on his arm.

'Bartley, I won't mince words. You must be prepared for a shock. Harry has been poisoned in some way, and there's very little we can do for him.'

'He'll be all right?'

'It's touch and go,' Ramsay said evasively. He watched Francis Quarles approach the body. 'Who's that?'

Sir Reginald told him.

Quarles bent over the unconscious figure, looked at its pale face and purple lips and nose, sniffed the scent of bitter almonds. He came over to Ramsay, who had now been joined by Ferguson. Sir Reginald introduced the detective.

'Have you gentlemen made up your minds about this case?' Quarles asked. He spoke in a faintly languid manner which made Ramsay, who was brisk and soldierly, bristle slightly.

'Not yet. In your superior wisdom I suppose you have done so.'

'Have you considered nitrobenzene?'

'Nitrobenzene,' Doctor Ferguson said thoughtfully. 'Yes, that would explain the prussic acid symptoms, but I don't see why it should have occurred to you.'

'I know little about horse racing, but something about poisoning,' Quarles said. 'And I had the opportunity of seeing Harry Bartley just before the race. His appearance then seemed to me very strange. His speech was blurred and he walked unsteadily. The thought crossed my mind that he might be drunk, but as you know such an appearance of drunkenness is a common symptom in nitrobenzene poisoning.'

There was silence. Ramsay shifted uncomfortably. Sir Reginald said, 'What are we waiting for? If there's no ambulance let's get him in to Liverpool in my car.'

Ferguson crossed over to Harry Bartley again, felt pulse and heart, and then drew a sheet up over the face.

Ramsay said to Sir Reginald, 'He's gone. I wanted to break it gently. There was never any chance.'

'But when we came in Ferguson here was telephoning—'

'I was telephoning the police superintendent on the course,' Ferguson said. 'There'll need to be an investigation. This is a bad business.'

Francis Quarles took no part in the flurry of conversation that followed the arrival of the police superintendent and the other officers with him. Instead, he went over to the wooden-faced trainer, Norman Johnson, and took him outside. They paced up and down in hearing of the excited crowds who were cheering the victory of Mountain Pride, and Quarles asked questions.

'Harry Bartley may have died by accident, but I would bet a hundred pounds that he was murdered. Now there's one obvious question I should like to have answered by a racing expert. Is it likely that he was killed to prevent Lucky Charm winning the National?'

Johnson paused for an appreciable time before he said bluntly, 'No.'

'It's unlikely?'

'You can put it out of your mind. I'm not saying horse racing's pure as snow, Mr Quarles. Far from it. Horses have been nobbled before now, horses have been doped. But favorites, not forty-to-one outsiders. And horses, not men.'

'You mean—?'

'If anyone wanted to stop Lucky Charm they'd go for the horse, not the man. Kill a horse and get caught, you may go to prison. Kill a man – well, it's murder.'

'Sir Reginald seemed very optimistic about his horse's chances in the National. What did you feel?'

The trainer rubbed his chin, making a sound like a saw cutting wood. 'With Baker up, he was a good outsider, a nice each-way bet. Hadn't quite the class for it, but you never can tell. He liked Baker, did Lucky Charm.'

'And he didn't like Harry Bartley?'

'Hated him. Bartley used the whip more than he needed to. Lucky Charm wasn't a horse you could treat that way. I tried to persuade Sir Reginald to give the ride to another jockey, but it was no good.'

'You shared the horse's dislike of Harry Bartley, I gather.'

The trainer said nothing. His faded blue eyes stared into the distance, and the Red Indian impassiveness of his features did not change. 'Was there a special reason for that?'

Slowly and without passion, Norman Johnson said, 'Sir Reginald Bartley is a man I respect and like, none more so. I don't know how he came to have such a son. He couldn't be trusted with a woman, he couldn't be trusted to pay his debts, he was a good rider but he couldn't be trusted to treat a horse decently.'

'But there's something personal in your dislike,' Quarles insisted.

Johnson brought his blue eyes out of the middle distance and focused them on Quarles. 'You'll learn about it soon enough. It might as well be from me. I had a daughter named Mary. She was a good girl until she took up with Harry Bartley. He was always around the stables, every day for weeks, and I was fool enough not to realize what he was after – until Mary went away with him and left me a note. I understood it then well enough. That was six months ago. He walked out on her after a few weeks. She put her head in a gas oven.'

'I see.'

'When I've worked out my contract with Sir Reginald, I'm asking him to take his horses away.'

Quarles said softly, 'Some people might call that a motive for murder.'

'I don't deny it, Mr Quarles. It happens that I didn't kill him, that's all.' Johnson drove the fist of one hand into the palm of the other, and his voice for the first time vibrated with excitement. 'But if you ever find his murderer you'll find he has a personal reason, a reason like mine. For me, I hope you never find him. I say good luck to the man or woman who killed Harry Bartley.'

Back in the course hospital Quarles met young Inspector Makepeace, who had been working with him in running down the Liverpool Forger.

Makepeace looked at the private detective with a wry smile.

'You seem to manage to be where things happen, Mr Quarles. I understand you saw young Bartley before the race.'

Quarles told him the impression he had formed that Bartley might be drunk, and the outcome of his conversation with Johnson. The Inspector listened with interest.

'I should say Johnson's right, and this was almost certainly the working out of a private enmity. As you say, he's got a motive himself, although I'm keeping an open mind about that. In return I don't mind telling you that we've got a pretty good idea of how the poison was administered. Miss Moore here has been very helpful about that. She was engaged to Harry Bartley.'

Miss Jennifer Moore had a round innocent face and dark hair. She had been crying. 'But Inspector, I only said—'

'Bear with me a moment,' Inspector Makepeace asked. Quarles, whose own sense of modesty was conspicuous by its absence, noted mentally that Makepeace had a good opinion of himself. 'I don't know whether you know much about nitrobenzene poisoning, Mr Quarles?'

'I know that nitrobenzene is comparatively easy to make,' Quarles answered. 'It is generally taken in the form of a liquid although it is equally poisonous as a vapor. I remember the case of a young man who spilled nitrobenzene on his clothes, became stupefied, finally collapsed in coma and died. But the most interesting thing about it is that there is an interval between taking the poison and its effects appearing, which can vary from a quarter of an hour to three hours, or longer in the case of vapor. Is that what you were going to tell me?'

The Inspector laughed a little uncomfortably. 'You're a bit of a walking encyclopedia, aren't you? That's pretty much what I was going to say, yes. You see, if we can trace the course of Bartley's eating and drinking today we should be able to see when he took the poison. Now it so happens that we can do just that. Doctor Ramsay, would you come over here, please?'

The poker-backed doctor came forward.

'I understand Harry Bartley came to see you this morning.'

Ramsay nodded. 'I'm staying with friends a couple of miles outside Liverpool. Harry rang me up this morning before nine o'clock. He was pretty jittery, wanted something to pep him up.

He was out at the place I'm staying before half-past nine and I gave him a couple of pills, and put two more in a box for him in case he needed to take them before the race.'

'They were in his clothes in the changing room,' Makepeace said to Quarles with a smile. 'I can see your eyes fixed thoughtfully on Doctor Ramsay, but Ferguson here assures me that any pills taken at half-past nine must have had effect well before the time of the race. Now, follow the course of events, Quarles. Bartley returned to the hotel by ten o'clock, met Miss Moore in the lobby, and said that he was going up to his room to write some letters. She arranged to pick him up at about twelve, because they were going to a cocktail party. She picked him up then and they went to the party, which was given by a friend of theirs named Lapetaine. There, Miss Moore can testify, Harry Bartley drank just one glass of orange juice.'

'What about lunch?' Quarles asked the girl.

She shook her head. 'Harry was worried about making the weight. He came and watched Bill and me eat lunch and didn't touch anything, not so much as a piece of toast or a glass of water.'

'Bill?'

She colored slightly. 'Doctor Ramsay and I have known each other for years. He can bear out what I say. We had lunch on the course, and after it Harry went off to the changing room. Of course he may have drunk something after that.'

'Most unlikely,' Ferguson said. 'Particularly if he was worried about making the weight.'

'So you see we're down to the one glass of orange juice.' The Inspector smoothed his fair hair with some complacency.

'Apparently,' Quarles agreed.

'At lunch, did he show any sign of confusion, blurred speech, unsteady walk – anything like that?'

Both Ramsay and Jennifer Moore returned decided negatives.

'Come on now, Mr Quarles,' Makepeace said with a smile. 'The fact is you're reluctant to admit that the police are ever quick off the mark, and this time we've surprised you.'

'It isn't that, my dear Inspector. Something's worrying me, and

I don't quite know what it is. Something that I've seen, or that's happened or that's been said. I shall be interested to know the result of the post-mortem.'

'The P.M.?' The Inspector was startled. 'Surely you don't doubt that—'

'That he died of nitrobenzene poisoning? No, I don't, but there's still something that tantalizes me about it. Ah, here are his personal possessions.'

The detective paused by a table on which a number of articles lay in two separate piles. One of them contained the things Bartley had been wearing during the race, the other came from his clothes in the changing room.

In the first pile were Lucky Charm's saddle, the cerise and gold shirt and cap, and the breeches Bartley had been wearing. Here too, isolated and pathetic, was the rabbit's-foot charm he had kissed; it was neatly ticketed: *Found in pocket.*

The things in the other pile were naturally more numerous – sports jacket, vest, shirt and gray trousers, gold wrist watch, keys on a ring, silver and copper coins, a wallet with notes and other papers, three letters.

Inspector Makepeace picked up one of these letters and handed it to Quarles.

It was a letter written in a sprawling hand by a woman who had used violet ink, and it was full of bitter reproaches, in painfully familiar phrasing. 'Cast me off like an old shoe . . . given you everything a woman can give . . . shan't let you get away with it . . . sooner see you dead than married to somebody else.'

Why is it, Quarles wondered, that at times of strong emotion, almost all of us express ourselves in clichés? The letter began 'Darling Harry' and was signed 'Hilary.'

'You haven't traced the writer of this letter yet?' The undercurrent of sarcasm in Quarles's voice was so faint that Inspector Makepeace missed it.

'Give us a chance, Mr Quarles. Between you and me I'm not inclined to attach too much importance to it – shouldn't be surprised to learn that there were half a dozen women in Master Harry's life. I'm more interested in getting a complete list of guests at that cocktail party. Nothing very informative here, I'm afraid.'

'On the contrary,' Quarles said.

Makepeace stared. 'You mean there's something I've missed—'

'You haven't missed anything, but something's missing that should be here. You should be able to deduce it yourself. Now I'm more anxious than ever to know the result of the post-mortem.'

Sir Reginald Bartley paced up and down the drawing room of his suite. His voice had lost none of its vigor, but his appearance was pitiably different from that of the jaunty man who had talked about leading in the Grand National winner twenty-four hours earlier. There was an unshaved patch on his chin, his face was pallid and his hand trembled slightly.

'I want this murderer caught,' he said. 'I want to see him in the dock. I want to hear the judge pronounce sentence on him. That police Inspector is smart, but I believe you're smarter, Quarles. I want you to investigate this case, and if you catch the man who poisoned my son you can write your own ticket.'

Quarles looked at him intently.

'Why do you call it a man? There is a general belief that most poisoners are women.'

'Man or woman.' Sir Reginald made an impatient gesture to indicate that this was merely splitting hairs. 'I want them in the dock.'

'Then you'll have to be franker with me than you have been so far. You might begin by telling me what you know about Hilary.'

'Hilary?' Sir Reginald's surprise seemed genuine. 'That's not a name I've ever heard in relation to Harry.'

'She wrote an interesting letter to your son.' Quarles did not pursue the point. 'Norman Johnson said that your son behaved very badly to his daughter.'

Sir Reginald blew his nose emphatically. 'She was a foolish girl, wouldn't leave him alone. I'm not denying that Harry was sometimes wild. But there was never any real harm in him.'

'Johnson's story was that your son lured this girl away from home, lived with her for a short time, then walked out on her. Do you accept that?'

'I've really no idea. Harry was of age. I knew little about that side of his life. I don't see,' he added stiffly, 'that it's our place to sit in moral judgment on him.'

'It's not a question of moral judgment,' Quarles said patiently. 'I'm trying to get at facts. What do you think of Miss Moore?'

'A very nice girl, very nice indeed,' said Sir Reginald emphatically.

'She'd only recently become engaged to your son, I believe?'

'About three weeks ago, yes. She is – was – very much in love with him.'

'Doctor Ramsay had known her for years?'

'Yes. Known Harry for many years too, for that matter, ever since he was a boy. Good chap, Ramsay, pulled me through a bad go of pneumonia a couple of years ago, just after my wife died.'

Quarles stood up. His eyes, hard and black, stared at Sir Reginald, who bore their gaze uneasily. 'I accept the commission. But you will realize, Sir Reginald, that I am no respecter of persons. You are engaging me to discover the truth, regardless of consequences.'

Sir Reginald repeated after him, 'Regardless of consequences.'

In the hotel lobby Quarles heard himself being paged. He stopped the boy and was told that Miss Moore was in the lounge and would like to speak to him. He found her talking in a deserted corner of the room to a dark-skinned, rather too beautifully dressed young man, with a fine large nose.

'This is Jack Lapetaine, who was Harry's great friend,' she said. 'As a matter of fact, it was through Jack that I met Harry, and it was Jack who gave the cocktail party yesterday.'

'Is that so?' Quarles looked at Lapetaine with interest, wondering about his ancestry. Indian perhaps? Turkish? 'Are you a racing man, Mr Lapetaine?'

'I am an art dealer.' Lapetaine smiled, showing pointed yellowish teeth. 'But I am interested in horse racing; yes. I like the excitement. I like to gamble, I was very fond of Harry. So I came up for the National. I am almost ashamed of it, but I had a good win.'

'You backed Mountain Pride?'

'I did. I had just a little flier on Lucky Charm, for sentiment's sake as you might say, but I did not think he had quite – how shall I put it? – the class for the race.'

'You watched it, of course?'

'No, Mr Quarles.' Lapetaine looked down at his elegant suede shoes. 'I was engaged on urgent business.'

Jennifer Moore said impatiently, 'Look here, Mr Quarles, there's something I want you to tell me. Has Sir Reginald asked you to investigate this case?' Quarles nodded. 'I hope you won't.'

'Why not?'

'It can't possibly do any good. Harry's dead, and nothing can bring him back. And it might – well, might embarrass people who haven't any connection with it.'

Lapetaine listened with a malicious smile. Quarles said quietly, 'I see. Your engagement is very recent, isn't it, Miss Moore?'

'Harry and I met for the first time five weeks ago. It sounds silly, I expect, but we fell in love at first sight. Within a fortnight we were engaged.'

'Should I be right in thinking that Doctor Ramsay feels some affection for you, and that you are afraid my investigations may involve him?'

Still with that slightly objectionable smile, Lapetaine said, 'I can tell you exactly what Jennifer is afraid of. Ramsay has been sweet on her for years. Now, you know that Harry went out to see Ramsay on the morning of the race to get some pep tablets. What was to stop Ramsay from giving him two more, one of them filled with nitrobenzene, and saying, "Take one of these at twelve thirty, my boy, and you'll ride as you've never ridden before." It simply happened that Harry took the poisoned tablet first. The timing would be just about right.'

The girl buried her face in her hands. 'You shouldn't have—'

'My dear, Mr Quarles is an intelligent man. I should be surprised if that idea had not already occurred to him.'

Quarles looked at him. 'You seem to know a good deal about the operation of nitrobenzene, Mr Lapetaine.'

Unperturbed, the art dealer showed his teeth. 'I trained for a medical degree in youth before I – what shall I say? – discovered my vocation.'

'There are certain objections to that idea,' Quarles began, when a page boy came running up.

'Mr Quarles, sir. Telephone for you.'

On the telephone Quarles heard Inspector Makepeace's voice, raw with irritation. 'We've got the result of the P.M. I don't know how you guessed, but you were perfectly right.'

'There was no question of guessing,' Quarles said indignantly. 'My suggestion was the result of deduction from observed facts.'

'Anyway, it seems to leave us just where we began.'

'Oh, no,' Quarles said softly. 'I have told you exactly what happened before and during the race. Surely it leaves only one possible explanation.'

He went back to the lounge, and addressed Jennifer Moore. 'You need not worry any further, Miss Moore, about Doctor Ramsay or anyone else having administered a poisonous pill to Harry Bartley. I have just learned the result of the post-mortem. There was only a trace of nitrobenzene in the stomach.'

They looked at him in astonishment, Lapetaine with his mouth slightly open. 'I will spell out the meaning of that for you. Harry Bartley was not poisoned by a pill or by the orange juice he drank at your cocktail party, Mr Lapetaine. He was poisoned by nitrobenzene, yes, but in the form of vapor.'

Lapetaine had been surprised by Quarles's revelation but, as the detective admitted to himself with some admiration, the art dealer was a cool card. After the initial shock he nodded.

'Will you excuse me? I must remember to make a note of an appointment.' He scribbled something on a sheet of paper torn from a pocket diary and said with a smile, 'I am relieved. You will no longer suspect me of poisoning my guest's orange juice, which would hardly have been playing the game, as you might say.'

Jennifer Moore seemed bewildered. 'I thought it must be the orange juice. If it was vapor, then – well, I simply don't understand. Perhaps it was an accident.'

'It was not an accident,' Francis Quarles said. 'You can see that my investigations may be useful after all, Miss Moore.'

'I suppose so,' she said a little doubtfully. 'Goodbye, Mr Quarles.'

Lapetaine held out his hand to say goodbye, and when Quarles took it he found a piece of paper in his palm. He opened it after they had turned away, and saw that it was the paper torn from Lapetaine's diary.

On it the art dealer had scribbled: *Can you meet me in ten minutes at Kismet Coffee House, down the street?*

Ten minutes later Quarles pushed open the door of the Kismet Coffee House. In one of the cubicles he found the darkly handsome Lapetaine, drinking black coffee.

'Mr Quarles, you'll think me immensely mysterious, but—'

'Not at all. It was plain enough from your note that you wanted to talk to me when Miss Moore was not present. From that I deduce that you want to talk about a woman connected with Harry Bartley, and that it would upset Miss Moore to hear about her. I admit, however, that I am making no more than an informed guess when I suggest that her name is Hilary.'

Lapetaine looked at Quarles with his mouth open, then laughed unconvincingly. 'My word, Mr Quarles, it's not much use trying to keep secrets from you. I didn't know you'd ever heard of Hilary Hall.'

'I didn't say that I had. But now that you have told me her full name, you may as well go on with the story. I take it that she was a friend of Harry Bartley's.'

'She certainly was. Hilary's a night-club singer, the star at the Lady Love, which is a newish club just off Piccadilly. She's a red-head with a tremendous temper. When she heard that Harry was engaged to be married, she really hit the roof. Harry had played around with a lot of girls in his time, you know.'

Quarles nodded. 'I do know. But about Miss Hall.'

Lapetaine leaned forward. 'This I'll bet you *don't* know, Mr Quarles, and neither does anybody else. Hilary Hall came up here the day before the race, and she came to make trouble. She telephoned Harry that evening and he went to see her, tried to quiet her down, but without much effect. She rang Harry again at that cocktail party I gave the morning before the race, but I spoke to her. I spent the afternoon of the race arguing with her.' Lapetaine smiled. 'She finally agreed that a thousand pounds might help to soothe her injured feelings. I think you should talk to her.'

'I think so too. Why didn't you give this information to the police, Mr Lapetaine?'

The art dealer looked down at his shoes. 'I didn't think Hilary could be involved, but after what you tell me about vapor – I don't know. If I'm going to get into any trouble myself, then with me it's strictly Number One. Hilary's gone back to London. You'll find her at the Lady Love night club.'

Francis Quarles talked on the telephone to the owner of the Lady Love, then took a plane from Liverpool to London. He arrived at the night club, caught a glimpse of a cabaret-turn ending, and pushed his way backstage among a crowd of blondes and brunettes, wondering as he had often done before why a dozen half-dressed girls should be so much less attractive than one.

He tapped on the door of a room that was labeled *Miss Hall*. A deep, harsh voice said, 'All right.'

Hilary Hall was sitting in front of a looking glass and her reflection frowned out at him. Her beauty was like a physical blow after the commonplace prettiness of the dancing girls outside. Yet on a second look it was not really beauty, Quarles saw, but simply the combination of flaming red hair, a milk-white skin, and certain unusual physical features – the thick brows that almost met in the middle, the jutting red underlip, the powerful shoulders.

This was a woman whom you could imagine as a murderess, although such an exercise of the imagination, as Quarles well knew, could easily be misleading.

'I was told you were coming,' she said in that rusty, attractive voice. 'And I've seen your picture in the papers. What do you want?'

'I would like you to answer some questions.'

'I'm on in ten minutes. You've got till then.' She had not turned round.

Quarles said, 'I can put it simply. You were in love with Harry Bartley. You wrote him a threatening letter after his engagement. You went up to Liverpool to cause trouble.'

Her thick brows were drawn together. 'So what? He's dead now. I never went near the course, Mr Detective.'

Quarles said softly, 'He came to see you the night before the race.'

She swung round now and faced him. Her eyes were snapping with temper. She looked magnificent.

'Of course he did, after I'd rung him up. He came to pour out all his troubles and say how sorry he was it had to be goodbye. He didn't want to marry that silly little bit he'd got engaged to. She had money, that was all. Can you imagine any man preferring her to me?'

She paused and Quarles, although not particularly susceptible, felt a kind of shiver run down his back.

'He had other troubles too,' she said. 'A frightful cold that he was afraid might develop into flu and make it difficult for him to ride that damned horse. Said he'd have to do something about it. Altogether, he was pretty low.'

'You were very much in love with him?'

Looking down at her scarlet fingernails she said, 'He was a man.'

With a deprecating cough Quarles said, 'But you were prepared to accept a thousand pounds to soothe your feelings.'

She struck the dressing table sharply with a clenched fist. 'That filthy Paul Lapetaine's been talking to you. He was after me himself, but he never got to first base. I like men, not dressed-up dolls. Yes, I said I'd take the money. I need it. I knew Harry would never put a ring on my finger. You can think what you like about it.'

'What I think,' Quarles said abruptly, 'is that you're an honest woman.'

Her heavy frown changed into a smile. 'You're all right.'

A head poked through the door and a voice said, 'On in two minutes, Miss Hall.'

'Look here,' she said, 'I'm on now, but why don't you stay here? We'll talk afterwards, have a drink. I want to find Harry's murderer as much as you do.'

'I should be delighted to have a drink, and honored if you

would allow me to take you out to supper,' Francis Quarles said. 'But we don't have to talk about the case. The case is solved.'

Quarles's secretary, Molly Player, was a neatly attractive – but not too attractive – blonde. He had told her something about the people involved in the case, and now as the suspects arrived and she took them all in to Quarles's office overlooking Trafalgar Square, she found some amusement in comparing the detective's remarks with the reality.

Sir Reginald came first, pale and anxious ('self-made man, vulgar and cocky, but really cut to pieces by his son's death,' Quarles had said), and he was closely followed by Doctor Ramsay ('every inch a soldier, so military he seems phoney, but in fact he was an army doctor, and a good one').

Then came Jennifer Moore wearing a becoming amount of black, accompanied by elegant Paul Lapetaine. 'She looks and talks like a mouse, but that doesn't mean she *is* a mouse,' Quarles had said thoughtfully of Miss Moore. Lapetaine he had dismissed briskly. 'One of nature's spivs.'

Then, on her own, in a glory of furs and radiating bright sex, Hilary Hall. 'You can't miss *her*, Molly, any more than you can miss the sun coming out,' Quarles said. 'An orange sun,' he added as an afterthought. 'High in the sky, a scorcher.'

Last of all, Norman Johnson, the brown-faced bowlegged trainer of Lucky Charm. About him Quarles's comment had been tersest of all. 'Poker face.'

Molly Player let them all in. Then she sat down and tried to type a report, but found herself making a number of mistakes. She remembered Quarles's last words to her: 'One of these six, Molly, is a murderer.'

Francis Quarles sat back in the big chair behind his desk, and said pleasantly to the six people, 'One of you is a murderer.'

His office was large, but it had only four chairs for visitors, so that Paul Lapetaine stretched his elegant legs from a stool, and Doctor Ramsey sat in a window-seat from which he could look down on the square far below with its pigeons, its children, and its lions. Jennifer Moore sat next to Ramsay, as far away as possible from Hilary Hall.

'It may be of interest to you all,' Quarles continued didacti-cally, 'to know how I discovered the murderer, after Sir Reginald had engaged me to investigate.

'I considered first the question of motive, and I found that five of you had motives for killing Harry Bartley. Johnson, trainer of the horse he rode, hated him because Bartley had treated his daughter badly. Miss Hall had been thrown over by Bartley, and had written him a threatening letter.

'Miss Moore might have discovered that Bartley went to see Miss Hall on the night before the race. She looks like a quiet young lady, but quiet young ladies have been known to poison through jealousy.

'Paul Lapetaine, I should judge, was jealous of Bartley's success with women, and especially with Hilary Hall. Doctor Ramsay was obviously fond of Miss Moore, and had been for years. He must have had bitter feelings when he learned that she was going to marry a man like Harry Bartley.'

Ramsay on his window-seat made a motion of protest. Sir Reginald said, 'You have no right to talk about my son like that.'

Quarles's voice was harsh. 'I'm sorry, Sir Reginald. I told you that this inquiry might be disagreeable for you. I don't condone murder, but I must admit that your son strikes me as an unpleasant character.

'Let us move on from motive to opportunity. Bartley was killed by nitrobenzene, and it was thought at first that he had drunk the poison in a glass of orange juice, or perhaps taken it in the form of a pill. There was a thought in Miss Moore's mind, or perhaps Lapetaine put it there, that Doctor Ramsay might have given Bartley a tablet filled with nitrobenzene when Bartley came to see him early on the morning of the race.

'The post-mortem proved conclusively that this idea was mistaken. Dr Ramsay's pills were perfectly harmless. Bartley had not been killed by nitrobenzene introduced into his stomach. He had been poisoned by it in the form of vapor.

'This was the essential feature of the crime. The last vital clue, however, was provided by Miss Hall. She told me that on the night before the race, when Bartley came to see her, he complained of a bad cold that he feared might develop into influenza.'

There was silence in the room. Then Jennifer Moore said timidly, 'I suppose I knew that too. I mean, I knew Harry was sniffing a lot and had a bit of a cold, but I still don't understand why it should be important – vital, you said.'

'Quite early in the case I said that I remembered an affair in which a young man spilled nitrobenzene on his clothes, became stupefied, collapsed in coma, and died. Something like that happened to Harry Bartley.'

'His clothes weren't poisoned.' That was Johnson, speaking for the first time.

'No. He was killed by a handkerchief impregnated with nitrobenzene, which he used frequently because he had a cold.'

Hilary Hall objected, in her rusty voice, 'I don't believe that that points to anybody in particular.'

'There are two other things I should tell you. When I met Harry Bartley in the paddock I noticed that he used a handkerchief to wipe his nose. After the race, when his things were laid out on a table, the handkerchief was no longer there.'

'It came out when he fell from the horse,' Ramsay suggested.

'No. Because the rabbit's foot which he had tucked into his pocket at the same time was still there. The handkerchief had been taken away – stolen.'

Sir Reginald rubbed his chin. 'I may be slow, but I simply don't see how that can be possible. Nobody came near Harry's body—' He stopped.

'That isn't true,' Quarles said. 'But it is true that only one person fulfills all *five* of our murderer's qualifications. He had to be a person who disliked Harry Bartley. He had to possess some knowledge of the properties of nitrobenzene. He had to know that Bartley had a cold, and would frequently wipe his nose with a handkerchief. He had to be a person from whom Bartley would have accepted a handkerchief – having been told that it was impregnated with what our murderer might have said was oil of eucalyptus, good for a cold. Finally, he had to be a person who had access to Harry Bartley very soon after he collapsed. He was able to bend over the body – making an examination, shall we say? – and steal the handkerchief.

'The police are outside, Doctor Ramsay. It's no good trying to use that gun in your hip pocket.'

Doctor Ramsay was on his feet now, and the gun was in his hand. 'I'm not sorry for what I did,' he said. 'Not in the least. Harry was a dirty little devil with girls, had been since he was a boy. I'd always loved you, Jennifer, although I've never said it. In the wrong age group, I know. When I heard he'd got hold of you I just couldn't stand it. Don't come near me, now. I don't want to hurt anybody else.'

'Bill.' Jennifer Moore held out a hand to him. 'Please don't—'

Ramsay flung up the window. 'You don't think I'm going to endure the farce of a trial, do you? It's better this way, for me and for everybody else.'

He stepped out onto the ledge, and looked for a moment at the pigeons and the children, the placid lions and Nelson on his pillar.

Then he jumped.

The Body in the Horsebox

JOHN FRANCOME

The Hennessy Gold Cup at Newbury is another of the big steeplechases of the racing year and arguably the highlight of the Christmas jumping season. Although initially run in the fifties at Cheltenham, the Gold Cup has become a major event since moving to Newbury with its wide, flat track and stiff fences before the daunting water jump right in front of the stands. It is, in fact, a spectacular venue that has seen wins for a roll call of great horses over the past thirty years, including Mandarin, Taxidermist, Mill House and the legendary Arkle, as well as staging some thrilling battles between some of the greatest jockeys of the period like John Lawrence (now Lord Oaksey), Stan Mellor, Pat Taaffe, Bob Champion and John Francome: the most recent of the racing fraternity to turn from rider to thriller writer. In fact, Francome won the Hennessy twice, in 1983 on Brown Chamberlain and the following year riding Burrough Hill Lad. But Newbury is a course that has both pleasant and *unpleasant* memories for him.

John Francome (1953–), who was born in the West Country, had an enviable record on the track that earned him the accolade from one commentator of being 'the greatest National Hunt jockey ever known', an epithet he dislikes. His record in the saddle was, however, very impressive: champion jump jockey seven times and the second out of only four men to pass the 1,000 winners mark. John started riding as a small boy and by the time he was in his teens had proved himself as a show jumper by winning a gold medal with the British junior team and a Young Riders Championship. But racing was what he really wanted to do, and at the age of sixteen he became an apprentice jockey to Fred Winter, with whom he remained until he retired in 1986 with only one major prize having eluded him, the Grand National.

It was while John was riding at Newbury that the events occurred which ultimately led to him starting to write. The story is one he loves to retell. He was in the unsaddling enclosure one Saturday when two men muffled in raincoats approached him and said menacingly that they had been tapping his telephone conversations and accused him of stopping horses. 'We had to go to the High Court to prevent the contents of those tapes being published,' he recalls, 'and they ended up in the wastepaper basket of a Fleet Street newspaper.' Both John and his QC, Tom Shields, felt the events had the making of a good thriller and together they worked on what became Francome's first book, *Eavesdropper*, published in 1986. Soon one book followed another as John dug into his rich store of turf memories, especially the shady side. 'Racing is not 100 per cent straight and never will be,' he maintains. 'Things happen in the sport which are stranger than fiction. Whenever there is cash involved, someone will always try and organize a coup. I never got asked to stop a horse because the big stables and jockeys have too much to lose. But if you are a small trainer or jockey having to bet for a living, then it is possible that some do not try as hard as they should.'

John prides himself on the fact that everything which happens in his books has happened in racing – or easily could. As a result, the sales of his dozen novels are now beginning to rival those of Dick Francis – 'he is Francis's nearest rival in the pen and quill stakes,' says the *Daily Mail* – although he has nothing but admiration for the older man and is, in fact, a close friend of Dick's son, Merrick, who runs a horse transporter business at Lambourn, near to his own home on the Berkshire Downs. And it is here that John turns the facts of his life into episodes such as the next from his first novel, *Eavesdropper*, a story in the same tradition as the one by Dick Francis which opened this section and proved to be the means whereby an ex-champion jockey became a best-selling thriller writer instead.

*

James Thackeray, racing journalist, tipster, amateur jockey and would-be *bon viveur*, was fast asleep as the racecourse commentator announced the weight changes for the Hartley Hurdle. When the race train from Paddington had arrived at its destination, the little station that adjoins Newbury racecourse, the other occupants of the carriage had grabbed their binoculars, TIMEFORMS and racing papers and gaily leapt onto the platform as if picking winners was a mere formality and the only problem was going to be how to carry home the winnings. They had paid little attention to the figure huddled in a thick, russet tweed overcoat, his brown curly hair falling over his forehead, who had dozed off in the corner over a grubby and obviously much travelled paperback soon after the train had idled out of London.

James was deep in his dreams and just about to undo the top button of Meryl Streep's blouse when the commentator somewhere in the distance asked the jockeys to mount. Those familiar words penetrated his subconscious and brought him back from his fantasy world to the land of the living. Still half asleep, he looked at his watch and realized that he was already ten minutes late for his meeting with Paddy Develera, a lad working in Monty Spry's racing stables at Compton. For a hundred pounds a year, happily paid for by James's employer, the *Sportsman* newspaper, Paddy, like several other lads up and down the country, supplied useful information about the chances of his governor's horses. The next day, Saturday 26 November, was the Hennessy Gold Cup, one of the big steeplechase races of the year, and as Monty Spry trained the second favourite the meeting could be informative. However, James was beginning to wonder whether Paddy was obtaining his information from the right part of the horse's anatomy, as his last two certainties had both finished in the ruck.

He crossed the bridge which led from the station to the racecourse and broke into an unsteady trot as he made his way to the field where all the horse boxes bringing runners to that afternoon's races were parked. It was a bitterly cold autumn day and James's breath danced like smoke signals in the air ahead of him. He had not yet gone into serious training for his own riding after having a three-month lay-off through injury and the 14-odd pounds overweight which his body was carrying soon took its toll. By the time he had reached the field he was definitely wheezing. Puffing shamefully, he began to pick his way towards the furthest corner where Paddy had said Monty Spry's box would be parked. Why he couldn't speak to Paddy on the telephone he never knew, but the Irishman treated his role as an informer with deadly seriousness, and passed on the name of a fancied horse as if it was the formula for a secret cure for AIDS.

As he reached the blue-painted horsebox which bore Monty Spry's name on its side in bold red letters, James could hear the commentary on the first race. In his morning's selections he had tipped the likely favourite, The Cavalier, and from what he could gather the horse was already prominent. Unfortunately the same could not be said of Paddy. He knocked on the door of the horsebox and whispered his name, just in case the careful Irishman was taking his role as undercover agent to its full limits. There was no reply and James cursed himself for being so late. He had not intended to get drunk the night before, but after a couple of glasses of champagne his judgement tended to take a sabbatical. He decided to make for the racetrack and a strong cup of coffee in the press room. After that he would go and hunt out Paddy, who could nearly always be found investing his wages in the betting shop in Tattersalls enclosure.

He had only walked about ten yards when he was stopped in his tracks. A hoarse voice, shaky from indignation and rage, grunted out the words 'Let go, you fool!' The sounds of a scuffle followed.

James stood still to listen. The horses in the first race were apparently coming to the last hurdle and judging by the roar of the crowd, the favourite was right there in contention. With so much noise going on James wondered whether his ears had deceived him. He fervently hoped so. He had never been particularly keen to involve himself in other people's disputes, especially when they became violent. The next sound, however, banished any such comforting thoughts. It was a low gasp of pain.

Then a few seconds later came a thump, like a sack of potatoes hitting the floor. James knew that in the films the hero would now leap forward to find out what was happening. But what of the dangers of having a go? The newspapers were full of stories of people who had done this and paid the penalty.

Triumphing reluctantly over his fears, he finally rushed to one of the horseboxes from which he thought the noise might have come. He knocked on the door and when his rather feeble cry of 'Is anyone there?' went unanswered, tried the handle and found the door unlocked. With trepidation he pulled it open. The box was empty. Enormously relieved, and once more putting his experience down to what he hoped was merely the first stages of delirium tremens, he set off hurriedly for the entry to the members' enclosure.

As he rushed through the entrance gates, the sight of a policeman in uniform made him wonder whether he should at least report the incident. He decided to turn back and tell the officer what he had heard. The sceptical look on the policeman's face suggested that he thought James was mentally unstable and, if anything, he seemed even more convinced of his diagnosis when James announced that he was a journalist. It took a great deal of persuasion before he reluctantly agreed that they should go and investigate together.

There was only one trouble. James realized that he could not identify the source of the noise with any certainty. With a highly sceptical policeman in tow, he tried two or three boxes, all of which turned out to be locked. 'The trouble with you journalists,' the policeman observed sarcastically, 'is you're always looking for a story. Just too much imagination.'

By now some of the horses from the first race were being led back by their lads and curious glances were being cast in the two men's direction.

'I'm sorry, officer. I know it sounds ridiculous. But I did hear those noises and I'm certain they came from one of these boxes.'

'Yes, sir, but which one? Can't you be a little more definite?'

'It was all over so quickly. As I told you, the only one I looked in was empty.'

At this moment the door of an extremely dirty, once cream-coloured box blew open in the wind and then slammed shut again.

'Let's try that one,' said James.

The officer gave him that indulgent look normally reserved for old ladies who report their cats missing. Together they walked the twenty yards towards the box. On the back of the twin doors were painted the words:

George Weatherby
Racing Stables
Malton

James went to open the right-hand door but the officer pulled him gently to one side.

'I think I ought to be the one to discover the body, sir,' he said jeeringly, a wide grin on his face. He peered inside. All that could be seen in the overcast light were several bales of hay piled in the corner behind the driver's cabin.

'Looks like there's nothing there, sir,' he said, turning to James. 'Have a look for yourself.'

Feeling relieved, James peered inside. Nothing. 'Perhaps you ought to look right inside, officer, just to make sure,' he said.

The policeman's expression made it plain that he had had his fill of his companion's antics. However, he climbed inside and walked over to the bales of hay in the corner. James tiptoed behind him.

'As I thought. Nothing . . . Jesus Christ!'

James rushed forward at the startled tone of the officer's voice. There, lying in the corner, partly obscured by the bales of hay, was the body of a man in a tweed suit and grey overcoat. His face and the top part of his chest were draped with a yellow silk racing jacket. Neatly resting at a rakish angle on the top of his head was a purple riding cap. A knife was protruding through the jacket and the yellow around it was slowly turning scarlet. The man was clearly dead.

'I think this is my job, sir,' the policeman said, gently but firmly pushing James behind him as they approached the grotesque corpse. Without worrying about fingerprints, he folded over the yellow jacket and lifted up the purple cap. The eyes of a middle-aged man stared up at them in fixed incredulity, his flabby jowls spilling over a stiff white collar from which emerged the knot of a regimental tie.

'Good God!' said James. 'Surely . . . it can't be . . .'

'You know him then, sir?' the policeman asked suspiciously.

'Know him? Who on the racecourse doesn't? That, officer, is none other than the Senior Steward of the Jockey Club.'

'And who's he, when he's at home?'

'Sir Denby Weatherington Makepeace Croft, to give him his full name.'

It was then that James spotted a crumpled piece of paper on one of the bales of hay behind Sir Denby's head. He bent down and picked it up and, without looking at its contents, handed it to the officer.

'This might be of importance,' he suggested respectfully.

The officer snatched it from him. 'I'd prefer if you didn't touch anything, sir.' He opened it up to reveal what looked like a betting slip with several typed selections on it and James edged closer for a proper look. But the policeman quickly folded it again and slipped it inside a compartment at the back of his notebook. 'I think you had better come with me whilst I go for further assistance.'

James was delighted with the invitation, as he had no desire to wait on his own beside the Senior Steward's body.

Fifteen minutes later he was back in the horsebox, and this time he found himself on the receiving end of a number of hostile questions from a certain Inspector Hardcastle, the most senior officer on duty at the course. A dirty old horse blanket was now covering the corpse.

'Please tell me again, Mr Thackeray, what you say you were doing here in the first place.'

'As I've told you, Inspector, and I'm sure your assistant wrote it down the first time, I had arranged to meet a stable lad called Paddy Develera beside his boss's horsebox half an hour before the first race. Mr Develera supplies me with information about the chances of his boss's horses.'

'Do you usually meet in such strange places?'

'Invariably. Paddy goes in for the cloak and dagger bit.'

James winced at his somewhat unfortunate choice of words in

the company of the dead man. 'And who am I to ruin his fantasies?'

'When did you arrange this meeting, then?'

'Last night. Tomorrow is the Hennessy Gold Cup, which, as you no doubt know, is one of the big races of the season, and Paddy's boss, Monty Spry, trains the second favourite. I hoped Paddy, who looks after the horse, might be able to tell me how well he was.'

'So what happened to this Mr Develera?'

'I suspect he got bored with waiting. He can't resist a bet and probably went off to put his wage packet on the first race.'

'Why did you say you were late?'

'I told you. I had a heavy night and fell asleep on the race train.'

'Did anyone see you there?'

'I doubt it. I certainly didn't recognize anybody in my compartment and I very much doubt if my fellow passengers paid any attention to me. They would almost certainly be thinking about the racing and what they were going to back.'

'How long did you look for him?'

'About two or three minutes. I was just giving up when I heard the noises, and you know the rest.'

'Do we? No doubt we shall see. That's all for the moment, Mr Thackeray. You can go and watch the racing, but I want you to come and see me again in the Chief Security Officer's room under the grandstand in half an hour's time. In the meantime, don't tell anybody on the course what happened, is that clear?'

'Perfectly. Aren't you going to tell the old boy's wife? They've got a runner in the fourth, the big race named after his father.'

'When's that?'

'In about a quarter of an hour.'

The inspector looked at his watch and thought for a moment. 'I don't see any point in upsetting her just yet. I'll break the news after the race. That doesn't mean I want you telling her. You can go now.'

Just as James was leaving the inspector called him back. 'Mr Thackeray, do you know anything about this man Weatherby?'

'He's a trainer. Or more accurately, he *was* a trainer until two weeks ago. Sir Denby took away his licence for a year for not running one of his horses straight.'

The inspector's face lit up. James reflected that it was a good job he hadn't mentioned the rumour of Weatherby's threats. 'So what would he be doing on the racetrack?'

That was a question James had already asked himself. 'He's still entitled to come and watch, only not to train horses under rules.'

'In which case, why would he bother to bring his horsebox with him and all the way from Malton?'

James just shook his head. 'You'll have to ask him. I'm sure there's some innocent explanation.'

'I'm going to, and for your sake, I hope there isn't, otherwise you'll have a great deal more explaining to do. See you later.'

James rushed back to the course, as he was anxious to watch the Sir Oswald Croft Memorial Handicap Hurdle. It was going to be a rather curious sensation watching Sir Denby's horse run when its owner lay lifeless in the corner of a muddy field, but James's interest was not solely ghoulish. He had napped The Teaser in preference to Paradise Lost and was desperately in need of a winner to boost his position in the Naps Competition, organized by a rival racing paper for racing journalists. There was talk of redundancies at work, and he was anxious to establish himself as a man in form.

Passing a call box he decided to phone the *Sportsman*'s office. He could not risk being overheard in the press room. The inspector had forbidden communication to anyone on the racecourse, so all James felt he was doing was taking him at his literal word. He was put through to his editor, Carlton Williams, who did not seem all that amused by the opening greeting of 'Hold the front page!' but immediately started speaking into the second telephone on his desk as James told him of his sensational discovery. James was ordered to return to the office as soon as the last race was over, instead of dictating his copy from the race-course press room.

Reaching his favourite viewing spot on the roof above the members' stand, just as the runners were approaching the fourth hurdle from home, James could pick out through his binoculars the colours of The Teaser going well in second place. About five lengths further back and going ominously easily was Paradise Lost. His jockey was wearing Sir Denby's second colours, identical to those which had draped his body, save for the addition of purple epaulettes.

As the horses came off the bend on the far side the pace quickened. Galloping downhill, some of the stragglers were having difficulty keeping up and not surprisingly three fell at the next flight. Neither The Teaser nor Paradise Lost were among them. James noticed how Paradise's jockey, the brilliant Phil Hope, had taken the precaution of pulling his horse a yard to the right just before the hurdle and then back to the left, so that he was jumping at an angle towards the inside of the course and could thus avoid being brought down by a faller.

The horses rounded the last bend for home. The Teaser was still going well and had now taken up the running, but jumping the third last and with only half a mile to run he was clearly beginning to tire. His jockey switched him from the inner to the stand side so that he could use the running rail dividing the flat from the hurdle course to help him gallop in a straight line.

As they approached the second last, The Teaser was now only two lengths up on Paradise. To James's dismay Phil Hope conjured an enormous leap out of the 7 to 1 chance and the roar of the crowd began to fade as Paradise ranged up beside the favourite at the last and then ran on to pass the post five lengths clear. Below him in the public enclosures James could hear the occasional jeer from angry punters.

Putting his own disappointment behind him, James rushed downstairs to join his press colleagues in the winning enclosure. There to greet the triumphant hurdler and his smiling jockey were its tall dapper trainer, Archie Duncan, and beside him the elegant fur-clad figure of Lady Croft. James reckoned that she was just the wrong side of forty, but with her hollow cheekbones and well-preserved figure she was by any standards an extremely attractive woman. It was obvious from her enthusiasm that she had no idea that she was now a widow. James wondered how she would react to the news, since word in the racing world was that they were a devoted couple.

He held back from asking any questions, but not surprisingly one of his colleagues asked where her husband was.

'He was called away on urgent business before the first race, and he's obviously been held up. I only hope he's been watching the race from the Stewards' room. He will be absolutely delighted with this win, that I can assure you.'

If only she knew, poor thing, thought James.

2

DEAD WEIGHTS

Mayhem in the Saddle

'The Turf is so beset with knaves that
when you go racing you are robbed when
you least expect to be robbed, and that by
men whom you would least expect to rob
you.'

J. G. BERTRAM

Calling the Tune

STEVE DONOGHUE

Whenever racing people meet there will always be a discussion about who was the greatest jockey. Fred Archer, Steve Donoghue, Gordon Richards, Lester Piggott and John Francome all have their admirers, while a new generation of riders like Pat Eddery and Frankie Dettori are already beginning to make the kind of reputations that may well place one or more of them alongside that list of great champions. Of those I have mentioned, Steve Donoghue (1884–1945) has been described as one of the most articulate men ever to ride the turf and certainly his two autobiographies, *Just My Story* (1923) and *Donoghue Up* (1938), are amongst the finest written by a jockey. But Steve's abilities went even further than just being able to convey accurately what it was like riding in a big race, for he was also an engaging public speaker, a perceptive race commentator, and an early member of that breed of jockeys-turned-authors now epitomized by Dick Francis and John Francome. He was also something of a character: a man who dressed stylishly in silk shirts, a grey pin check coat and trousers and high-heeled tan brogues. He was said to have been a man of a fiery temperament that frequently got him into trouble, and though he made several fortunes he spent the money just as quickly. Yet he never lost the affection of the public – the racegoers' cry of 'Come on, Steve!' became a national catch phrase – and at the time of his death he was hailed by no less a paper than *The Times* as 'the most successful jockey of the century'.

Steve Donoghue was born of poor parents in Warrington and such was his determination to become a jockey that he offered himself to the famous trainer John Porter at Chester when he was just fourteen years old. The future champion did not enjoy immediate success in the saddle, however, and actually had to go to France to experience his first winner at Hyeres in 1904. He rode in his first Derby in 1910 – an event he was later to win six times – and thereafter at all the major events in France, Belgium, Spain, Italy and the USA, and in so doing earning himself the reputation of being 'a genius of a jockey' according to his friend and fellow jockey-author Jack Leach in his delightfully entitled book, *Sods I Have Cut on the Turf* (1961).

Steve further enhanced his legend during a six-year period when he rode Brown Jack, a horse whose popularity rivalled his own and was later commemorated in a book by R. C. Lyle. The great man was fifty-three years old when he rode his last winner in the Queen Alexandra Stakes at Ascot. When he died in March 1945 as the country was just on the verge of winning the Second World War, the press and radio paid tribute to his fame and popularity which had 'gained for him a place in the hearts of his countrymen and made him a beloved national figure'. *The Times* lengthy obituary went even further: 'They loved him for the dash that brought him unerringly out of the severest maelstrom and the pluck that made him unrivalled at Tattenham Corner.'

That remark gives added poignancy to the following mystery story about the Derby which Steve wrote for the magazine *Passing Show* in 1932. It has been suggested to me that Edgar Wallace, who was a close friend of Donoghue, may have been involved in the writing of the tale, but it is nonetheless a colourful reminder of the man as well as providing a breathtaking ride around that most famous of corners by a jockey who mastered it better than anyone else.

*

Above Epsom hung a crystal and violet English twilight. The wagons of the gypsies, some red with yellow wheels, some red with yellow trim, but all predominantly red, were still pouring in upon the Downs, as they had been for the past week; for the past fortnight. The stalls of the bookies were up. The gamblers, tipsters, fakers, mendicants, had gathered. Queer smells were in the air – human smells, animal smells, the stale reek of rank tobaccos. Strange languages were muttered. Strange foreign faces, mingling among the English, grinned and grimaced in the fading light. It was as if a vast melting-pot had been overturned in the heavens and its heterogeneous contents spilled out on the Downs. And yet, the members of this fantastically mixed assemblage had something in common, not only between themselves but with the thousands soon to flow into Epsom like a human river with every corner of England as its sources. Tomorrow was the great day – the day of the Derby.

'Tors' Talbot and Johnny Cann pushed their way through the milling, jostling throng. And among all these chaotic thousands gathered on the Downs there was no more ill-assorted pair. Talbot was a giant of a man, six feet four in his stockings, with the neck and shoulders of a prize-winning bull. His face might have been carved out of some wind-swept mountain in the West Country from which he came, and from which and by reason of his size he had derived the entirely suitable nickname of 'Tors'. His thick, grizzled hair was like the mane of an ageing but still alert lion. He walked with a slight stoop and his great legs were bowed a little, as befits one who has been much around horses.

On the other hand, Johnny Cann looked as though he might have been designed to fit Tors Talbot's waistcoat pocket. He was hardly more than a boy and his head, with its shock of unruly, wheat-coloured hair, barely came up as high as Talbot's armpits. He had grinning blue eyes and a tooth was missing from the scraggly ramparts in the front of his mouth. But, undersized though he was, Johnny Cann and the gigantic Talbot who stalked at his side shared a mutual interest. They were, respectively, trainer and rider of Lord Lord Melchester's Arrowburn, the odds-on favourite to win tomorrow's Derby.

Tors Talbot waved a shovel-like hand over the scene surrounding them.

'Well, my boy,' he said, in his thick West Country burr, 'this is what it's like the night before the Derby.'

Johnny Cann's blue eyes were missing nothing.

'Not much like the East, it isn't,' he commented at last.

It was in the East that Cann had done most of his riding. A drifter by nature, he had gone out four years earlier, after a brief experience of the English tracks. He had ridden at Kuala Lumpur, Singapore, Colombo. For a time, he had gone down to Australia to ride at Randwick in Sydney; at Flemington in Melbourne. Then back to the East again, and it was at Colombo that Lord Melchester, coming through on his yacht, had first seen him.

Johnny had piloted three winners that day. And Lord Melchester had liked the look of him; liked the way he got the most out of a horse; the way his hands seemed to lift the beast across the line when the finish was close. He'd offered him a job in England. And Johnny, itching to be on the move again, had accepted. He had come home during the previous season and ridden at Doncaster and Newmarket. But this was his first Derby. And because of the ability of his knotty freckled-backed hands to transform Arrow-burn from a snarling black devil into something that seemed like a dark poem of swift motion, he had the leg up on the favourite.

Some of the gypsies had lighted fires by their wagons. The flames laid coppery tints over the seamed, swarthy faces ringed about them. The voluminous skirts of the women, moving about the fires, cast grotesque, malignant shadows. Near one of the wagons a girl was dancing in the firelight, some weird, nameless dance out of Romany. Her body seemed to move in a golden flow. Her hips twisted sinuously, snake-like. The fire bathed her blue-black hair in lived light. Her eyes were like rapiers. The tambourine she clutched chattered against her knuckles.

'Barmy, ain't they?' said Tors, stopping to watch the performance.

Johnny Cann did not reply. Johnny Cann had things on his mind. He was thinking of how he was going to do as the bearded man had instructed – and not be found out.

Tor's hand rested on his shoulder.

'Let's have a look at that black devil before we turn in,' he suggested.

Johnny nodded, and they began edging through the crowd in the direction of the stables. Presently, however, they were aware of a group of small boy tatterdemalions from the gypsy wagons, shouting in mingled derision and delight. At the same moment a shrill, piping sound came to their ears.

'Wait a tick,' Tors said. 'Here's something you'd ought to see – a character.'

Johnny's eyes wandered to the group of gesticulating children. In their midst was a little old man, dressed in a faded blue jacket with brass buttons. A brown felt hat, disreputable with age, sat uncertainly on his sparse, greyed locks. He had a dirty white goatee and his eyes were weak and dimmed. But he was active in a strutting, monkeyish way and evidently pleased with the reception accorded him by his doubtful audience. He was gambolling and capering about the Downs, abandoning himself to a dance that might have been a weird combination of the Highland Fling and the goose step. As he capered, he blew shrill reedy notes on a small flute. And, at intervals, he would take the flute from his lips and twirl it in his fingers, goose stepping as he did so after the manner of a pompous, cock-sure drum-major.

'Character, did you say?' said Johnny Cann, laughing. 'More than that, if you ask me. Looks right off his chump.'

'He is a bit dotty, that's a fact,' said Tors, 'but he wasn't always. You wouldn't believe that that little old bloke was one of the best jockeys in England thirty years ago, now would you?'

Johnny studied the wretched old man. No, he wouldn't have believed that. He said so.

'Fact,' said Tors Talbot, decisively. 'Rode a Derby winner once, he did. Brought him in as pretty as ever I see. But' – Tors shook his great head – 'a month afterwards he was finished.'

'What happened?'

'Pulled a horse,' said Tors, laconically. 'The stewards set him down for life.'

Pulled a horse? Pulled a horse? Talbot's words started a kind of devil's chorus in Johnny Cann's brain. And the low, even, insinuating voice of the black-bearded man came back to him: 'Pull him easy all the way around – easy, mind. No one'll suspect. That black brute's got a reputation for temperament. They'll put it down to that.'

Johnny shook his head suddenly, as if to shake the remembrance of those low-spoken words out of his mind. He pointed to the capering old man. 'What's this bloke do now?' he inquired.

'Just what you see him doing,' Tors replied. 'On every race track in England. Dances about like that, he does, blowing his flute and the people toss him coppers. If you' – Tors squinted – 'was to have time to see anything tomorrow, which you won't have, you'd see him capering around Tattenham Corner and the crowd laughing fit to die.'

Tattenham Corner? Again the persuasive voice of the black-bearded man seemed to glide back into Johnny Cann's mind like a sinister snake: 'Pull him last at the corner – Tattenham Corner. Easy does it. Apollyon will be laying back. He'll come up on the outside. Remember, pull him at the corner, there's a smart lad.'

'Yes,' Tors was saying, 'he'll be dancing his blooming head off tomorrow. That's how he gets enough to follow the gee-gees. But' – his big hand smote Johnny Cann's shoulder – 'you won't see him, boy. You'll be too busy bringing Arrowburn home. Your first Derby winner. God, how I wish I was young, and your size!'

They began to move away. Over his shoulder Johnny Cann glanced back at the little old man. He wasn't dancing now. He was waving the pitiful flute in the air, making futile efforts to answer the jests of the small, scurrilous crowd of hobbledehoys.

'But wasn't the old chap – er – paid off for pulling the horse?' Johnny asked.

'Paid off?' Tors snorted. 'Of course, he was paid off – paid plenty. I don't know what he got – five thousand quid, maybe. Six or seven, for all I know. But they got it away from him soon enough.'

'They? Who?'

Tors looked down at him pityingly. 'God, you're young, Johnny. Who? Why, the whole blasted lot of them – the tipsters, the bookies, the girls, the liquor. 'Struth! It wasn't two years before I used to see him around the tracks, leaning over the rails and looking hungry. No, I don't mean hungry to fill his belly. He made fish and chips money for a long time. I mean hungry for – for something he couldn't ever have again.'

Johnny Cann's brain wasn't of the steel-trap variety at its best. It was a shrewd enough brain, though. It knew that there were twenty shillings in the pound. It knew, or thought it knew, where its bread and butter came from. But just now it was a little confused, a little startled; a little frightened, even.

'Hungry?' he repeated. 'You mean . . .' He stopped. He didn't at all know what Tors meant.

'Why, I mean this,' said Tors. 'Hungry for the horses – the chap was a jock, lad. As fine a jock as ever put foot in stirrup. But he let his horse down. See what I mean?'

Johnny Cann didn't know if he saw or not. He was silent all the rest of the way to the stables.

Talbot thumped on the door that led to Arrowburn's great comfortable box-stall. There was a shuffle of feet inside. An anxious voice inquired, ' 'Oo's there?'

'Me, you ape,' said Tors, 'and Johnny.'

A bolt slid. The door opened a crack and the pinched, furtive face of Cocky Mitchell, stable-boy detailed to keep guard over Arrowburn on this last night before the Derby, peered out. Then, seeing that it was indeed Talbot and Johnny Cann, he swung the door wide.

'Well,' said Tors, passing in, 'how's the Derby winner?'

That was how Tors Talbot always thought of Arrowburn – as the Derby winner. That was how he had thought of him even when the horse was a spindly foal, wobbling on uncertain legs; how he had continued to think of him as, under his great, quiet, understanding hands, Arrowburn had grown into this thing of speed and black fire.

'There ain't a horse in England that can touch him,' Tors had told Lord Melchester, the owner. 'Not one.'

And so far there hadn't been. Every time he had gone to the post, Arrowburn had come home, a winner. Bad-tempered and surly in the stables, an uncontrollable black flame out of hell in the hands of the exercise boys, he would change in an instant under the knowing touch of a first-class jockey, like Johnny Cann. Then he would be quiet, and the raging fire within him seemed to grow cold, and it was as if the horse were dominated by a deadly purpose. And speed, speed that flowed and flashed like light, became the essence of his being. Always it would be the same, Arrowburn rearing and plunging at the barrier. But as soon as the field broke, he would settle down – and it was as though a dark juggernaut had been turned loose to race the wind.

Cocky Mitchell answered Tors' question.

'Gawd's truth, sir,' Cocky said, ' 'ee's been takin' on something owful. A-rowin around in there fit to turn you grey, that 'ee's been, sir. Seems like 'ee knows something's up.'

' 'Course he knows something's up,' growled Tors contemptuously. 'Think a horse like that don't know what day the Derby is? No damn fear.'

From the big stall came a sudden stamping. A screaming whinny filled the room. Then a frenzied pawing at the floorboards of the stall.

' 'Orrible,' breathed Cocky Mitchell. Tors laughed and went over to the stall. He made a clucking noise with his tongue. Instantly, Arrowburn's hoof ceased beating its tattoo on the boards, and the horse came forward, thrusting his velvety muzzle out of the stall.

As Tors reached out, Arrowburn's head jerked up as if he were suspicious for the moment. Then he seemed to recognize Tors. His nose stretched further over the partition. The fire died out of his eyes; he nuzzled against Tors' shoulder.

Tors patted the long, tar-black body.

'He'll do,' he said, his eyes a-gleam with something that might have been both pride and impatience. 'Watch him tomorrow.'

Johnny Cann stood to one side, his eyes riveted on that thing born of brimstone and the night wind, so quiet now beneath Tors Talbot's big, sympathetic hands. But Johnny wasn't thinking of the horse. His mind had gone back to a night in a London public house; to a stranger with a short, black beard who had so casually fallen into conversation with him over a glass of ale; to the thousand pounds that he had carefully deposited in the bank the next day.

The man had put his proposition very reasonably indeed.

'Look here, Cann,' he had said. 'I won't beat about the bush. I know who you are and who you work for. Now, don't be a fool for your own good. Who should know better than a jockey that a jockey's life is short. No, I don't mean that, exactly. I mean the years when he can earn money – big money. And that's all the more reason to be sensible. Why not make enough all in one clip to see yourself comfortable for the rest of your life? Particularly when you can make it easily and safely, and no one the wiser?'

Johnny Cann had hesitated, torn between desire and suspicion.

'What is it you want me to do?' he'd enquired.

The stranger's eyes had narrowed; his voice became barely audible.

'Listen,' he said. 'There're some of us, I mention no names, but there're some of us who'll pay to see Apollyon win the Derby – and pay well. You realize, of course, that it will be a two horse race this year. Outside of Arrowburn, there's nothing that can even extend Apollyon. Well' – the man's eyes had narrowed to mere slits, then – 'there's money in it for the man who can make this race safe for Apollyon.'

Apollyon? That was Mr Cathcart-Griscom's big bay, Johnny knew. A fine horse, but not in it with the black Arrowburn. He would have bet anything he owned that Arrowburn could have spotted Apollyon a hundred yards in a race the length of the Derby and won going away at the finish.

'Well,' he had said, interested in spite of his innate distrust of strangers, 'what do you mean by "pay well?" '

The bearded man had pulled at his sleeve. 'Come over here. We can talk better.' And to the barmaid, 'Two more pints of bitter, miss. Serve 'em at the corner table.'

'Now then,' he had continued, after the drinks were brought, 'I have already intimated that money is no object to my – er – associates and myself. To come straight to the point, we will pay you' – he paused for a brief second, squinting one eye at Johnny Cann – 'eight thousand pounds to see that Arrowburn doesn't win this year's Derby.'

Johnny Cann had gasped. Eight thousand pounds! Why, it was a fortune. A ruddy fortune – and coming all at once, in a lump sum! Just for the rather simple business of pulling a horse. Well, all he could think was that this gentleman and his shadowy friends must be prepared to bet a gold mine on Apollyon's chances.

'Come,' the stranger had urged, 'what do you say? It's easy money, isn't it?'

Johnny's native shrewdness had prompted him then.

'How do I know', he said, looking directly at the man, 'that I'll be paid?'

The stranger had laughed. 'A fair question, and a fair precaution. You know it, my boy, because I've been instructed to pay you a thousand pounds down – tonight. The balance comes after Apollyon has won.'

Johnny had shaken his head.

'What guarantee do I have that you'll pay the balance?' he asked.

'You'll be given a note,' the stranger said promptly. 'Signed by a name that will surprise you. When the amount is paid, you will surrender the note. Oh, this is business and you'll get your share right enough. You play the game with us and we'll do the same with you. Now then, speak up! What's the answer?'

Well, it hadn't been difficult for Johnny Cann to make up his mind. He loved Arrowburn, as he had never loved any of his other mounts. But after all, Arrowburn was a horse. And what did the sacrifice of one horse mean, one horse out of the numbers he'd ridden? And it would have taken him years to amass eight thousand pounds.

'Right-o,' he'd said finally, his teeth clicking. 'I'm on at that price – provided that note you mentioned is satisfactory.'

'Don't worry about that,' the stranger had said. 'It'll be as good as gold.' And forthwith he had plunged into details. He and his associates had it all figured out. Apollyon was to pass Arrowburn at Tattenham Corner.

A few nights later, Johnny had again met the stranger, who said that his name was Mr Moreton, by appointment. This time Mr Moreton was accompanied by a stout, elderly gentleman with hard eyes. Mr Moreton introduced this gentleman sketchily as 'one of my colleagues'.

Johnny Cann was handed a promissory note – for seven thousand pounds. The name signed to the note did surprise him. It was a name well known in racing circles. Mr Moreton had waited for his natural astonishment to abate.

He said, then: 'Don't think that we aren't aware of the risks we're taking, young fellow. With that note in your possession, you could blackmail us to kingdom come. But remember this, we've got your receipt for a thousand pounds. As sure as you try to break us, we'll break you. On the other hand, play fairly with us and we all profit.'

It sounded reasonable to Johnny Cann. He had no intention of resorting to blackmail. That possibility had never entered his head. The price for pulling Arrowburn, as named by Mr Moreton, was far more than he had ever dreamed one could get for riding a crooked race. He was content with it. It would assure his future. And, as Mr Moreton had pointed out several times, only bad luck could make anyone the wiser . . .

So Johnny Cann stood and watched as Tors fondled the black nose of Arrowburn, and thought of his thousand pounds safely stowed away, and of the seven thousand he would yet receive, and of Mr Moreton, and of the horses bunched at Tattenham Corner on the morrow. And once, just once, there came to him a vision of a shabby little old man in a brass-buttoned, blue jacket who capered and played a flute. But he brushed a hand over his eyes and dismissed the picture.

Derby Day came up in a flash of blue and gold. Early in the morning the London-to-Epsom road crawled with traffic. The legions of great, red-sided buses lumbered along in an endless chain. In and out between them, mice whizzing around the feet of elephants, ran the little cars, sputtering, gasping, tooting. The stately motors of the wealthier bowled easily over the highway, lending a touch of dignity to the ceaseless procession. And all morning people poured in upon the Downs, people representative of all England. For this was the race that everyone, high or low, rich or poor, could see and enjoy. Here was no grey-toppered Ascot. No exclusive Goodwood. This was everybody's race – the Derby.

The gypsies did a brisk business in fortune-telling, in tipping the winners. Mobs milled in front of the betting-stalls and the bookies, shirt-sleeved and perspiring, kept up their indefatigable chatter; their peppery, hair-trigger replies to the sallies of the crowd. The Downs were a carnival of colour, a riot of excitement.

Just before the horses were saddled for the Derby, Tors Talbot laid a hand on Johnny Cann's shoulder. He spoke of the only thing that he had on his mind – Arrowburn. He spoke of him as though he were a human being.

'Let him size up his field for the first furlong,' he said. 'Then give him his head. He knows the way home all right. And there's only two other horses you've got to think about. Apollyon's the most dangerous. And the Rajah of Montenore's horse, that Bey-Selim, he's got an outside chance. But that's all – there's nothing else in this race.'

Johnny was in the maroon and white colours of Lord Melchester. His shiny black boots flashed in the bright afternoon light. Under his little peaked hat his eyes were an inscrutable blue.

'Righty-o,' he said. 'Don't worry, Tors. I'll bring him in.'

Best to appear on the level; to make Tors think that his heart and soul were behind Arrowburn. Then, in the event of investigation afterwards or of an unforeseen slip-up of some kind, his before the race attitude would have seemed proper. Also, he wanted to make Tors Talbot feel good for as long as possible. He was sorry for Tors. For months Tors had been counting on Arrowburn winning the Derby. It would have been the greatest triumph of his life. He had never trained a Derby winner before.

But hell! Johnny Cann couldn't afford sentiment now. He had an eight thousand pound stake in this race. A stake far, far greater than he would have been paid for giving Arrowburn an honest ride. Far more than he could have made in a year of honest riding. And he couldn't throw it over his shoulder for the sake of a man or a horse. Under his peaked cap his eyes were an inscrutable blue. But they didn't look at Tors Talbot.

Then – it was time to go to the post.

Arrowburn came out stepping nervously – a great black engine endowed with a brain, with fire, with passion. He reared once at the barrier. Sun sparks shook from his dark mane. Johnny Cann's firm, practised hands quieted him. And out of the corner of his eye, Johnny looked the starters over. On the very outside, the sun tinting his bay sides to fiery copper, was Apollyon, with Joe Bentnor up. Joe wore the green and yellow colours of Mr Cathcart-Griscom's stable. And over there was the Rajah of Montenore's Bey-Selim, whom Tors had conceded an outside chance. Well, unless Apollyon had an off-day, Bey-Selim would be nowhere. And as for Arrowburn – Johnny Cann smiled a hard, calculating smile – Arrowburn would have an off-day right enough. An off-day worth eight thousand pounds to his rider.

The gate went up.

Like multi-coloured bombs of light, exploded by the Roman candle of a giant, the field got away. Sunlight danced on bright silks, on visored caps, flashed off the straining flanks of the horses. Lincoln Green, a rank outsider, took the lead. Next to him came Bey-Selim. Apollyon was lying back. Arrowburn was in the middle of the moving, pounding kaleidoscope of colour.

For a moment, Arrowburn seemed content to run with the herd. Then, his long dark body flowed rhythmically forward, and he settled into his stride, running now with the easy, oiled precision of a perfect machine.

Ahead of him, Bey-Selim drew up to Lincoln Green, pushed his nose in front. Arrowburn drew out from the bunched horses, hounded the heaving flanks of Lincoln Green.

Going towards the corner, Johnny Cann pulled Arrowburn slightly, tentatively. It was hardly more than a firming of his hands, an imperceptible yet definite tightening of the bit. But it was something foreign to Arrowburn. Always, he had been given his head, allowed to run as he chose. The unaccustomed checking put him off his stride momentarily. He faltered a little, and Johnny Cann was aware of the fiery head of Apollyon, of the green and yellow of Joe Bentnor, coming up on his right.

So it was that easy, was it, to halt the march of the great Arrowburn? That easy to bank eight thousand pounds? Well, thank God for the sensitiveness of the big black; for his precarious, hair-trigger disposition. The pull at the corner would do the trick – and no doubt they would put it down to temperament, as the bearded Mr Moreton had suggested.

Carefully he relaxed his hands on the bridle. Arrowburn flowed beneath him again, like an easy black river. Apollyon fell away. They surged up to Lincoln Green, passed him. There was a length between Arrowburn and Bey-Selim – and the race was half over.

Fifty yards further on, Johnny Cann again applied a tightening hand to the bridle. Arrowburn slugged up his head; his mouth tore at the bit. His beautiful, rhythmic stride broke. Once more Apollyon drew up to his flank.

They were approaching Tattenham Corner now. Johnny kept the bit cutting into Arrowburn's mouth. But his muscles ached as the big black, enraged and puzzled, fought against the restraining grip. And Johnny dared not increase the pressure. It would have been too obvious. The best he could do was slow the horse slyly and hope that Apollyon would be able to pass. The field swept towards the corner, like a flashing, colourful pinwheel.

The time was at hand. Leaning far over Arrowburn's neck, Johnny Cann gave the impression of urging him on furiously. Actually, in the most covert fashion possible, he was pulling the bridle back, exerting all the strength of his small arms to check the horse's headlong rush. On the rails the crowd was roaring. Clods of turf flew up from the thundering hoofs. The mouths of the horses foamed with white lather.

Arrowburn was slowing. Johnny could feel the great body under him slackening its pace – ever so slightly, but enough. Enough to draw him back among the bunched horses. To give the straining Apollyon, a length behind, the chance to pass. Enough to make sure of eight thousand pounds.

And then, out of the corner of one eye, Johnny Cann saw him.

It was nothing but the briefest flash, as one sees an object from a rushing train. But it registered a starkly clear picture on the mind of Johnny Cann. An old man in a faded blue jacket with brass buttons; an old man wedged in between the crowd at the rail; and old man who had capered and played a flute last night to the derision of gypsy boys. But he wasn't capering now. His weak old eyes were fixed upon the speeding horses, and upon his face was an expression of wistful hopelessness, a suggestion that the dimmed eyes were searching for something – for something that even they knew was irretrievably lost, that would never come again.

And, suddenly, Johnny Cann felt that he knew what was going on in that weakened, senile mind. It was as if the little old man were re-living a part of his life, the most splendid part, casting back pitifully to the year when he too had swung around

Tattenham Corner, riding a winner, the Derby winner. Groping back into the dim past to recall some glorious, forgotten day before . . .

Had it been worth it? The question buzzed like a trapped insect within Johnny Cann's head. Worth it to pull some magnificent horse, if the final reward was a tinny flute, a grotesque dance, the jeers and ribaldry of crowds? No matter what the old chap might have been paid long ago. . . . Very suddenly something seemed to explode in Johnny Cann's brain, explode burstingly like a shell. And after that, everything was clear. There on the rails, but for the grace of God, might go a hideous mockery of himself.

And all at once Johnny Cann knew that nothing in the world, not eight thousand pounds or eight times it, could compensate a man for the loss of his job and his self-respect for ever.

Something roared on his right – a long, fiery streak shot by him, Apollyon. Past, going into the straight. A mighty roar droned from the crowd.

Tears, tears of rage and frustration, welled up in Johnny Cann's eyes. Perhaps he was too late – too late to square himself with this splendid, protesting black thing beneath him! Too late, perhaps, to square himself with himself! But . . . his teeth clicked. He wasn't beaten yet. There was a short stretch of green turf left, in which to right a wrong.

The next instant he was flat over Arrowburn's neck, and for the first time the big black was given his head properly.

No cutting restraint of the bit now. The hands on the bridle had the old familiar urging touch. The faltering stride picked up, blended into swift, easy motion. And Johnny Cann felt the big body flowing again like black lightning stitching a pattern across a great cloth of green. And Arrowburn was running now, eating up the track in huge thundering bounds.

Horses fell away on the right, on the left. A length and a half ahead moved the fire-coloured flanks of Apollyon. Between Apollyon and Arrowburn ran Bey-Selim, not yet out of it.

Johnny Cann's heels dug into Arrowburn's sides. They rocketed past Bey-Selim like a cloud of whirling, dark smoke. And now they were well into the straight, with Arrowburn's nose hard on Apollyon's flank. And to Johnny Cann's ears came the dull, thundering boom of the stands.

Ahead of him, Joe Bentnor's green and yellow bounced crazily. Johnny, alternately cursing and praying, cut Arrowburn once with the whip.

It was as though the final insult had been heaped upon a thwarted, outraged being. With an angry snort, the great horse surged forward. His head came abreast of Joe Bentnor. Then, in a flash, they were neck and neck. And for one blinding moment they raced down the stretch, with Johnny Cann clinging to Arrowburn's neck like a white bird riding a mad, black comber of the sea. . . .

The winning post loomed. Johnny Cann's lips, loose and ashen, babbled a prayer. And then his hands, strong and freckle-dotted, seemed to lift Arrowburn, lift him over the line, a neck ahead.

'Honest to Gawd,' said Cocky Mitchell, 'me 'eart was down in me boots.'

For a moment, Talbot didn't reply.

'Where's Johnny?' he said at last.

'Dunno. Ain't seen much of 'im since the race.'

'No?' Tors' eyes clouded. 'I haven't, either. But' – he drew a breath – 'I'm going out to find that bloke now.'

It was late afternoon. Tors went round a corner of the stables – and suddenly he stopped short.

Twenty yards away a small chap, hardly more than a boy, was struggling in the grip of a man with a black beard.

Tors was too far off to hear Johnny Cann babbling, 'There's a cheque for your damn thousand, and that receipt for seven. And you can keep your dirty money.'

'Why, you blasted, double-crossing little rat!' began the bearded man, shaking his collar.

He didn't finish. Tors Talbot's great fist sent him sprawling. After a moment he got up and reeled away, shouting curses back at them. Tors fixed his eyes on Johnny Cann.

'Before I find out what you're doing with Black Jack Phelps, the lowest swine that ever set foot on a racecourse,' he said, 'I'll find out something else. What was the reason for that rotten ride?'

Johnny Cann kicked turf.

'Temperamental horse,' he said, looking away. 'But' – his eyes met Talbot's then – 'I brought him home, didn't I?'

Tors Talbot looked at him keenly. He knew jockeys. And he was putting two and two together. He felt pretty certain that from now on he would have no doubts of Johnny Cann.

'Listen, youngster,' he said, 'let me give you a tip. I don't know what Jack Phelps wanted of you, and I'm not going to ask. But keep away from the likes of him and you'll be better off. Understand me?'

Johnny breathed a silent breath of relief. Again, he kicked turf.

'Cripes,' he said, 'I'll keep away from him, no fear. Why, the damned crook wanted me to pull a horse. Fancy that!'

To Win A Race

ALFRED WATSON

Until the middle of the nineteenth century there were very few professional jockeys at race meetings. The vast majority of competitors were amateur owner-riders: either wealthy gentlemen, prosperous farmers or military men of independent means. But with the introduction of increasingly large sums of prize money and valuable trophies, ambitious owners soon brought about the dawn of the professional era, and this was compounded in 1879 when the Jockey Club introduced a ruling that if amateur riders wished to compete with the professionals, they had to be similarly licensed. 'Gentleman riders now had to be good even to be allowed to take part,' Wray Vamplew has written, 'for unskilled riders, no matter how enthusiastic, were simply too dangerous; and racing bloodstock was far too valuable to be put at risk by bungling amateurs.'

The demands of a jockey's life – the need to diet rigorously, travel long distances to meetings and the ever-present risk of serious injury – soon discouraged all but the very keenest and ablest of the 'gentlemen riders', the remainder turning their attentions to point to point racing which was generally held to be much more of a social event. Yet despite the importance of the role of the amateur in the development of horse racing, they feature very little in turf fiction, and this next story, 'To Win A Race', is one of the few in which there is also a strong criminal element. The author, however, was a man well-prepared to write about the subject with a reputation as one of the best writers on the turf at work during the closing decade of the Victorian era and the early years of the twentieth century.

Alfred Edward Thomas Watson (1849–1922) was the son of a well-known Victorian racing figure, Captain B. L. Watson, and was encouraged to follow the sport from his childhood. In fact he began writing about racing when still in his teens, though it was not until he joined the staff of the *Illustrated Sporting and Dramatic News* (which later became the *Illustrated London News*) as the racing correspondent and launched a forthright weekly column under the pen-name 'Rapier' that his reputation was made. Watson also occasionally contributed to the London *Standard* and *The Times*, as well as utilizing the inside information he collected around the race courses in a series of popular novels and several authoritative non-fiction books, including *Race Course and Covert Side* (1883), *The Turf* (1898) and *The Racing World* (1904). He was for a time, too, the editor of the prestigious Badminton Library of sporting histories and wrote the entry on horse racing for the *Encyclopaedia Britannica*. An ebullient and forceful character, he was a close friend of a number of leading British trainers whose exploits he recorded in *Types of the Turf* published in 1885. Some of the tales he heard from these men were actually too scandalous to be printed as fact and so Watson turned them into short stories, the majority of which appeared in a series under the generic title *Racing and Chasing* in *Longman's Magazine* around the turn of the century. 'To Win A Race' (May 1897) is one such tale and apart from recalling the world of the amateur jockey also lifts the lid on the scheme of an unscrupulous trainer planning a betting fraud in England and France.

*

I

The industry of horse training is much more widely spread than would be imagined by those who are accustomed to see a score or so of familar names in sporting records. There are numbers of little men whose fame for good or evil is merely local, half trainers, half horse dealers, sometimes livery stable keepers as well, to the extent, at least, of letting out a hunter or two in the season. Such a one was James Dossie, of the Common Farm, Downleigh, who on a certain November morning a year or two since was strolling to and fro before the gates of his stable-yard as if waiting for somebody.

' "Good enough to win a little race," ' he muttered to himself, glancing at a letter which he held in his hand. 'Yes! I think we can manage that. Thomas!' he called out, and from the saddle-room a neat-looking light-weight groom appeared. 'How's the grey horse?'

'Oh, he's fining down. He'll get right enough till he's put into strong work again, and then he'll go,' Thomas answered, in a careless offhand manner, which showed that the relations of master and servant were on anything but a formal footing.

'Take his bandages off. There's someone coming to buy a horse directly; a young fellow who's staying at the Manor House, and wants something good enough to win a little race with. Soldier, I judge he is. How did King Cole go this morning?' Dossie continued; for Thomas had superintended the exercise on the neighbouring downs, as he usually did, unless there chanced to be anything special in the wind.

'Went very short. He won't get through this bout, I guess,' Thomas answered, 'and that chestnut mare makes a worse noise every day. I don't know what's to be done with her. Hulloa! here's somebody! I suppose that's the one you expect?' and Thomas disappeared into the saddle-room, leaving the proprietor of the establishment to receive his visitor, a quiet soldier-like man of thirty, who had ridden up to the gates of the yard, and thrown his reins to a lad who came forward to take the horse.

'Mr Osborne?' Dossie said, interrogatively. 'Glad to see you, sir.'

'Yes, I am Mr Osborne. You got my letter, of course? It just occurred to me that you might have something in your stable that would suit me – something just about good enough to have a chance of winning a little race at Aldersham next month. Colonel Lockhart, a friend of mine, who bought Oddity from you some time ago, recommended me to look through your stable, and as I am staying a few miles off, I thought I would ride over and see what you had.'

'Glad to see you, sir,' Dossie repeated, much relieved to hear that one of his customers had been pleased with his purchase, which probably was not much of a rule when he sold a horse, his business lying to a great extent among those animals that did not improve upon acquaintance when taken home. 'He was a sweet little horse, was Oddity, and I told the Colonel he would do us credit. Will you step this way, please, sir? Here's a little grey I should like you to look over,' and Thomas, coming forward at this moment, opened the door of one of the stables by which the yard was bounded on three sides.

The grey was stripped. Osborne looked him over carefully, and Dossie followed his glances keenly to note on what they rested. Osborne's eyes lingered on hocks that told a tale not to be mistaken by a practical horseman, and Dossie saw that he had something of a judge to deal with.

'Is he sound?' Osborne asked.

'Well, sir, I can only say that he's been doing well enough since I've had him, but I believe the man I bought him from had a bit of trouble with him,' Dossie answered, seeing that a little candour would make a good foundation for future assertions. 'I never sell a gentleman a horse without saying what I know and what I think. Now, there's a fine upstanding horse, sir. King Cole we call him, won a couple of steeplechases in the spring,' he continued, as Thomas turned back the clothing.

'No. I don't care much for King Cole,' Osborne remarked, for the horse's legs all round showed traces of a hard life. 'I want a horse that I can hunt when he has won a race or two, perhaps, and I should ask you to keep him here, in the first place, and prepare him for his engagement.'

That altered the case considerably. There was more to be made out of Osborne than the casual profit of a deal, and, as a matter of fact, Dossie had the animal that was wanted in his stable, though he had not proposed to show her and let her go into other hands before he had talked the affair over with Thomas and with Mr Sharpe, the 'gentleman rider' who performed on Dossie's horses. Thomas was a shrewd, hard-headed man of thirty, whose face and manner belied him. He looked a decent, civil servant, one who was meant by nature for a groom, and was at once recognized as that and nothing else. He had been in two or three good services, but an inclination towards roguery had proved irresistible, had destroyed his prospects when allowed full play, and so he was landed as factotum to Dossie, who was a keen hand at a bargain and knew his way about well enough, but had in the course of some two years been taught more sharp practice of the modern school by Thomas and Mr Sharpe than he had gathered in a good deal more than forty years' experience of men and horses.

'Well, sir, I think I have just what you want. Will you step this way, please, sir?' Dossie said, leading the way across the yard to the opposite stable and opening the gate of a loose box.

'That's more like it, Mr Dossie!' Osborne remarked, as he looked over a handsome bay mare that came forward amicably with her nose out to investigate her visitors.

'Handle her, sir – handle her!' Dossie exclaimed. 'The more you know of her the more you'll like her. She's as quiet as a lamb. Good all round, I think you'll say, sir. No fear of her not jumping, with those shoulders and quarters – but perhaps you'd like to throw your leg over her, sir? Certainly! By all means! Put a saddle on, Thomas!'

Dossie was so unused to selling a horse that really would bear strict inspection, that he almost overdid the part of the honest dealer. There was, as a very general rule, some weak point about the animals he offered for sale, and one that might be handled in the stable and freely tried outside was not often forthcoming. He had picked the mare up cheaply a few weeks before, at the sale, one miserably wet day, of the stud of a youthful plunger who had broken himself in three years after coming of age. Mr Sharpe had not been to the stables for some time, and Dossie was waiting his arrival in order to discuss the best mode of proceeding. To sell it at a handsome profit, to keep it in the stable, to train and win a race with it at someone else's expense, seemed a satisfactory thing to do, and Phyllis, as she was called, was offered accordingly. So far as looks went she was well enough. There was, indeed, nothing particularly striking about her, but she appeared sound and honest, and submitted to the operation of saddling with perfect good-humour, for Osborne had expressed his wish to give her a bit of a gallop, as Dossie suggested.

The downs were almost at the stable-door, just across the road. Osborne mounted, walked through the gate, passing the reins through his fingers, while Dossie and Thomas looked on.

'Jump her, sir. Do what you like. Throw her down if you can; but you can't do *that*, I know,' the trainer said. Osborne, nodding, leant forward in the saddle, and off they went. The canter increased to a gallop as the mare left the watchers, but she was easily restrained, and came back heading for a row of hurdles that ranged in a line away to the left. The mare pricked her ears and slid over in excellent style, finishing the gallop with a jump over a biggish made-up fence. Osborne's good-natured face was slightly flushed, and his dark eyes sparkled as he trotted back to where Dossie stood.

'Well, sir?' the trainer asked.

'Yes, Mr Dossie, I like her much. She seems sound and good-tempered. What do you ask for her?'

Then followed the arrangement of terms, the arguments concerning which, as set forth by Dossie, need not be quoted at length. Her performances were naturally magnified; the races she had won were described in flowing terms; plausible excuses were made for her defeats. Osborne hated haggling, and made little demur when the price was named. Three hundred pounds down, fifty pounds more if the mare won the Regimental Challenge Cup, to win which was Osborne's object in making the purchase. Meantime she was to stay and be trained at the usual rate. Osborne, as he mounted his hack and trotted along the road towards the Manor House, some ten miles off, where he was paying a duty visit to a somewhat dull party of elderly relatives, was perfectly well satisfied with his morning's work; and Dossie, who had picked up the mare for rather less than a quarter of the sum he had received, was by no means displeased with his share of the transaction. Osborne wanted an animal that would have a good chance of winning the Challenge Cup at the Aldersham meeting, and his friend Lockhart had written to him to say that Dossie might possibly have a likely horse. 'I hear he's a shocking old thief, but he behaved well enough to me, and you can take care of yourself. As you are so near, you may as well go over and say I told you of him. Perhaps he's not such a rascal as they say, and at any rate fellows like that are glad to keep straight with a few people if they can,' Lockhart had written.

Some three weeks after Phyllis had been bought and entered, Mr Sharpe paid his visit, unusually long deferred, to the Common Farm, where, one morning, he might have been observed leaning back in a chair in Dossie's business-room, puffing moodily at a cigar. Dossie was seated at the other side of the fire, looking bewildered, and seeking inspiration from apparently pressing trouble in brandy and water, while Thomas, a Newmarket snaffle bit in one hand, and a piece of wash-leather in the other, was standing at the table.

'It's a confounded nuisance!' presently Sharpe said. 'The whole thing fitted in so well. The mare is qualified to run in France; she could hardly be beaten, and is certain to start at a good price, for it isn't likely to leak out that Vivandière and Quick March won't be spinning. Instead of that, Phyllis goes to Aldersham, where she isn't wanted, for she'll beat the horse I sold to Major Congreve, and that's quite good enough to win with her out of the way – at least, it ought to be.'

'Yes, it's a nuisance, as you say; but what's to be done? I can't kid young Osborne the mare's dead and then send her to France. What a pity you didn't tell me sooner!' Dossie answered.

'I did tell you that I had a game on for the mare if she was as good as you said, and I thought, of course, you'd keep her till you saw me,' Sharpe responded, in a surly tone. 'It's no good wrangling about it, though it's desperate bad luck, and as for backing the mare at Aldersham, I don't care for that much when an outsider has the ride.'

Thomas, from the other side of the table, looked up.

'You haven't been to Horley these last few days, have you, Mr Sharpe?' he asked.

'No; nor these last few weeks for the matter of that. Why?'

'Because I see rather a funny thing there. In the last lot of horses that Tim Wetheral had from the Curragh there's a mare the very spit of Phyllis – an aged mare, same shade of colour, same star, and same white heel. Funniest thing I ever saw! I thought the gov'ner had sent Phyllis over for something or other when I came across her first; but there she is,' Thomas said.

Both the listeners turned with interest to the speaker.

'And what then?' Sharpe presently asked. 'What sort is she?'

'Very bad, they say. As slow as a man; can get over a fence, but isn't likely to win unless everything else falls down. Tim says it's no good running her, only if their horses don't win once or twice, somebody generally thinks they're being kept for something, and buys them. They've got rid of one or two that way that was no good at all.'

'Well?' Sharpe continued, as the groom laid down the bit and cloth on the table.

'Well, supposing the gov'ner bought the mare, and—'

'I see!' Sharpe broke in, nodding with a cunning twinkle of the eyes to Dossie, who was also just breaking his way through the mystery. 'You're no fool, Thomas. I see what you mean. Send Phyllis to France, and let our young friend have the other one. But are you sure the likeness is as close as you say?'

'I tell you I had to look more than once before I was sure it wasn't Phyllis, and he's seen her just twice – the day he bought her, and one morning when he came to see her gallop in her clothing,' Thomas answered.

'If that's so, it's a rattling good dodge, and you are on a pony if it comes off. When can we see her? Where's a railway guide? There's no time to be lost.'

In less than two hours Dossie and Sharp were on their way to Horley, where Wetheral, a kindred spirit who kept an establishment somewhat similar to that presided over by Dossie, was to be found. There was no false delicacy about the transaction, and the visitors came to the point at once when Wetheral had exchanged greetings, and poured out the inevitable drink. Leading the way to the stall where the mare stood, Wetheral stripped off her clothing; and the two gazed with astonishment at the animal – Ophelia she was called – whose likeness to Phyllis, even to their practised eyes, was amazing.

'Thomas was right. Smart chap, that – very smart,' Sharpe said, and Dossie nodded assent, his gaze still fixed on the mare.

'It's wonderful! They are as like as two peas. How's she bred?' he asked. 'Both Solons? Well, that's odd, though it doesn't account for the likeness.'

It was, indeed, a strange accident. Wetheral was ready enough to sell, and the mare returned to the Common Farm with her new master. Even when put side by side with the other, the likeness was not lost – scarcely diminished. Phyllis was a shade the taller and bigger horse, and her colour was a thought darker. The blazed faces varied very slightly. On the whole it was really hard to tell which was which when the pair were not together, and anyone but an exceedingly careful observer might readily have made a mistake even when they were.

When the two were seen out at work the difference was distinct enough. Phyllis was a freer jumper, galloped in better form, and was, all things considered, a good 21 lb in front of Ophelia. The two varied so much that, there was no disguising it, a really good horseman like Osborne might be led to suspect, or at least to wonder at, the alteration in his mare's way of galloping and jumping; but for various reasons horses do lose their action and jump indifferently at times; and to suspect and to prove are different things. Wetheral was safe enough; Sharpe and Thomas were implicated in the fraud; the other boys at Dossie's place knew nothing and were not likely to learn anything – it was Dossie's whim to try and have boys about him who could neither read nor write; it might save trouble, he said, and, besides, in this case there was no writing to show anything. Phyllis was going to run in France, and once there (in the name of Ophelia, of course) was not likely to be recognized; if she were, proof was again well-nigh impossible, even if the suspicious person strove to arrive at facts. What could be said? Ophelia, b. m., aged, by Solon – Lady Jane, simply took the place of Phyllis, b. m., aged, by Solon – Aspasia. Who was to show that one was the other? If it came to hard swearing, Wetheral would have been bad to beat; and so the business was settled. Both took their gallops together, for the race in France (which a stealthy rumour declared was a good thing for Ophelia – *i.e.* Phyllis – because the owners and jockeys of the two most dangerous opponents were 'going for her') was, as it happened, run on the same day as the Aldersham race, which Osborne would have won on Phyllis had all gone well, but which it was arranged he was to lose on the substituted Phyllis (*i.e.* Ophelia).

The completeness of the arrangement was derived from the fact that Sharpe had sold to a man in the regiment a chaser which would be quite good enough, under ordinary circumstances, to win the Regimental Challenge Cup, and Sharpe was 'on' a hundred to nothing if it won. The excellence of Osborne's mare had crept out, however, and as soon as betting began on the race it was sure to be favourite; when, by backing the other and laying against the supposititious Phyllis, something extra might be made. The whole thing was delightfully plain and simple, and no less safe. It was difficult to see how a slip could occur, and the rogues chuckled to themselves as they thought of their own cleverness and the lucky way things had fallen out.

Both went on well in their respective fashions. Phyllis – the true Phyllis – improved greatly in her business, and got better every day; Ophelia looked the picture of health and condition, but galloped as if her legs were tied, and could never learn to get away from her jumps. The day arrived when they were to be sent away, Phyllis to France and Ophelia – to give the animals their right names – to Aldersham, for Osborne had decided to take her in good time so that she might have a school over the course. But just then a somewhat awkward event happened. Soon after the horses had come in from exercise a hack cantered up to the stable-door, and Osborne dismounted. Dossie, who was preparing to despatch the two mares, happened to see his client, and recovered his surprise before he was obliged to speak.

'Very glad to see you, sir,' was his exceedingly untruthful greeting. 'You've come to have a look at the mare, I suppose? She's very well, I'm glad to say, sir. I was just going to send her on to the station,' and he showed his visitor a label with the mare's name, and Captain A. V. Osborne, Aldersham Station, written on it, slipping into his pocket at the same time another label with a different address that was to have been attached to Phyllis's collar.

'Thanks. Yes, I should like to see her. In the same box?' Osborne said, half leading the way to the spot where she had stood before, and where, in point of fact, she was still standing. 'I should have been over before; I hoped to come and ride a gallop or two, but the illness of a relative has prevented me. I feared, indeed, that I should not be able to ride at all, but things have taken a turn for the better. I was half afraid the mare would have gone, but now I can see her off. Yes! she looks well, indeed,' he continued, as Dossie stripped her. 'I'm indebted to you, Mr Dossie, for the care you've taken. She ought to be about good enough to win.'

'Yes, sir, and I'm very much obliged for what you are pleased to say. I always do my best for gentlemen, and it's satisfactory when they recognize it,' Dossie, slowly recovering from his confusion, answered. 'I didn't even know you was in the neighbourhood, or I should have been proud to see you.'

'Never mind, Mr Dossie. There she is, and that's the great thing. When I wrote to you last week fixing the train for you to send her by, I did not know that I could get down. What's that? The grey I saw before? Those hocks don't look like winning races, do they? What's that mare?' he added, pointing to Ophelia, who, Dossie was relieved to see, stood, well clothed, in a dark corner box.

'Oh, that's nothing, sir. My daughter's hack. I've just put her in there as I was pressed for room,' was Dossie's unblushing reply, and to divert attention he busied himself about Phyllis.

'Time to be starting, if she goes quietly to the station, isn't it? You call it four miles, don't you?' Osborne asked. 'I'll see her off, and then I must get back, for I can't follow till an evening train.'

Sharpe and Thomas, peeping round the corner of the saddle-room door, saw the unfortunate Dossie fixing his card to Phyllis's head-stall, and in a few minutes – earlier than was necessary, for Dossie was burning with anxiety to get his client out of the stable – the mare was prepared for the journey, turned round, and trotted off by one of the boys towards the station. Sharpe, who wanted to call at the saddler's shop in the town, mounted a hack, and set off on his journey, accompanied by Thomas, riding Ophelia.

'I'll see that it's all right,' Mr Sharpe said, nodding significantly to Dossie, as he got into the saddle.

'You understand how it is?' the trainer said. 'You see, I had to put the wrong label on; but when you get to the station you'll have a chance, or, if not there, at some station where you stop, you can just—'

'Yes, I know; leave it to me,' Mr Sharpe added, turning his hack's head, and following Thomas into the road.

III

The horses were duly boxed, and Sharpe took his place in his carriage, well supplied with his favourite sporting papers. He perfectly well understood what he had to do. Perhaps it would have been better to have done it before the train started, but, after all, it did not much matter. Before reaching Aldersham the train stopped for five minutes, and, slipping into the box in which Dossie's animals were travelling, he neatly and expeditiously changed the labels on the two mares' head-stalls, fastening the strings a good bit tighter than Dossie had fastened them. Osborne's groom was waiting at the Aldersham station to take charge of the mare, and she was safely handed over to him; after which Sharpe returned to his seat, for he was bound for London, in order that he might himself see the so-called Ophelia despatched on her journey across the Channel. A boy was to go with her; but he was a country lout, more than likely to get into the wrong train unless started on his way and placed under the supervision of the guard. Sharpe had plenty to amuse him, particularly in wondering what Osborne would think when he got on his mare, and what would be the sentiments of backers of Vivandière and Quick March when they found how far those animals were from their book form in the French race. His sale of the horse, Dobbin by name, to Major Congreve, of Osborne's regiment, was a perfectly *bona fide* transaction. Hearing indirectly that such a horse was wanted, he had negotiated the business, and Congreve, who had the most casual 'racecourse acquaintance' with Mr Sharpe, had put him on £100 to nothing if the horse won.

The excellent chance of the prospective hundred was not the least agreeable matter in Mr Sharpe's thoughts, as he sped on his return journey to Aldersham on the morning of the race, a couple of days after, especially as the hundred would bring more money with it, both by reason of Dobbin's win and of 'Phyllis's' inevitable defeat. She was favourite at 2 to 1, Dobbin was at 7 to 1, and he had laid against one and backed the other. Of course he was going to assist Congreve all he could, saddle the horse, and give such advice as seemed likeliest to be of avail. Mr Sharpe, it will be understood, though a 'gentleman rider,' duly elected, was, in plain English, a professional steeplechase jockey, who rode under false pretences; but that is too common an occurrence to excite surprise. In any case, he had a thorough knowledge of his business, and Congreve was extremely glad to meet him in the paddock before he went to dress for the Challenge Cup.

'Halloa! Here we are! That's all right!' the Major, who was rather a novice at the business, exclaimed as he met Sharpe. 'The horse is third favourite, but they're backing something called Phyllis all over the ring. A man in the regiment – Osborne his name is – got hold of it at Dossie's – you know him, don't you? Haven't I seen you ride his horses? Do you know anything about this one? They say she went in wonderful style over the course yesterday morning. Perhaps you know her?'

'No, I don't think I do. Let's see. Is it a bay mare with a white off heel? I fancy I've seen something with a name like that down there,' Sharpe answered.

'Yes, that's the mare – rather good-looking – blaze on her face. Is she any good?'

'I should say not, if it's the one I mean. If you can lay £50 against her, I'll go halves in the bet; that'll show you what I think,' Sharpe replied. 'There's nothing at Dossie's just now likely to interfere with us.'

'I'm uncommonly glad to hear you say so – uncommonly glad, I can tell you. It put me into an awful funk, for the mare looks so well, and she has won races, you know. But if you know her, that's all right. I can lay £60 to £40 against her, no doubt, and that's how they bet now she's getting a warm favourite,' the Major replied.

Sharpe was strongly inclined to laugh, but suppressed the inclination. Everything seemed ready to his hand. The true Tommy Tiddler's ground was evidently a racecourse where affairs were going right.

'There she is! That's the one!' the Major suddenly exclaimed, pointing across the paddock to the familiar figure of the bay mare. 'That's it, is it? I'm awfully glad. Ah! There's ours,' he added, as a big chestnut, which might have been called a bit clumsy by enemies, was led up. 'I'll go and get into my things.'

Congreve retired, and Sharpe went to superintend the saddling of the horse. While engaged in that operation, Osborne, in a pink and white hooped jacket, walked past him, but he had never seen Sharpe, or at least did not know him. Congreve, in a purple jacket and white cap, was not long in appearing. Dobbin was now second favourite, for when stripped the animal that had been most fancied after Phyllis was found to be very big and a trifle lame, while the rest of the field were for the most part a rather sorry lot – none, at least, looking dangerous; besides, Congreve could ride a little – well enough to do all that was necessary on such a comfortable horse as Dobbin, if only he could be persuaded to let his mount alone, a lesson which Mr Sharpe used his best efforts to enforce.

The course at Aldersham is not a good one for spectators. To see all the way round it is necessary to run backwards and forwards, in the midst of a crowd, to say nothing of chairs and seats, up and down the top of a hill; and Sharpe lingered in the ring when the horses had gone down to the post, to have a few last bets, and to give those he knew a hint to lay against the favourite. He did not, therefore, see the start, nor observe how one man tumbled off at the drop-fence, how two men came to grief with their horses at the open ditch, how one was shot over his horse's head into the brook, and another ran out, leaving only six competitors in the race. A rider in a white jacket was a hundred and fifty yards ahead, when he, too, toppled over a fence, and Dobbin was left with the lead; for Sharpe had told his rider not to keep too far behind the others, but not to be flurried if one or two got a long way in front in the first mile and a half, as they would probably begin to come back before the second of the three miles was finished.

Dobbin was going well enough. What much surprised Sharpe, when presently he fixed his glasses on the race, was that Phyllis seemed to be going well also. There was nothing in it yet.

Condition would do much for a horse that came out of a training stable in a race against a lot of animals prepared at home; but still the mare seemed to jump more easily, and to gallop much more freely, than she had done at the Common Farm. Without a semblance of effort she kept her place a length or two behind Dobbin; and though the pace was very moderate the others were beginning to tail off. Over the drop the second time Dobbin blundered a bit. Congreve sat tight, and pulled his mount together again very neatly, but this let up the mare, who now was holding her own quite easily, while Dobbin was beginning to labour. Congreve gave his horse a dig with a spur, and that put him a couple of lengths to the good again, but nearing the brook for the last time, Dobbin had to be waked up with the whip, and the mare, not yet touched, swung over and landed by his side.

What could it mean? Sharpe had the line between them clearly enough. They were running at even weights, and Dobbin had, or should have had, a good 21 lb in hand. It did not look like it, however. As they neared the last fence Congreve was riding hard to keep his place. The mare was first over, and to all appearance winning anyhow. But Congreve was not to be beaten without making a fight for it. Sitting down, he did all he knew, and old Dobbin answered gamely to his calls. But it was no sort of use. Osborne, sitting quite still, watched over his left shoulder the struggles of his friend, and some sixty yards from the winning post let out the mare, who came away and won hands down by a couple of lengths.

Sharpe stood still for a minute before he could believe it. The mare had won, and won easily. There was the number up, and the spectators were cheering. The race was over, and his schemes were upset – how, he could not tell, but upset they were. It was not in an amiable frame of mind that he made his way to the paddock, but it was necessary to see the Major and say what could be said. Osborne was naturally radiant as he received his friends' congratulations – and friends are sincere when they have backed you and won their money – while the Major was not unnaturally depressed.

'If *that's* no good, mine must be a very bad one,' he gloomily remarked, nodding towards where the mare was being led away;

and at the moment a horrible suspicion began to dawn upon Sharpe! Before he could frame it in his own mind the Major's servant approached him with a telegram in his hand. It was addressed to Sharpe, from Auteuil Racecourse. He had asked his French confederate to send him a wire to Aldersham as soon as their race was over, and this was it. He opened it and read:

'*Mare beaten a hundred yards in a bad field.*'

Then the suspicion took distinct form.

After all, Osborne must have got the true Phyllis, and the Ophelia, which had been sent to Auteuil, was in truth what she purported to be, the veritable Ophelia! Could that possibly be it? What else could it be? And yet he had most certainly changed the cards, as he had told Dossie he would do, and he was positive, moreover, that the mare he intended to give to Osborne's servant had been given to him.

The stupefaction with which Dossie received the news of how the two good things – the four good things, for there were two horses to back and two to lay against – had been upset, and the rage of Thomas, when it was found that his neat trick had been ruined, are not easily to be described; nor would a detailed description of the scene which took place when Sharpe made his next appearance at Common Farm be edifying.

By degrees the facts came out. Thomas, on arriving at the station on the real Ophelia, had, while putting the mares into the box, removed the label from her head-stall and substituted that which Dossie had fastened on to Phyllis. It was his scheme, and he supposed that the working of it had been left in his hands. Sharpe, on the other hand, had told Dossie to 'leave it to him', and had undertaken to 'see that it was all right'. Having no idea that Thomas had changed the labels already, he had simply changed them back again, as before described. Osborne, therefore, had the mare he had bought, and the real Ophelia had been sent to France.

Dead Cert

LEON BREAKER

Australian-born Leon Breaker holds the distinction of being the first jockey-turned-novelist. Although he rode at a number of major steeplechase meetings in Australia during the latter part of the last century and thereafter wrote a group of popular novels about the turf which were also published in England, Breaker is today virtually forgotten and his books impossible to find unlike those of his two contemporaries, the Englishman Nat Gould and fellow countryman Andrew 'Banjo' Patterson. For a time Leon Breaker worked on the same newspaper as Gould, but he actually became a closer friend of Patterson, with whom he frequently went racing.

Patterson was a fun-filled, gregarious man known as the 'Bush Balladeer', and is today best remembered as the author of 'Waltzing Matilda', despite the fact that he wrote many other verses, especially about racing, and innumerable articles dealing with the turf. Curiously, however, although 'Banjo's' very first published story was entitled 'How I Shot a Policeman' (it appeared in the *Sydney Bulletin* in January 1890), his fiction was mostly in the same humorous vein as Damon Runyon and there is sadly nothing suitable for inclusion in this anthology. Breaker, on the other hand, wrote a number of mystery novels and short stories about racing which drew on his experiences as a steeplechase jockey. 'Dead Cert' is certainly the best of these which I have been able to track down.

Leon Breaker (1861–1938) was born in Adelaide, where he was trained as a jockey and rode to a notable victory in the Adelaide Grand National Hurdle Race in 1885. When injury curtailed his career a few years later, he turned to writing fiction and based his first novel, *Riding To Win* (1893), on Australia's famous Melbourne Cup, which had then been running for over thirty years drawing huge crowds each year to the Flemington race track. (Today this event, held on the first Tuesday of November, attracts crowds in excess of 100,000 and virtually brings the nation to a standstill while the race is televised nationwide.)

Breaker's novel drew in particular on the legendary first Melbourne Cup in 1861, which had been won by a horse named Archer. Only after the event was it revealed that the animal had actually been walked the 500 miles from its stables in New South Wales to Flemington as part of its preparation! Archer instantly became a national institution; and his popularity was further increased the next year when he returned to win the event for a second time.

Leon Breaker followed *Riding To Win* with *A Strange Finish*, *The Scarlet Jacket*, *Zenobia*, and a number more which were published in the UK by R. A. Everett & Co., who were also Nat Gould's publishers for several years until he was lured away to George Routledge and finally, Mellifont Press, who kept up a vigorous reprinting programme in paperback for some years after his death. Breaker enjoyed no such extended publication, so I am pleased to be able to represent this pioneer of the genre with a story related by an Australian steeplechase jockey just like himself who becomes embroiled in a vicious plot to fix a major race. The title is, no doubt, immediately familiar to readers as being the same one Dick Francis chose for his ground-breaking first novel.

*

It had long been the ambition of Angus McGregor, of Glen Park, to add the Great Eastern to the formidable list of cross-country events captured by bearers of his pretty red, white, and blue jacket. Ill luck had, however, attended his efforts. Year after year he had brought horses to the post for the race trained to the hour, and fit to run for a king's ransom, and disaster had overtaken each one.

One year Glen Roy, one of the finest 'chasers that ever bore silk, after getting the course under the steadier of 12 st 10 lb, and when holding a winning hand, was brought down on the flat by a riderless horse, and, breaking his leg, was shot. Undeterred by the many reverses he had met with on this course, two years ago he nominated Chieftain for the big race, and this time he felt that success must crown his efforts.

Chieftain was a bay horse and a six-year-old, and Angus, the canny Scot, had saved him for this race. He had performed with credit in several big events between the flags, and he was just the sort of horse to do the Oakbank course – not too big, built for hill-climbing, and as nice a model of a steeplechaser as you could wish to see. He was a quick, bold jumper, and Rob Roy was put in to ensure a sound run race from end to end. The handicapper played right into Mac's hands, giving Rob Roy 9 st., and Chieftain 10 st.

Angus backed Chieftain so heavily that about a week before the race he was a firm favourite at a short price. Many a talk did Angus and I have over our impending triumph, for at the weights, and even considering the big field, we knew that there could be no other 'rod in pickle' like ours to upset our calculations. Chieftain was a pure, unadulterated specimen of a 'dead cert.'

I had trained him over hilly country similar to that at Oakbank, and he had answered satisfactorily every question put to him. Tim Brady, who was to ride Rob Roy, and I had rehearsed the race, until we felt assured that nothing short of the sky falling could prevent the successful issue of our plans. We felt that the Great Eastern was coming to Glen Park at last. Tim was just the man for the task allotted him. He was a fearless, devil-may-care Irishman, and a first-class jockey. Poor Tim! We little anticipated the fate that was to befall him in the much-looked-forward-to race as we chatted together about it.

It wanted but a few days to the date of our departure for the scene of action with the horses when I received a strange communication, which worried me not a little. A letter arrived by post for me one morning, and on opening it I read something to this purport:

'Dear Dalton, – You will be on Chieftain at Oakbank, and I understand that he has a big say in the race. I stand to win some thousands over a horse that must beat your mount, but naturally would feel more assurance with yours out of the way. Is it safe to conclude that he can't win? You ought to know. I can afford to be generous, and if you can relieve me upon this point it will be worth £500 to you, and more to follow after the race. Your riding fee and probable winnings will hardly amount to this. A reply to "Nemo," G.P.O., will be looked for. An appointment can be arranged. The enclosure will more than cover postage, and is a proof of my *bona-fides*.'

The letter was signed 'Nemo,' and the enclosure was a twenty-pound note. Of course I knew that 'Nemo' desired me to make Chieftain safe, and would look for my acquiescence to his proposal. Doubtless he had great faith in his generous offer of a monkey. I could not think whom 'Nemo' might be, and resolved to be upon my guard lest an attempt might be made to get at the horse. Somebody evidently meant serious business. The monkey told me that. All day long I puzzled my head about the sender of that letter. I could not reasonably fix suspicion on anyone. The sender must be a stranger to me, and yet he was not, for that evening the mystery was made clear to me.

I unwillingly overheard a conversation of a strictly private nature between Howard Fane, the most plausible, polished, and unscrupulous villain I have ever met, although I did not know him in his true colours then, and his affianced wife, Hilda Maynard, the ward of the late Colonel Fane, Howard Fane's father. I had had occasion to go out that evening, and was returning to the stables, and taking a short cut through the Park, suddenly came upon a couple strolling in front of me. It was a clear, moonlit night, and I knew at once who the lovers were, as Miss Maynard had been staying at Glen Park for some time, and Howard Fane was a frequent visitor there.

I did not like to pass them, nor did I want to retrace my steps, so waited in some thick shrubbery for a few moments to allow them to get well ahead of me. I did not calculate upon their turning back, and when I saw them coming towards me I was half of a mind to slip away, when I thought I might as well wait until they had passed, for doubtless they were returning to the house, and then I could resume my journey.

The hand of Fate was in this *rencontre*, and it was well that I

waited in the shrubbery. As the two lovers neared my place of
concealment, I drew farther back amongst the dark bushes, and
was congratulating myself that in a moment or so they would
have passed, when to my chagrin they halted immediately
opposite my hiding-place. They had been walking slowly, her
hand resting on his arm, and both had been strangely silent. This
silence was now broken. Fane wheeled abruptly, and, facing his
companion, said:

'It is no use, Hilda; I won't release you from your engagement.
You ought not to ask me to do so. My father's heart was set upon
our marriage, and you promised him on his deathbed that you
would be my wife. Is that promise now to be broken for a whim? I
love you, and I need you. Looking at things from a wordly point
of view, my father's fortune comes to us on our marriage. Should
we not marry, I get a beggarly pittance of a thousand a-year, and
you get a like proportion, and the rest goes to enrich God knows
whom. Perhaps, being sure of the thousand a-year, you want to
throw me over.'

'Howard, you wrong me, and your hard words break my
heart,' replied Hilda Maynard. 'I do not need the money, as you
know. I have not forgotten my solemn promise to your father, and
in honour bound will fulfil it to the letter, though it be to sacrifice
myself.'

'Sacrifice yourself!' he interjected sneeringly, 'that's not at all
complimentary to me.'

'Yes! sacrifice myself,' she repeated. 'I loved you, and still love
the Howard of the old days, but how can I love you in your new
life? Your father was the noblest of men, and was a father to me.
He knew my influence over you, and begged me to exert it to save
you from yourself. I loved you then, and promised to marry you,
believing that my love could hold you faithful to your better self.
That it does not seem to have the power to do. You have chosen a
life of pleasure and vice, and were your father alive now to see the
road you are taking, it would break his heart. You speak of my
respect for his dying wishes. Are you respecting his memory? Are
you a worthy son of your sire? No, Howard, you are a drunkard,
a gambler, and worse, and if you cannot appreciate the sacrifice I
am making in marrying you, I can realise what it means to me. I

will be faithful to my promise, and marry you, and trust in God to redeem you in spite of yourself.'

'You're quite dramatic, my dear Hilda, and not a bit logical,' sneered Fane, and I felt a strong desire to kick him. 'If you feel that morally you should and must marry me, why ask to be released from your promise to me, which means that you break your given word to my father?'

'Because at times, Howard, I feel that the task set myself is hopeless, and I shrink from the sacrifice of my life, and from you with abhorrence, and I tell myself that were your father alive he would not wish it. I know he would not,' she added vehemently.

'By God! then,' said Howard Fane passionately, suddenly flying into a rage, that half involuntarily I made ready to spring from my hiding-place, 'since I repel you, am so distasteful to you, I'll give you a chance of your freedom. I'll make you a sporting offer, and hold you to your promise only in the event of a certain happening. You say I am a gambler. Aye! I am that – a born gambler. The spirit to hazard all on Fortune's smile always burns within me. The gambler's fever, that fierce passion which cannot be defined or stayed in its course, runs through my veins like fire, and is life to me. I am a devotee at the shrine of the Goddess of Chance, an ardent worshipper. Your marriage with me practically gives me command of my father's wealth. I'll risk losing you for a gambler's whim. You shall have your freedom, the freedom you want and don't want. You shall have it if Fortune wills it. 'Twas only yesterday, when inspecting the horses, you said that Chieftain was a noble animal, and looked fit to run for a man's life. Well, he shall run for yours, since you say to marry me will be a sacrifice. If he beats Black Eagle at Oakbank, you are free; if not, I'll hold you to your promise. That is a noble gamble – a fortune against your life. It will be a great match, and the result will decide, not whether you marry me, but whether I marry you. Black Eagle must win the race also, for then I'll win two fortunes, for I've backed him down to my last penny. If he fails me, I swear you shall never see me again. Now, Hilda, go back to the house. I will not come in just yet. I'll stroll round the park and meditate, and a cigar will assist my thoughts materially. I'll watch you to the gate from here.'

This was the gist of the conversation I overheard. It would take too long, nor would my memory serve to tell all that passed between them. She pleaded with him to abandon the worthless life he was living, and got about as much sympathetic response from him as she would have received from a stone image. I could well understand that he valued her love not at all, and that whatever influence she had had over him before his present evil ways obtained such a hold on him, she had no power now to turn him from them. For some strange caprice, some reason best known to himself, he had offered her her freedom, and, like the gambler he was, had called on the fickle goddess to decide the matter. I there and then decided to give that deity a good lead, and swore that wherever the black finished the bay would be in front of him.

When Hilda Maynard left him, Howard Fane stood watching her until she passed through the gate leading into the garden which encircled the house, and then, instead of taking his intended stroll, he paced too and fro in front of my hiding-place, and held an audible conversation with himself. I'm glad he did. He appeared to be reviewing his position, which, I gathered, was a desperate one. I also ascertained that he was 'Nemo,' the sender of the letter reclining in my pocket. No wonder he had adopted this method of approaching me on the subject. If I refused to pull Chieftain, I would not know him in the matter at all, and he would thus be free to adopt some other course to make Chieftain safe. I wondered at his offering to release Hilda Maynard from her engagement, for I gleaned that he was heels over head in debt – gambling debts principally – and therefore the money to come to him on his marriage with her should have helped him retrieve his position. I did not know then that an entanglement with an actress made a legal marriage with Hilda Maynard an impossibility, and any form of marriage a perilous experiment for him. The situation contained more danger for Miss Maynard than I knew of, and doubtless Fane exercised his brain pretty frequently to arrive at a scheme safe and satisfactory to himself to solve the problem.

I learned enough to satisfy me that he was a thorough scoundrel and heartless villain, and to decide me that Chieftain must win at

Oakbank, and so smash him up. This might expose him in his true colours, and if he went back on his word, and still held Hilda Maynard to her promise, and to what she considered her duty to her dead guardian, might be the means of so disgusting her with him that she would feel justified in turning her back on him for ever.

A big responsibility rested upon Chieftain, and I trusted fervently that the ill-luck which had so persistently clung to the striped jacket at Oakbank would on this occasion be conspicuous by its absence.

That night I made a very false move. I enclosed the letter signed 'Nemo,' with a note attached, 'The £20 goes on Chieftain,' in an envelope, and addressing it to Mr Howard Fane, Glen Park, got one of the servants to deliver it to that gentleman. I regretted this step when it was too late to recall it. Second thoughts are usually the best, and had I not returned his letter to Fane a life might have been saved on that Easter Monday. My *coup de théâtre* could do no good, and did do much that was ill. It put Fane on his guard, and may have influenced him considerably in adopting the drastic measures he did to prevent Chieftain winning. With ours out of the way, the race certainly looked a real good thing for Black Eagle.

I did not meet Fane again until I came face to face with him in the saddling paddock at Oakbank half an hour before the race. To my astonishment he stopped me.

'A moment, Dalton,' he said coolly, removing his cigar from his lips, and carelessly flicking the ash off it. 'I see you're wearing a new jacket. It is very pretty,' and his hand gently stroked out a crease in the sleeve. 'I hope it will be as pretty after the race.'

'That's a threat,' I said, as I looked straight into his eyes; 'and after the race I'll horsewhip you round the paddock if it costs me my license.' I trembled with rage, and shook my whip ominously. He merely puffed a cloud of cigar smoke into my face, and drawling out the one word, 'Really!' strolled leisurely away. I was strongly inclined to accelerate his movements with a whip-stroke across that portion of his anatomy situated just below his back, but fortunately for both of us I restrained myself.

A moment later Miss Maynard, with a lady friend, met me.

'How pretty your new jacket is, Mr Dalton,' said Miss Maynard. I thought of Fane's remark to the same effect. 'Poor Jim' (everybody called the genial Irishman Jim) 'has to be content with the old one.'

'The old one, Miss Maynard,' I replied, 'has a good record, and Jim has won many races in it, though he won't win to-day.'

'I want Chieftain to win. I want it very much,' she said, and I fancied I detected a tremor in her voice.

What reply I would have made to this I don't know, for at this juncture Angus McGregor's hearty Scotch dialect broke in upon our conversation.

'Weel, James, ma lad,' he said, 'ye had better be making ye're way back to the beast; and, Hilda, ma lassie, the Chief will win. His chances are as bright as the new jacket, and I canna say mair than that.'

Alas for the much-talked-about new jacket! – its brightness was quickly dimmed. When I was tossed into the saddle in the paddock the realisation of the responsibility resting upon my shoulders, and how much depended on the issue of the race, descended upon me with crushing force, and for an instant I feared for the result; but the moment I felt Chieftain move under me all doubts and fears fled, and I rode on to the course sanguine of success, and feeling a strange elation of spirits, in marked contrast to the 'slump' of a few moments previous.

My little passage-at-arms with Howard Fane made me resolve to be upon the *qui vive* throughout the race, for I knew that there were men riding in it capable of doing any dirty work if sufficient inducement offered, and I had a premonition that Fane would stick at nothing to ensure the success of Black Eagle. Tim Brady on Rob Roy led me down the straight in the preliminary. Chieftain moved freely and fought for his head. As I held him in hand, and felt him strain like a hound in the leash, the blood tingled in my veins, and I felt thoroughly in my element.

Chieftain was a warm favourite, both in the tote and with the books, and Black Eagle ranked second. Chieftain received a round of applause, and Rob Roy came in for his share. It was an open secret what his mission was, and Tim Brady's pluck was recognised. Few people on the course, however, guessed how warm Tim meant to make the pace. I did not know myself. Micawber (12.7), Exile (11.7), and Barb (11.0) were a dangerous trio, and Tim meant to run them off their legs. Black Eagle was giving Chieftain a stone.

The big field, eighteen strong, faced the starter, and he did not keep us dawdling about very long. Down went his white flag, and away we went down the straight past the stands, and rounding the bend raced up the hill to the first big fence. I wanted to get a clear run at it, so was well in front when it suddenly rose up in front of us.

Tim was already playing his part of pace-maker, and Rob Roy was the first over it. A thumping crash told me something had come to grief as I raced away from the fence, and I wondered if it were Black Eagle. I quickly found that the pace was going to be sound enough for Chieftain. Rob Roy's striped jacket and red cap (I wore a white cap) were well ahead, with several light-weighted outsiders in hot pursuit. I saw Tim put the whip on Rob Roy, and the red cap drew away from us.

As we tore past the stands for the second round, the field was considerably diminished, for the pace had already weeded out some of the indifferent jumpers, and was as early as this telling its tale upon not a few. A babel of shouting was borne to us from the stands. We could not interpret anything from the volume of sound. I was told after the race that it expressed the exciting thrill which gripped at each man's heart in the vast crowd, caused by the unusual pace at which the race was being run.

It was reckless race riding, I'll admit, especially over such country as this. I didn't half like it, I don't mind telling you, and I wasn't the only one of that mind. We had no alternative, though, but to dance to the tune set for us by Rob Roy and the other light-weighted leaders. I took a look round as we swept up the straight. Rob Roy, a good thirty lengths in front, was slipping along like greased lightning. Chieftain was running about sixth in the middle of the course, and Black Eagle's scarlet jacket was just behind. He was going well – moving like a machine. I saw Blake, his jockey, watching Chieftain.

For the second time we faced the fence on the hill past the bend. Songstress, a South Australian mare, was a few lengths ahead of mine, and she took off with something running just in front of her. She landed on the fence with a sickening crash, and, smashing down a couple of rails, fell in front of Chieftain just as he took off.

My heart was in my mouth. I made sure I was down, and was ready to leave, but Chieftain made a wonderful leap, and cleared the fallen mare and her rider with plenty to spare. On we went, and as we raced for the wall Black Eagle came with a rush alongside me and headed Chieftain for the wing of the jump. Two or three severe bumps caused him to make a bungling jump of it, but he got over it. Owing to being interfered with he stumbled on landing, and was jumped into by something whose jockey bore a yellow jacket. On to his knees went Chieftain, and it was only by a superhuman effort that I got him right end up again. This foul riding roughed me not a little, and I shouted an angry warning to Black Eagle's rider.

Blake's answer was a lurid curse, and I gave him a wide berth. Racing along the side of the hill yonder, Rob Roy ran off at the jump past the fallen tree, but Tim whipped him around, and sent him at the fence again, and he cleared it, for when passing the Stand for the final round he ran up to us again.

At the pyramid logs the man in yellow had interfered with Chieftain for the second time, nearly succeeding in bringing his own mount down. I meant to have a bitter reckoning with both him and Blake after the race.

The pace had caused an unusual number of falls, and had choked off the bulk of the horses, therefore the survivors were few as we swept up the straight, strangely bunched considering the period of the race. Despite the rough passage he had had, Chieftain was going well, but I did not like to send him along just yet. We were still a long way from home, and the most critical part of the journey was before us.

I intended making my run from the fallen tree. I did not care to call on him to sustain a longer one, but in that final dash meant to race the tails off the others.

At this juncture The Ace, ridden by Merritt – a bad lot – Callboy and Exile were in front, the latter a beaten horse. Then came Chieftain, hard on their heels. Rob Roy raced at Chieftain's girths until nearing the bend, where he dropped back, and Clune, the man in yellow, came alongside me again, and just in front of Rob Roy. 'None of your tricks!' I shouted at him, as a gentle reminder that trouble lay ahead of him if he indulged in any more foul riding.

Chieftain had the rails, but at the bend he ran wide, and Black Eagle slipped up into the position, racing stride for stride with mine. The toilers behind us were all beaten, and I could see that the race lay between Chieftain and Black Eagle. Mikado, Clune's mount, was done, and was being hard ridden to keep him alongside me.

Mikado bored in on Chieftain, and Black Eagle at the same time swung out from the rails. I was nicely trapped, and was wedged in a dangerous position. The beaten Exile blocked the road in front, and with a yell to his jockey to pull out I drove Chieftain forward.

We all seemed to take the fence in a heap, and we got over it, no thanks to Blake and Clune. It is surprising that a smash did not happen, considering the jostling and bumping which occurred.

If Exile had blundered Chieftain must have come to grief. My blood was up. 'You blackguards!' I shouted at Blake and Clune, 'you'll have us all down.'

Exile still blocked the way, but he seemed to have gained a momentary fresh lease of life. He shot forward, and I followed in his wake straight as a die. I could do no other. I had to trust to his getting safely over the wall, for I hadn't room or time to pass him in the short run between the two jumps.

I tried to shake off Black Eagle and Mikado, but they clapped on speed also, and under full sail we dashed recklessly for the wall. I sent Chieftain along for all he was worth. I meant to risk no more bumping, but they were not to be denied, and edged in on either side of me, Clune riding like a butcher boy, hard at it with whip and spur in his desperate effort to keep Mikado alongside Chieftain.

At the wall we went, the three horses running abreast. With Exile out of the way, Chieftain's chance of clearing the wall was a poor one, wedged in as he was between Mikado and Black Eagle; but a sudden glimpse, like a flash of two heels in the air, told me that Exile was down, and I knew that Chieftain's only chance was gone, and I was in for a bad spill.

Black Eagle swerved off to the left and cleared the wall without mishap, only just avoiding the fallen horse though, but the pressure from this quarter was not relieved in time to save Chieftain coming to grief.

He made a gallant effort to get over the wall, but Blake had done his work well, and Clune's desperate riding had enabled him to do his part in the foul deed. Chieftain struck with his fore-legs and turned right over, falling on top of Exile. Luckily I fell clear of him. Mikado, ridden as he was, had no chance of getting over, and fell with a terrible crash, Clune underneath him.

I was scrambling to my feet, dazed and hardly knowing what I was doing or where I was, when crash! came another horse over the fallen Exile, whose neck was broken, and I saw a sight the memory of which unnerves me even now. It was Rob Roy that had come to grief, and as he rolled over I saw poor Tim crushed beneath him in a huddled heap. The horse struggled clear of him, and then I saw Tim's face. O God! it was awful. The short sharp agony of a horrible death was stamped on it – poor Tim's neck was broken.

This terrible shock helped restore my scattered faculties. I staggered and nearly fell. This made me aware that I was grasping something with my right hand, and that that something was slipping from my hold. I had recovered or retained possession of the reins, and Chieftain was pulling back affrightedly from the dead horse.

In an instant, quite mechanically, I tossed the reins over his head, and was in the saddle like a flash. A crowd surged around me; a jumble of sounds rang in my ears. What they were I did not know.

Chieftain seemed to be spinning around and around with me, and the crowd became a black patch with a circle of white faces.

This last fit of dizziness quickly passed off, and then I found that the crowd had opened out before me, and I heard a voice shouting, 'Go on! go on! You can catch 'em. The red 'un's down.'

The red 'un! Ah! that marshalled my ideas in order. The scarlet jacket. Where was it? It must not win. I rode forward. It must be in front of me. Yes! I could see it now, and I gave Chieftain the spur, and up the rise he went towards the hedge. I must have received a pretty smart tap on the head, but as soon as I got going again I began to get a proper grasp of things. I neared the hedge, and could see a black horse on the rise the other side of it, and a scarlet-clad jockey scrambling into the saddle. Black Eagle, then, had fallen. 'Thank God,' I muttered, 'I'll catch him now.' As Chieftain came at the green barrier Blake got Black Eagle going again, and raced for the fallen tree. My brain was clear now, and I anxiously summed up the situation. Could Chieftain win? All the fire and go was knocked out of him, and the scarlet jacket was a long way in front. Could it be caught? Chieftain struggled over the hedge and the fallen tree, and then I could see that there were three or four horses ahead of me, including Black Eagle, and that he was with them. I learned afterwards that the block at the wall had stopped the other stragglers, who were pulled up or ran off. Well it was that Chieftain had no more to beat. He had quite enough to do as it was.

I put the whip on Chieftain. It was like a knife in my heart to do it, but I couldn't help myself. Could whip and spur avail I dared not spare them. The race must be won. Chieftain answered gamely to my call, but it was only a flash in the pan. I was riding a beaten horse, and my heart was like lead within me. My only hope was that the others were in the same plight, for the race had been a severe one.

As the leaders went down the hill yonder I saw Black Eagle go to the front, and Blake was riding him – fool that he was. The others were stopping to nothing, and Black Eagle should have been nursed down that dangerous slope and over that last big fence. Blake's error of judgment, however, would be to my profit, and I exulted. The laugh was not on my side, though. As I passed the others and took second position, I saw Black Eagle footing it merrily down the hill under his big weight, and he safely placed the last jump behind him and rounded the bend for home.

Would Chieftain ever get up to that scarlet jacket dancing so tantalisingly in front? Could he do so I knew he would foot it better. It seemed to be drawing away from me. My God! it was. I drove Chieftain along as fast as he could pace it, emulating

Blake's performance, which I had condemned. I risked a fall over the stiff pyramid. I fully expected to fall there, but to rattle him along was my only chance.

On, Chieftain, on! We must win! The poor brute battles gamely on, but he is like a log under me. Blood will tell, and the stamina inherited from his thoroughbred sire was carrying Chieftain on to the bitter end in this desperate struggle.

The big black fence faces us threateningly, but, thank God! Chieftain proves equal to the task set him. He gets over it, but all the life and spring has left him. He crosses the fence, just touching it, and staggers on landing. I hold him up with a half-thought-of prayer and a muttered curse on my lips. I straighten him, and look for the scarlet jacket. A volume of cheering rolled up the course from the stands, and I knew that it was meant for the favourite. 'I shall win! I shall win!' I told myself fiercely. Black Eagle was toiling on not so far ahead, after all. Those struggling quarters told me he was all out, and I saw him roll in his gallop. Chieftain was rolling like a water-logged ship. Both horses were utterly baked, and no wonder. Their falls, if nothing else, sufficed to take it out of them.

Chieftain seemed to be catching Black Eagle; but it was not so. The scarlet jacket was coming back to us; Chieftain could not go one whit faster, though I urged him on with voice and touch and mesmeric pressure of leg.

We had reached the distance. Three lengths separated us. Inch by inch that space was lessened. At the half distance Chieftain's nose was at Black Eagle's girths.

I heard the roar of the excited onlookers – one vast volume of sound, which seemed powerful enough to topple over the tottering Chieftain. God! was the horse going to fall? A mighty sob burst from him, and he faltered, staggered, recovered himself and battled on. I saw Blake look back and heard him curse. I saw his whip at work dangerously near Chieftain's head.

The horses rolled together. I got my whip ready. Black Eagle fell back, and inch by inch that fatal distance which meant so much was reduced. One loud swell of sound proclaimed that we were level. I saw the judge's box on my right. We were perilously near the post now, and my brain swam. Another instant and up went my arm and down came the whip with one mighty cut.

A convulsive shudder beneath me and desperate plunge forward, two or three faltering strides, a stagger, and Chieftain fell with a crash, several yards past the post. One mighty heave of his foam-covered flanks, a quick, sharp shudder, and life had gone from the gallant bay. I rose to my feet and looked around.

A few paces away stood Black Eagle. He required no pulling up. He had run to a standstill.

I looked at the judge's box. Three numbers were in the hoist beside it. Three white numbers on a black ground, but the first two shone like letters of fire – 5 and 12. God! I might have spared poor Chieftain that last cruel cut. Black Eagle had won the Great Eastern.

The clerk of the course rode alongside Black Eagle and escorted him past the judge's box, and into the weighing enclosure.

I stood staring stupidly at the dead horse. A crowd began to gather. Quickly they were scattered. The scarlet-coated clerk of the course rode up.

'Bring your gear and weigh in,' he said. 'I am representing the steward of the scales. Trooper,' turning to one of the mounted police at hand, 'don't let anyone touch the horse.'

He waited whilst I, unassisted, secured the saddle and bridle, and then escorted me to the scales. I seated myself in the chair. 'Weight,' cried the clerk of the scales tersely, and as I passed from the weighing enclosure a great cheer went up.

Angus McGregor met me. 'Ye're no hurt, ma lad?' he asked anxiously.

'No,' I replied.

'God be thanked!' he said; 'but, ma lad, this is a verra bad business.' 'It will be a very bad business for someone,' I said; and I told him of Tim's death and the incidents of the race.

My news about Tim nigh unmanned him. 'Puir laddie, puir laddie,' was all he could say for some moments, and tears rolled down his cheeks. There were some who called Angus a hard-headed, cold-hearted Scotchman. Those people lied. Beneath his rugged exterior beat a warm, generous heart. The ambulance van had not yet come in with its sad freight. Its harvest for this race was a big one, and it had had to make several journeys.

'We'll bring puir Tim's murderers to boot, ma lad,' he said fiercely. 'No mercy shall be shown the black-hearted villains. We must see to this at once.'

A little later it was known all over the course that a protest had been lodged against the winner for interference, and that Blake, the jockey, by his foul riding, was virtually responsible for Tim Brady's death.

Sensational as had been the race, even more startling and dramatic were the proceedings at the stewards' inquiry. My complaint against Blake and Clune having been recorded, Angus McGregor formally stated the grounds on which he objected to Black Eagle being returned the winner, and in impassioned language charged the two jockeys with being responsible for poor Tim's death.

Blake and Clune had been summoned, and as we awaited their appearance the chairman, addressing Angus McGregor, said: 'You have our sympathy, Mr McGregor, for we fully realise what a terrible shock poor Brady's death must be to you. We deeply deplore it, the more so as the charge of foul riding against Blake and Clune makes the position a most involved and serious one, both for the accused and for we who have to investigate the charge. It is my duty to warn these men of the position in which they stand, for, if they are found guilty of foul riding, the terrible charge of murder may be preferred against them. It is my duty, therefore, as I have said, to warn them against making any statements which may tend to incriminate themselves. I beg of you to be calm, for we dare not listen to your demands for vengeance. We must consider calmly, and investigate without bias or desire to be revenged upon anyone, this charge, and if these men are proven guilty, remember, vengeance is not ours. I sympathise with you, and beg of you to refrain from any further outburst of feeling, and if you do not feel equal to meeting these men unmoved, I think it would be less painful for yourself to retire.'

Poor old Angus, his fiery Celtic nature had been fully roused by the dastardly scheme which had resulted in the death of poor Tim, and lost him his two horses, Chieftain and Rob Roy, for the latter had sustained such injuries in his fall that the friendly bullet had been requisitioned to put him out of his misery. His anger had run away with his characteristic caution and reason, and the kindly rebuke of the chairman recalled him to himself. By a great effort he calmed himself.

Blake made his appearance still in his colours, and his face was white as that of a corpse. He had pulled his cap down so that the long scarlet peak shaded his face, and he did not look up when the chairman spoke to him. A doctor accompanied him, who stated that Clune was unable to attend. 'He has not long been brought in by the ambulance van,' he said, 'and he is still unconscious. He is being examined by Dr C—, and I fear he is dying.'

This startling news was a shock for everyone. 'My God! this is awful,' said the chairman. He then addressed Blake.

'Blake,' he said, 'the charge of foul riding in the race just run has been laid against yourself and Clune by Dalton. He alleges that you, in conjunction with Clune on Mikado, interfered with Chieftain several times during the course of the race, and that such interference caused Chieftain to fall, losing him the race. By this interference Rob Roy was also brought to grief, and in view of his rider, Brady, having been killed, it is my duty to caution you that your position is a grave one. To put it plainly, you stand accused of foul riding, and in the event of this being proven against you, you may be brought before another tribunal upon a far more serious charge. Therefore you are now before us, to a certain extent, as a person suspected of the graver offence, which it is not necessary for me to specify, and I am on that account warranted in intimating to you that you need not make any statement which you think might incriminate yourself.

'At the same time, do not think for a moment that in thus cautioning you we are prejudiced against you, or predisposed to think you guilty. It is an axiom of British fair play and justice that a man is innocent until proven guilty, and this hearing will be a thoroughly impartial one.'

I then gave my evidence. A strange revulsion of feeling had set in, and I shrank from bearing such damning testimony against a dying man, as the doctor had reported Clune to be, and as to

Blake, I felt a strange pity for him in his desperate position. I guessed that Howard Fane was the villain behind the scenes, who had worked these poor puppets to his will, and here again I felt tongue-tied. Did I denounce him, Hilda Maynard's name would probably be dragged into the miserable affair. I was sore put to it to endeavour to expose him and shield her; to punish the master villain and spare his poor tools, scoundrels though they were.

Vengeance would not bring poor Tim back to life. I am afraid I gave my evidence in a halting manner, as I was dragged this way and that between these conflicting emotions, for the chairman questioned me sharply several times.

Suddenly the whole matter of levelling accusations was taken from me in a startling and impressively dramatic manner.

Dr C— entered the room hurriedly. He seemed excited, and, speaking rapidly, said: 'Gentlemen, I am compelled to thus unceremoniously interrupt this inquiry, and I regret the necessity. Clune has regained consciousness, and knowing that he is dying, insists on being brought here. He was conscious for a few moments after being picked up, and he and the unfortunate Brady were brought in together. He knows of Brady's death, and we have had a terrible scene with him. He has been calling himself a murderer, and his cries and frenzies have been awful to hear and witness. These paroxysms have now passed, and he is sinking fast. He may not live another quarter of an hour. He says he must be brought here that he may unburden his mind. He has made several important statements, and I think it only right that you should hear him. It will also be a humane act to let him unburden his conscience, for it may make his end easier. I have ordered him to be brought here. He has alleged many things against Mr Howard Fane, who is, no doubt, well known to you all, and I think that that gentleman should be present if you have the power to call him, though Clune must not see him, for that would probably bring on another violent paroxysm, which would hasten the poor fellow's end.'

As the doctor ceased speaking the door was pushed open, and two of the hospital attendants carefully carried into the room a stretcher, upon which lay the still, motionless form of the dying jockey. It needed but a glance at the ghastly face, the crushed and mangled figure, to show that the doctor's words were only too true. Clune's case was hopeless. The yellow jacket, blood-stained and torn, was unbuttoned, and the sheet covering his body having become disarranged, the fearful nature of Clune's injuries were too plainly manifest. His chest was literally crushed in, and it was a matter for wonder that he still survived.

But for a quiver of the eyelids, and the faint, incessant moans of the sufferer as he gasped his life away, life to all other appearances might have already fled. A shudder ran through the assembly, and many eyes were averted from the soul-sickening sight.

Blake staggered as though about to fall, and someone led him to a chair. He collapsed into it with a groan, and sat with bowed figure and his face buried in his hands. Gently the bearers lowered the stretcher.

A louder groan from the dying man, and then the poor blood-stained lips moved as if speaking. Several unintelligible words, and then gaspingly and chokingly, but audible to all, the half-conscious man spoke: 'That – that's right. I – I'll ride him – down.' Then in louder tones: 'Blake must win – must win, I tell you!' and an intense shudder ran through the crushed frame, as though the maimed and broken strength struggled to reassert itself. A meaningless mumble of words, and then Clune's eyes slowly opened. He looked at the faces bent over him, a frightened expression in his eyes.

'I – I didn't mean to kill Tim,' he gasped faintly. 'Look, look at me; I am dying, and – and I want to tell you – tell you the truth. It was Fane – Fane, I tell you, made me do it.'

The doctor, bending over the stretcher, moistened Clune's lips with brandy and water, and the poor fellow seemed to gain strength from the kindly attention. His voice was stronger and clearer, and he seemed to be mustering all the energies fast slipping from him, that he might denounce the man who had urged him to his ruin and death.

At this moment there was a bustle at the door, and I was surprised to see Howard Fane enter the room, accompanied by a race-course detective, who had been sent to ask his presence.

Fane, as a person of no small importance in the racing world, dared not refuse this request, and no doubt he had decided to put

233

a bold face on the matter, for he must have guessed that Clune intended divulging everything. It was better that he should know the full extent of the danger that threatened him. He was cool and calm, and I give him credit for his self-possession. He remained in the background, so that Clune should not see him.

In faint and faltering tones the jockey spoke. 'I will tell you the truth,' he said; 'I am done for, and it's no use hiding anything. I did my best to bring Chieftain down several times during the race, and I succeeded at the wall. I've settled myself, and I deserve it. I've killed Tim Brady. He was a good pal of mine, and I swear before God that I wouldn't have hurt a hair of his head. I had no choice in this matter. Fane urged me to throw Chieftain down, and I couldn't refuse to do his dirty work. He had me under his thumb. Make him suffer for this. He is a devil!

'I can't tell you now the power he had over me. My time is short, and I want you to know of Fane's share in this business. I fouled my hands for him years ago, and he has held me in his clutches ever since. I've tried to go straight – God knows I've tried – but this pitiless devil was not to be shaken off, and he has ruined me.

'A week or so ago he told me that he wanted Chieftain taken care of in the race, and I refused to do any more crook work for him. He threatened that if he could not get Dalton to pull the horse he would fall back on me to help his plans along, and if I failed him he would put the police on to my track for the old job, the consequences of which he has long threatened me with. This cowed me. I knew I had a poor chance of winning on Mikado, and he promised to pay me well if I prevented Chieftain scoring. I was to ride in Black Eagle's interests, and assist Blake all I could.

'When he found he could not get at Dalton he tackled me again. He had suddenly developed a bitter hatred against Dalton, and said he hoped that he would break his neck when Chieftain fell. I was forced to do Fane's bidding, and Blake and I laid our plans; but he dared not risk bringing Black Eagle down, so could not help me much to interfere with Chieftain.

We closed in on him at the wall, and that settled him. If Exile had got over all right it would have made no difference; Chieftain must have fallen. I hated to do this, God knows, for I'm not all bad. That d—d scoundrel Fane is Tim Brady's murderer as much as I!'

Clune was speaking clearly now and excitedly. He had struggled on to his side, and his face was turned eagerly to the chairman. His eyes burned brightly, and were fixed with an intensity of gaze on the chairman's face.

'I want justice to be done,' he said. 'Remember, it is a dying man asks you. Justice on Howard Fane. He is a murderer. I accuse him with my dying breath. He killed Tim Brady, and he should suffer as I suffer now. Where is he? Why is he not here to face me? He daren't come, the coward, the villain! Howard Fane, *alias* Harley Brookes, the swell swindler. Ha! ha! that's torn his mask off. Now you all know him. Harley Brookes the forger and Howard Fane the murderer are one—'

'Gentlemen, this man is dying, but I cannot stand quietly by and listen to these outrageous, amazing accusations without denying them. In common justice to myself I must here and now deny them absolutely. The man is mad.'

Howard Fane had stepped forward, stung to action by the lash of the jockey's tongue.

'Stand back,' said the doctor abruptly, stepping forward so as to prevent Clune seeing Fane, and motioning Fane back. 'For God's sake, think of the condition of this poor fellow! This is no time for argument.'

The doctor's action was futile. The effect of Fane's voice on Clune was electrical.

'Brandy, doctor; give me brandy quickly!' he cried. 'O God! I want my strength to face this cowardly hound.'

The doctor sprang hastily to his side. He moistened Clune's lips with the reviving spirit, and allowed him to take a little. The flame of life sprang up again, but it was a dying flicker. The end was plainly near. Blood flecked his lips, and Death looked from his eyes.

'Speak, speak!' he cried. 'Where are you? O God! I can't see. Yes, yes! I see you now. Raise me, doctor, I – I want him to see me. Let him look on his work. See, you devil! Look at me, crushed to my death doing your foul work. Go yonder and see poor Brady. His death, too, is on your hands. Ah! you may well shrink from me – you murderer! Thank God! I'm out of your power now. You've run your course, and your punishment is near at hand – oh, doctor! the pain – the pain. Hold me, I'm falling – fall—'

Clinging to the doctor in his dying agony, Clune drew himself into a sitting posture. For a brief moment he held himself thus, his face wrung with pain, and his glazing eyes fixed appealingly on the doctor's face; then, with a long-drawn-out moan of intense anguish, ending with a rush of blood from his mouth, his nerveless hands loosed their hold, and he fell back dead.

For several moments everyone seemed spellbound, deeply affected by the painful scene just passed; then the doctor quietly and reverently covered the still figure of the dead jockey with a white sheet, and drawing a screen before the stretcher, hid it from our view.

'For God's sake let me get away from here!' gasped Blake, breaking the silence, and staggering to the foot of the table around which the stewards were seated. His face was ghastly, and it was clear that Clune's awful end had made a deep impression on him, and had broken down his nerve completely.

He trembled violently, and clung to the table with one hand as though to steady himself. With the other hand pointing to the screen-hidden stretcher with its sad burden, he cried, in a hurried torrent of words:

'He said what was true. I will make a clean breast of everything. I admit that I interfered with Chieftain, and it was at the instigation of Fane, as Clune has told you.'

'You're an infernal liar!' said Fane passionately, starting forward as though to strike Blake.

The detective interposed, seizing Fane's uplifted arm. 'Hands off!' said Fane, with an oath, and shaking himself free.

'Mr Fane,' said the chairman severely, 'I must ask you to remember where you are. These proceedings have been of an exceptionally painful nature. Please do not make them more so by a repetition of such abuse or conduct.'

An angry exclamation broke from Howard Fane. 'You're mighty high-handed,' he said. 'It is a pity you do not expend your energies in the proper direction. I came here to defend myself against false and malicious accusations, and I have been accused of various atrocious acts which I have denied, and now deny again. The lying scoundrel who endeavoured to clear himself at my expense, and who could quote nothing to prove his charges, is dead, and I forgive him his endeavour to injure me. This man, for some reason best known to himself, is taking up the same tale, and is it any wonder that I strongly resent it?

'The dead are beyond our reach, but Blake will learn to his cost that he cannot make false accusations of this serious nature against me with impunity. It is your duty to protect me from insult, and to warn him to desist. I resent the tone of this inquiry towards me. Ever since I've been in the room I've been ordered to do this, or requested to do that. Why! were I guilty of these amazing charges I could not have been treated more brusquely.'

'A moment,' said the chairman, rising. 'You are a racing man, an owner of repute, and being, by the confession of that dead jockey, involved in this very serious affair you come under our jurisdiction. Recognising this, you will see that had you been ordered as you say, we should not have been exceeding our powers. You have, however, been treated with all courtesy, and in making this frivolous objection, and by your unseemly conduct and language of a moment ago, you are prolonging these painful proceedings.

'Blake will now resume giving his evidence. When he has finished you may question him if you wish to do so. If you interrupt him again, especially in such unseemly manner, or threaten him, we shall deal summarily with you. As a friend, I advise you that your conduct is not in your best interests.'

'You are biassed against me,' said Fane angrily, 'and I protest that this inquiry is not a fair one.'

'It is perfectly fair,' replied the chairman, 'and you have brought this censure upon yourself. Now, Blake, you may go on.'

'I ain't afraid of Fane's threats,' said Blake. 'He is afraid of what I may say about him, and so threatens me, thinking I may hold my tongue. He can do his worst for all I care. I'm going to tell all I know. It is no good me keeping my tongue quiet. I've helped to do mischief enough, and I'll now try to right things a bit.

'Mr Fane wrote to me between a week and a fortnight ago, saying that he had backed Black Eagle to win him a mint of money, and promising if I won the race he would give me £100. I've got that letter. I knew Mr Fane pretty well. A night or two after that I met him in town, and over drinks we had a pitch about the race. We reckoned Black Eagle a good thing bar one, and that was Chieftain, and I told Fane this. He said he knew it, but thought he could make it all right with Dalton to pull Chieftain. "If I can't," he said, "we must trust to luck to knock him over."

'After a bit he asked me point-blank if I would work in with someone else, and shepherd Chieftain so as to put him out of the running. I refused, but he held out such inducements that at length I told him I would do what he wanted. He then told me that Clune would assist me. Some days later I saw him again, and he then told me that Dalton had refused to pull Chieftain, and that if Black Eagle did not win he was ruined. He said that Clune and I must adopt no half measures, and that if we knocked Chieftain endways, and Dalton too, he would be better pleased, and we were promised a big figure for our work.

'Clune and I put our heads together. Mikado was as safe as a church, but had no pace. I reckon he ran the race of his life today. Clune must have punished him terribly to keep him with the field. I know that Clune had interfered with Chieftain several times without much success. I took a lot of risk at the wall, and Black Eagle was nearly down. This, I think, made him fall at the hedge. Chieftain would have won easily but for his fall. Poor Clune was afraid of Fane. He told me that Fane had ruined him, and was holding some threat over him to force him to carry out his designs against Chieftain. That is all I have to say, and every word of it is true.'

'It is a parcel of lies,' said Fane angrily.

'It is the truth,' said Blake, in ringing tones, drawing himself up and facing Fane defiantly, 'and it will finish the work that Clune started – settle your hash once for all, my fine gentleman.'

'By heaven! you shall pay dearly for this,' said Fane excitedly, completely losing his self-possession, and forgetting his surroundings.

He sprang forward and grappled with Blake. Blake struck at him as Fane's hands sought his throat. The suddenness of the attack enabled Fane to have things all his own way for a moment.

His superior strength fought down the jockey's opposition, and he gripped Blake's throat in a savage clutch, and ere he could be torn from his victim, had given the jockey more than a taste of the horror of death by strangulation. Almost simultaneously with Fane's attack the detective had rushed forward, and with assistance he succeeded in wrenching Fane's hands from Blake's throat.

As the jockey staggered back, bearing unmistakable marks of that steel-like clutch upon his throat, Fane, jerking his right arm free, dealt him a smashing blow full in the face and Blake dropped like a log.

Fane struggled with his captors, and in a moment the detective snapped the twitches on to his wrist, and he was helpless. Like a trapped wolf he glared about him. His violent rage was in marvellous contrast to the wonderful self-possession he had exhibited on entering the room. His face was deathly white, and distorted by his passion.

'Curse you all!' he said, writhing ineffectually to get free. 'This is a damned trap. You give ready ears to lies, and when I punish the liar treat me like a dingo. Damn you, let me go! let me go, I say!' and he struggled again with the detective. Smart manipulation of the twitches, however, made him as helpless as a child.

I expected to see him have a fit, his rage was so great; but that did not happen. Finding that his struggles availed him nothing, he gradually became quieter, though in a sullen mood.

In the meantime the stewards had deprived Black Eagle of the race, and awarded it to Chieftain. When this was announced a great cheer went up outside. Then the chairman addressed Howard Fane again:

'Mr Fane,' he said, 'your violent temper is getting you into sad trouble. It is terrible to see a gentleman of your position acting thus. Your hasty, ill-judged accusations we overlook. We have here two letters, undisputably yours, which have just been found in a pocket of Clune's coat. They support the affirmations of Blake and Clune, and prove clearly the despicable part you have played in this terrible affair. Your deliberate plot to overthrow Chieftain has caused a terrible loss of life. As to that, it is out of our province to deal with you.

'Such men as you disgrace and degrade a noble sport, and we have decided to punish you severely. In the face of the damning evidence we have here, your denial is utterly futile. Howard Fane, you are warned off during the stewards' pleasure, and that decision will be endorsed by every club and every supporter of the turf in Australia. You will be escorted off the course at once. You may release Mr Fane, Mr R—.'

Fane said not a word. He drew himself up, shot a glance of malignant fury around the room, turned on his heel, and escorted by the detective, disappeared. I did not see him again. That evening he shot himself at his hotel in Adelaide.

Blake, dazed by the blow Fane had dealt him, again stood at the foot of the table, and received his sentence of banishment for life from turf affairs without seeming to comprehend its significance.

At the inquest upon poor Tim and Clune some quibble arose, and Blake escaped further punishment in connection with the affair. It was a sad party returned to Glen Park. Hilda Maynard lived at Glen Park for some time after our return, and was married from there to a countryman of ours who was touring the colonies. He was a sterling young fellow, and literally worshipped her. In her new home in the dear old country his love should compensate for the sadness of a portion of her life out here.

Nat Wedgewood Trapped

JACK FAIRFAX-BLAKEBOROUGH

While arguments will always go on as to who was the best jockey, in fictional terms Nat Wedgewood was probably the most popular rider with readers of racing fiction during the years between the two World Wars. Wedgewood was no traditional hero, however, but a man beginning to show his years and prone to become involved, sometimes unwittingly, sometimes not, in the seamier side of racing. His inside information about the track was unsurpassed, and though he found it increasingly difficult to obtain good rides, could still be relied upon to find a way to get to the bottom of a mystery and help prevent the nobbling of favourites or the fixing of races. Nat's creator, Jack Fairfax-Blakeborough (1881–1975) was one of the foremost sporting writers of his day and the author of a number of now much-collected books including *The Analysis of the Turf* (1927), *Turf's Who's Who* (1932) and *Paddock Personalities* (1935), not to mention a dozen novels based upon his intimate knowledge of the turf with titles like *The Last Gamble* (1930) and *Beating the Nobbler* (1934). Apart from the books about Nat Wedgewood, he wrote several stories about another memorable character, Colonel Jasper Bellew, a prominent figure in racing circles whose well-to-do appearance belies a cunning mind and devious nature.

Fairfax-Blakeborough was born of 'racing blood' at Guisborough in Yorkshire where his father, a passionate racegoer, tried to support his family by writing plays and novels about the turf. As his son was to note years later, 'When I was born my father was busy writing a really good sporting play called *Tomboy* and a novel entitled *More Than A Dream* – but he lost a pot of money over both.'

Not deterred by this example, the young Fairfax-Blakeborough became an expert steeplechaser before he reached his teens and then tried to join the racing stables run by the renowned Jack Walton. Frustrated in this ambition, he instead got employment on the *North Eastern Gazette*, where he was assigned to write a weekly column for the sports section. From covering local meetings, he soon graduated to the bigger national events and after 1906 until his death aged ninety-three wrote probably more words about the sport than anyone before or since. He also rarely passed up an opportunity to ride; became noted as a trainer; and in time was something of a legend among his friends for 'riding all day and writing all night.'

Jack's journalism brought him into regular contact with the 'flotsam and jetsam of the turf', as he called them, who, suitably encouraged by a bottle or two, gave him the raw material from which he later fashioned his crime and mystery novels. Nat Wedgewood, his best creation, was partly based on a real person, the Northern steeplechase jockey, Harry Taylor, 'who gave me much interesting detail regarding his experiences on the turf and in racing stables where the conditions were anything but a bed of roses,' Jack recalled in his memoirs, *Sporting Days and Sporting Stories* (1925). 'Nat Wedgwood Trapped' (1933) is a typical episode in the life of the browbeaten jockey, though different from most in that it brings him into contact with his creator's other character, Colonel Bellew. The pages which follow offer a reminder of Wedgewood's adventures which were, for a time, as popular as those by Nat Gould – who was, in fact, one of Fairfax-Blakeborough's friends and may well have given him advice on the writing of his 'turf thrillers'.

*

The station platform was crowded for the South train after Pickford Races. For once a railway company had really displayed some intelligent interest in racing, and allowed those going South to get away within half an hour of the last race instead of keeping them hanging about for an hour or more. The South express was being stopped at Pickford, through which it usually screams its disdain of such small stations. It was the usual racing crowd which waited on the platform. Apart from their field-glasses, the bookmakers' clerks carrying easels, jockeys, trainers, and owners whose faces are familiar to Tom, Dick, and Harry through the frequency with which their portraits appear in the sporting papers, there is no mistaking a body of Turf regulars. There is an indescribable, indelible stamp upon them which marks the majority as connected with racing. A number of bookmakers and their satellites were bombarding the refreshment room, whose staff and capacity was unequal to the occasion. The attendants had completely lost their heads and seemed to be walking round each other in circles, getting more and more bewildered as the friendly banter of their waiting customers increased. There is perhaps no class – certainly not professional humorists – who are possessed of more spontaneous wit or can cause more laughter than those whose business it is to 'travel the meetings.' Sometimes their jokes are too pointedly personal to be in good taste, sometimes they are strongly flavoured with sarcasm, but this disregard of the feelings of others does not alter the fact that there is a keen sense of humour in the makeup of the average racing man, and that he has a mind which works rapidly and a tongue which can equally quickly express his thoughts and sharpened wit. All of them are trained to be observant, many of them are clever mimics, most of them possess a self-confidence and self-reliance which make them able to hold their own in a crowd of any character. They are not easily squashed, snubbed, or restrained from securing what they believe to be their rights, or from obtaining such comfort or desirable places as may be going, either in trains, queues, or elsewhere.

Whilst some of the cheaper ring layers and their staffs were making the little station ring with their voices and laughter as they heckled and completely bamboozled the stout lady and her two even slower assistants behind the refreshment-room counter, Nathan Wedgewood paced up and down the far end of the platform with those quick, short steps which are a characteristic of many men who have spent much of their lives in racing stables. Nathan is 'getting on.' He prefers not to discuss his age and is irritated by the frequent references made to him by Turf correspondents as 'a veteran jockey,' 'one of the old school,' 'a doyen,' and so on. No one knew better than he did that he was riding before many of the other jockeys of to-day were born or thought of. The fact was cruelly impressed upon him day by day when he stood about weighing-room doors waiting for rides which didn't come. He knew he was looked upon and treated as a light of other days, and as each spring has come round for the last four or five years he has wondered if his licence *would* be granted, and if it was worth his while taking out a licence, supposing one would be granted. He was not too well off. Money he had saved and invested in his palmy days had gone west, and other investments in a direction not wise for a jockey to say anything about in view of the Jockey Club's rule (printed on each jockey's licence, but not to be found in the decrees printed in the book *Calendar*) regarding jockeys making bets, had not yet turned up trumps. So he found himself at nearer fifty than forty, without sufficient to live on, unable to shake off the lure of racing and the old 'here to-day and gone to-morrow' life, yet hardly making more by his profession than will pay his expenses. Often he went to a meeting for one ride in the hope that he might get others, only to find that the hope did not materialise and that his fee for the single mount did not do more than pay his railway fare, let alone his hotel bill. Gradually he has found it absolutely necessary to discontinue his patronage of the best hotels at which he had always stayed, and to find cheaper places, even 'a private lodge,' where possible. This was galling, but an essential economy when he found that he could neither afford the charges of 'the flash places' nor to join in with either the extravagances or quite ordinary expenditure of his brother jockeys staying at them. Boxes at the theatres, taxis here and taxis there, billiards for high stakes, fizz, expensive cigars, and all manner of impetuous schemes for amusement all cost money – often a considerable sum. The game may be worth the candle to those who want to live every minute of a short life and a merry one, but Nathan no longer had the candle to burn. As a matter of fact, he never was really a roysterer, or one of the 'easy come, easy go' brigade. When he had it he was always willing to stand his corner, but he never threw money about as though there was no end to it. Indeed, Nathan was always considered to be a shrewd, level-headed, quiet, decent living jockey, and many were of the opinion that he was pretty warm at his bankers. If they could have read his mind as he walked quickly to and fro, keeping away from the crowd at Pickford station on the afternoon our story opens, they would have been disillusioned.

Nathan Wedgewood was cogitating whether to leave the regular game and turn to pony racing, as some others of the older generation had done, or whether to go over to Belgium, Denmark, or somewhere else on the Continent to try his luck there. He had been two days at Pickford and not had a single ride. It was Saturday, he'd been racing five days and only had one mount during the whole of the five. Careful as he had been – cheap tickets, five meals at the expense of race executives, and staying at temperance hotels, his total expenses since leaving home on Monday afternoon had been £5 15s. 9d., including his present to the valet who looked after him. Three pounds from £5 15s. 9d. left a balance on the wrong side of £2 15s. 9d. He'd better have stayed at home, he thought. But there was the difficulty. He couldn't stay at home. He was still full of energy and considered himself to be as good as ever he was.

There is no more lamentable thing than a man who has been a bold horseman, finds himself compelled to admit that his nerve is gone, without it be the horseman who has lost his dash and courage and won't acknowledge it even to himself. Some of the latter take 'jumping powder' in the shape of brandy, a few even resort to the needle and dope themselves. Many of us have seen those jaundice-eyed, arm-mottled, half-dazed looking individuals who, in the aftermath, pay such a heavy penalty for their Dutch courage.

Truth to tell, there has never been any sign that Nathan Wedgewood has lost his dash, or that increasing years have made him either slow at jumping off, or careful at the turns. He has never been chary of getting up on some horses with the reputation for cold backs, taking charge of the man on the top, or being difficult in some other direction. Rather the contrary; and it is often said that 'Nat will ride anything.' It is, however, good horses which make good jockeys in the eyes of all but those few who can sometimes see better horsemanship on the part of the rider who manages to get second or third than that displayed on the winner.

On this particular afternoon Nathan was depressed, and not without cause. When it is made brutally clear to a man that he is considered a back number in any walk of life it hurts, no matter how long an innings he has had. It hurts all the more when it is a question of bread and butter with him that he should continue in his profession. As he was pacing up and down with his hands thrust into his smartly-cut, but growing shabby, top-coat pockets, Issy Salvo, well-known in England, Ireland, and on the Continent as a professional backer, a paddock personality, and rather a mystery merchant to boot, saw him and joined him in his 'sentry-go.'

'How are things, Nat?' asked Issy.

'Rotten! Couldn't be worse!' was the reply.

'There are a few of the boys on this train,' said Issy. 'Better come in with us. We've got a porter squared to lock us into a carriage.'

'The boys don't bother me,' answered Wedgewood. 'I've never known them go through a jockey yet. They wouldn't get much if they did go through my pockets. I'm broke to the wide! Stoney!'

'Better come in with us, anyhow,' repeated Issy. 'We were talking about you yesterday and thought you'd be on the train. As a matter of fact, I've been looking for you on the platform to get hold of you.'

'Who's *us*?' demanded Nathan. 'I'm no good for cards. Couldn't pay if I lost.'

'No, we don't want any cards,' said Issy. 'We want a little talk. We might put something in your way so that you'd make a bit.'

'Who's *we*?' again asked Nat rather irritably.

'Oh, the Colonel, Mo Kelly, Bob Durkin, and Ray Lint.'

'Nice school that to travel with! I'd almost as soon travel with "the boys!" ' exclaimed Nathan, laughing.

'They're all right,' retorted Issy, 'and they've got some money behind them – three of 'em, anyhow – although they've been going bad lately with so many favourites winning. We've got one or two little schemes which are money for nothing. Come on, here's the train. We've got to get in at the back end. Some extra carriages have been put on there, and they'll be locked. There's Mo and Bob, Ray will be somewhere handy, and there's the porter we've squared.'

The two men walked towards the porter, who gave them a broad wink. As the train drew up Ray Lint joined them, having Colonel Jasper Bellew in his company. There was the usual mad rush for carriages, the usual yelling for missing friends, or those seen making a dash to get into compartments with 6 to 4 against their chance. Awaiting his opportunity the porter opened an empty carriage, and when the six men had hastily scrambled in, locked the door. He knew that many racing men carry a door-key to lock or unlock doors at will when travelling. So the porter remained on guard till the last of the dashers up and down had found a seat.

'We're in luck's way for once!' remarked Colonel Bellew. 'That porter ought to be made a station master or a director or something! He's about the only one I've ever struck with any intelligence.'

'You know Colonel Bellew?' asked Issy Salvo, looking towards Nathan Wedgewood.

'Who doesn't?' laughed Nat, making a movement as though to raise his hat without actually doing so. The very action was evidence of the jockey's estimate of the Colonel. It is the same with hunt servants. A stranger who arrives early at a fixture of hounds and watches the arrival of each new-comer can form a pretty accurate idea of the social position, the amount of subscription, and importance of every individual by the mode of reception by the staff. There is the sweeping salute of caps for peers who are considerable landowners, almost an equal sweep to the principal supporters and covert owners, hats raised to other big subscribers, caps touched deliberately to those whose cheques are small, hands raised to caps to those who cannot be ignored but who give no presents at Christmas and either can't or don't pay much for the fun they enjoy, and a more or less familiar nod to farmers, puppy walkers, and others. Every one who goes racing regularly knows Colonel Bellew. He is one of those well-born men who, after leaving the service, find themselves at a loose end, take to the Turf, and eventually make, or try to make, racing a source of income. Some of them become trainers, some act as advisers and managers for young men just starting on a Turf career, or too much engaged with other concerns to be bothered with the detail of racing. Yet others represent big S. P. houses (and do a little touting for wine merchants into the bargain). There is a small remaining percentage who live by their wits, and seem to sharpen and use them so well that they prove quite a profitable commodity on the market both to themselves and others. Of this genus was Colonel Bellew. Some of those high up in the social scale are still quite ready to chat with him and pick his brains, or to employ him to work commissions for them, to bid up a horse after a seller, to engage them a jockey, and on occasion to help them to saddle a horse. Despite the fact that he has some decidedly questionable friends and associates in the paddock and ring, he is recognised as such a power on the Turf that, though he has fallen from grace in many social circles, he is not a man it is considered safe to quarrel with. He may be useful any day, and, even if not used, it is not desirable to have him in opposition in view of his rumoured powerful string pulling in quarters that matter.

It was therefore merely to get the two into conversation that Issy Salvo said to Nathan Wedgewood, 'You know Colonel Bellew?' When the jockey had answered, 'Who doesn't?' and made the abortive movement to raise his hat, the Colonel said:

'You've been riding a long time now, Wedgewood. You must be one of the oldest jockeys holding a licence.'

Nathan rather squirmed in his corner seat. Here was some one else reminding him that he was getting into the sere and yellow.

'There's some older than me,' he replied. 'I could mention a few. A man's as old as he feels, and when a jockey gets past mark of mouth, he's rather like the ladies, Colonel, he doesn't like it rubbing in. It's all these bits in the paper about the older jockeys being veterans, as old as Adam, and all that rot, that makes people frightened to put them up. There's some of the old 'uns could ride a lot of these ruddy kids' heads off. I've seen two or three races this week tossed away by putting weak kids up. They've let their horses beat themselves because they hadn't the strength to hold them together or take a pull at 'em.'

'I saw one race absolutely flung away,' agreed Issy. 'The kid was stone cold long before his horse was beat. He would have won ten minutes with a man on his back. I wouldn't back him when I saw on the board a little apprentice was riding him. I knew he wasn't a kid's horse. He takes hold, and what's more, when Joe Clayton rode him he told me he had to carry his head all the way round. I told Mo he could make his book for him if he liked as he hadn't an earthly with a kid on top.'

'I took your tip,' remarked Mo. 'It was a good race for me, was that.'

'I could tell you two other races that were thrown away this week just as glaring as that was!' exclaimed Nat. 'Still, they goes on putting kids up what haven't the experience or the head-piece of some of us what's forgotten more than they'll ever know.'

'You haven't had many rides lately,' said the Colonel.

'No,' agreed Nat; 'and most of those I *have* had have been '"dead meat" what doesn't do a jockey any good. It's a bad job when a jockey gets a name for only riding stumours, horses which aren't fit, or are only having an outing to get farther down the handicap. He seems to get nothing else to ride after a bit, and then people begin to ask, "How long is it since he rode a winner?" and to say he's in the bookmakers' pockets, or he's never on anything that's intended to win or that has an earthly. I can tell you I'm about fed up with the game and only wish I could chuck it.'

'We were talking about you this morning,' broke in Colonel Bellew.

'So *you* were among the *we*, were you?' said Nat, in a tone of voice which might have been considered bordering on either suspicion or insolence.

'Yes. We happened to travel up to Pickford together,' replied the colonel, 'and both Mo and Ray here said they'd been hard hit lately—'

'And what about me, guv'nor?' interrupted Bob Durkin. 'Don't forget your humble! I've not had a winning meeting this month, and can't get any of the money in that's owing to me either. There's one or two will find themselves in the black list if they don't part before the end of next week. It's getting serious, I can tell you. There's one party I could name what's got into my ribs to nearly three hundred of the best, and to-day I see'd him taking his ready money to Josh Timkins. I sent my runner after him to say I wanted a word with him. But did he come? Not blooming likely. That's the way some of these toffs treats you. They bets on the nod till you won't stand them no more, and when you sends the wire round that they're defaulting, then they goes to some one else with their ready and leaves you to whistle. I'll fetch one or two of them to their milk in a day or two, mark my words!'

'I'm glad I don't owe you anything, Bob,' said the Colonel, 'if you're in that frame of mind.'

'We know you always *do* settle, Colonel,' remarked Durkin. 'There's no one standing up but what's willing to wait till it's convenient for you to pay up. It's these toffs what's in such a big hurry to receive when they're winning and what's quite impident if you tackle them for some money on account when they're losing, what gets my goat.'

'Well,' resumed Colonel Bellew, directing his conversation to Nathan Wedgewood, 'as we came up this morning I just happened to say how easily it could be worked to get hold of a few hundreds amongst us next week at Toxton. We could work it without any one being hurt in any way, and without any one doing anything wrong. Simple as A B C. I have registered authority to act for one or two owners, and could work it myself, but as we said this morning there's Nat there not been going too good, we'll bring him into this and one or two other little schemes we have in our minds, and let him have a share of the doings. What do you say, Nat?'

'I says nothing till I knows what you're driving at,' replied the jockey. 'I don't want to be mixed up in no twisting games.'

'Oh, Nat! Don't mention such a thing as twisting!' exclaimed Issy Salvo, feigning both surprise and hurt feelings. 'You know as well as I do that Mo, Ray, and Bob here, are amongst the biggest men in the ring. They bet to money and – well, what is it you have printed on your cards, Ray?'

'Civility, honesty, punctual payments,' was the reply.

'Yes, that's it! Civility, honesty, and punctual payments,' repeated Salvo. 'That applies to all of us,' he added. 'As you know, Nat, none of us can afford to do anything that even sails near the wind.'

'Don't you mean that you can't afford to be found out?' asked Nathan, smiling and giving Issy a broad wink. 'I could tell a little tale about some one offering a jockey a hundred pounds on Edinburgh platform not to be in the first three on a certain horse trained in Yorkshire. When he found he couldn't win he was sorry he hadn't taken it!'

'Don't tell tales out of school,' remarked Mo with a forced laugh. 'I know who you're getting at. A certain party would be better if he kept his mouth shut, or others might open theirs about him. He's no blooming saint and he's ridden for the books more than once. I know that for a fact!'

'I don't dispute it,' retorted Nat; 'but you won't find a jockey who has any sense or who values his reputation or future who'll be so mad as to be in the pockets of bookmakers. More than half the talk about jockeys riding for the books is all me eye and Betty Martin. Who's going to keep a jockey when he's warned off? The bookies won't and jockeys know it. All these tales about pulling horses and Johnnie Armstrong is Thomas Rot. Most jockeys are only too keen to win. There may be an odd case when we're told a horse isn't fit, and that they daren't back him, so don't want him in the first three, that we ride accordingly, but even then most jockeys would win if they found they had a chance, though they put those they're riding for in the cart.'

'We needn't discuss the morality of jockeys any more now, I think,' said Colonel Bellew. 'According to many people all those who are in any way connected with racing are deep-dyed villains, and racing itself a twist from beginning to end. Now let's get down to tin-tack business. At Toxton next week Billy Shales has Dirblew in a handicap with top weight on. He's in another handicap with four pounds less to carry on the same day at the other meeting. I happen to know he's going to send Dirblew to Toxton the day before and have him reported an arrival there. Then the following morning he's going to slip him away to the other meeting and run him there. He could probably win either race, but it's a certainty at the other meeting. Now, on the book, with Dirblew out of the way, it's a good thing for Callist. Dirblew would be certain to open out favourite with Callist second favourite at two or three to one. If Dirblew's name could go into the frame with Paddy Black as his jockey – he's ridden him in all his races, you know – we could snap up all the twos and threes, p'raps more, before it was found out that Dirblew was a non-runner. He'd be a red-hot favourite, wouldn't he, Mo?'

'Yes! He'd be certain to open out favourite. It would be three or four to one, bar one, evens the field, at the start, and Dirblew would soon be odds on.'

'And how are you going to manage to get this number in the frame and Paddy Black's name there?' asked Nat, who added, 'If they're sending Dirblew to Woolsingham, Paddy Black will be engaged to ride there.'

'All the better. If none of the Dirblew party are there it'll be all the longer before the mistake is found out. All you have to do is to fill in one of those declaration forms – I have some in my pocket – and either pop it into the box in the weighing-room for the third race, and it'll go up in the frame all right. I've declared a lot of horses since this new business came into force, and I know that there's no possibility of a hitch.'

'No, but there'a a nasty word called forgery,' broke in Nathan Wedgewood. 'And they have a nasty habit of putting you in gaol for that.'

'As a matter of fact,' laughed the Colonel, 'there's nothing whatever in the rule about declarations being signed, though it might raise suspicion if the form didn't bear a signature of some sort. It might just call the official's attention to the declaration, and that's what we don't want. I happen to know there was a sort of test case recently as to whether a declaration form filled in by a fully authorised person is valid without a signature, and it was decided that as the rule reads it is. Listen to the rule.' The Colonel took his book *Calendar* out of his pocket, and read:

' "No horse shall be weighed out (except as provided below) for any race unless the name of the race and of the horse and of the jockey have been given in writing by the owner, trainer, or duly authorised agent to the clerk of the course not less than three-quarters of an hour before the time fixed for the race. The numbers of the runners, together with the names of the jockeys and the draw for places, will be exhibited on the number board for the first race as soon as practicable, and for the subsequent races immediately the preceding race has been run. When the numbers have been exhibited, no additions or alterations (except as allowed for in Section ii of this rule or in Rules 28, 35 (ii) and 30 (iii) can be made without leave of the Stewards, whose reasons for such permission shall be reported at the Registry Office."

'You see there's nothing about the declaration form being signed, and also that once a number is up in the frame, even if the horse falls down dead, there's bound to be some delay in collecting the Stewards to get permission to have it withdrawn.'

Nathan shook his head, a plain indication that the suggestion didn't appeal to him. 'I wouldn't fill in one of those papers without written authority, no, not for no money,' he said. 'Mind, I have declared horses for one or two trainers who had horses running at two meetings on the same day and asked me to act for them and ride at the meeting they weren't going to be at. They've always given me a letter saying I had authority to represent them, and I've had to hand that in and leave it with the official. I'll never forget the first time I had to declare a horse just after the rule came out. I forgot all about it till one minute before the time. They were just going to make the draw when I dashed into the weighing room and shouted to them to hold hard as I had a runner. If I'd been a minute later the horse couldn't have run. But I wouldn't put in one of these forms without I *had* authority; what's more, they wouldn't take the declaration. They have a little book from Weatherby's with every one's name in it who has registered authority to act, and if your name isn't in, then you must bring a written authority from the owner or trainer with you.'

'We don't want you to hand it in. All we want you to do is to pop it into the right box without being seen when the occasion offers. Wait till the official is away from the boxes for a minute, filling in the draw or something, and then slip it in. You needn't bother about filling in the form, I'll get that typed, and I'll put the name at the bottom, so that will make everything plain sailing. The owner and trainer of the horse won't care two straws, they're doing a bit of double-crossing themselves, and this will rather help them than otherwise. It'll prevent S. P. money going from the ring at Toxton to Woolsingham, and that's just what they want. Don't you see, we shall draw all round, and of course you'll get your whack. The whole thing will only be a huge joke in the paddock, but there's money in it for us. All of us here want to get hold of a bit, and this is one very easy way if we keep the thing to ourselves. We have one or two other little schemes we want you to be in later. All quite mild – milk and water, but money in 'em, old boy! Now think it over, and I'll see you at Toxton. Where do you stay there?'

'I always used to stay at the Adelphi, but I can't afford it now,' replied Nat, who added hesitatingly, 'I stop private.'

'You join us as our guest at the Adelphi,' said Colonel Bellew. 'We'll have a private room there. We usually have a hand at cards after dinner, but you can play or not, as you like. It won't cost you a penny at the Adelphi, and we can talk this and the other plans over then. You come in with us, Nat! It'll be the making of you. We're all too old hands at the game to do anything likely to get any one into trouble.'

'Yes!' broke in Issy Salvo. 'None of us would dream of carting you, Nat. We're really out to help you a bit, and we're all gentlemen, as you know – men of the world who know the racing game backwards from A to Z. We wouldn't put our own or anybody else's head into a noose. We talked things over coming down in the special this morning, and thought of you. As the Colonel there has said, by helping us you will help yourself. Isn't that right, Mo?'

By this time, however, the corpulent, apoplectic-looking, hoarse-voiced Mo Kelly was fast asleep. The other two layers nodded assent before Issy doubled up a sporting paper and threw it at the sleeping bookie, and awakened him with a start.

'Are you in this, Mo, or are you a sleeping partner?' asked Issy.

'When the Colonel started reading the rules of racing he made me feel as though I was in church and sent me over,' replied Mo. 'How far have we got now? Isn't there a saloon on the train? Let's go along and have a drink, that would waken me up best of anything. Three bleeding weeks and not a bleeding winning day in the three of 'em! S'trewth. What a life! And the bookmaker is supposed always to win if he's clever enough to make his book right. There's very few been clever enough to win these last few weeks, I'll wager.'

'Any here for tea, gentlemen?' asked a car attendant, sliding back the door leading into the corridor.

'There's one poor lad here,' replied Mo, adding, 'though tea's not much in my line.'

'We're all coming for a drink, anyhow,' replied the Colonel, who added, 'I'll toss you, Mo, for who pays for the six. Sudden death,' he spun a coin as he spoke, and slapped it on to the back of his hand. 'Heads or tails?' he demanded.

'Is that your double-faced tossing coin?' asked Mo. 'Well, it means I pay in any case, so I'll say "heads." '

'Tails, old boy! Hard luck!' exclaimed the Colonel as they filed out into the corridor. Mo Kelly hadn't even looked at the coin. From previous experience he knew that on similar occasions it meant him footing the bill even if the Colonel lost, though he always insisted it was 'only a loan.' More than one racing man in the dining-car nudged a companion as Nathan Wedgewood passed in company with Colonel Bellew, Issy Salvo, and the three well-known bookies.

'Never saw old Wedgewood in that company before,' whispered Sir Thomas Ripley to a friend opposite.

'That party have the reputation of having some of the jockeys on a string.'

'You don't believe all the silly tales you are told, Tom, do you?' asked the friend, raising his eyebrows.

'If you *did*, then half the jockeys on the Turf are riding for the bookmakers and no one would ever have a chance of owning or backing a winner if they weren't in the swim and in the know. I'm inclined to think that the game's a great deal cleaner than is made out. In fact, I'm certain it is. Stewards don't go about with their eyes and ears shut. You're a Steward yourself, and I'm surprised to hear that you even listen to such stories.'

'Well, I don't really believe half I hear,' replied Sir Thomas, 'but I always think that where there's smoke there's fire, and that men like Bellew and Issy Salvo don't batten on to jockeys and treat them without some *quid pro quo*. You know what I mean, Johnstone.'

'There's such a thing as hero-worship,' remarked Johnstone. 'There's a certain class of men, particularly young men, who love to be seen in the company of those who are in the limelight. They feel a certain reflected glory, and love to brag about having dined, and wined, and travelled with jockeys, theatricals, and even scoundrels. Only the other day young Sir Valentine Beach told me that Steve Denton had rung him up on the 'phone twice during dinner about some horses he was to ride on the following day. 'Awful bore being taken away from dinner *twice*,' said Sir Valentine, expecting me to be impressed. It so happened that Steve the same afternoon pointed to Sir Valentine in the paddock and asked me who he was. I told him, and he then said, 'He's been continually stopping me to pump me, and I thought he must be one of those reporter fellows.' 'But didn't *you* ring him up to talk to *him* last night, Steve?' I asked. 'Never rang him up in my life – never even heard his name till you told me it,' replied Steve. So there you see the sort of inferiority complex, the craving to know, or pretend to know, and to be known by notabilities.'

'Yes, but in that case,' said Sir Thomas, 'it was only the action of a silly young fool. There was no desire to buy the jockey!'

'And how many jockeys who really count, do you think, *could* be bought?' persisted Johnstone. 'Take the leading dozen. How many of them would risk their reputation, licence, and future for any bribe a scoundrel might offer? There's none of the racing hooks could put down a sum big enough to tempt them. It would be a rotten bad bet – a jockey's reputation, character, and possible warning-off to, say, a certain couple of hundred or even a monkey.'

As the two men continued their discussion Mo Kelly and his divided party talked of the day's doings over their drinks without any reference to the plans only part of which Colonel Bellew had disclosed. A meal or even drinks on a train always help to lessen the weariness of those long journeys which the regular racing army have to travel week by week. Before they parted Nat had promised to stay at the Adelphi as the guest of the others, or whichever of them eventually had to settle the bill. He left the train before Colonel Bellew and Issy Salvo, and when he had gone the Colonel winked at Issy as he said, 'He'll do what we want him to all right. He's hard up and he'll probably do anything we want if we pay him well enough. This is only a mild show, though there's money in it. I could do this myself, but it will be a means of getting hold of him with an easy bait. It will be as easy as thinking to slip that dud declaration into a box, but I've been rather cold-shouldered out of one or two weighing-rooms lately, and the clerk of the course at Toxton and I aren't exactly brothers since I gave him a bit of my mind about refusing me admission to the club enclosure. We keep out of each other's way now, at any rate, I keep out of *his*, which is the same thing.'

The Phantom Jockey

BAT MASTERS

Dozens of straight-as-a-dye jockey heroes were to be found in the novels of Bat Masters, whose cheap paperback editions published during the twenties and early thirties rivalled the sales of those of the great Nat Gould. In fact, a whole generation of older schoolboys and young office workers, clerks and factory apprentices grew up on Masters' long-running series of Racing Novels with their colourful covers of horses and riders in dramatic situations which cost $4\frac{1}{2}$d (under two pence) per issue. The series was published by the Aldine Publishing Company in London which, according to E. S. Turner in his classic study of comics and magazines for the young, *Boys Will Be Boys* (1975), 'for over forty years put out a profusion of "libraries" on every subject from highwaymen to horse racing'.

The Aldine Racing Library was one of the firm's most successful lines and ran for 116 issues between 1922 and 1932, according to publishing historian W. O. G. Lofts, thanks no doubt to the authentic knowledge of racing possessed by its contributors, who included Sydney Horler (later to challenge the popularity of Edgar Wallace with his thrillers, all of which carried the exclamation, 'Horler For Excitement!') and Bat Masters, whose name is still remembered by older readers of fiction, though it was actually the pen name of one Ernest Charles Buley (1869–1933).

Curiously, though Buley in his Masters persona was given a colourful 'biography' by his publishers, who claimed that he was an intimate friend of the leading jockeys and trainers 'and knew all the secrets of the turf' thereby being able to write his thrilling tales, the truth about the man was more interesting still. Buley had been born in Ballarat, Australia and educated at Granville

College and Melbourne University, where he apparently first developed a taste for horse racing. A story, probably apocryphal, says that he left Australia in rather a hurry because of a number of unpaid debts to Melbourne bookies, and arrived in London where his skills as a journalist soon got him work in Fleet Street. In time he became chief subeditor of *Reynolds News*, but from 1910 he was also supplementing his income by contributing serials and stories to a whole range of popular magazines and boys' papers.

Friends who recall Buley holding court with other journalists in Fleet Street pubs say he never lost his enthusiasm for the turf and one of his most frequently heard remarks as he left the bar was that he had to 'dash off another story to pay my bookmaker'. The mysteries which he contributed to the Aldine Racing Novels undoubtedly represented his most popular work – several like *A Derby Objection*, *The £20,000 Bet* and *The Snowstorm Derby* sold over 100,000 copies – and they are now among the most sought after by collectors of the company's titles. Interestingly, the Bat Masters by-line was kept alive during the later thirties by the author's son, Bernard, who was also a Fleet Street journalist and worked in the editorial department of the popular *Boy's Magazine* until his death in the forces during the Second World War. 'The Phantom Jockey' is a typical Bat Masters story, except for the fact that it introduces a little of his background and, by a strange quirk of fate, contains a character with the very Australian name of Chris Packer.

*

A white mantle of snow covered the earth and a sharp hoar frost made it sparkle like myriad diamonds and sound crisp to the tread. It was a glorious, brilliant scene that the moonshine shone down upon, the soft rays of the consort of the sun bathing the snow with its millions of minute particles in a scintillation of splendour. Brankston stud farm, nestling amidst the Surrey hills, was warm and snug although the air was keen and sharp, and the faint moan of a cutting wind came through the trees heavily laden with glittering gems, equalling in purity stones of the finest water.

The loose boxes which ranged round three sides of the spacious yard, were hanging heavy with snow, but within all was warmth, and the horses were oblivious of the state of the weather without.

There were some famous horses and mares within these somewhat old-fashioned boxes. In yonder box at the far side of the yard stood a famous winner of the triple crown, and next to him, in another box, was a winner of a Melbourne Cup who wondered at this strange and unaccustomed sight of white earth whenever he caught a glimpse of it through the open door of his box. King of Diamonds was a famous horse in Australia, and how he lost the Derby will ever remain a mystery, for he won the Melbourne Cup by four lengths, three days after his most extraordinary defeat. A couple of Oaks winners were housed not far from this celebrated pair, and scores of splendidly bred mares had to be well looked after in this severe weather.

Dan Sharples, the stud-groom at Brankston, had much responsibility resting upon him at this time, and felt it, although this did not prevent him from 'keeping it up' on occasions in right royal style.

The stud-groom's house was an old dwelling that in years gone by had been a manor house, and the rooms were spacious and the place rambling. A stranger, having partaken freely of Dan's hospitality, would have found it difficult to discover his particular room unaided, for there were sundry staircases leading to nowhere, having been blocked at the top where the house was falling almost into ruins.

On this particular January night Dan Sharples had invited several neighbours from the village to partake of his hospitality, and also a couple of jockey friends who were 'out of collar' during the frost, hunting being out of the question. A welcome guest was Ben Engel, who had brought over a couple of colonial horses to Brankston in the spring, and remained to see an English winter.

Ben Engel was as well known in Australia as Dan Sharples in England, and the two men had much in common although their dispositions were dissimilar. Ben Engel was inclined to take a gloomy view of human nature, while Dan Sharples tried to look upon the bright side of everything. The defeat of King of Diamonds in the Victorian Derby was a sore point with Ben

Engel. Ben had reared the King from 'foalhood' to 'horse-hood,' and had backed his pet for pounds, shillings and pence to win the great double – the Derby and Cup. That Ben ought to have won his money everyone acknowledged after the Cup, but they did not agree with him when he positively affirmed that Chris Packer, who rode the King in the Derby, sold the race to the ring.

Chris Packer made a mistake when he rode King of Diamonds in the Victorian Derby. He was over-confident, knowing how good the horse was, and he threw the race away. No one, with the exception of Ben Engel, questioned Packer's honour in the matter, and it was said that the mistake which he made broke the jockey's heart, for he went downhill afterwards, lost his nerve, and died by his own hand. Many men blamed Ben Engel for Chris Packer's downfall. Ben had a sharp tongue and he let Packer know what he thought of that fatal race. The jockey was sensitive and Ben's words rankled deep, and he never forgot them. He knew Ben Engel's opinion was honest, although wrong, and he fancied everyone began to regard him as a rogue. This happened some years ago, and yet the mere mention of King of Diamonds' name set Ben Engel off on a subject that he was never tired of talking about. 'You worried Chris Packer into his grave,' said a friend of Engel's, 'and you'll worry yourself into your grave if you talk so much about him. The man's dead; let his name rest in peace.' But this was just what Ben Engel could not do. It was the worst trait in Ben's character, this vilifying a dead man, and yet Ben believed that he was honest in what he said.

Dan Sharples looked a great contrast to Ben Engel as they sat facing each other at the long table in the old oak room at Brankston. The fire roared and crackled up the chimney, the hot punch, a fragrant odour arising from the large bowl, pervaded the room, and pipes and cigars made the atmosphere somewhat cloudy, while as the steaming liquor circulated the fun became boisterous.

'Your first winter in England,' said Dan Sharples to Ben Engel. 'Fill up, lads, and we'll drink to Ben's first sight of a big snow storm, and wish him many more such nights in the old country.'

Ben Engel was not popular but they drank his health heartily enough.

Then Ben had to respond.

'We've got a horse here, lads, that Ben knows a good deal about,' went on Dan Sharples; 'King of Diamonds, and a real good one he is to look at, and Ben says he is one of the best that was ever foaled in Australia.'

The mention of King of Diamonds made Ben Engel's eyes sparkle, and he gripped his glass and then swallowed the contents, the hot toddy making his eyes water and coursing through his veins.

'What about King of Diamonds? Tell us about him, Ben,' shouted several voices.

'Yes, I'll tell you about him,' said Ben, 'and I'll tell you how the jockey who rode him in the Derby sold the race and lost me a pot of money,' he added, bringing his fist down on the table with a bang that made the glasses dance.

A tap was distinctly heard at the window behind Ben, and he turned sharply round.

'Someone is knocking at the window,' said Ben.

'Chaps from the village, perhaps,' answered Dan Sharples. 'Open the window and see who is there.'

The window was unfastened and pushed open, and the firelight shone on the snow outside. Ben put his head out, but drew it in again quickly.

'Nations,' he cried, 'it is cold.'

They laughed as he shivered, and Dan said:

'You don't see much of that in Australia, Ben.'

Several of the men looked out but saw no one, nor could any signs of footsteps be traced in the snow.

'Curious,' observed Ben. 'I could have sworn that I heard a knock.'

'Never mind – go on with the yarn. There are no ghosts out to-night; it's too cold for them,' laughed Dan.

'King of Diamonds was a wonder,' went on Ben. 'I reared him, and broke him in, and taught his trainer how to train him. I loved him like one of my own children. He was a dead certainty for the Derby, and I backed him to win our big double, the Derby and Cup, before the public got to know how good he was. When they did find out they were on him to a man, and he started at odds of two to one on him. Chris Packer was engaged to ride him in this race, but not in the Cup, as he could not get the weight. Packer was always regarded as an honest man, and he was a fine rider.'

The wind commenced to moan dismally as Ben went on with his story, and it had a weird sound as it echoed through the rooms and passages of the old manor house.

'I'll never forget that race,' said Ben. 'It was a hundred to one on King of Diamonds as they came round the bend and entered the straight. He ought to have won in a canter, and he lost. When they reached the distance Barcoo was the only horse going strong, and he would have had no chance had King of Diamonds been ridden well. But Chris Packer suddenly dropped his hands and King of Diamonds stopped dead. Before he could get him going again Barcoo was alongside, with Haden riding for his life. I hardly know how I felt, but I know I cursed Packer with all my heart. They slid past the winning post with Barcoo half a length in front when King of Diamonds ought to have cantered in. I said then, and I repeat it now, that Chris Packer sold the race and—'

There was a loud rap at the window which interrupted Ben's flow of eloquence. Everyone in the room heard it and they looked at each other. It was a peculiar knock and there was a deathly silence after it.

Dan Sharples was the first to speak, and said:

'Follow me, lads, someone is having a game with us. We'll make it hot for him if we get hold of him.'

Dan put on his hat, went into the hall, took up a heavy stick, opened the door, and went out into the snow, followed by the others.

It was almost as light as day and the scene was wild and weird.

After examining the snow under the window and round the garden, and finding no trace of footsteps, they came to the conclusion, suggested by Dan, that it must have been a stray bird flying and hitting against the panes. They returned to the house and entered the hall, and were about to resume their seats at the table, when a sharp scream of alarm was heard.

Dan Sharples rushed into the hall and called out:

'What's amiss? Who is it?'

'It's me, sir,' came in a timid voice from the top of the big stairs, and a figure in white, candle in hand, loomed out distinctly.

'What's the matter with you, Jane?' asked Dan.

'Oh, please sir,' said the shivering girl, 'I heard you all go out at the door, and I got out of bed. When I heard you come in I looked out of the window and saw such a strange little man, like a stable boy, running across the yard. He went into that box the Australian horse is in, and then I screamed.'

'Went into King of Diamonds' box?' exclaimed Dan in surprise. 'Nonsense, you must have been dreaming, Jane. The box is safely locked, but anyhow we'll go and look round to see that all's right, it will freshen us up a bit after this stuffy room.'

They went out of the warm comfortable house again into the snow, and Dan Sharples led the way across the yard. There was no necessity for lanterns, the moon gave more than ample light for their purpose. The wind had risen and was howling amongst the frost-clad, leafless trees, sending showers of hard spray on to the ground.

Ben Engel was shivering with the cold. It was a strange experience for him to be tramping about a snow-clad stable-yard at nearly midnight. He felt in a strange mood. He was not a nervous man; men who have spent most of their time amongst horses seldom are, but he would have found it difficult to define his feelings.

'Don't know what's come over me,' he muttered. 'Those raps on the window upset me a bit, and I've had a fair share of punch. I'll put it down to the liquor, but this is a creepy old place, and I'd sooner be inside than out on a night like this.'

Dan Sharples reached King of Diamonds' box first, and gave a start and exclamation of surprise as he did so. From beneath the door came a fine streak of light, which faintly reflected on the snow in a quivering line.

'Look!' he said in some agitation, 'there's a light in the box. What had we better do?'

'Open the door,' was the pertinent answer.

Slowly Dan pulled back the top part of the door, peered in, but saw nothing. The light had disappeared and King of Diamonds appeared to be all right, but neighed in a somewhat alarmed manner, which might have been caused by this instrusion at such an untimely hour.

'What's amiss, old fellow?' said Dan in a soothing, encouraging voice which the horse recognized at once, and showed he did.

He pulled the lower half of the door open and stepped in. Ben Engel followed him and stood by his side.

Then a strange thing happened. A ray of light played about the horse's head, and flitted around the corner of his box.

Dan Sharples saw it and thought it was the moonlight paying King of Diamonds a visit.

Ben Engel saw it and stared hard at the corner of the box near King of Diamonds' head. As he looked his face turned pale as death, and his eyes almost started out of his head, and his hair seemed to stand on end. He trembled in every limb and caught hold of Dan Sharples' arm; the remainder of the men clustered round the door and gazed in wonder at Ben Engel's face.

When Dan looked at the man at his side he said:

'Good heavens, man, what ails you? Are you ill, Ben?'

Ben Engel did not speak, he could not, his tongue clave to the roof of his mouth; although he wanted to shriek aloud in his terror he could utter no sound. He seemed to be suffering from a terrible shock – a horrid nightmare. He pointed to the corner of the box, and then with a desperate effort to throw off his dumbness, said in a hoarse whisper: 'Do you see him? There, there, there!' and he pointed thrice to the spot where the light was.

'There's nothing there,' asserted Dan, thinking the whisky and the warm room, with the sudden change to cold air, had made Ben's head reel.

'Take him away,' cried Ben. 'Take him away. He's pointing at me. He's got his hand on a wound in his temple; his face is all over blood. I thought him dead. He is dead; take him away.'

The last words were uttered in a tone of such abject terror that Dan and the rest knew that there was something more than an overdose of liquor here.

'You shan't mount him. I tell you you shan't mount him!' said Ben savagely. 'You stiffened him, you – you—'

The words died away on Ben's lips. He made one forward dart

and fell headlong on the straw beside King of Diamonds. The horse snorted and looked round.

Dan saw that he was about to lash out and tried to soothe him. Again the stud-groom's voice acted like magic and soothed the frightened horse.

They carried Ben Engel back to the house in an insensible condition and put him to bed. They tried to restore consciousness, but without effect.

Dan dismissed them and sent for the local doctor who came and examined Ben Engel.

'Bad case,' pronounced the doctor. 'He's had a terrible shock. What has happened?'

Dan related as briefly as possible all that had taken place, and the doctor listened with a surprised, grave face.

'He saw, or fancied he saw, someone or something in that box,' was his comment. 'I'm no believer in ghosts, Sharples, but this man's state, and the causes of it, border on the supernatural.'

Ben Engel lay hovering between life and death for many days in Dan Sharples' house.

It was many weeks before he was sufficiently recovered to be able to come downstairs. Dan Sharples did not question him as to what had happened. He waited until Ben should speak. Ben Engel spoke out at last.

'Dan,' he said, 'do you know what I saw in King of Diamonds' box that night?'

'No. What could you see? There was nothing there.'

'There was,' declared Ben. 'Chris Packer was there.'

Dan stared at him and thought, 'Poor fellow, he's bad yet.'

'I saw the jockey in the corner of the box. It was Chris Packer who rapped at the window both times when I spoke ill of him. I'll never forget his face and the look on it in that box; it made me feel like a murderer. So pitiful it was. He'd come back to tell me not to speak ill of the dead. I know it now. I've been thinking it over, and the Lord knows I've had time enough for that. It's gospel true, Dan, believe it or not, as you like. I saw him and you didn't.'

Dan was still silent.

'Conscience,' he thought.

'You've been very good to me, Dan,' went on Ben. 'I'm sorry to have given you so much trouble, but I'm glad it happened, for I have learned a lesson.'

'Don't mention the trouble,' replied Dan. 'I'm glad you are better. You'll soon be yourself again.'

'I hope so,' said Ben, 'and I shall never forget the lesson which the phantom jockey has taught me.'

'And that was?' asked Dan, merely as a matter of form, and guessing what was coming.

'Never speak ill of the dead,' replied Ben Engel.

Thoroughbred

MAX BRAND

Crime and mystery stories featuring jockeys were also to be found in considerable number in America's famous 'pulp' magazines of the twenties and thirties, not to mention their up-market competitors, the 'slicks', which numbered among their ranks *Cosmopolitan, Saturday Evening Post* and *Collier's Magazine*. A whole generation of now largely forgotten writers produced hundreds of tales about the Turf for both these markets – of whom Barclay Northcote (a prolific contributor to *All-Story Weekly* who has been described as 'the American Nat Gould'), Gordon Grand (creator of the enigmatic Colonel Weatherford, and a man who later abandoned writing to raise colts) and John Taintor Foote (better known as a playwright and Hollywood screenwriter) are perhaps remembered by older readers for their horse racing stories. One name does, however, stand head and shoulders above the rest in this category, Max Brand, though even he is more famous as a writer of westerns and hospital dramas. The fact remains that few authors have written better about horses than Brand: notably in novels like *The Thunderer*, *Alcatraz* and *Mistrel* and in any number of his westerns, especially the big-hearted animal 'Parade' who features in the Silvertip series and the brave and resourceful 'Satan' in the best-selling adventures of Whistling Dan Barry.

Max Brand, whose real name was Frederick Schiller Faust (1892–1944), was the son of a German immigrant, and by all accounts led a dramatic life from his poor birth in California's Central Valley to his tragic death while serving as a war correspondent for *Harper's Magazine* at Anzio in 1944. As a writer he was amazingly prolific and it has been estimated that between 1917 and 1944 he used at least twenty pen-names to publish over 125 novels and probably as many as 900 short stories. His stories for *Black Mask* and *Detective Fiction Weekly* were pioneers in the 'hardboiled' school of fiction, though his fame rests on his westerns and for the creation of Dr Kildare, the young intern whose career is guided by a crusty old doctor, and which later became the basis of several movies in the forties and three TV series in the sixties and seventies.

Brand was an inveterate racegoer and loved to ride horses whenever he had the oportunity. He truly believed the horse was 'a noble creature', but was not quite so sure about jockeys as he demonstrates in 'Thoroughbred'. This story of Freeman Paget, a jock with a drink problem, who is urged to throw a race by a notorious race fixer named Harry Delwin, was written for *Collier's Magazine* as long ago as November 1935, but is as terse and dramatic as anything from Dick Francis' pen. This also marks its long-overdue first appearance in book form.

*

Harry Delwin said: 'Listen, Free! Will you listen or are you boiled?'

'I can listen,' said Freeman Paget, 'but I've had enough to stiffen my upper lip a little and the words don't have much meaning. Why don't you take a walk, Harry?'

'What's the matter? Don't you want me around?' demanded Delwin.

'You're so sleek that you shine,' said Paget, 'and my eyes are too weak to stand the glare. I mean you ought to take more exercise.'

'I know what you mean,' said Delwin. 'But I'm here to talk business.'

'Give me fifty dollars,' said Paget.

'You've had a lot of fifties out of me. Why should I keep on forking out?'

'Give me fifty dollars,' said Paget.

'When do I get it back?' asked Delwin.

'This afternoon, if you play Portulaca in the second race. . . . Waiter! Another, please. What will you have, Harry?'

'I don't want anything,' answered Delwin. 'Neither do you.'

'What will you have, Harry?'

'Well, a thin one. I don't like to drink in the middle of the day, though.'

'Waiter, two of these.'

'Here's the fifty,' said Delwin. 'Now will you listen to me?'

'You've paid for this long-distance call. Go ahead and use your three minutes.'

'You're riding Which Way for Jim Baring in the Clarenton Cup.'

'I won't have to ride. I'll only have to sit still and watch that horse win.'

'That won't bring you any closer to marrying Judith Baring. Unless you want to live on her money.'

'We were talking about a horse race,' said Freeman Paget.

'We were. The point is that it's going to be a real race, after all. Perry Gibson entered a gray stallion, Bristol, yesterday afternoon.'

'I never heard of Bristol.'

'You'd hear of him if you went to England. Bristol can beat Which Way.'

'All right, but where's the dirt?'

'What do you mean?'

'Whenever I see that hungry look in your eye, I know that the meat is well hung,' said Freeman Paget.

'You can't talk like that to me!'

'Your three minutes is nearly up. Go ahead and speak your piece,' said Paget.

'I'm trying to give you a helping hand, Free,' said Delwin.

'And you keep shying away and kicking mud in my face. Listen to me. Nobody knows Bristol. Which Way is going to the post an odds-on favorite. Bristol will open at about thirty-to-one even after the dopesters have watched him gallop and jump . . . How much money have you in the world?'

'About twenty-five hundred. Want it?'

'Open your ears, Free. . . . You're not drunk, are you? . . . Then listen to me. You put your twenty-five hundred down on Bristol and you'll clean up fifty thousand dollars when he wins.'

Paget pushed back his chair. The feet of it stuttered out a small thunder against the floor.

'You've used up your time,' he said. 'This call is ended, Delwin.'

'Free, listen! Now, for Pete's sake don't kick opportunity in the face! You and the Baring girl have been waiting for a couple of years for you to get placed. You won't marry her money and live on it – and she can't keep on waiting for you forever. Even if she didn't have a penny, the men wouldn't let her alone. Not with a face like—'

'That's enough Delwin.'

'Free, sit down again. Don't pull out on me. Don't—'

'How many times have you bribed jockeys?' asked Paget.

'You think I'm a dog. I'm not a dog. It's only when a man sees a chance for a big killing. Sit down, Free, will you?' Paget sat down.

'Wipe your face. It's dripping,' he said . . . 'How many riders have you turned into dirty crooks, Delwin?'

'You won't understand. I'm talking about your own future. You can clean up fifty thousand. With that for backing, there are a lot of businesses that would be glad to take you in. You could step out and marry— I'm sorry. I won't talk about that any more. But—'

'The idea is that I bet my wad on Bristol.'

'And get in on the juicy part of the odds.'

'I bet on Bristol and ride Which Way. When I've committed myself, you'll know that you can plunge with everything you have. That I'll ride Which Way so he's sure not to win. Then you'll go the limit.'

'You know what the limit is? I've got twenty thousand. I can beg and borrow and steal another thirty. I'll put the whole thing on Bristol. With Which Way fixed, it's the surest thing I ever heard of. The odds can't be backed down too far. They won't be shorter than two-to-one at the post. I'll average about ten to one all the way down the line. I'll clean up a fortune, Free, and I'll cut you in on it. You see how clean I'm coming? I want you to feel how much depends on your doing the right sort of a job. I'll cut you in big. And all you'll have to do will be to use the old head a little. Get Which Way into one jam. Just make one mistake. Bristol can win on his merits, anyway – but you'll make it sure.'

'Well, all right,' said Freeman Paget. 'If this doesn't work out you're washed up forever, I take it?'

'Don't talk about that. I'm not going to be washed up. Give me your hand on this, Free, will you?'

'You'll see my money go down on the line,' answered Paget. 'That ought to be enough guarantee for you.'

'There's Turk McFadden just went by the door. Nobody will give you better odds than Turk McFadden. Go and nail him now, will you?' Paget looked at the ceiling.

'All right,' he said, and left the room. He found Turk McFadden's red face in the middle of a group and beckoned him aside.

'I was just talking with Dave Solomon about you, Mr Paget,' said McFadden. 'Solomon says that you have the finest pair of hands he ever saw. He says with hands like yours, you could juggle raw eggs and not get your fingers dirty. If you ever cut out this gentleman rider business, and go right into the profession, Mr Paget—'

'Have you seen that new entry in the Clarenton Cup?'

'Bristol? Yes. He's a nice piece of goods. Gray, with black silk stockings on every leg. That's the kind of points for a horse to have. He's a big bruiser but as sleek as a referee's whistle.'

'McFadden, I want to do some business with you; not for the newspapers, either.'

'I hope you can trust me, Mr Paget. Not a word to a soul. What is it, sir?'

'What are your odds on Bristol?'

'About thirty-to-one.'

'I want to put twenty-five hundred dollars on Bristol.'

'Twenty-five hundred – on Bristol? Did I get that right? But you're riding Which Way, I thought.'

'I'm riding Which Way. But that English horse looks too strong to me.'

'Ah, that's the way of it, eh? . . . Look here, I can't give you more than ten-to-one, if it's that way.'

'That will do all right,' Paget said.

'Very well, Paget.'

'Goodby, McFadden.' Free did not seem to notice the omission of the prefix to his name.

McFadden forgot to echo the farewell, perhaps because he was making a notation in his book.

The green gray of the dawn had barely turned to blue and gold, but Jim Baring and his sister Judith were already leaning against the fence to watch Which Way at his work, for Freeman Paget was giving the gelding a stiff bit of jumping; between that morning and the running of the Clarenton Cup the steeplechaser would have nothing but a bit of warming-up. Now he flew the jumps on wings, his big-boned ugliness made beautiful with speed.

Jim Baring said: 'Free knows how to lighten Which Way in the forehand. That's the great secret. I never saw such a pair of hands. He sends electricity down the reins and does the thinking for the horse. One brain serves the two of them. . . . What's the matter, Judy?'

'Nothing,' said Judith Baring.

'You've got tears in your eyes.'

'It's the cold of this morning wind,' she said.

'There's something wrong with you. Why don't you come clean?'

'I wish you wouldn't bother me, Jim,' she said.

'It's Free,' said Jim Baring. 'There – I touched you that time. It's old Free, and I knew it. I wish he wouldn't be such a damned fool, really. We want him in the family, don't we? But he's such a clean-bred one that he'd rather steal than live on the Baring money, I think. I'm going to talk to him today.'

'I wish you wouldn't; please don't, Jim.'

'I'm going to. What's the matter with you, Judy? Your lip's trembling. You look like a sick puppy. I tell you, I'm going to put an end to all this damned nonsense. You'll be married to Free within a month or I'll know the reason why.'

'I'm never going to marry,' said Judith.

'Wait a minute. Judy, are you crazy?'

'I'm never going to marry,' she said, and walked quickly away.

Jim Baring looked after her blankly. . . .

Which Way took the water jump, trailing his feet cleverly through the brush. Freeman Paget cut outside the next barrier and eased the gelding to a canter, a trot, a walk. Which Way walked like an ambling cow, his head working back and forth on a ewe-neck, a big, Roman-nosed head that seemed to overweigh the neck entirely.

'He's had enough,' said Freeman Paget.

'He's not fine enough,' declared Baring, when they had the gelding back in the stable with two grooms rubbing him down.

'He's had enough,' answered Paget. 'For a distance like the Clarenton, a horse has to have something more than legs. There has to be a bit of gallop left in his belly. Remember that he's by Waylay out of Whichever and neither of them trained very fine.'

'He looks like cold blood,' declared Baring. 'He looks like a big gawk of an Irish hunter.'

'Where's Judy?' asked Paget.

'She's gone away somewhere. Free, will you listen to me? She's changing a lot. That blue under the eyes isn't right. She's breaking her heart, Free; do you know that? And all because you're such a damned fool. Now look me in the eye and tell me. Are you a damned fool?'

'Yes,' said Paget.

'God bless you, Free. Now you go right on over to the car and tell her what a damned fool you've been. You ask her to marry you, will you? . . . Don't start talking back to me. You've been smacking her down with your rotten pride all this while. Will you go ask her to marry you now?'

'Yes,' said Paget.

He went over to the big car and slipped into the front seat under the wheel, beside Judith.

She said: 'Hello, Free—' And she smiled at him.

'Judy, will you marry me?' he asked.

'No, Free,' she said.

'Have you stopped loving me?'

'No,' she said.

'Then what's the matter?'

'I don't know. I'm never going to marry,' she answered.

'Kiss me, Judy, will you?'

'Yes, Free.'

'Now look here. When we're close like this, you can't say you've stopped loving me.'

'I do love you,' she said.

'And you won't marry me?'

'No, Free.'

He patted her shoulder softly.

'All right,' said Paget. 'It's all right, Judy. Don't you go worrying about it. The old instinct is talking inside you. And it's all right. You stop crying, Judy, will you?'

'Yes,' she said.

When the bookies are nervous, something happens to the atmosphere at a race track. A noise goes through the crowd like the humming of wires in a high wind. And the bookies were nervous on the day of the running of the Clarenton Cup. On their boards the new horse, Bristol, stood an even-money favorite with the former first choice, Which Way. Money-pressure had done. that, but before the odds were cut to evens, thousands had been laid at thirty and twenty to one. Only Turk McFadden, that wise old head, had hedged from the first in a very clever way. So the whisper was in the air and Bristol was the word on everyone's lips.

Jim Baring was watching the saddling of Which Way.

'How are you, Free?' he asked.

'Right enough,' said Paget.

'Are you, really? I knew I shouldn't have let you sit up last night. But I had to talk.'

'That? Oh, that did me good.'

'This Judy business hasn't cut the heart out of you?'

'No, not a bit.'

'Old Free!' said Jim Baring. 'Nobody can tell what's inside a woman's head. . . . Here's Which Way trying to eat your hand – let's talk about him. Remember that he can do with a bit of the whip if a pinch comes. Let him have his head most of the way and don't think he's running himself out if he drops the others behind him, pretty fast. He takes his fences so big and strides so large that he's apt to float away from the rest of the field after the first scamper. Just keep a nice hold on him and let him work; he won't stop. If he does – the whip! Burn it into him. He won't sulk. He's honest. But you know all this.'

'That's all right,' said Paget.

'Listen, Free,' said Jim Baring. 'I want you to watch the gray horse during the race. You see him over there? He's all silk but I don't think he's a yard wide.'

'I think he's a yard wide, all right,' said Paget.

'Don't like his middle piece,' objected Baring.

'He's a little light, but he'll last. And Perry Gibson is up on him.'

'They tell me Gibson is as good as a professional,' said Baring. 'But that doesn't worry me. So are you. However, there's been a big play on him the last twenty-four hours. Have you heard about the big play on him?'

'Something,' said Paget.

'There's Wilson ready to give you the leg up. Goodbye, Free. You'll give me the best you have. I know that. God bless you! Remember the whip in the pinch.' . . .

Baring joined his sister in the grandstand only as the parade went past; and as big Which Way went by people turned bright faces and nodded and smiled and waved at the Barings.

'It's going to be yours, Jim,' said fat Mrs Johnson, who sat just behind. 'Think of winning the Cup outright with one horse! That's never been done before: but they can't beat Which Way when he looks the way he does today. Freeman Paget has a lovely pair of hands *and* a seat. There they are at the post. I never can stand it simply, when it comes to the start.'

A moment later David Grayson Watkins appeared, a white face and swollen eyes of horror.

'You're not going to let him ride, are you, Jim?' he asked. 'Not after the word I gave to Judith yesterday. It was the truth; I just happened to find out. Freeman Paget has bet twenty-five hundred dollars on Bristol! Judith, didn't you tell Jim? You can't have forgotten a thing like that!'

'Of course she told me,' said Jim Baring, 'but Paget told me before.'

'What!' cried Watkins.

'No matter what horse he's riding, he has a right to his own opinion about the winner.'

'But—'

'Oh, I know what you mean. I'm sorry you don't understand. Freeman Paget is a gentleman.'

'Ah, yes – yes,' said Watkins. 'I understand, then. Terribly sorry, Judith. Frightfully sorry, Jim. I've made an ass of myself about this. I didn't – ah, well—'

'Why didn't you tell me, Judy?' asked Jim Baring, quietly, as Watkins left.

'I love him,' said the girl.

'Do you, dear?' said Baring. 'Well, it will come out all right.'

Which Way, disdaining the ground like a cloud of fire, danced and floated all the way to the post but Paget paid little attention to the horse, there was such a weight and cold sickness in his heart. He had to lose twenty-five hundred dollars to win that race. The winning would crush that swine of a Delwin forever. But would it bring him closer to Judith? Looking down at his hands as the reins played them in and out, Paget saw that they were lean and hard like the rest of him. They might well have been, he thought, the hands of an old man. From the smoothness of another time the flesh had wasted; the knuckles were sharp ridges; but the change in his body was nothing compared with the change in his soul.

There had been a gradual alteration, a lowering to days of idle drifting until at last he was a bit of the worthless chaff that blows and whirls and disappears in the rear of the racing season. Now, if Which Way lost, there never would be any explaining. Not if Bristol won. Well, he had a vague feeling that years ago life had been flashed in his eyes like a bright sword from which he had shrunk and all the rest of his days he had been cowering and cowering away.

He faced the race as one faces the surgeon, anxious to be through with the pain.

At last they were lined up, from inside to outside in order: Chancery, Elegance, Which Way, Calvinist, Bristol, Calumet, Portulaca, Cargo, Trickster, Pennyroyal, White Magic. The start would come now in an instant. Paget felt an electric current running from the mouth of the horse up the reins and into his own brain cells.

They were off!

The white and lavender of Sargent shone in the lead as Which Way, untouched by the will of his rider, rated himself deep in the ruck, running with a stride that rolled as big and free as a ground swell on the Pacific. He seemed to know all about the miles that had to be covered and fell to his work.

The field rose in a great-crested wave at the first jump, pitched over it. Which Way trailed his wise feet deeply through the brush, saving strength which would be a life-giver at the end of four miles of running and jumping. At his right, Bristol flashed past, jumping big and fighting for his head, but Perry Gibson pulled the stallion back beside the two-time winner of his race. Bristol galloped well. His long stride kept him hanging lightly in the air.

Now the field was rounding the lower turn. On the long straight-away towards the grandstand, Paget took Which Way out of the ruck and carried him at a smart clip over the water jump and the hedge and ditch. He wanted to see what Bristol had to say to this early pace. He was well in the lead when Bristol, dipping over the fences like a swallow just behind, came up and looked Which Way in the eye. They passed the stands. Those crowded benches flowered suddenly and it seemed to Paget that nothing but the orange and blue of Baring was waving in the sun. He could see Jim Baring like a face cut from hard wood. Judith's head was down as though she could not endure the excitement, and that was odd, because in spite of her gentleness usually she could confront anything with a straight, clear eye. He saw another face at the fence near the finish: Harry Delwin . . .

They had completed the first round with not a single horse down but now they hit the big timber jump called Guthrie's Gate and disaster mowed down half the field; for Portulaca swerved, knocked Calumet right into the rails, and then landed beyond the fence in the path of Cargo. There was a huge spill that involved Trickster. Pennyroyal had come a cropper all of his own accord. And as Which Way slithered by the rolling mess on the ground,

Paget saw beautiful Bristol suspended in the air above the top bar, heading right at that confused ruin on the ground.

That meant half a million out of Delwin's pocket, but as Paget watched over his shoulder with a cold, clear eye he saw Perry Gibson skim the gray stallion over the tumult to safety beyond it. A magnificent effort for the horse, a splendid bit of bold riding for Perry Gibson. And five hundred thousand dollars back in the pocket of Harry Delwin.

Paget let Which Way pick up the tiring leaders as they reached the last long turn towards the straight. Elegance was reached and disposed of. White Magic, as though frightened by the shadow of the gelding, ran straight into a fence and crashed in a heap with Tilson lying nearby, blood on his face. Calvinist unexpectedly remained up there, galloping well until Which Way looked him in the eye; then the devil got into Calvinist's brain. He swerved and lurched sidelong at Which Way as Paget settled the big gelding for the next jump. He was taking it well on the outside, close to the edge, but at the last instant Calvinist bumped the gelding heavily.

That was the end of Calvinist. He struck the near side of the fence with a crash and Which Way rose drunkenly right beside the post that thrust up its head like an ugly fist a foot above the crest of the jump. Between that timber and the hard ribs of Which Way the ankle bones of Paget cracked like dry sticks.

He was jerked sidewise in the saddle. Which Way landed, pecked and almost banged his forehead against the ground. But the knees of Paget were glued to the saddle leather.

He looked down at his right foot. It was twisted. The stirrup iron shook off the boot. It jumped up and down at the end of the stirrup leather with every stride that Which Way made. And every jump shook the numbness out of the broken ankle and let the blood and the agony come thrusting in.

There was Bristol sweeping by. The voice of Perry Gibson screeched in the air like the cry of a sea bird: 'Too damned bad, Free! Pull up, old-timer!'

Which Way met the challenge of his own accord. Head to head he galloped with Bristol towards a rising madness of noise down the track. Paget might as well pull up. He felt himself a weight of lead that swung out of rhythm with his horse; the electric current no longer ran up and down the reins; and Which Way, with flattened ears, faltered in his stride. Bristol glided smoothly away. The crowd groaned like a beast that has been hurt.

He knew how the thing looked, two horses tied together by a single great effort, a battle that is costing blood and brain and nerve until the head of one of them begins to bob like a cork in a rough current, quickly left behind by the winner of the duel. Such a beaten horse never comes again, or almost never. Bristol already was half a dozen lengths ahead, running five hundred thousand dollars into the pockets of Delwin. Paget said, behind his teeth: 'Oh, Lord, it's all for nothing. . . .' And then something entered him, as the blue enters the morning sky.

Paget became once more a part of the gelding's life, an added thing in his blood, a portion in his heart and brain.

With his will power as with a knife he cut that right leg off at the knee and told himself that there was no pain. He was all one rhythmical part of Which Way, now. The ugly, honest old head was stretched straight out. Which Way was running as he had never run.

Yet the gap would not be closed.

How honestly the gelding struggled, giving greater and greater efforts that came up through the nerves of the rider in small, electric shudderings! The sharply pricked ears of the horse drove through the heart of Freeman Paget like two spears. All that courage could do was being done, but pain is a sword that can drive the soul still farther. Paget cut the side of the good horse with the whip and felt the blow as though it were on his own body.

There was an answer – a freshening, a greater stretch and lightness in the gallop. As though pain were food and breath which he needed, Which Way raced, still with pricking ears. The heart of Paget swelled. A blind mist washed his eyes till the face of the crowd blurred and the cry of the thousands seemed to be a thunder rising in his own throat, shouting: 'Which Way! Which Way! Which Way!'

They were seeing their miracle, which each horse-lover witnesses once in a lifetime: a beaten horse that comes back, while

Paget struck savagely again and again, and always into his own heart, it seemed.

They reached to the tail of Bristol. The crowd in the grandstand seemed to Paget like a toss of flame and a rising smoke, but the voice of the yelling was a wind that carried Which Way irresistibly forward.

He could see a thousand arms stretched out, pointing at him. Women caught their hands over their faces, and looked again. He himself glanced down and saw, as though it were no part of him, the crazy bobbing of the broken foot. The bone-edges must have cut through the outer flesh. His boot was full of blood. It was sloshing over, staining the silks, dribbling down the side of the boot.

But all of this was nothing. That sword which so many years ago had flashed in the eyes of Paget and from which he had shrunk away was flashing before him again – so it seemed to him – and he was using it to strike for a cause. All the carrion-eaters, all the Harry Delwins of the world – he was striking at them. Down with them! And all the cowards who, like himself, had shrunk from the business of life – for them the blows were being struck.

Pain is nothing. It's a food. You can eat it. It's a wine. You can drink it, and laugh. He saw Perry Gibson look back, a face twisted white with exhaustion and the agony of fear; then Bristol staggered and was struck back as though by a hand. The wire of the finish gleamed as small as a vanishing thought. . . .

The horse slowed at last. Perry Gibson went by, cantering Bristol towards a halt, shouting: 'Wonderful, old boy!'

And as big Which Way turned, laborious as a harness plow horse, someone ran out and raised the twisted face of a maniac to Paget. That was Harry Delwin, groaning: 'Why, Paget? Why? Why? For heaven's sake?'

Paget looked down at him and smiled.

'Because I wanted to blunt the edge of your teeth, Delwin,' he said. 'Before you gnawed into the souls of a hundred poor devils, as you have gnawed into mine. But you went too fast. I might be ready to lie for money but to keep a horse from running for that reason – No, Delwin, I had not come to that.'

*

Of the several colonels in Clarenton County, Colonel Victor Tolliver Stanhope was pre-eminent, therefore it was fit that his raised voice should spread around it a silence through the big, crowded rooms of the Baring house: 'Ladies and gentlemen, when I ask you to raise your glasses, I am not asking you to honor the finest fighting finish that these eyes of mine have ever seen ridden. I am asking you to consider a man who doubted himself and his horse so much that he laid a handsome wager on another, but then, regardless of profit – my friends, I toast the pure honor of a gentleman, Freeman Paget!' . . .

When at last the house was still, Paget was saying to Jim Baring: 'I wanted to tell them all the truth; when I laid my bet on Bristol I wasn't quite sure that I wouldn't pull Which Way in the race.'

'That isn't the truth,' said Baring.

'I think it is, Jim,' said Paget.

'Perhaps,' said Baring, 'but I think Judith will know. It's she that's at the piano in there, and playing it to let you understand. A day before the race she knew that you'd laid a heavy bet on Bristol. Suppose you go in there and talk to her about it?'

'I can't see her,' said Paget.

'What a damned fool you are, Free!' said Baring. 'Go in there to Judith. It's plain that she knows you better than you know yourself.'

It seemed to Paget, when he came to the threshold of the room, that an infinite distance lay between the door and the piano, and the reflection of the lights laid a dim, watery moonpath across the floor. Through this he forced himself to hobble on his crutches until the music stopped. With it he stopped also. It seemed to him a moment as long as birth or death before she turned to him.

My Old Man

ERNEST HEMINGWAY

To make a good living today's jockeys are forced to travel long distances: where once the courses of Britain would have been sufficient – with the occasional foray across the Channel to Europe – now leading riders regularly fly over the Atlantic and will even go as far afield as the southern hemisphere to Australia and New Zealand. This itinerant lifestyle is brilliantly captured in the following story by Ernest Hemingway (1898–1961), who was fascinated by racing – 'a demanding friend,' he described the sport in *A Moveable Feast* (1964), 'the falsest, most beautiful, most exciting, vicious and demanding because she could be profitable' – and who was a regular figure at the Auteuil and Enghien racecourses during the years he lived in France.

It is not generally realised that some of Hemingway's earliest pieces as a journalist were about racing; while working for the *Toronto Star* in the early twenties he wrote 'The Sport of Kings' (24 November 1923), a perceptive insight into the emotions of gambling, and followed this with a lengthy investigation, 'Betting in Toronto' for the 29 December issue. According to Hemingway, writing a few years before his death, he actually produced several short stories with a racetrack background but, 'everything I had written was lost and there was only one racing story that survived because it was out in the mails.' This was 'My Old Man'.

Hemingway, who was born close to a race course in Oak Park, Illinois, met the famous author Sherwood Anderson in the early twenties and was encouraged by his example, if not his advice. Sherwood's belief in hard work and dedication to writing about subjects with which he was intensely familiar set the young Hemingway on the road that would result in such brilliant personal novels as *The Sun Also Rises* (1926), *A Farwell to Arms*

(1929) and *For Whom The Bell Tolls* (1940), earning him a
Pulitzer Prize in 1953 and the Nobel Peace Prize a year later.
Anderson had no influence, however, on his staccato, vernacular
style of writing, and after the publication of 'My Old Man', with
its account of a boy's disenchantment with his crooked jockey-
father, he resented it being compared by some critics to a couple
of stories by the older man which also featured the racing world.
Hemingway responded vehemently to one critic, Edmund Wilson: 'No, I don't think "My Old Man" derives from Anderson – I
don't think they're anything alike. I know I wasn't inspired by
him.' Curiously, the story had earlier been rejected by *Cosmopolitan* and *Pictorial Review* before appearing in a fifty-eight-page
booklet, *Three Stories and Ten Poems* by Ernest M. Hemingway,
which was privately printed in 1923 in a limited edition of 300
copies by McAlman's Contract Publishing Co. It was, however,
seen there by the anthologist Edward O'Brien, who overlooked
the fact it had not appeared in a magazine and republished it in his
annual volume, *The Best Stories of 1923*. He was apparently so
impressed by the tale that he dedicated the book to his discovery,
although mis-spelling his name in the process: 'To Ernest
Hemenway'!

*

I guess looking at it, now, my old man was cut out for a fat guy,
one of those regular little roly fat guys you see around, but he
sure never got that way, except a little toward the last, and then it
wasn't his fault, he was riding over the jumps only and he could
afford to carry plenty of weight then. I remember the way he'd
pull on a rubber shirt over a couple of jerseys and a big sweat shirt
over that, and get me to run with him in the forenoon in the hot
sun. He'd have, maybe, taken a trial trip with one of Razzo's skins
early in the morning after just getting in from Torino at four
o'clock in the morning and beating it out to the stables in a cab
and then with the dew all over everything and the sun just starting
to get going, I'd help him pull off his boots and he'd get into a pair
of sneakers and all these sweaters and we'd start out.

'Come on, kid,' he'd say, stepping up and down on his toes in front of the jocks' dressing-room, 'let's get moving.'

Then we'd start off jogging around the infield once, maybe, with him ahead, running nice, and then turn out the gate and along one of those roads with all the trees along the sides of them that run out from San Siro. I'd go ahead of him when we hit the road and I could run pretty good and I'd look around and he'd be jogging easy just behind me and after a little while I'd look around again and he'd begun to sweat. Sweating heavy and he'd just be dogging it along with his eyes on my back, but when he'd catch me looking at him he'd grin and say, 'Sweating plenty?' When my old man grinned, nobody could help but grin too. We'd keep right on running out toward the mountains and then my old man would yell, 'Hey, Joe!' and I'd look back and he'd be sitting under a tree with a towel he'd had wrapped around his waist wrapped around his neck.

I'd come back and sit down beside him and he'd pull a rope out of his pocket and start skipping rope out in the sun with the sweat pouring off his face and him skipping rope out in the white dust with the rope going cloppetty, cloppetty, clop, clop, clop, and the sun hotter, and him working harder up and down a patch of the road. Say, it was a treat to see my old man skip rope, too. He could whirr it fast or lop it slow and fancy. Say, you ought to have seen wops look at us sometimes, when they'd come by, going into town walking along with big white steers hauling the cart. They sure looked as though they thought the old man was nuts. He'd start the rope whirring till they'd stop dead still and watch him, then give the steers a cluck and a poke with the goad and get going again.

When I'd sit watching him working out in the hot sun I sure felt fond of him. He sure was fun and he done his work so hard and he'd finish up with a regular whirring that'd drive the sweat out on his face like water and then sling the rope at the tree and come over and sit down with me and lean back against the tree with the towel and a sweater wrapped around his neck.

'Sure it's hell keeping it down, Joe,' he'd say, and lean back and shut his eyes and breathe long and deep, 'it ain't like when you're a kid.' Then he'd get up and before he started to cool we'd jog along back to the stables. That's the way it was keeping down to weight. He was worried all the time. Most jocks can just about ride off all they want to. A jock loses about a kilo every time he rides, but my old man was sort of dried out and he couldn't keep down his kilos without all that running.

I remember once at San Siro, Regoli, a little wop, that was riding for Buzoni, came out across the paddock going to the bar for something cool; and flicking his boots with his whip, after he'd just weighed in and my old man had just weighed in too, and came out with the saddle under his arm looking red-faced and tired and too big for his silks and he stood there looking at young Regoli standing up to the outdoors bar, cool and kid-looking, and I said, 'What's the matter, Dad?' 'cause I thought maybe Regoli had bumped him or something and he just looked at Regoli and said, 'Oh, to hell with it,' and went on to the dressing-room.

Well, it would have been all right, maybe, if we'd stayed in Milan and ridden at Milan and Torino, 'cause if there ever were any easy courses, it's those two. 'Pianola, Joe,' my old man said when he dismounted in the winning stall after what the wops thought was a hell of a steeplechase. I asked him once. 'This course rides itself. It's the pace you're going at, that makes riding the jumps dangerous, Joe. We ain't going any pace here, and they ain't really bad jumps either. But it's the pace always – not the jumps – that makes the trouble.'

San Siro was the swellest course I'd ever seen but the old man said it was a dog's life. Going back and forth between Mirafiore and San Siro and riding just about every day in the week with a train ride every other night.

I was nuts about the horses, too. There's something about it, when they come out and go up the track to the post. Sort of dancy and tight looking with the jock keeping a tight hold on them and maybe easing off a little and letting them run a little going up. Then once they were at the barrier it got me worse than anything. Especially at San Siro with that big green infield and the mountains way off and the fat wop starter with his big whip and the jocks fiddling them around and then the barrier snapping up and that bell going off and them all getting off in a bunch and then commencing to string out. You know the way a bunch of skins gets off. If you're up in the stand with a pair of glasses all you see is them plunging off and then that bell goes off and it seems like it rings for a thousand years and then they come sweeping round the turn. There wasn't ever anything like it for me.

But my old man said one day, in the dressing-room, when he was getting into his street clothes, 'None of these things are horses, Joe. They'd kill that bunch of skates for their hides and hoofs up at Paris.' That was the day he'd won the Premio Commercio with Lantorna shooting her out of the field the last hundred metres like pulling a cork out of a bottle.

It was right after the Premio Commercio that we pulled out and left Italy. My old man and Holbrook and a fat wop in a straw hat that kept wiping his face with a handkerchief were having an argument at a table in the Galleria. They were all talking French and the two of them was after my old man about something. Finally he didn't say anything any more but just sat there and looked at Holbrook, and the two of them kept after him, first one talking and then the other, and the fat wop always butting in on Holbrook.

'You go out and buy me a *Sportsman*, will you, Joe?' my old man said, and handed me a couple of soldi without looking away from Holbrook.

So I went out of the Galleria and walked over to in front of the Scala and bought a paper, and came back and stood a little way away because I didn't want to butt in and my old man was sitting back in his chair looking down at his coffee and fooling with a spoon and Holbrook and the big wop were standing and the big wop was wiping his face and shaking his head. And I came up and my old man acted just as though the two of them weren't standing there and said, 'Want an ice, Joe?' Holbrook looked down at my old man and said slow and careful, 'You son of a bitch,' and he and the fat wop went out through the stables.

My old man sat there and sort of smiled at me, but his face was white and he looked sick as hell and I was scared and felt sick inside because I knew something had happened and I didn't see how anybody could call my old man a son of a bitch, and get away with it. My old man opened up the *Sportsman* and studied the handicaps for a while, and then he said, 'You got to take a lot of things in this world, Joe.' And three days later we left Milan for good on the Turin train for Paris, after an auction sale out in front of Turner's stables of everything we couldn't get into a trunk and a suitcase.

We got into Paris early in the morning in a long, dirty station the old man told me was the Gare de Lyon. Paris was an awful big town after Milan. Seems like in Milan everybody is going somewhere and all the trams run somewhere and there ain't any sort of a mix-up, but Paris is all balled up and they never do straighten it out. I got to like it, though, part of it, anyway, and say, it's got the best race courses in the world. Seems as though that were the thing that keeps it all going and about the only thing you can figure on is that every day the buses will be going out to whatever track they're running at, going right out through everything to the track. I never really got to know Paris well, because I just came in about once or twice a week with the old man from Maisons and he always sat at the Café de la Paix on the Opera side with the rest of the gang from Maisons and I guess that's one of the busiest parts of the town. But, say, it is funny that a big town like Paris wouldn't have a Galleria, isn't it?

Well, we went out to live at Maisons-Lafitte, where just about everybody lives except the gang at Chantilly, with a Mrs Meyers that runs a boarding house. Maisons is about the swellest place to live I've ever seen in all my life. The town ain't so much, but there's a lake and a swell forest that we used to go off bumming in all day, a couple of us kids, and my old man made me a sling shot and we got a lot of things with it but the best one was a magpie. Young Dick Atkinson shot a rabbit with it one day and we put it under a tree and were all sitting around and Dick had some cigarettes and all of a sudden the rabbit jumped up and beat it into the brush and we chased it but we couldn't find it. Gee, we had fun at Maisons. Mrs Meyers used to give me lunch in the morning and I'd be gone all day. I learned to talk French quick. It's an easy language.

As soon as we got to Maisons, my old man wrote to Milan for his licence and he was pretty worried till it came. He used to sit around the Café de Paris in Maisons with the gang, there were lots of guys he'd known when he rode up at Paris, before the war, lived at Maisons, and there's a lot of time to sit around because the work around a racing stable, for the jocks, that is, is all cleaned up by nine o'clock in the morning. They take the first bunch of skins out to gallop at 5.30 in the morning and they work the second lot at 8 o'clock. That means getting up early all right and going to bed early, too. If a jock's riding for somebody too, he can't go boozing around because the trainer always has an eye on him if he's a kid and if he ain't a kid he's always got an eye on himself. So mostly if a jock ain't working he sits around the Café de Paris with the gang and they can all sit around about two or three hours in front of some drink like a vermouth and seltz and they talk and tell stories and shoot pool and it's sort of like a club or the Galleria in Milan. Only it ain't really like the Galleria because there everybody is going by all the time and there's everybody around at the tables.

Well, my old man got his licence all right. They sent it through to him without a word and he rode a couple of times. Amiens, up country and that sort of thing, but he didn't seem to get any engagement. Everybody liked him and whenever I'd come into the Café in the forenoon I'd find somebody drinking with him because my old man wasn't tight like most of these jockeys that have got the first dollar they made riding at the World's Fair in St Louis in nineteen ought four. That's what my old man would say when he'd kid George Burns. But it seemed like everybody steered clear of giving my old man any mounts.

We went out to wherever they were running every day with the car from Maisons and that was the most fun of all. I was glad when the horses came back from Deauville and the summer. Even though it meant no more bumming in the woods, 'cause then we'd ride to Enghien or Tremblay or St. Cloud and watch them from the trainers' and jockeys' stand. I sure learned about racing from going out with that gang and the fun of it was going every day.

I remember once out at St. Cloud. It was a big two hundred thousand franc race with seven entries and War Cloud a big favourite. I went around to the paddock to see the horses with my old man and you never saw such horses. This War Cloud is a great big yellow horse that looks just like nothing but run. I never saw such a horse. He was being led around the paddocks with his head down and when he went by me I felt all hollow inside he was so beautiful. There never was such a wonderful, lean, running built horse. And he went around the paddock putting his feet just so and quiet and careful and moving easy like he knew just what he had to do and not jerking and standing up on his legs and getting wild eyed like you see these selling platers with a shot of dope in them. The crowd was so thick I couldn't see him again except just his legs going by and some yellow and my old man started out through the crowd and I followed him over to the jocks' dressing-room back in the trees and there was a big crowd around there, too, but the man at the door in a derby nodded to my old man and we got in and everybody was sitting around and getting dressed and pulling shirts over their heads and pulling boots on and it all smelled hot and sweaty and linimenty and outside was the crowd looking in.

The old man went over and sat down beside George Gardner that was getting into his pants and said, 'What's the dope, George?' just in an ordinary tone of voice, 'cause there ain't any use him feeling around because George either can tell him or he can't tell him.

'He won't win,' George says very low, leaning over and buttoning the bottoms of his breeches.

'Who will?' my old man says, leaning over close so nobody can hear.

'Foxless,' George says, 'and if he does, save me a couple of tickets.'

My old man says something in a regular voice to George and George says, 'Don't ever bet on anything I tell you,' kidding like, and we beat it out and through all the crowd that was looking in, over to the 100 franc mutuel machine. But I knew something big was up because George is War Cloud's jockey. On the way he gets one of the yellow odds-sheets with the starting-prices on and War Cloud is only paying 5 for 10, Cefisidote is next at 3 to 1 and fifth down the list this Foxless at 8 to 1. My old man bets five thousand on Foxless to win and puts on a thousand to place and we went around back of the grandstand to go up the stairs and get a place to watch the race.

We were jammed in tight and first a man in a long coat with a grey tall hat and a whip folded up in his hand came out and then one after another the horses, with the jocks up and a stable boy holding the bridle on each side and walking along, followed the old guy. That big yellow horse War Cloud came first. He didn't look so big when you first looked at him until you saw the length of his legs and the whole way he's built and the way he moves. Gosh, I never saw such a horse. George Gardner was riding him and they moved along slow, back of the old guy in the grey tall hat that walked along like he was a ring master in a circus. Back of War Cloud, moving along smooth and yellow in the sun, was a good looking black with a nice head with Tommy Archibald riding him; and after the black was a string of five more horses all moving along slow in a procession past the grandstand and the pesage. My old man said the black was Foxless and I took a good look at him and he was a nice-looking horse, all right, but nothing like War Cloud.

Everybody cheered War Cloud when he went by and he sure was one swell-looking horse. The procession of them went around on the other side past the pelouse and then back up to the near end of the course and the circus master had the stable boys turn them loose one after another so they could gallop by the stands on their way up to the post and let everybody have a good look at them. They weren't at the post hardly any time at all when the gong started and you could see them way off across the infield all in a bunch starting on the first swing like a lot of little toy horses. I was watching them through the glasses and War Cloud was running well back, with one of the bays making the pace. They swept down and around and came pounding past and War Cloud was way back when they passed us and this Foxless horse in front and going smooth. Gee, it's awful when they go by you and then you have to watch them go farther away and get smaller and smaller and then all bunched up on the turns and then come around towards into the stretch and you feel like swearing and god-damming worse and worse. Finally they made the last turn and came into the straightaway with this Foxless horse way out in front. Everybody was looking funny and saying 'War Cloud' in a sort of sick way and them pounding nearer down the stretch, and then something came out of the pack right into my glasses like a horse-headed yellow streak and everybody began to yell 'War

Cloud' as though they were crazy. War Cloud came on faster than I'd ever seen anything in my life and pulled up on Foxless that was going fast as any black horse could go with the jock flogging hell out of him with the gad and they were right dead neck and neck for a second but War Cloud seemed going about twice as fast with those great jumps and that head out – but it was while they were neck and neck that they passed the winning post and when the numbers went up in the slots the first one was 2 and that meant that Foxless had won.

I felt all trembly and funny inside and then we were jammed in with the people going downstairs to stand in front of the board where they'd post what Foxless paid. Honest, watching the race I'd forgot how much my old man had bet on Foxless. I'd wanted War Cloud to win so damned bad. But now it was all over it was swell to know we had the winner.

'Wasn't it a swell race, Dad?' I said to him.

He looked at me sort of funny with his derby hat on the back of his head. 'George Gardner's a swell jockey all right,' he said. 'It sure took a great jock to keep that War Cloud horse from winning.'

Of course I knew it was funny all the time. But my old man saying that right out like that sure took the kick all out of it for me and I didn't get the real kick back again ever, even when they posted the numbers upon the board and the bell rang to pay off and we saw that Foxless paid 67.50 for 10. All round people were saying, 'Poor War Cloud! Poor War Cloud!' And I thought, I wish I were a jockey and could have rode him instead of that son of a bitch. And that was funny, thinking of George Gardner as a son of a bitch because I'd always liked him and besides he'd given us the winner, but I guess that's what he is, all right.

My old man had a big lot of money after that race and he took to coming into Paris oftener. If they raced at Tremblay he'd have them drop him in town on their way back to Maisons and he and I'd sit out in front of the Café de la Paix and watch the people go by. It's funny sitting there. There's streams of people going by and all sorts of guys come up and want to sell you things, and I loved to sit there with my old man. That was when we'd have the most fun. Guys would come by selling funny rabbits that jumped if you squeezed a bulb and they'd come up to us and my old man would kid them. He could talk French just like English and all those kind of guys knew him 'cause you can always tell a jockey – and then we always sat at the same table and they got used to seeing us there. There were guys selling matrimonial papers and girls selling rubber eggs that when you squeezed them a rooster came out of them and one old wormy-looking guy that went by with postcards of Paris, showing them to everybody, and, of course, nobody ever bought any, and then he would come back and show the under side of the pack and they would all be smutty postcards and lots of people would dig down and buy them.

Gee, I remember the funny people that used to go by. Girls around supper time looking for somebody to take them out to eat and they'd speak to my old man and he'd make some joke at them in French and they'd pat me on the head and go on. Once there was an American woman sitting with her kid daughter at the next table to us and they were both eating ices and I kept looking at the girl and she was awfully good looking and I smiled at her and she smiled at me but that was all that ever come of it because I looked for her mother and her every day and I made up ways that I was going to speak to her and I wondered if I got to know her if her mother would let me take her out to Auteuil or Tremblay but I never saw either of them again. Anyway, I guess it wouldn't have been any good, anyway, because looking back on it I remember the way I thought out would be best to speak to her was to say, 'Pardon me, but perhaps I can give you a winner at Enghien to-day?' and, after all, maybe she would have thought I was a tout instead of really trying to give her a winner.

We'd sit at the Café de la Paix, my old man and me, and we had a big drag with the waiter because my old man drank whisky and it cost five francs, and that meant a good tip when the saucers were counted up. My old man was drinking more than I've ever seen him, but he wasn't riding at all now and besides he said that whisky kept his weight down. But I noticed he was putting it on, all right, just the same. He'd busted away from his old gang out at Maisons and seemed to like just sitting around on the boulevard with me. But he was dropping money every day at the track. He'd feel sort of doleful after the last race, if he'd lost on the day, until we'd get to our table and he'd have his first whisky and then he'd be fine

He'd be reading the *Paris-Sport* and he'd look over at me and say, 'Where's your girl, Joe?' to kid me on account I had told him about the girl that day at the next table. And I'd get red, but I liked being kidded about her. It gave me a good feeling. 'Keep your eye peeled for her, Joe,' he'd say, 'she'll be back.'

He'd asked me questions about things and some of the things I'd say he'd laugh. And then he'd get started talking about things. About riding down in Egypt, or at St Moritz on the ice before my mother died, and about during the war when they had regular races down in the south of France without any purses, or betting or crowds or anything just to keep the breed up. Regular races with the jocks riding hell out of the horses. Gee, I could listen to my old man talk by the hour, especially when he'd had a couple or so of drinks.

He'd tell me about when he was a boy in Kentucky and going coon hunting, and the old days in the States before everything went on the bum there. And he'd say, 'Joe, when we've got a decent stake, you're going back there to the States and go to school.'

'What've I got to go back there to go to school for when everything's on the bum there?' I'd ask him.

'That's different,' he'd say and get the waiter over and pay the pile of saucers and we'd get a taxi to the Gare St. Lazare and get on the train out to Maisons.

One day at Auteuil after a selling steeplechase, my old man bought in the winner for 30,000 francs. He had to bid a little to get him but the stable let the horse go finally and my old man had his permit and his colours in a week. Gee, I felt proud when my old man was an owner. He fixed it up for stable space with Charles Drake and cut out coming in to Paris, and started his running and sweating out again, and him and I were the whole stable gang. Our horse's name was Gilford, he was Irish bred and a nice, sweet jumper. My old man figured that training him and riding him, himself, he was a good investment. I was proud of everything and I thought Gilford was as good a horse as War Cloud. He was a good, solid jumper, a bay, with plenty of speed on the flat, if you asked him for it, and he was a nice-looking horse, too.

Gee, I was fond of him. The first time he started with my old man up, he finished third in a 2500 metre hurdle race and when my old man got off him, all sweating and happy in the place stall, and went in to weigh, I felt as proud of him as though it was the first race he'd ever placed in. You see, when a guy ain't been riding for a long time, you can't make yourself really believe that he has ever rode. The whole thing was different now, 'cause down in Milan, even big races never seemed to make any difference to my old man, if he won he wasn't ever excited or anything, and now it was so I couldn't hardly sleep the night before a race and I knew my old man was excited, too, even if he didn't show it. Riding for yourself makes an awful difference.

Second time Gilford and my old man started, was a rainy Sunday at Auteuil, in the Prix du Marat, a 4500 metre steeple-chase. As soon as he'd gone out I beat it up to the stand with the new glasses my old man had bought for me to watch them. They started way over at the far end of the course and there was some trouble at the barrier. Something with goggle blinders on was making a great fuss and rearing around and busted the barrier once, but I could see my old man in our black jacket, with a white cross and a black cap, sitting up on Gilford, and patting him with his hand. Then they were off in a jump and out of sight behind the trees and the gong going for dear life and the pari-mutuel wickets rattling down. Gosh, I was so excited, I was afraid to look at them, but I fixed the glasses on the place where they would come out back of the trees and then out they came with the old black jacket going third and they all sailing over the jump like birds. Then they went out of sight again and then they came pounding out and down the hill and all going nice and sweet and easy and taking the fence smooth in a bunch, and moving away from us all solid. Looked as though you could walk across their backs they were all so bunched and going so smooth. Then they bellied over the big double Bullfinch and something came down. I couldn't see who it was, but in a minute the horse was up and galloping free and the field, all bunched still, sweeping around the long left turn into the straightaway. They jumped the stone wall and came jammed down the stretch toward the big waterjump right in front of the stands. I saw them coming and hollered at my old man as he went by, and he was leading by about a length and riding way out and light as a monkey, and they were racing for the water-jump. They took off over the big hedge of the waterjump in a pack and then there was a crash, and two horses pulled sideways out of it, and kept on going, and three others were piled up. I couldn't see my old man anywhere. One horse kneed himself up and the jock had hold of the bridle and mounted and went slamming on after the place money. The other horse was up and away by himself, jerking his head and galloping with the bridle rein hanging and the jock staggered over to one side of the track against the fence. Then Gilford rolled over to one side off my old man and got up and started to run on three legs with his front off hoof dangling and there was my old man laying there on the grass flat out with his face up and blood all over the side of his head. I ran down the stand and bumped into a jam of people and got to the rail and a cop grabbed me and held me and two big stretcher-bearers were going out after my old man and around on the other side of the course I saw three horses, strung way out, coming out of the trees and taking the jump.

My old man was dead when they brought him in and while a doctor was listening to his heart with a thing plugged in his ears, I heard a shot up the track that meant they'd killed Gilford. I lay down beside my old man, when they carried the stretcher into the hospital room, and hung on to the stretcher and cried and cried, and he looked so white and gone and so awfully dead, and I couldn't help feeling that if my old man was dead maybe they didn't need to have shot Gilford. His hoof might have got well. I don't know. I loved my old man so much.

Then a couple of guys came in and one of them patted me on the back and then went over and looked at my old man and then pulled a sheet off the cot and spread it over him; and the other was telephoning in French for them to send the ambulance to take him out to Maisons. And I couldn't stop crying, crying and choking, sort of, and George Gardner came in and sat down beside me on the floor and put his arm around me and says, 'Come on, Joe, old boy. Get up and we'll go out and wait for the ambulance.'

George and I went out to the gate and I was trying to stop bawling and George wiped off my face with his handkerchief and we were standing back a little ways while the crowd was going out of the gate and a couple of guys stopped near us while we were waiting for the crowd to get through the gate and one of them was counting a bunch of mutuel tickets and he said, 'Well, Butler got his, all right.'

The other guy said, 'I don't give a good goddam if he did the crook. He had it coming to him on the stuff he's pulled.'

'I'll say he had,' said the other guy, and tore the bunch of tickets in two.

And George Gardner looked at me to see if I'd heard and I had all right, and he said, 'Don't you listen to what those bums said, Joe. Your old man was one swell guy.'

But I don't know. Seems like when they get started they don't leave a guy nothing.

Saratoga in August

HUGH PENTECOST

There is nothing crooked about jockey Jimmy Coombs in this next story, although he finds himself at the centre of a brutal plan to fix a race by injuring his horse. The setting is the Saratoga race course not far from New York which is for many racegoers the most beautiful track in America. Churchill Downs in Louisville where the Kentucky Derby is run, may be more famous; the Arlington International at Chicago the richest with 'The Miracle Million', the world's first million-dollar horse race; and the Santa Anita track in the San Gabriel Mountains of California, the most spectacular. But for countless thousands of Americans there is nowhere else to be than Saratoga in August, where the race meetings which have been held since 1860 attract the most colourful cross-section of horses, jockeys and punters to be seen anywhere in America. As this mystery story reveals, it is a venue that attracts the good and the bad: specifically Joe Salmin, a gangster who will stop at nothing to achieve his purpose; Willie 'Slick' Jacobs, described as 'a character straight out of Damon Runyon'; and a giant, red-bearded, artist-detective named John Jericho. John is, in fact, primarily attracted to Saratoga for the opportunities it offers him as an artist, but suddenly he finds himself in the middle of a callous plot, the solution to which lies in one of his spur-of-moment sketches.

Hugh Pentecost was the pseudonym of Judson Pentecost Philips (1903–89) perhaps best-known for his engaging sleuth, Pierre Chambrun, the French-born gourmet-detective, who was forever trying to find the time to run one of New York's foremost luxury hotels while investigating a whole catalogue of baffling crimes and murders. Philips, who was born in Massachusetts, the son of an opera singer and an actor, was educated at Columbia

University – where he wrote his first crime story – and thereafter joined the *New York Tribune* as a sports reporter, covering mainly baseball and horse racing. Some of his first short mysteries were written for the pulp magazines, but he came to the attention of crime readers with a novel, *Cancelled In Red*, published in 1939. He was later one of the founding members of the Mystery Writers of America and in 1973 was given the special award of Grand Master for his contributions to the genre.

Philips said he got his best ideas from listening to 'saloon talk' and once actually claimed a deduction on his income tax return for the money he said he had spent on drinks for his informants! The claim was allowed by the IRS – although he was asked in future to list such expenses as 'research'! He also made a point of carefully researching the tracks mentioned in his racing novels, which included *The 24th Horse* (1940) featuring New York Inspector Luke Bradley, and *The Homicidal Horse* (1979), a case for public relations sleuth Julian Quist, although Saratoga always remained his favourite. (The town also has another curious claim to fame, for it was here in 1853 that a Red Indian Chief-turned-chef named George Crum invented the first potato crisps which he merchandised as George's Saratoga Crisps!)

The painter-detective John Jericho also made his debut in a novel, *Dead Woman of the Year* (1967), but most of his later cases have been told in short story form and a lot of his admirers believe that it is tales such as the following one, steeped in the atmosphere of the track and graphically portraying the underside of racing, that will ensure his reputation as one of the most creative mystery writers of the century.

*

It has been said that the reason there are so many stray dogs in the town of Saratoga Springs, New York, during the month of August, is that they have rented their dog-houses to visiting canines. It is the custom of the human residents of the town to rent their gracious homes, surrounded by lush green lawns and shaded by ancient elms, to people who come there in August for the month of racing. It has been said that the rents for the month could amount to half of the purchase price of the property. But the racing buffs ignore the costs. There is only one Saratoga, only one place on earth for the genuine horse player to be in the month of August. From these undeniable facts comes the probable apocrypha about stray dogs.

'Like the horses,' Jericho would say when he was asked, 'I come to Saratoga in August to eat the grass.'

Since Jericho was considered to be an eccentric, some people thought he might actually be telling the truth. He was a giant of a man, well over six feet tall with 240 pounds of well muscled body. His red hair, red beard, and mustache gave him the look of an oldtime Viking warrior. Perhaps, some people thought, a diet of sweet clover and grass might account for his aura of incredible good health.

Anything could be true in Saratoga if you said it with authority – for instance, who will win the fifth race? There will always be someone to tell you, and it will be true until a different horse makes it a lie.

Going to Saratoga in August, wrote the late Joe Palmer, incomparable chronicler of the world of horses, 'is a successful turning back of the pages, a stroll through the mirror, the slow drop of Alice down the rabbit hole. It is a month of living in about 1910.'

Jericho, sitting in the grass, his back propped against a giant elm, making casual charcoal sketches of grooms cooling thoroughbreds who had just been working out on the track, of horses looking at him curiously over the tops of box-stall doors, felt that he was living comfortably in another age. He knew that the famous Mrs Langtry, the Jersey Lily, and the probably infamous Diamond Jim Brady had walked in the grass right where he sat more than three quarters of a century ago.

In a world of turmoil and violence, of crime and man's inhumanity to man, there was an old-world grace, a strange peaceful tradition, a kind of forgotten style here at Saratoga that let you relax and forget – for the month of August. Horse people will tell you that after eleven months of racing in the big cities, at tracks like Aqueduct and Belmont, surrounded by cement and macadam and carbon monoxide fumes, Saratoga was good for man and beast. For the horses there was grass to eat; for the people the grandstand wasn't as crowded as those at the city tracks; for the State the share of the betting money was smaller, but surely there should be one time in the racing year when the prime concern was not the cash register. As Joe Palmer also wrote, 'Any man who would change that would stir champagne.'

On that morning when Jericho sat propped against a tree, sketching, there was, not far away, a man preparing to stir champagne.

Saratoga is not guarded by armed troops, like the city tracks. You don't need a pass to walk into Shed How, where the horses are kept, fed, groomed, pampered, and even worshipped. You don't need an introduction to the person standing next to you. You presumably both belong to the same club, have a mutual interest in horses and the life that goes with them. You could have no other reason to be there and, therefore, you are friends with everyone. Saratoga in August.

The truth is that John Jericho is not a passionate devotee of the horse, but of the way of life that surrounds them, particularly at Saratoga in August. He is a man who has traveled the world, painting in brilliant colors and with a kind of fierce outrage the daily history of violence. The result is that he is not only a painter but a persistent and deadly fighter against men who destroy their brothers for the sake of profit and power. Thieves, murderers, and war makers of all races and creeds are his enemies, and a great many of them have learned, too late, that they would be well advised to stay out of his way. Saratoga in August is the place where, once a year, he takes time to regroup his energies, refresh his enormous vitality; where he sits in the shade, totally relaxed, idly sketching the horses and the people who surround them. It is his way of preparing for the next turn of the wheel. Violence is inconceivable in this old-world setting.

And yet, there was a man preparing to stir champagne.

Willie Jacobs, known as Slick to his friends, was one of the delights Jericho looked forward to each August at Saratoga. Jericho was a man who detested phonies and Willie Slick Jacobs was a total fraud. But a harmless one, an engaging one, Jericho noted. Slick was a character straight out of a Damon Runyan story. His language was a combination of Runyanese and the eloquent prose of the aforementioned Joe Palmer. Jericho, taken in from time to time, discovered after a little research that Slick was loaded with direct quotes from those two great men, quotes he appropriated as his own colorful inventions, and that he acted a role invented by those great men from the past.

There was nothing sinister about Willie the Slick. He knew horses. He worked at the business of being a character for the simple reason that it gave him entree to the world of people who live with and by horses. Willie the Slick didn't want to steal from them, or defraud them. He just wanted to be one of them.

Jericho had met Willie one day, half a dozen years ago. Jericho had been propped against his favorite elm tree, sketching. He found himself attracted to a little man with a sharp ferret's face wearing a checkered cap and a rather gaudy, vested summer suit. A tout, Jericho thought, and drew a wicked caricature of the little man.

Slick Jacobs approached him. 'You drawin' a picture of me?' he asked.

Jericho handed him his sketch pad. Slick looked stunned. 'Gawd a'mighty, do I look like that?' he asked.

Jericho grinned at him. 'To me,' he said.

Slick shook his head. 'Maybe I oughta steer clear of you,' he said. But he was fascinated by the other sketches of horses and people on the pages of the sketch pad. He sat down in the grass beside Jericho.

'They really pamper the horses,' Slick said. 'A hundred and fifty years ago they'd rub 'em down with whiskey and let 'em drink it, too. Twenty eggs the day they exercised. Some people believed in a pound of butter each day, washed down with a quart of English claret.' Slick gave Jericho a sly look. 'In those days when they said a horse was stiff, he was stiff!'

Jericho smiled back. 'As Joe Palmer wrote in one of his inimitable columns.'

'Jeese, I better steer clear of you,' Slick said.

'Expert plagiarism is a gift,' Jericho said.

It was the beginning of a beautiful friendship.

On that day, six years later, when trouble was brewing, Slick sought out Jericho under his favorite tree.

'Time to head for the grandstand, Dad,' he said. He called Jericho 'Dad' for no particular reason. They had a date to watch Foreclosure, considered the greatest horse of the day, run the seventh race.

Jericho rarely watched the races. His concern was with the backstage of the world of horses, but Slick had insisted that he simply couldn't bypass the chance to see the great Foreclosure do his stuff.

Slick and Jericho made their way around the far end of the track to the grandstand. The parade to the post for the seventh race had already begun.

'Look at him!' Slick said. 'Ever see anything like it? He looks like a plow horse.'

Different horses have a different approach to the moment of truth. Some of them, tense, prancing, are led to the starting gate by an outrider on a stable pony. Some of them, with only the jockey in control, seem prepared to take off for the moon at any moment. Then there is the rare one, like Foreclosure, who just ambles down the track, relaxed, unexcited by the noise of the crowd or the nearness of the contest for which he is prepared, coddled, trained.

Foreclosure, a big bay stallion, unbeaten in three years of racing, was the picture of relaxation. Jimmy Coombs, the jockey who had ridden him in all his big races, exerted no pressure on the reins. Foreclosure just ambled along, fourth in the parade.

'He don't waste anythin' on the way to work,' Slick said. He obviously loved the big horse, as did the applauding spectators in the grandstand and along the rail. Foreclosure turned his head, ears pricked, as if to acknowledge the cheers that he evidently knew were meant for him

The horses turned at the far end of the track and approached the starting gate, where handlers on foot waited to lead them into their appointed starting stalls.

'In like a lamb and out like a lion,' Slick said.

Foreclosure walked into the Number 4 slot and stood quietly

while the other horses, exhibiting varying degrees of tension and excitement, were led into place, the gates closed behind them.

'The horses are in place,' the track loudspeaker told the crowd. 'Hammerlock in the Number 6 spot is giving the handlers a little trouble and – *they're off*!'

The horses broke from the gate, and at that same moment the crowd was on its feet, screaming. The great Foreclosure, normally a fast starter from the gate, had gone completely haywire. He came out bucking and kicking. He barged into the Number 5 horse on his right, knocking that one off stride. He swerved in and smashed into the Number 3 horse, unseating the jockey. He headed outside again and charged into the rail, throwing Jimmy Coombs over his head and into the crowd.

Then Foreclosure raced down the track, nostrils flaring, dark with sweat, still bucking like a rodeo horse broken loose from a cattle pen. Riderless, he pounded his way through the horses that were ahead of him and then, at the first turn, he kept right on to the fence and sailed over it and into the screaming crowd.

Slick, jumping up and down in an effort to see over the heads of the the people in front of him, was swearing, tears streaming down his cheeks. The crazed Foreclosure was a symbol of everything he cared for on this earth.

Very few people, except perhaps those who had bet on him, noticed that Slim Jim, a 40-1 outsider, won the seventh race at Saratoga that afternoon by six lengths.

Rumors spread like a forest fire around the track. An ambulance had taken Jimmy Coombs to the hospital. Some said he was dead. Some said he had broken limbs or a concussion. What about the jockey who had been knocked off the Number 3 horse? He'd walked away from the spill, miraculously unhurt.

But the big question was Foreclosure. Had he been caught without serious injury? What could have driven him into such a frenzy?

'Only pain – pain he couldn't stand,' Slick said, as he and Jericho wedged their way through the crowd toward Shed Row where there would be answers.

Foreclosure had finally been brought down by cowboy skills as he reared and kicked his way through the crowd at the far end of the track. A couple of dozen people had been injured – how seriously there were no reports as yet – before some stablehands managed to lasso the berserk horse and bring him down, sweat-smeared, bleeding from the mouth and from wounds in his forelegs where he had hit the fence breaking out of the track. A track veterinarian had managed to sedate the struggling Foreclosure and he had been carried back to his stable on Shed Row in a horse ambulance.

A huge crowd had gathered around the stable, waiting for some news about the horse's condition. Slick Jacobs knew everyone backstage, including the security men who had roped off the area to keep the curious from barging right into the animal's stall.

Eventually an old man, his face tear-stained, came out of the stall. He was Mike Greenleaf, the groom whose job it was to care for the champion thoroughbred. He seemed to grab onto Slick, someone he knew and trusted.

'You wouldn't believe,' he said, nodding to Jericho when Slick introduced them. 'His mouth. Of course Jimmy Coombs tried to stop him when he bolted, yanked him around pretty bad. But that isn't what did it. It's like his mouth was burned out with acid.'

'Acid!'

'That's what the vet thinks. Burned the poor baby's mouth raw as hamburger.'

'How?' Slick asked, not believing. 'He walked into the starting gate quiet enough, Mike.'

Mike Greenleaf nodded. 'Either it was squirted into his mouth at the last minute, or it was contained in a capsule, maybe fastened to his bit, that he bit into, or that dissolved just as the starting gate opened.'

'You saddled him for the race, didn't you, Mike?' Slick asked. 'Wouldn't you have noticed if anything was fastened to his bit?'

'You'd think I would, wouldn't you? Well, I didn't. I got to go, Slick. The track stewards are holding an inquiry.'

'The only person who could have squirted anything into his mouth is the handler who led him into the starting gate,' Slick said.

Greenleaf nodded. 'Eddie Stevens. They're trying to locate him.'

'What about Foreclosure? Is he going to make it all right?'

'Who knows?' Greenleaf said bitterly. 'He may never let anyone put a bit in his mouth again – we may never be able to handle him in another race.'

'The horse's owner?' Jericho asked, speaking for the first time.

'Jeb Faulkner,' Greenleaf said. 'He's out on the West Cost. He has a couple of horses running out there. They're trying to get him on the phone now.'

Slick and Jericho watched the old groom walk off.

'Acid!' Slick said. 'Some bum really did stir the champagne.'

Jericho had made friends over the years of his visits to Saratoga. Finding a place to stay for a month wasn't easy. Among the people who rented estates there for August was Ruth Prentiss, one of the great ladies in the world of racing. Mrs Prentiss was also a patron of the arts and the owner of several of Jericho's paintings. There was a small apartment over the garage of the estate she rented and it was Jericho's for the asking. Slick and Jericho went there.

'I've got some forty-year-old bonded anti-freeze there that I think I could use,' Jericho told Slick. 'Anti-freeze' was a synonym for bourbon whiskey. Jericho didn't want to drink in a bar surrounded by mobs of people all talking about the disaster to Foreclosure. A deep anger was burning in his gut. The senseless cruelty to the great horse, who could be worth more than a million dollars to his owner when he was syndicated and put out to stud, was as evil a crime as anything that Jericho had seen man do to man.

'Someone probably made a killing on that race,' he said to Slick as he poured bourbon over ice in two old-fashioned glasses. Neither man wanted his liquor diluted. 'That Slim Jim paid forty-to-one.'

'The totalizator will show that up if there was any heavy betting on him at the track,' Slick said.

'Offtrack betting parlors all over the country,' Jericho said. 'Hundreds of hundred-dollar bets scattered around the country. Would they show up?'

'In time,' Slick said. 'But let me tell you about Slim Jim. He's a sprinter, not a distance horse. That race was a mile and a quarter. Slim Jim can't run that far. He was in there to set a fast pace for the first few furlongs. Foreclosure would have run him into the ground over the distance. He'd have been at the end of the parade when the race ended if it hadn't been that all hell broke loose.'

'But if someone knew it was going to happen?'

'Slim Jim is owned by a guy named Rod Cross. Decent guy, good young owner. His father was Martin Cross who raced good horses ever since I was a kid. No shenanigans from him. What happened? Slim Jim broke fast from the gate, like he was supposed to. He was ahead of the field when Foreclosure stampeded. Everyone behind him was pulling up, trying to get out of Foreclosure's way. Slim Jim just kept running with nobody able to take out after him until it was too late. I'll bet if you look at a film of the race you'll see that Slim Jim was staggering the last quarter mile, but he was ten lengths ahead by then in the confusion. I'll bet you Rod Cross didn't have two bucks on him. Slim Jim wasn't supposed to win, just set the early pace.'

'It wouldn't have to be anyone who owned or trained Slim Jim, would it?' Jericho asked. 'Anyone who knows racing, like you, would know that Slim Jim would be in the lead at the start. If the race could be disrupted behind him—?'

Slick Jacobs didn't seem to hear. He'd picked up Jericho's sketch pad which the big man had tossed down on a table when he set about making drinks.

'When did you do this?' he asked. He'd been flipping the pages, casually interested. Now he was riveted on a sketch of two men, leaning against a fence rail somewhere, watching a horse who was being walked cool in the background.

'Why?' Jericho asked. 'What about it? Sometime just after breakfast this morning. Friends of yours?'

Slick's finger wasn't quite steady as he pointed at one figure, dressed in blue jeans, a plaid sports shirt, and Western boots.

'That one is Eddie Stevens,' Slick said. 'He's the guy they're looking for. He handled Foreclosure in the starting gate.'

'You know the other one?'

'Sure I know him,' Slick said. 'He's Joe Salmin, gangster type who isn't very popular around race tracks anywhere. Strong-arm wheeler-dealer. You suppose—?'

'That horse in the background,' Jericho said. 'That's Foreclosure. Just finished an easy canter on the track, preparing for this afternoon's race.'

'And two and two makes four,' Slick said.

'If you can prove it,' Jericho said.

'The track stewards would like to see that sketch, I'll bet,' Slick said. 'And the State Police, too.'

Over the years John Jericho had developed a healthy respect for the professional skills of the police, but the legal restrictions under which they operated were another matter. You had to read a criminal his rights. You couldn't third-degree a confession out of a man, no matter how monstrous his crime. '*Poor baby's mouth raw as hamburger,*' old Greenleaf had said. An innocent animal ruthlessly tortured – for profit! '*Read the prisoner his rights.*' Damn his rights, Jericho thought.

'Where can we find Eddie Stevens?' he asked.

'Somewhere between here and Mexico,' Slick said. 'Paid off and took off.'

'And this Joe Salmin? He wouldn't take a powder, would he? It might draw attention to him.'

'He rents a cottage down at the south end of town for the month of August,' Slick said. 'Some local yokel lets him have it each summer. Probably knows he'll get his arm broke if he doesn't.'

'Let's see if Mr Salmin will be interested in my sketch,' Jericho said.

'That's not a safe idea, Dad,' Slick said. 'Joe Salmin's apt to blow your head off when he sees it.'

A muscle along Jericho's jaw rippled under his red beard. 'That could be dangerous if I wasn't ready for it,' he said.

The Lyman cottage at the south end of Saratoga was a pleasant little place, surrounded by a white picket fence. At the rear of it was a small garden, bright with summer flowers. Joe Salmin, overlord of crime, sat there in a wicker armchair, drinking what looked like a pleasantly cool gin and tonic. Counting his money,

Jericho thought. He was a big man, dark-haired, wearing a gaudy sports shirt and light beige slacks. His size pleased Jericho, who never liked to fight a smaller man.

Salmin turned his head as he heard the garden gate open. 'What the hell are you doing here, Slick?' he asked.

'Friend of mine wanted to meet you, Mr Salmin,' Slick said. 'He has something I thought you'd like to see.' He held out Jericho's sketchbook, opened to the right drawing.

Salmin took the drawing and looked at it, a nerve twitching at the corner of his mouth.

'I remember seeing you out at the track this morning,' he said to Jericho. 'You do this for fun, or you make your living at it?'

'You might say both,' Jericho said. He moved casually, so that he was standing behind the gangster, looking over his shoulder.

'It's good,' Salmin said. 'How much you want for it?'

'Oh, the price isn't prohibitive, Mr Salmin,' Jericho said. 'Just some information – like, where is Eddie Stevens? And what are the names of the people who placed bets on Slim Jim for you all around the country?'

Salmin started to heave up out of his chair. Jericho's left arm went around his neck, jerking him back. His right hand closed on Salmin's right wrist and twisted the arm behind the man's back. In spite of himself the gangster cried out in pain.

'Be good enough to pull Mr Salmin's tooth, will you, Slick?' Jericho said softly. 'He's carrying a gun in a holster under his left arm.'

Slick, as if he were walking on eggs, came slowly forward. Salmin lashed out at him with a booted foot.

'Now, now, Mr Salmin, none of that,' Jericho said. 'I can start out by breaking your arm. And if you insist, I can break your neck. If you please, Slick.'

Slick came forward and snatched the gun out of Salmin's holster. He backed away, holding the gun in a shaking hand.

'Be good enough to point that somewhere else, Slick,' Jericho said. 'And now, Mr Salmin, where is Eddie Stevens?'

'I don't know any Eddie Stevens,' Salmin said, half strangling for breath.

'The other man in my sketch,' Jericho said. 'The man you were talking to about acid.'

The gangster started to struggle, but Jericho pulled up painfully on his arm.

'I guess you can stand pain, Mr Salmin,' Jericho said. 'But I think I have something that you can't stand.' He looked steadily at Slick. 'Be good enough, Slick, to hand me that little bottle of acid we found in Eddie Stevens's room.'

Slick stared at his friend like a man in a trance, his eyes wide with disbelief.

'Come on, Slick, we haven't got all day,' Jericho said.

Slick put a hand in his pocket and brought it out, his fist closed around something. He came forward, stiff-legged, and held out that fist to Jericho. Jericho put his knee into the middle of Salmin's back and jerked his head back. He released the gangster's right arm and reached out for what Slick apparently was holding in his closed fist. Salmin, his head bent back so that he looked up into the sky, struggled weakly.

'What I've got here, Mr Salmin, is the acid you prescribed for Foreclosure. When I start to pour it into your eyes you will never see another summer sunset, or the flowers in this garden, or another horserace, or the profit figures at the bottom of the accounting sheet your men send you.'

'All right! All right!' Salmin cried out, a pent-up scream. 'Eddie's on his way to the Albany airport where a chartered plane is waiting to fly him out of the country.'

'Go into the cottage, Slick, and call the police,' Jericho said. 'Tell them to stop any chartered plane preparing to leave the Albany airport. Meanwhile, Mr Salmin, the names of the people who placed bets for you, please.' He held his closed fist over the gangster's terrified eyes.

'I thought you must have gone out of your mind!' Slick said. 'Asking me for acid we found in Eddie's room. What room? What acid? I almost blew it.'

The two men were back in Jericho's room, sipping the bonded anti-freeze again. The Saratoga cops had carted off Joe Salmin. Airport security people had snatched Eddie Stevens when he arrived there.

'It turned out to be a great tongue loosener,' Jericho said. 'I knew I could count on you, Slick. You spend your life acting a role, and I knew you'd improvise well when it was required of you.'

'Brother! I almost asked you what the hell you were talking about!' Slick shook his head. 'How could he believe that you'd really pour acid in his eyes?'

'I suspect Mr Salmin has done just as terrible things as that to other men,' Jericho said. 'A man who is capable of brutal torture has to believe that other men are capable of the same monstrous actions.' He raised his glass. 'It seems our Mr Salmin stirred the champagne once too often.'

The Photographer and the Jockey

JAMES HOLDING

The people of South America also have a passion for horse racing, with two of the finest race courses both located in Brazil at Sao Paolo and Rio de Janeiro. Rio is also the home of the famous and very exclusive Jockey Club in the Avenida Rio Branco, which is said to have been inspired by either the English or French Jockey Clubs. Created in 1868 by a small group of enthusiasts and funded from members' and spectators' purses, it built the city's first major race course on the northeastern outskirts five years later. By the early 1880s an English visitor was enthusing in his journal, 'I do not suppose that any other racecourse in the world enjoys such a view, with the glorious mountains all around, while the grandstand is a very fine building which could hold five thousand people.' The anonymous scribe also added wryly, 'I suppose because racing is entirely an exotic from England, the horses run round as they do at Epsom, from right to left.' In the years which followed such was the success of the club that Jeffrey D. Needell could write in his book, *Brazil: A Tropical Belle Epoque* (1987), 'Monarchies might fall, Republics might rise, Society and the Jockey Club remained.' The Brazilian fascination with racing is, in fact, at the heart of this next story about Paulo Pereira, 'the most famous jockey in Brazil' and Manuel Andradas, a professional photographer who also happens to be a professional assassin.

James Holding (1907–) was born in Pittsburgh, Pennsylvania and started to write while studying at Yale where he became the editor of the *Yale Record* and later won the prestigious John Masefield Poetry Prize. For a number of years he worked in an advertising agency, but then in 1960 began to indulge his interest in crime fiction by creating his own mystery stories. These immediately found favour with the doyen of American crime-writers and anthologists, Ellery Queen, who was thereafter responsible for first publishing many of Holding's stories in the magazine which bears his name. In 1962 James Holding sent his mentor the first of the case histories of the character who has since made him famous: Manuel Andradas, the Brazilian who uses photography as a cover for his main occupation. Ellery Queen later provided a pen-portrait of Andradas to accompany his exploits: 'A fastidious man, especially with words, Manuel does not think of himself as a murderer. That term is too harsh, too crude, too brutal. Rather, he looks upon himself as a Nullifier – a freelance who accepts businesslike assignments from The Corporation, "The Big Ones" (they are too fastidious in their choice of names – never anything as indelicate as The Mob or even The Syndicate).'

Nothing, however, can disguise the fact that these men are Brazil's organised crime group, and with horse racing and gambling representing two of their main sources of income, Andradas has found himself at the races acting on their behalf in several stories. 'The Photographer and The Jockey' is one of the best of these and when originally published in *EQM* in August 1974, was introduced once again by Ellery Queen. 'If there's a jockey, can a horse race be far behind?' he asked. 'Actually, it is a two-horse race – between money and murder. Place your bet – but if there's a photographer, can a photo finish be far behind . . .'

*

With his camera case on the floor beside him, Manuel Andradas, known in Rio de Janeiro as The Photographer, sat at a corner table in an open-air café below the towering figure of Christ the Redeemer on Corcovado. He sipped beer while waiting for Rodolfo. He would have preferred a glass of cashew juice – he considered it soothing to the nerves – but cashew juice was unavailable at the café.

Rodolfo had made the rendezvous with Manuel by telephone the evening before. Manuel had been quite pleased, in his peculiarly unemotional way, to hear from Rodolfo. Six weeks had elapsed since his last assignment. And Manuel needed money. At least, he thought he did.

A new, miraculously complicated color camera had caught his eye; he wished to buy it. It did not occur to him to use a bit of his accumulated capital to make the purchase although, in fact, he possessed a tidy fortune, earned in pursuit of his second profession. For Manuel was so fond of money that it was an actual physical wrench for him to part with any of it: unless, that is, it was what he termed 'new money' – cruzeiros earned so recently that he had not yet added them to his permanent collection, as it were.

Rodolfo came onto the café terrace, his ape arms swinging, his prognathous jaw jutting. He spotted Manuel and walked to his isolated table with a word of greeting.

'Sit down,' said Manuel politely. 'Will you have a beer?'

Rodolfo took the other chair at the table. 'A *cafezinho*,' he said.

Manuel motioned to a waitress. While she was securing Rodolfo's coffee from the bar, Manuel murmured, 'Where is it this time, Rodolfo?' His last assignment had sent him, somewhat uncomfortably, to Bahia aboard a coastwise freighter loaded with stinking hides and castor beans.

Rodolfo's lips lifted in the grimace that was his smile. 'Right here in Rio, Photographer,' he replied.

'Good.' Manuel took a sip of beer. 'Not a child this time, I hope. I grow sensitive, Rodolfo.'

Rodolfo's coffee came, black and steaming. 'You, sensitive!' he began, laughing sarcastically until he looked across the table into Manuel's muddy-brown eyes. Then he stopped laughing abruptly and said, 'It's a man, don't worry. But a man who is still, in one respect, a child.'

'Retarded?' The Photographer made a moue of distaste.

Rodolfo shook his head. 'A jockey,' he said.

Manuel permitted himself a half smile. 'Very funny. His name and address?'

'Here.' With a prestidigitator's gesture Rodolfo slipped a small white card into Manuel's hand. There was a name written on it in pencil, an address underneath.

Manuel glanced at the card and sucked in his breath. 'This one I have photographed for *Rio Illustrated*,' he said, pleased. 'I am known to him already.'

'That should simplify your job,' said Rodolfo.

Manuel ignored the hint of a sneer in the other's voice, and asked eagerly, 'How much?'

'Fifty thousand.'

'What! To nullify the most famous jockey in Brazil? The Whip?' Manuel was shocked. 'You insult me, Rodolfo!'

'Fifty thousand. No more.'

'That is a fair price for a minor businessman, a politician of the fourth rank, a troublesome relative!' Manuel spread his hands in an eloquent gesture of protest. 'This man is worth far more than fifty thousand – a quarter million at the very least!'

'Fifty thousand,' Rodolfo repeated impassively.

Manuel's lips tightened. Anger burned in him. Yet he said only, 'Is there a time limit?'

'Before Sunday,' Rodolfo replied. 'You understand?'

Manuel nodded his comprehension. On Sunday the annual horse race known as the Grande Premio Brasil would draw everybody who was anybody in Rio to the Jockey Club to witness this most glittering of August sporting events. And the jockey whose name Manuel had read but a moment before on Rodolfo's little white card would be riding the favorite.

Manuel said, 'Very well, then. The usual arrangement?'

'A third now. The rest when you show me proof.'

They stood and shook hands as an excuse for Rodolfo to leave in Manuel's palm a packet of banknotes.

When Rodolfo left the café, Manuel sat down again and thriftily finished his beer, nursing his indignation at the niggardliness of The Corporation.

The jockey, Paulo Pereira, lived on the top floor of one of Rio's luxurious new apartment houses which was imaginatively set up on stilts between the green of the mountains and the aquamarine of the sea in the waterside suburb of Leblon.

At four in the afternoon, when he knocked on the jockey's door, no one answered Manuel's summons. So he retired to a shady corner of the carport under the building to await his victim's return. He did not wish to waste a single unnecessary hour in carrying out his shoddy cut-price assignment from The Big Ones.

He almost wished he had refused the commission entirely, so indignant was he at the minuscule sum, the mere *pitança*, they were paying him to dispose of Paulo Pereira, known to the sporting world as The Whip because of his invariable habit of going to the whip in the stretch – whether his mount was leading the pack already or dead last – and pretending to belabor his poor beast unmercifully while actually never touching whip to hide. By this merciful magic The Whip had brought home more than a hundred winners and become the most successful jockey in Brazil.

Manuel waited. The cocktail hour arrived and passed, the dinner hour followed, darkness fell over Leblon, and lights winked on in the apartments over Manuel's head. The jockey did not return. Manuel used the time of waiting to think very carefully about his assignment. As a result, when Paulo Pereira did at length appear – a very small man driving a very big North American car – Manuel had discarded his original straightforward murder plan for something considerably more subtle.

The jockey's huge car slid quietly between the stilts supporting the apartment building and came to a cushioned halt in the parking space marked 'Pereira.' The headlights went out. Manuel was relieved to see that the jockey was alone in the car. Paulo Pereira stepped from the driver's seat and Manuel Andradas, materializing in the semigloom beside him, spoke quietly. 'Senhor Pereira,' he said. 'Do you remember me? I am Manuel Andradas, the photographer who took your picture for *Rio Illustrated* several months ago.'

The jockey tilted his head to look up at Manuel's face, then smiled cordially. 'Certainly,' he said. 'And damned good pictures you took of me, too! You made me look almost of normal size.' He laughed self-consciously with the air of a man who deplores his meager stature. 'What's on your mind tonight, Senhor Andradas?'

Manuel answered, 'In a purely accidental manner I happened to overhear something today that concerns you very closely. You are in great danger, Senhor Pereira.'

In the dim light of the garage Manuel thought the little man's expression was more of contemptuous impatience than of startled surprise. 'What kind of danger?' he demanded brusquely.

'We can't talk here.'

Paulo shrugged his narrow shoulders. 'Come up to my apartment, then.'

Manuel said, 'If I am seen with you tonight, or known to have visited your apartment, or, indeed, even suspected of having exchanged a single word with you, I would find *myself* in great danger also. Naturally, I wish to protect myself. Yet I feel I should warn you, too.' He paused. 'I suggest my studio as a place where we can be quite safe from observation, Senhor.'

'Well,' Pereira said giving The Photographer a level look. 'I guess I'll agree to that, since you think it so important.'

Manuel felt his spirits lift. 'Good. My car is parked there in that guest space. Shall we go?'

They entered Manuel's eight-year-old station wagon and drove in silence to his studio just off Rua Ouvidor in the center of downtown Rio. 'Kindly keep down in your seat, Senhor,' Manuel requested with well-simulated nervousness.

The jockey complied, slouching in his seat until only the top of his head could possibly have been visible from the black and white mosaic sidewalks as they passed. He seemed to be amused rather than apprehensive at the precaution.

Manuel approached his studio from the narrow alley that ran behind it. Parking his old car in its usual place in the alley, he led the way through the back door of his quarters, through his darkroom, and ultimately into the spacious studio beyond. Here, in complete darkness, he said to Paulo, 'Wait,' and pulled the heavy draperies across the windows before he switched on lights.

The lights revealed a thoroughly professional work-room, cluttered with cameras, mobile lighting units, reflecting screens, electric cables. Near the doorway that led to Manuel's simple bedroom stood a small circular table and two straight chairs. The photographer motioned Paulo into one of the chairs and himself sat in the other. As hospitably as his dour nature permitted, he said, 'Will you have a glass of wine, Senhor? or coffee?'

Paulo shook his head. 'Nothing, thank you, except an account of what you overheard today that concerns me.'

Manuel nodded, leaning forward to deposit his camera case under the table. 'I could scarcely believe my ears, to tell you the truth. You know the café at the foot of Christo Redentor? I was there today, sitting at a table drinking beer. Behind me, at another table, were two men talking. I must tell you that I have unusually keen hearing and their words reached me clearly.'

Paulo, whose feet failed to reach the floor as he sat in the chair, nodded his head to be indicate his interest.

'One seemed to be giving the other instructions.' said Manuel. 'An assignment. Your name was mentioned. Paulo Pereira, The Whip. I recognized it immediately, since I had photographed you for *Rio Illustrated*. I eavesdropped quite shamelessly from then on, as you can imagine.'

The jockey squirmed uneasily in his chair. 'Get to the point, please, Senhor Andradas. What did they say?'

'I gathered that the man receiving instructions was a professional assassin. He was being commissioned to kill you, Senhor Pereira.'

'Kill me!' The expression on the jockey's face was no longer one of amusement.

'Yes. In reprisal for some action of yours that I did not hear mentioned specifically between them.'

In a low voice Paulo murmured, 'Incredible!'

Manuel, considerately, was silent, watching his small visitor woodenly until the jockey went on, 'He *looked* like a gangster, I must say. Overdressed and with a hard, menacing, assured manner, you know? Just like the gangsters in North American cinemas.'

'Excuse me,' said Manuel, 'may I know who this overdressed gangster was?'

Paulo shrugged. 'A fellow I'd never seen before yesterday, I beg you to believe. A perfect stranger. This man approached me last evening in a restaurant where I was having dinner alone and offered me money to throw the horse race on Sunday. Imagine! The Grande Premio Brasil! I'm riding Wait-a-Bit, the favorite, you know.'

'Every Carioca worthy of the name knows that,' said Manuel.

'He wanted me to pull Wait-a-Bit in the stretch,' said Paulo, 'under cover of my well-known whipping routine. Otherwise, I will be killed before the race, he said. I thought the whole performance a practical joke of some kind, frankly. Or an attempt at psychological warfare by a rival stable. Or, most likely of all' – the jockey eyed Manuel calmly – 'sensational publicity stunt to promote the race on Sunday. Tonight, I was convinced that was it when you confronted me in my carport. I thought, quite naturally, that you wanted photos for the press of the threatened jockey; you know, very dramatic, the jockey who refused a bribe to throw the race. Incidentally, I did refuse the bribe. And laughed at the man who threatened me to make me do as he said.' There was a curious sort of bantam dignity about Paulo as he uttered these words.

Manuel could not refrain from asking, 'How much were you offered to pull your horse?'

'A paltry quarter of a million.' The jockey was disdainful.

Inwardly Manuel groaned. A paltry quarter of a million, indeed! This from a man no taller than a ten-year-old boy whom Manuel had been hired to nullify for a pitiful fifty thousand! He forced down his anger and said, 'You spoke of a rival stable. Would any of the owners with horses entered in the Premio pay a quarter of a million to fix a race in which the purse is only a hundred thousand?'

Paulo nodded at once. 'Oh, yes. To owners, the purse and even the betting in the Premio are incidental. It is the fortune to be made in stud fees that makes this race so special. The horse that wins automatically commands enormous fees, once he is retired to stud.'

'I see,' said Manuel, 'the big money comes later.'

'Yes. And it oftens runs into the millions.'

Manuel thought for a moment. 'Which horse is the second favorite in Sunday's race?'

'Scalawag,' Paulo said. 'Pre-race odds of four to one.'

'Who owns Scalawag?'

'A group called The Big Boy Corporation.'

'Ah!' said Manuel softly. 'The Big Boy Corporation. And how long have they been racing horses in Brazil?'

'A year or two only. They are comparative newcomers. Scalawag is the first horse to carry their colors in the Premio.'

'So. Now it becomes clear. My suspicion is confirmed.'

'What suspicion?'

'That our Brazilian brotherhood of criminals – The corporation, The Big Ones, so-called – is behind the attempt to bribe you. And now intends to kill you for refusing their bribe.'

The jockey at last looked startled. 'You mean The Big Boy Corporation who owns Scalawag is really The Big Ones?'

'I would bet my life on it,' Manuel said positively. 'And I'll tell you why. After I heard these men talking about your murder today, I turned my head casually to get a glimpse of them. To my horror I recognized one of them, And worse still, he recognized *me*.'

'Who was he?'

'A man I know only as Rodolfo. But I am sure of this: he is an important member of The Big Ones. He walks like an ape and has a jaw like one. Would that be your well-dressed gangster?'

The jockey shook his head. 'My man walked like a woman. And had scarcely any jaw at all.'

'I had trouble with this man Rodolfo once,' Manuel explained, 'over an actress friend of his I was photographing. After I knocked him down and humiliated him before her, she told me this Rodolfo was a member of The Corporation. She feared he would have me killed. I hastened to apologise very humbly to him when I found out who he was, you may be sure. And thus I managed to stay alive. In any event, this is the man we are up against, Paulo – Rodolfo, and The Corporation of which he is a member. That is why I was so anxious not to be seen with you tonight. Why I brought you here. Rodolfo may well have suspected that I overheard his talk of murdering you today. You see?'

The jockey, still only half convinced, gave Manuel a quizzical look. 'Tell me,' he said, 'if you go in such fear of these Big Ones, I am surprised you were willing to risk your life tonight to warn me. Why did you do it?'

Manuel said simply, 'To find out which horse has the best chance of winning on Sunday if you happen to get killed in the meantime.'

The diminutive jockey laughed aloud. 'You are frank, at least, Senhor Andradas,' he said. 'No, you must not bet on Wait-a-Bit unless I ride him! He's never finished better than fourth without me up. There is something mysterious between that horse and me that makes him put forth his maximum effort only for me, do you understand? Without me riding him, he's just another race horse, and a mediocre one, at that. If you follow racing at all, you must know that. It's been widely commented on. The only reason he's favored on Sunday is because I'm riding him.'

'And without you he'll be beaten?'

'Soundly. Scalawag will win the race easily. He's very fast at the Premio distance. The rest of the field are born also-rans, in my opinion.' Then, as anger overcame him, the jockey went on fiercely, 'But I *will* be riding Wait-a-Bit on Sunday! I promise you that! This is no obscure, unknown man whose murder can be planned so blithely! This is Paulo Pereira, Senhor, the premier jockey of Brazil! A man with hosts of friends and patrons! Why, even if I don't call the police, which I intend to do immediately, the owner I ride for, Francisco Almeida, could himself easily provide me with airtight security, twenty-four hours a day, until the moment I step into Wait-a-Bit's saddle on Sunday!'

Paulo jumped up from his chair, his small figure stiff with stubborn pride. He looked around the cluttered studio. 'Do you have a telephone?'

'Yes,' said Manuel. He, too, rose from his chair. 'But I am afraid it is too late for you to call the police.'

'What do you mean?'

With one foot Manuel snaked his camera case from under the table and pushed it gently across the floor toward the jockey. 'Please look in this case, Senhor, and I think you will understand what I mean.'

Paulo's brows knit in puzzlement. He eyed Manuel uncomprehendingly for a moment before he bent over, unzipped The Photographer's case, and lifted out its contents. Item by item he deposited on the floor alongside the case a Leica camera, a Minox, an electronic flashpack, a telephoto lens, five rolls of film. And from the very bottom of the case, finally, he brought forth a large pistol with a silencer on its barrel, a delicate, razor-sharp throwing knife shaped like a bougainvillea leaf, and a wire garrote with twisted handles of electrician's tape on each end.

Like a man who has suddenly become unbearably weary, Paulo Pereira straightened his slight frame and looked with sick eyes at Manuel. 'You?' he asked in an incredulous voice. It was only a choked whisper.

Manuel said, 'I am sorry, Senhor,' and like striking snakes his two hands flew across the space between them to seize the jockey's slender throat. The muscles in The Photographer's forearms came up like steel wires under the stuff of his jacket sleeves. The diminutive jockey was lifted bodily off the floor and held suspended in midair while he strangled. To no avail his hands tore at Manuel's hands, his legs and feet thrashed wildly, his body writhed.

When he was dead, Manuel dropped his body on the floor and reached for his Polaroid camera. But before he took his picture of the jockey, he thrust one hand under the table and switched off the tape recorder.

The next day was Friday. Manuel met Rodolfo in an obscure café on the Praça Tiradentes.

'So soon?' asked Rodolfo. Manuel grunted and passed a Polaroid print across the café table to Rodolfo. 'Here is your proof,' he said.

Rodolfo examined the picture of Paulo Periera, the eyes bursting from their sockets, the swollen, bitten tongue protruding too far from the open mouth, the limbs sprawled at painful angles like those of a ragdoll.

Rodolfo nodded. 'This should serve. It's certainly convincing. I'll have the rest of your money for you tomorrow. On the Sugar Loaf cable car at noon.'

'Be sure you do,' said Manuel. 'I'll need the money before Sunday.'

'Sunday?' Rodolfo raised his eyebrows.

'I'm going to bet the whole thing on the Grand Premio Brasil.'

Rodolfo gave him a surprised look. 'You? You never gamble.'

'This time I shall. In the forlorn hope of turning your insulting fee into a respectable sum.'

Rodolfo laughed. 'If you lose, though, you will have nothing. Have you thought of that? What horse are you going to bet on?'

'The same one you are,' said Manuel. He withdrew his gaze from the Joao Caetano Theatre across the square and locked eyes with Rodolfo. Rodolfo was the first to look away. The Photographer made to rise.

'Wait,' said Rodolfo. 'What did you do with our friend here?' He tapped a finger against the Polaroid print.

'That is nobody's business but mine. It is sufficient for you to know that I have disposed of him where he cannot possibly be found until the day of the race. Do you understand?'

'So there will be no radical change in the odds until the last minute, eh?'

'I am not a dunce,' said Manuel, 'even if you treat me as one. Goodbye, Rodolfo.'

From the Praça Tiradentes Manuel went directly to his studio, checked to be certain the stiff body of Paulo Pereira still lay under his darkroom sink, then picked up his telephone.

His call to the owner of Wait-a-Bit was put through very quickly by Francisco Almeida's butler at the mention of Paulo Pereira's name. 'Paulo?' asked Almeida anxiously when he came on the wire. 'Why didn't you show up at the stables this morning? Are you ill or hurt? And where are you now? I haven't been able to reach you all day! For God's sake, Paulo, this is no time for you to—' Abruptly he cut off his words. After a pause he said tentatively, 'Paulo?'

Manuel, through the handkerchief he held over the mouth, said 'Paulo is neither ill nor hurt, Senhor. He has been kidnapped.'

There was a long moment of stunned silence. Then Almeida yelled 'What!' so loudly that Manuel's ear rang.

'Kidnapped. That is what I said. You know the meaning of the word?'

Another pause. Then, 'And you, I suppose, you are Paulo's kidnapper? Is that what you mean?'

'Exactly. Paulo is quite safe. Ready to ride Wait-a-Bit into the winner's circle for you on Sunday. But only if you first pay me a ransom of a quarter of a million cruzeiros for his release.'

'You're mad!'

'I am sane. And in deadly earnest, Senhor. If you wish to win the Grande Premio Brasil, you must believe me.'

Senhor Almeida breathed heavily on the other end of the line. 'The law does not look lightly on extortion!' he cried fiercely. 'I shall set the police on you at once!'

Manuel adopted the reasonable, patient tone of a man arguing with a stubborn child. 'This is not extortion, Senhor Almeida. This is plain, oldfashioned kidnapping. I have your jockey. And you must pay to get him back alive if you want to win on Sunday. It is as simple as that.'

'You think I am a cretin?' shouted Almeida furiously. 'You don't have Paulo! I have met men of your type before. You are merely trying to—'

The Photographer interrupted him. 'I *do* have Paulo. Wait. I'll put him on the phone. Will that convince you?'

Silence. Manuel took it for an invitation to proceed. 'Listen, then,' he said to Almeida. 'Here he is.' Then, aside, he growled, 'He thinks I play games, this owner of yours, Paulo. Tell him the truth.'

Manuel switched on the playback beside the telephone and brought the mouthpiece closer to it. From the tape then, spoken into the telephone in Paulo's unmistakable voice, came the words which Manuel had painfully culled from the recording of his conversation with the jockey the evening before.

'This is Paulo Pereira, Senhor Almeida. I beg you to believe this man. If I am to ride Wait-a-Bit on Sunday for you, you must do as he said. But please don't call the police. Otherwise I will be killed.'

Almeida tried to interrupt with a question. Manuel came back on the wire smoothly. 'Are you satisfied?'

Almeida answered in a new placatory voice. 'Yes. Yes. You promise to release him unharmed? Before Sunday? If I pay you a quarter million?' He spoke of a quarter of a million cruzeiros as though it were nothing. Briefly Manuel was tempted to ask for more, but he resisted.

'You have my word on it,' he said solemnly.

'How shall I deliver the money?'

Manuel told him in meticulous detail of the foolproof delivery plan he had concocted in anticipation of this question. 'I must warn you, however, Senhor,' he finished, 'if you go to the police or the press about this, or fail to deliver the money as directed, Paulo, your jockey, will die. Understood?'

At Almeida's reluctant murmur of 'Yes, yes, I understand perfectly,' Manuel hung up.

Only one small problem remained: how to dispose safely and permanently of the body in his darkroom. Before addressing himself to its solution, The Photographer went to his tiny refrigerator, took from it a pitcher of cashew juice, and poured himself a glass of the thick sweet liquid. Today it would not only soothe his nerves, he told himself, but would serve as a drink of celebration as well.

For his nullification of Paulo Pereira, which had at first seemed so financially unpromising, was going to prove quite profitable for him after all.

Especially if Scalawag won the Grande Premio Brasil on Sunday.

Which Scalawag certainly would do. Because Manuel himself had arranged it.

Ellen Keegan's Revenge

MARY RYAN

This final story of the section is about a young stable lad who has a special way with horses and a burning ambition to become a jockey like the father he never knew. The setting takes us back to Ireland, where horse racing and native superstitions are brilliantly combined in a tense thriller by a very talented mystery writer. Mary Ryan is, in fact, following in a great tradition, for it was in Ireland that the very best nineteenth-century novel about horse racing, *Esther Waters* by George Moore, was written and published in 1894. Moore, who grew up on a stud in southwest Ireland where his father bred horses for racing, broke new ground with his story, although it was attacked in some quarters as being vulgar and offensive. The plot drew heavily from his own experiences of the turf and its people, in particular the activities of some unscrupulous owners and devious racing touts exploiting the public. This authentic insight introduced its readers to a wider world than any of the fashionable novels of the time. A prominent character in the book was a young stable lad nicknamed 'The Demon' who is also determined to make his name as a jockey and competes against 'The Tinman' (Fred Archer) in a memorable racing sequence. Like Moore's novel, 'Ellen Keegan's Revenge' draws on the activities of a group of people at a stud, focusing especially on the mystery surrounding a strange woman once famous for her racing tips, but now apparently nursing a terrible grievance from the past.

Mary Ryan, who lives in Dublin, is doubly qualified to write about crime and the turf. She is a practising solicitor by occupation and her husband's family breed and race horses from their stud farm, Ballyneale House in Ballingarry. She has now written five novels which have been published on both sides of the

Atlantic, the most recent of which, *Whispers in the Wind,* was for twelve weeks on the Irish bestseller list – and for half of that time at number one. 'Ellen Keegan's Revenge' is Mary's first short story specifically about the world of horse racing and is being published here for the first time. It is a tale with a climax as exciting as a photo-finish and dramatic as a steward's enquiry.

*

The boy was fifteen, eager, dark haired, small for his age. He hurried across the cobbles to the loose box where the big black stallion was creating mayhem. The stables reverberated with the thunder of Lucifer's hooves against his door. The fury of his screams had set off the other horses. Glad, like all prisoners, of an excuse for remonstrance, they neighed in adjoining loose boxes, sympathetically flattening their ears and rolling their eyes.

Liam was carrying a galvanised bucket of water. He put it on the ground, unbolted both halves of the door, picked up the bucket and slipped inside, closing the bottom door behind him. Instantly the plunging quietened; the stallion put his head down and drank from the pail. The boy stroked his glossy neck.

Two men crossed the stable yard to gaze in through the open half door at the horse and boy.

'He's the only one who can manage Lucifer,' the trainer, Matt Touhy, said to his employer as they watched the stallion drink. 'That animal is aptly named! But the boy has no fear! Wants to be a jockey like his father.'

'Who is he?' Charles Butler asked.

'Liam Keegan, the widow Keegan's son. His father used to work here; was killed before my time, back in thirty-seven before the boy was born!'

'I see!' Matt did not turn to glance at his employer.

'Do you remember it . . . the accident . . . the drowning . . . it can't have been long before you left . . .'

'Ah yes . . . unfortunate business . . .'

Charles Butler quelled his impulse to say something more. The less said the better. The French had an expression – 'Qui s' excuse s'accuse' – and to accuse himself was the last thing he wanted. He had a new persona to polish now. His recent inheritance of Tullystown Stud had ended his wandering life on the Contintent. It had been a stroke of Fate, a gift from Providence. His father, who had shown him the door sixteen years before, not long after the unfortunate business to which Matt had just referred, had sworn he would leave the place to a cousin. Charles had gone to England, lived with a college friend, enlisted on the outbreak of war, been demobbed in forty-five and set off to wander the Continent in the post-war gloom, glad of his aunt's money when it came. But two months ago his father had died, sinking suddenly to his knees in the stable yard, hands clutching his chest, his face contorted in horror at the sudden death which yawned before him in the sunlight.

The old man's coronary had given Charles the inheritance he had not dared hope for, and given it just as his aunt's bequest, which had kept him in shoe leather and hotel expenses for many years, was running out. Because his father had not made a Will his estate devolved by law to his estranged son. The men working on the stud said it was the way the old man had wanted it anyway, that that was why he had died intestate.

Charles enjoyed the irony of it. He was yesteryear's golden boy, banished, but now, despite the direst forecasts, the prodigal son come home.

'I knew him, Dan Keegan,' he said. 'He was a jockey here, a good one too. Didn't he marry that queer girl, Ellen what's-her-name, the one who read the tealeaves and scared the living daylights out of all the eejits?'

Matt stared at Charles Butler for a moment before replying. 'Well she's strange enough all right . . . she used to give good tips about winners, for all the good it did her. But she's quite weird now . . . Won't even give hints anymore . . . Probably lost it!'

'Very proper,' Charles said after a moment. 'So we don't have the benefit of her prognostications for the Balgadden Apprentice Stakes?'

Matt heard the sarcasm and something else in his employer's voice, the *frisson*, a small catch when his tongue turned the syllables of Ellen Keegan's name. He wondered if there was any truth in the rumour that Charles Butler and Ellen Keegan had once been more than mere acquaintances. One of the old men, who propped up the bar at Donlon's on Sundays, had woken up long enough to deliver himself of something which had whetted Matt's curiosity. When he had heard that Charles was coming back to run Tullystown the old fellow had muttered, 'Ah well, now we'll see whether what's bred in the bone will come out in the flesh . . . But say nothing to Ellen Keegan?' and he had shaken his head.

'Lucifer is the winner for the Apprentice Stakes,' Matt said confidently. 'He's a real flier . . .'

'What's his pedigree?'

'By Slieve Gorm out of Lady Jane . . . Sure where would he leave it?'

In the loose box Liam stood beside Lucifer's head as the horse drank from the bucket, and listened to the voices – that of Mr Touhy which he knew well, and the voice of the new owner, Mr Charles. It was a funny voice, with an accent he must have acquired in his travels, one where the t's were caressed but never embraced. The stallion, highly strung, heard the stranger's voice outside his door and moved uneasily. But the boy murmured softly, sibiliantly, and stroked Lucifer's neck.

Liam knew Lucifer better than any of them; the coal-black, seventeen-hand stallion was his friend, his alter ego, almost his mentor. He knew the labyrinths of savagery which lurked in Lucifer's heart, the pride that had never been broken. He had ridden him around the yard a few times and once at night; he had stealthily taken him out of the stable, slipping the bolts so softly that no one heard, easing the bridle on him, mounting him at the block and walking him down the back avenue to the track. He knew there would be hell to pay if Matt Touhy found out; Lucifer was the most valuable animal in Tullystown. Great hopes were pinned on him. He had already won all his races in his first season. If his promise held good he would be worth a fortune at stud. But a horse galloping by night would not be able to see the true lie of the ground. There weren't many rabbits in Tullystown; they kept greyhounds to see to that. But it would only take one rabbit hole . . . A broken leg would end Tullystown's hopes for new prosperity.

Lucifer was already lathered with excitement before they reached the yard gate. All the way down the field to the track Liam was put to the test. He hadn't the strength to pull the stallion, so he kept the right rein short and Lucifer's nose to his right stirrup, releasing it a little when the horse seemed to quieten, tightening it again when the horse strained to gallop, and in this stilted way they progressed towards the track. By the time they reached it, sheets of hay-scented lather were peeling off Lucifer like spindrift in the sea.

But once on the track Lucifer had taken off. The packed sand had flown like artillery smoke, while Liam had clung to the mane and felt the fierce equine exultation rise in him also, the surrogate glory of being free and fierce and proud. Afterwards he had wiped him down with a sugán, a thick rope of hay, and walked him around the field until he was dry before returning him to his stable.

Sometimes he slept above Lucifer, in the high loft that served as a fodder storage where hay could be dropped down to each stall.

Ellen, his mother, knew of this, but no one else. If anything she seemed to tacitly encourage it.

As far as Matt Touhy was concerned, Liam was a quiet boy, obsessed with horses, useful in the stud every day after school, earning the occasional few bob, ready to muck out, feed, groom. He was unobtrusive, but ubiquitous, as knowledgeable about horses as though a sixth sense made him privy to the scriptures of their strange, powerful hearts.

But no one knew the extent of the passion he nurtured for Lucifer. No one suspected how the sight of the stallion, the thunder of his gallop, his speed and strength, his glossy black coat, the quivering of his aristocratic lips, the flashing of his great teeth, satisfied the part of him that craved some tangible absolute.

He was Ellen Keegan's only child. She had a county council cottage, ten acres and a small widow's pension. At school he was a poor pupil, irked by the disciplines of study, the constraints of essay writing, detesting maths and its attendant torments of equations and theorems. But his mother had scrimped for years to pay the modest fees required by the Christian Brothers who had a school in the town and Liam attended, albeit unwillingly. He knew that, if he wanted the use of his hands and backside after school, he had to perform at his lessons; the Brothers did not spare the strap. But he wanted only one thing: horses and one horse in particular, the black demon who had stolen his soul.

That evening he said to his mother, 'Mr Butler – the old man's son – is back!'

His mother had just put the blackened pot of potatoes down to boil on the range. Liam's supper was more or less invariable. He would eat his fill of spuds and drink the buttermilk he collected from the creamery on his way home, and she would give the left-over potatoes, skins and all, to the hens.

Now she turned her strange eyes on her son. Some people thought Ellen Keegan was blind, for her eyes had an opaque quality and did not seem to focus. The years of toil had marked her, bent the slender shoulders, thickened the waist which Charles Butler had liked to put his arm around when he met her at dusk in the woodland along the banks of the Bawnogue. But she still possessed presence, as though the passion within her had crystallized. The cunning of her madness was not apparent, only its fire.

She remembered Charles as one of the few things she had ever fully seen in the ordinary physical sense. As beautiful as the day, a young man cut like glass, long legged, graceful, striding in boots and jodhpurs towards her in the dappled evening.

'And who might you be, Fair Lady?'

The tone had been one of genuine surprise, small banter, and the covert impertinence of privilege.

She had held the fragrant bluebells so tightly that the stems oozed sap into her hand.

'I'm Ellen Keegan . . . What's it to you?'

She looked into his eyes. In the ensuing silence she heard his mind and his thought and the first stirrings of his lust. She did not move, feeling in herself something that answered it, something that coveted his beauty, even his arrogance, and, coveting it, was afraid. There was a rustle nearby. Above their heads a red squirrel jumped with a flutter from one branch to the next.

He looked up and laughed. 'I know who you are now. You're Dan Keegan's bride.'

331

Encouraged perhaps by the unabashed way she looked into his face, he moved a little closer. 'And very beautiful you are, Ellen Keegan,' he said softly. 'But I should introduce myself . . .'

'I know who you are, Charlie Butler!'

He moved back.

'How did you know? Was Dan talking about me?'

'Maybe.'

'They say you read the cards. Will you tell me my fortune?'

Ellen turned away from him to break the spell, walked away along the forest path, calling over her shoulder, schooling nonchalance into her voice:

'Mocking is catching!'

He hurried after her, thinking he had identified a note of coquetry. She heard his boots bruise the woodland floor, felt the young shoots' shock, the pain of the crushed cowslips, recognised the cry of a small snail as it died under his heel. But the life in him, the confident striding force, the grace of form, the semi-cultivated mind, cried out to something in her which was famished.

A game, Ellen thought. It will be safe if I turn it into a game.

He caught up with her, touched her shoulder. 'Will you read my palm?'

The touch resonated through her, shocking her. She suppressed the shiver, turned, took the proffered hand. But she deliberately closed the doors of her perception and did try to unravel what his lines of Life and Fate had to tell her.

'Do I have to cross your palm with silver?'

Ellen looked at him, offended by his condescension.

'No.' She glanced at his outstretched hand. 'You'll get what you deserve,' she added with a forced laugh.

'Is that what you see?'

She realised suddenly that his interest was genuinely caught. For a moment she was tempted, but she dropped the hand.

'That's true of most of us!'

'Is it?' He studied her face. 'Is that all you have to tell me? And to think they're all saying that Dan married a witch! You know what I believe?' he added with a small, merry laugh. 'I think you're a fraud!'

'There's some think otherwise!'

She laughed then, seeing that he had meant no offence.

'But you won't tell anyone. It would be very bad for business!'

He moved closer and said softly, 'I won't tell anyone if you give me a kiss!'

She had run, flying down the damp forest path without looking back, hearing his half-laughing, half-vexed voice, 'Why are you running away . . . I won't hurt you . . .'

That night as she lay in bed beside her husband, Ellen reviewed the events of the day. She had just made love with Dan, if such it could be called, for there could be no release for her in his conjugal embrace. Passion and Dan did not mix. The true extent of her own capacity in this department she suspected, but hid from her slight, wiry husband. Dan, although urgent in his needs, although fiery by temperament, was embarrassed by carnality. He wore the brown scapular of St Francis around his neck; he knew that pleasure was sinful and liked to get the business over and done with as quickly as possible. The spectre of Confession and Father McGuire's face behind the grille tormented him with shame. He loved his fey young wife; she was like an elfin being, someone that you could never know no matter how long you lived with her. He was mortified that he should foist his appetites on her daintiness and tried, as much as possible, to spare her. It never occurred to him that his wife experienced his shamed, impersonal performance as an affront.

The following evening saw Ellen walking the same woodland path as before. Dan was away. He had sweated and dieted to get his weight down and was now at the Galway races. Old Mr Butler had gone as well and many of the horses and staff from Tullystown. Young Mr Butler was at home, ostensibly studying for an autumn examination, a repeat of a summer one which he had failed. He came along the banks of the Bawnogue, hoping to find the girl of the day before, knowing that her husband was away, knowing that he had moved her in some way which challenged him. He had little real experience of women. The prostitutes in Dublin had pretended, but he had felt their silent resignation and their profound and private scorn. He had tried to pull several female fellow students, but their virtue was cast iron, and never lapsed beyond frustrating necking sessions. He had sensed in Ellen Keegan something more, something untrammelled by strictures of received morality, something pagan. It was at odds with her elfin appearance, and her strange half-seeing eyes. He reminded himself that she was married to one of his father's servants; but the part of him that wanted Ellen Keegan didn't give a damn.

That had been the beginning. And all through that summer it had gone on, the meetings, the oblique conversations on strange subjects, the shared silences, the increasing intimacy, the hand around her shoulders, around her waist. He recited Keats to her:

> 'I met a lady in the mead,
> Full beautiful, a faery's child.
> Her hair was long and her foot was light,
> And her eyes were wild.'

Ellen felt herself lulled into enchantment. And then he had added, slightly paraphrasing the original, 'La Belle Dame Sans Merci me hath in thrall,' and swooped on her for the first real kiss. She had rested against the bole of a tree and felt what his strong tongue said to her as it forced itself into her mouth. Then his hands raised her skirts to find the secret places of her body.

'Don't,' she said, pushing him away.

'Why not? You want me to. Oh Ellen, don't be afraid; I will never betray you.'

'I can't. Think of Dan. He'd kill you! He'd kill us both.'

'All right . . . all right . . . Don't go. Don't go . . .'

But a little later it came back, ambushing them, the great crushing python of desire, until at last she had confessed in a storm of despair:

'I would give my immortal soul, Charlie Butler, for just one night between you and the wall!'

He had laughed.

'Oh Ellen Keegan, I love you. But I come much cheaper than that!'

He hadn't – come cheaper. Dan had returned earlier than expected from a race meeting, had found the lovers in the woods in full flagrante, his wife making sounds he had never heard, sounds which scandalized and maddened him. He had launched himself at his employer's son. But the small jockey, however great his wrath, was no match for the young man with eight years' hard hunting behind him and a genetic inheritance of size and strength. The Butlers were all tall, rugged, hard-riding country folk. The struggle ended with Dan being thrown into the fast flowing Bawnogue, being swept out by a current. Ellen had started to scream.

'For God's sake, save him.'

'I can't swim,' Charles had said, looking around desperately, seizing upon a fallen branch and pushing it out into the current, shouting, 'Grab hold of that, man . . .' But Dan had been lost, turning a desperate and hate-filled face to him before he disappeared, and the bubbles of his last breath broke in the heedless river.

Neither Ellen nor Charles had subsequently told the truth. At least not until some two months later when Ellen went to Tullystown to see him. He had not visited her since the fateful day when Dan had died and she took her courage in her hands and went to the Victorian mansion which was the Butler home. There she had asked Charles, point blank, what his intentions were, and he, feeling cornered, and fearful of his father's wrath, had answered her with scorn. His father had intruded and she had told him as much of the truth as her vengeful pride would allow.

'I promise you,' she said to Charles in a low voice, 'that I will not rest until you pay for this!'

'Get out, you impertinent slut,' the old man had thundered, and had shown her unceremoniously towards the door. Then there had ensued a row between the old man and his son which had echoed through the house.

'Dan was my man, a good man, one whose loss I cannot afford. You have destroyed him, and maybe Tullystown too. Get out. Do your whoring somewhere else . . . and don't ever expect a penny piece from me . . .'

Charles had removed himself from the family home.

'I am poor,' Ellen said bitterly as she went home that day. 'That makes me a slut! I am bereaved on two counts. He never loved me. He lied. He has used and widowed me.'

That night she had a strange dream. In it she rode a black

stallion down the woodland path at night. But at the river the rhythm of the ride changed. Looking down she saw the bony hands clutching her ankles and knew that she was being carried on the back of the dead Dan Keegan, the dead husband whose body had still not been recovered. She knew who it was, although he had become a bloated thing which cursed and mocked her with the stench of the grave. She had woken with a cry, knew the desolation, the loneliness of her widowhood, and listened to the wind moaning down the chimney until something in her mind seemed to snap.

Now Ellen, tired from her day's work, wrapped in a dark blue apron, considered her son Liam from her place beside the range. She had the fire door open, watched the flames, felt the heat on her face. She sat like that for a long time in silence. The boy was doing some homework, doing it badly because he hated it, doing it at all only because he was afraid of Brother John's strap. He was used to his mother's silences, could somtimes hear her thought. When he was a child and had done that, read or felt the tenor of her mind, she had said he had the gift too. But lately such incidents had become fewer and fewer.

'That is no ordinary horse!' she whispered now, and Liam glanced at her and saw the way her eyes had turned towards the fire.

'Lucifer?'

'He came for a special purpose.'

Liam finished the algebra. The equation hadn't worked out as an even number and so was probably wrong, but he didn't care. He wouldn't get into as much trouble for it being wrong as he would incur if it were not done.

'What special purpose, Mam?' he asked warily.

His mother did not answer for a moment, but when she turned to him he saw that her face was bitter and her strange eyes wretched with madness.

'That horse has Dan Keegan's soul. Wasn't it foaled the day they found his skeleton under the water?' Then she added in a low voice, 'A horse like that would kill . . . and – as it says in that poetry book of yours – "there is a man to die . . ." '

'Oh, Mam . . . What are you talking about? That's from Yeats – where Eimer sends her son out to fight his father!'

And then she turned off the light, came to him and pulled him towards the range. He dragged his feet on the kitchen floor, hating what was in store. She had done this twice before with him, forced him to stare at what she saw in the fire. It was an experience which made him feel he was lost, that he had left his body behind and was inhabiting a crazed dimension where the ordinary rules of reality did not obtain.

'Come, child.'

To humour her he sat beside her on the settle, letting her take his head and hold it in her hands.

'What do you see in the fire?'

'Flames.'

'Do you see the hot pale ones inside the bigger ones?'

'Yes.'

'Keep watching them, my son. Keep watching.'

When she felt Liam become limp against her she said very softly, 'Do you see the riverbank?'

'Yes.'

'Do you see the men . . . two men?'

'Yess . . . two men and a woman. The men are fighting. I cannot see the woman's face . . .'

'What is happening?'

'One is thrown into the river.'

'That is Dan Keegan.'

'My father is thrown in the river. He is drowning.' He keened on a high keen note of anguish. 'I see the other man now . . .'

'It's Charlie Butler, that's who it is, Liam, Mr Charles Butler Esquire . . .'

The boy jerked convulsively.

'All right, a cushla . . .' Ellen said soothingly. 'Is there anything else?'

'Dan Keegan screams that he will be avenged.' Liam moaned.

'Good,' Ellen said softly, shuddering a little. Then she added in a very low voice, 'You must ride Lucifer at Balgadden,' and she added some words in Irish that sounded like a chant.

Liam threw up his arm as to ward off a blow and, in mounting distress, babbled something incomprehensible. She had to shake him to bring him from the trance. Then she rained kisses on him, told him he was her life, her stoír, her sweet boy, her pride. But despite her endearments he pulled away, complaining of a headache and was in low spirits for the rest of the evening.

'What do you remember of it?' she asked him eventually, 'of what you saw in the fire?'

'Nothing,' he said in a surly voice. 'And I'm not doing that again.'

'Can I ride him, Mr Touhy?' he asked Matt next day. 'Can I ride him in the Apprentice Stakes tomorrow?'

'Lucifer? I thought it was already settled . . .'

Matt Touhy looked at him carefully, saw the wiry build, the future jockey. If he came off itself, what harm, except that someone would have to catch the horse. Matt could not see the future where people would pay real attention to such distressing legal irritations as the law of Negligence and Employer's liability. It was the early fifties; it was *laissez faire*. Anyone worth a damn rode. For a moment he thought of the boy's mother. The only thing standing between her and the mental hospital was her son. But it was not his problem and the boy had his own way to make.

'I'll exercise him now!'

Matt smiled.

'Ride him if he'll let you!'

Liam rushed to the tack room and returned with a saddle and bridle, let himself into the loose box and put them on Lucifer. He led the stallion from the loose box. Lucifer tossed his mane and rattled the bit. His hooves made a staccato melody on the cobbles reminiscent of mangolds being chopped, an impatient and interrogative clopp-clopping, hinting at the performance he would shortly put up on the track. Matt reached up to stroke his nose, but the horse threw back his head and bared his teeth.

But the shiver along the stallion's already lathered flanks, as Liam bent his knee for a leg-up and shot into the saddle, was one of acceptance of his rider and excitement for the chase.

'Wear the stirrups long,' Matt said as Liam bent down to attend to the leathers. 'It'll give you a bit of control!'

Liam held the reins in sensitive hands. He saw Charles Butler enter the stable yard, attired in a new tweed hacking jacket, and he bent and whispered into his mount's ear the Irish words his mother had muttered in his own ear the night before. He did this without thinking, wondering at the words as he said them, wondering why he was even saying them, not remembering that she had uttered them.

'A marbh leis nár smachtaigh a thoil,' which, roughly translated meant that it was death to him who had not disciplined his will.

The stallion flattened his ears in excitement, snorted, pawed the ground.

Charles Butler stood well back from Lucifer but he frowned as Matt Touhy tightened the girth.

'You're letting that youngster ride him?'

'Why not? Make a man of him!'

'So long as he's not crippled!' Charles muttered and Matt Touhy turned in surprise at this unpropitious utterance.

'Sorry,' Charles said. 'Stupid remark!' He tossed a shilling into the air at the rider. 'For luck,' he called. The boy caught it; the stallion danced as though the coin were a horse fly diving for his flank, but the boy quietened him with a touch. Charles turned and followed the trainer towards the track.

Liam rode with long stirrups as he had been instructed, but he bent over the stallion's withers in silent joy. The wind whipped past his ears; his nose ran. He felt the pounding of the hooves beneath him, felt the surge of energy, the force in the warm body on which he rode as it gathered itself up beneath him on each stride, the rhythm of the canter, the undulating head of his mount, thrust out for the joy of it, drinking the breeze that came like a gale as horse and boy rushed through it. Then he shortened the reins and Lucifer surged into a flat-out gallop. He saw the sweat slick on Lucifer's neck, smelled the pungent horse smell, felt the coarse mane whip his face.

Matt Touhy looked at his stop watch as he came around, called out, 'Just once more!' Liam saw Mr Charles standing there like a phantom in a dream and suddenly the memory came of the night before when he had seen him in the heart of the fire.

Oh, Mam, he thought, when will you stop all this? It can't have been true . . . what I saw. And it's not lucky . . . It's just not lucky!

Charlie Butler's shilling had done its work. He had a warm place inside him for the new owner of Tullystown Stud. The charm that had won Ellen Keegan was working its subtle alchemy on her son.

The ride over, horse and boy were congratulated.

'Did you see that?' Matt Touhy said to Charles as Liam walked Lucifer back to the stables. 'Can you credit it? Wasn't it the lucky day your father had Lady Jane covered by Slieve Gorm. Funny thing. Dan Keegan always said a foal from those two would be a winner!'

'Is that a reproach, Matt?'

Matt stared at his employer. 'No. Sure you can't tell a mule from a jennet!'

'I'm learning, Matt. I've been away. I've wasted time and life and opportunity . . . but I'm learning. So be patient. I'm committed to Tullystown! My wild oats are sown and it's time to make porridge. I've come home!'

Liam walked Lucifer back to the stables. There was froth on the stallion's lips. In the stableyard the boy took off the saddle, wiped him down and spread a blanket over him. Charles Butler watched him with an inscrutable expression. He moved towards the boy.

'That was well done,' he called.

Lucifer saw him coming, rolled his eyes, skittered and bunched up his hindquarters.

'Look out,' the boy shouted as Charles moved towards them. 'He'll kill you!'

The hooves lashed out viciously, but caught only the air. Liam held onto the reins, pulled down the stallion's head. Charles had ducked back, just out of reach.

'Why should he kill me?' he demanded with as much *sang froid* as remained to him. 'Is he really wicked?'

Liam looked sheepish, shrugged. 'I don't know,' he said. 'But I think that he will kill you if he can.' Then he added under his breath, 'There's death in him. Sometimes I feel it!'

He brought the stallion into his stable, then slipped the bridle from his head. Charles stood and watched above the half door.

'Why is there death in him? It wasn't your mother who put that notion into your head, was it?'

The boy shrugged.

'My mother says she sent for him,' he muttered in a jocose voice as though he would deflect the nature of this utterance. He essayed a laugh. 'She's like that! She imagines things!'

Liam felt his disloyalty. But stronger than his filial love at that moment was his need for autonomy, for his acceptance by Mr Butler. Fatherless, he craved admittance into the world of men. He liked Charles Butler in ways he hardly understood; he wanted to work for him; he wanted to distance himself from his mother, from her eccentricity which, he knew, was common conversational currency, and, indeed, from all the labirynthine confines of her feminine world. He was high with new self-esteem, with the longing to swagger before men.

Charles saw the youthful eyes which were turned to him. It struck him suddenly that they were hazel, like those of his own mother and that the cast to the boy's face was similiar to his own.

'What do you really think, Liam?'

'I don't know what to think,' Liam answered truthfully after a moment. 'I saw things in the fire; I know it's stupid but I do it when she wants me to. And I hate it.'

'Things are seldom what they seem,' Charles said drily. 'Even in the fire!'

The boy emerged from the stable with the bridle over his shoulder and bolted the door.

'I'm looking forward to riding Lucifer at the race tomorrow, Mr Butler.'

He said it in a rush and his face reddened.

'What will your mother say?'

'She'll be pleased. She knows I want to be a jockey. She knows I look after Lucifer, that he trusts me.

'It's a pity my father can't see me. He used to be a jockey here . . . Dan Keegan.' Then Liam added with a half laugh as though the subject embarrassed him, 'My mother even says that Lucifer has his soul.' He laughed again. 'Which means I should win!'

Charles Butler started visibly and paled.

'Does she indeed?' he said to himself, adding aloud, 'How is your mother, Liam? Is she keeping well?'

'She's fine. You wouldn't want to take too much heed of what they say about her. She's just like any other mother, really.'

It is time I went to see her! Charles said to himself. I have been cowardly long enough.

He went the following morning.

The door of the council cottage was open. In the yard a scattering of rust-coloured hens fled, clacking. Ellen was at the turf shed, filling a creel. He watched her for a moment, saw the tired way she pulled out the sods and threw them into the wicker creel. He remembered her arms around his neck by the banks of the Bawnogue in the morning bloom of her life, and guiltily imagined her, winter after winter, picking potatoes, bringing up the child, alone and bitter while the bloom fled from her, reading the cards, or the teacups, for a pittance, and hating him. While he had never forgotten her, could not forget her, although she was only little Ellen Keegan, half-peasant, half-changeling.

He made no movement but she suddenly froze, and said without turning, 'So you have come after all, Charles Butler.'

'Yes,' he murmured, moving to stand beside her. 'I have come. Let me bring in the creel for you, Ellen . . .' He lifted it and brought it into the kitchen.

'You never married?' she said, watching him, as he drank the tea she put before him. 'You spent years wandering around the great places of the world and you never found a wife?'

There was a covert note of triumph in her voice.

'Ellen,' he said, 'I found my wife a long time ago and did not know it. I found her by the banks of the Bawnogue and courted and won her there. No woman has ever touched the spring of life in me that she did. And that is the truth of it!'

He saw the sudden fierceness in her face. Was it joy? Whatever it was it transformed her, touched her with life and beauty.

'Oh God,' Ellen said, starting up as though she had forgotten something. 'Where is Liam?'

'Didn't he tell you? He's gone with one of my stallions to Balgadden. I'm going on later, in time for the big race.' He looked at her gently. 'The horse had a go at me yesterday, you know.

Your boy said he was trying to kill me.' Then he added drily, 'I rather gathered you might have had some hopes in the matter.'

Ellen's expression changed, became mild. 'I'm sorry. You shouldn't heed Liam. It's true I've tried to do silly things. But I lost the gift years ago. Liam is the one who has it. He saw something in the fire the other night which upset him at the time. It had to do with today's race . . .'

She glanced at him. Charles met the glance; something in it sent shivers up his spine. But when she smiled it was the smile of the old Ellen.

'And he is not just my boy. He is our boy. You suspected as much when you came here.'

'Yes.'

'Will you take me to Balgadden? I would like to see the race.'

Charles went back to the house, took out his car, picked Ellen up and drove to Balgadden. His mind was a ferment of unexpected emotion. In the space of a couple of days he had found a son, and along with the son the woman he had tried to obliterate from memory. He glanced at her now. She was transformed. She was wearing a navy blue coat and hat which suited her, a trace of powder and lipstick. She looked like the old Ellen, he thought with approval, like a lady. For a moment he was touched with the breath of the old desire.

'Tomorrow is Sunday,' he said. 'How would you feel about a bit of a spin?'

Ellen did not demur, but she turned her opaque eyes on him. 'Can you go faster?' she asked in a flat voice. 'Liam will win the race . . . but there is something else to be done.'

'It's all right, Ellen. There's nothing to worry about.' He touched her knee. 'There's really nothing at all to worry about now.'

Ellen did not reply, did not flinch from his touch. But as she sat there she thought, 'You think you can come back now, claim your son, pick up the pieces . . . You think you can make a slut of Ellen Keegan again . . . You should not have trifled with me, Charles Butler . . . But you will learn that before today is out . . .'

Because they had a puncture and had to change the wheel, the Apprentice Stakes was already in progress when they got to

343

Balgadden. They saw Lucifer thundering down the field, his young rider in the Tullystown silks bent over his shoulders. They saw the black stallion take the lead, sustain the lead, flee across the finishing line two lengths ahead of the field.

Charles experienced a stab of pride, a swelling in his chest. His son had shown what he was made of; his horse was a wonder. A new vista was opening before him, a world where he would have a real home, and everything that went with it, a son, success, respect, a modicum of peace.

Ellen rushed forward, shouting something he could not catch, although for an eerie moment he had the feeling that she was addressing the horse. But he followed her, congratulations for Liam ready on his lips. Liam, glowing with success, had just dismounted in the paddock and waved at them.

The boy felt as though his feet hardly touched the ground. Someone came forward to present him with the cup. He heard Lucifer's name and Tullystown Stud and his own name read over the public address system. He heard the sussuration of the crowd, tasted, for a moment, the glory.

But in the pit of the boy's stomach something quite different was fermenting, something which tightened and closed until he was in pain. It was the expectancy of some imminent event he could not identify, like the knowledge he had had at twelve – a split second before the hurley ball had got him at the side of the head – that the ball had marked him, and was coming for him, slowly, and that he could do nothing either to change his own position or alter its trajectory.

As the trophy was lifted towards him he saw the reflection in its silver surface – the black horse and its rider. In a start of terror he understood his mother's ferment for the past few weeks. There was someone on Lucifer. He saw him as he had seen him in that dream, saturated from the river, but his eyes were white, like an old corpse, and the grin of his rotting mouth an obscenity. Liam shouted, turned to the dreadful thing on the saddle. But the apparition had gone. Then Charles Butler was beside him.

'Well done,' he said, clapping his son on the back.

It was then that Lucifer reared, wrenching the reins from Liam's fingers. The boy reacted with lightning reflexes, pushing

Charles back, but the plunging, race-shod hooves came down on his own skull, spattering his brains down the Butler racing silks to splatter the trampled ground.

Ellen Keegan, too, saw the shadowy rider, felt the triumph of its malevolence as its gaze found her.

A woman's scream mingled with those of the crowd, rose higher and shriller until the race course seemed to echo.

She stood immobile, like someone who would never move again.

'Liam! . . . Not my son, oh . . . not my *son* . . .'

Lucifer stood trembling, head drooping, drenched in sweat. Charles Butler told them to take his stallion away. He knelt at the boy's side, whispered something in his ear and closed his eyes. Then, without a glance at Ellen Keegan, he rose and left the paddock.

3

FIXED ODDS

Crime and the Gamblers

'Betting is the manure to which the
enormous crop of horse-racing and
racehorse breeding in this and other
countries is to a large extent due.'

ROBERT BLACK

Straight From the Horse's Mouth

EDGAR WALLACE

Few writers are more closely identified with the fiction of the Turf than Edgar Wallace, the 'King of Thrillers'. A much repeated story about the man who wrote over 200 books which sold in their millions says that when he died suddenly in 1932 he was over £140,000 in debt most of which was owing to his bookies. The truth is rather different, as Margaret Lane insisted in her biography *Edgar Wallace* (1939): 'There were no racing debts since Wallace's bookmakers' accounts had, following the usual practice, been settled weekly.' There was, however, no argument that the prolific author had been a compulsive gambler all his life, forever confident in his ability to pick a winner even after years of proof to the contrary. For, as Margaret Lane has also written, 'He was never, in the narrow sense of the phrase, a real racing man. He had none of the patience and caution of the backer who makes racing a profession, and even calculates his profit; he had no deep knowledge of horse-flesh (though his vanity flattered him on this point) and his betting was directed less by system than by fancy. Betting was his excitement, his drug; the pleasant stimulant which filled every afternoon with suspense and every morning with opportunity.'

Another writer, the former jockey Jack Leach, who was a friend of Wallace, was even less complimentary about him in his amusing autobiography, *Sods I Have Cut On The Turf*: 'Edgar Wallace was a fantastic man, but there was one very weak link in his make up – he thought he knew everything about racing. I never met a man who knew less.'

Wallace had, it seems, developed his passion for racing while he was a journalist in Fleet Street, a job that enabled him to attend many meetings free of charge and later encouraged him to hire his own box at Ascot. For a time, Wallace even ran a tipster business from an address in Brick Lane, Piccadilly, which belonged to a horse-painter of great charm and plausibility named 'Ringer' Barrie, who had earned his nickname by his ability to disguise race horses for big races. Although this soon proved an ill-fated venture that Wallace had to abandon after six months of fighting off punters furious at constantly losing money on his 'tips', he did come out of the business with a role model and a lot of ideas for his series about a cockney tipster, Educated Evans. In the interim he had also built up a number of contacts in the shady world of racing and it was the stories that they told him – in return for the usual five or ten pound note – that gave him the ideas for most of his subsequent novels and short stories about the Turf.

Wallace continued to frequent the race tracks with the same lack of success to the end of his days, and was even at the races a few days before his sudden death. It was, though, one outing of unalloyed pleasure. He was then in Hollywood working on the screenplay of the movie *King Kong*, when he was visited by his old friend Steve Donoghue and the pair decided to visit the track at Agua Caliente, just across the border in Mexico. Much to his surprise, Wallace found that the second most important race of the day had been named the Edgar Wallace Stakes in his honour. And to complete his joy, he picked three winners in a row while Donoghue, the true man of the turf, failed to pick a single one.

Edgar Wallace (1875–1932) has been described as probably the most popular thriller writer of all time, and certainly was for the first half of this century. Following the success of his first (self-published) book, *The Four Just Men* in 1905, he poured out an unending stream of novels, stories and plays which earned him immense popularity, and a fortune which he squandered on a mixture of gambling and high-living. Even so, within two years of his death a coordinated re-publication programme of his best novels had wiped out all of these debts and even started paying royalties to his heirs. Among Wallace's many famous characters, Johnny 'Educated' Evans was very successful in print and enjoyed an even larger audience when several of his stories were made into films in the thirties, starring the ribald comic Max Miller.

In this typical Evans story, there are appearances by his two most regular sparring partners: 'The Miller', aka Detective Sergeant William Challoner of the CID, whose nick-name derives from his knowledge of horses and his habit of nibbling a piece of straw, and the dour Inspector Pine, who also serves as the Secretary of the Racecourse Elevation Brotherhood for the Suppression of Gambling. Herein, once again, the best laid plans of Evans the tipster to substantiate his claims of infallibility seem destined to failure when he becomes involved in a fight with a client. But Wallace, the gambler who could never win on the horses, never fails to surprise when it comes to the unexpected story dénouement.

*

It is generally believed in Somers Town that a policeman would shop his own aunt for the sake of getting his name before the magistrate, but this is not the case. A policeman, being intensely human, has what the Portuguese call a *repugnancio* to certain jobs.

Sergeant Challoner, CID, was called into the office of his superior and entrusted with a piece of work which revolted his soul – namely the raiding of Issy Bodd's flourishing ready-money starting-price business, which he carried on at his house off Ossulton Street.

Complaints had been made by a virtuous neighbour.

'Tibby Cole,' said The Miller. 'He's annoyed because Issy caught him trying to work a ramp on him, and one of Issy's minders gave him a thick ear.'

'My dear Sergeant!' said the shocked Inspector Pine. 'There is really no reason why you should employ the language of Somers Town.'

The Miller went forth to his work in no great heart. He was too good a servant of the law to send a warning, and he came upon the defenceless Issy at a most compromising moment.

'I'm very sorry, Bodd,' he said as he effected the arrest. 'I'll take all the slips you've got – you can get bail, I suppose?'

'You couldn't have come on a better day,' said the philosophical Mr Bodd. 'All Camden Town's gone mad over Sanaband, and as I never lay off a penny, it looked as if I was going through it.'

Sanaband, as all the world knows, started a hot favourite for the Northumberland Plate and finished last but one, and everybody said: 'Where are the Stewards?'

Thousands of people who had had sums varying from a shilling to a hundred pounds on the favourite, gnashed their teeth and tore their hair, and said things about Mr Yardley, the owner and trainer, of Sanaband, which were both libellous and uncharitable.

Bill Yardley himself saw the finish with a whimsical smile and, going down to meet the disgraced animal, patted his neck and called him gentle names, and people who saw this exhibition of humanity nodded significantly.

'Not a yard,' they said and wondered why he was not warned off.

Yardley in truth, had backed Sanaband to win a fortune, but he had spent his life amongst horses and backing them. He knew that if Sanaband had been human, that intelligent animal would have said:

'I'm extremely sorry, Mr Yardley but I've not been feeling up to the mark this past day or two – you probably noticed that I didn't eat as well as usual this morning. I've a bit of a headache and a pain in my tummy, but I shall be all right in a day or two.'

And knowing this, Yardley neither kicked the horse in the stomach nor did he tell his friends that Sanaband was an incorrigible rogue. He casually mentioned that he had fifteen hundred pounds on the horse, and nobody believed him. Nobody ever believes trainers.

'What's the matter with you, you old devil?' asked Mr Yardley as he rubbed the horse's nose, and that was the beginning and end of his recriminations.

In far-off Camden Town the news of Sanaband's downfall brought sorrow and wrath to the heart of the World's Premier Turf Adviser and prophet, and the situation was in no sense eased by the gentle irony of Detective-Sergeant Challoner.

'I don't expect miracles,' said The Miller, 'and I admit that it was an act of lunacy on my part to imagine that you could give me two winners in a month.'

'Rub it in, Mr Challoner,' said Educated Evans bitterly. 'How was I to know that the trainer was thievin'? Am I like the celebrated Mejusa, got eyes all over my head?'

'Medusa is the lady you are groping after,' said The Miller, 'and she had snakes.'

'Ain't snakes got eyes?' demanded Educated Evans. 'No, Mr Challoner, I got this information about Sanaband from the boy that does him. This horse was tried to give two stone an' ten lengths to Elbow Grease. My information was that he could fall down—'

'*And* get up, *and* win,' finished the patient Mr Challoner. 'Well, he *didn't* fall down! The only thing that fell down was your reputation as a tipster!'

Educated Evans closed his eyes with an expression of pain.

'Turf Adviser,' he murmured.

The whole subject was painful to Evans. Just as he had re-established confidence in the minds and hearts of his clientèle, at the very moment when the sceptics of the Midland Goods Yard at Somers Town were again on friendly terms with him, this set-back had come. And it had come at a moment when the finances of Educated Evans were not at their best.

'It's a long worm that's got no turning,' said Educated Evans despondently, 'an' there's no doubt whatever that my amazing and remarkable run of electrifyin' successes is for the moment eclipsed.'

The Miller sniffed.

'They never electrified me,' he said. 'Two winners in ten shots—'

'*And* five seconds that would have won if they'd had jockeys up,' reproached Evans. 'No, Mr Challoner, my education has taught me not to start kicking against the bricks, as the saying goes. I'm due now for a long batch of losers. If Sanaband had won – but it didn't. And I ought to have known it. That there thieving Yardley's keepin' the horse for Gatwick.'

The sneers that come the way of an unsuccessful Turf Adviser are many. There is an ingratitude about the racing public which both sickened and annoyed him. Men who had fawned on him now addressed him with bitterness. Hackett, the greengrocer, who only a short week ago had acclaimed him great amongst the prophets, reviled him as he passed.

'You put me off the winner,' he said sourly. 'I'd have backed Oil Cake – made up my mind to back it, and you lumbered me on to a rotten five to four chance that finished down the course! It's people like you that ruin racing. The Stewards ought to warn you off.'

'I'm sorry to hear you say that, Mr Hackett,' said Educated Evans mildly. 'I've got a beauty for you on Saturday—'

Mr Hackett's cynical laughter followed him.

A few yards farther on he met Bill Gold, an occasional client and a bus conductor.

'I wouldn't mind, Evans,' he said, sadly, 'only I've got a wife and eight children, and this was my biggest bet of the year. How I'm going to pay the rent this week Gawd knows! You ought to be more careful, you really ought!'

It was a curious circumstance, frequently observed by Educated Evans, that his clients invariably had their maximum wager on his failures, and either forgot to back his winners or had ventured the merest trifle on them. In this they unconsciously imitated their betters, for it is one of the phenomena of racing that few ever confess to their winnings, but wail their losses to the high heavens.

Misfortune, however, has its compensations, and as he was passing through Stebbington Street he met a fellow sufferer.

'Good morning, Mr Bodd,' said Evans respectfully – he was invariably respectful to the bookmaking class. 'I suppose you had a good race yesterday – that Sanaband wasn't trying.'

Mr Issy Bodd curled up his lip.

'Oh, yes, I had a good day,' he said sardonically. 'Three hours at the station before my bail came, and a fine of fifty and costs – and six hundred slips destroyed and every one of 'em backing Sanaband. I've had a crowd round the house all the morning getting their money back on the grounds that if you can't win you can't lose. The public knows too much about the rules to suit me. It's this popular education, Evans, and novel reading that does it.

If I hadn't paid out, I'd have lost my trade, though how I'm going on now, heavens only knows.'

He looked at Evans with a speculative eye, listening in silence as the educated man recited his own tale of woe.

'That's right,' he said, as Educated Evans paused to take breath. 'You've struck a streak of bad luck. I don't suppose you'll give another winner for years, and I don't suppose I'll have another winning week for months.'

They stared at one another, two men weighted with the misery of the world.

'It'd be different if I was in funds,' said Evans. 'If I could afford to send out a classy circular to all clients, old an' new, I'd get 'em back. It's printing and advertising that does it, Mr Bodd. My educated way of writing gets 'em eating out of my hand, to use a Shakespearean expression. I'm what you might term the Napoleon Bonaparte of Turf Advisers. It's brains that does it. I'm sort of second-sighted, always have been. I had to wear glasses for it when I was a boy.'

Mr Bodd bit his lip thoughtfully. He was a business man and a quick thinker.

'A few pounds one way or the other doesn't make any difference to me,' he said slowly. 'You've got to put it down before you pick it up. What about a share in my book, Evans?'

Educated Evans could scarcely believe his ears.

'Not a big share – say three shillings in the pound,' said Bodd, still speaking deliberately. 'Your luck's out, you won't be giving winners for a long time – I've studied luck and I know. Most of your Somers Town mugs bet with me. That last big winner you sent out gave me a jolt. And it doesn't matter much whether you give winners or losers – you can't hurt yourself. A little punter is born every minute. *And* I'd put up the money for all the advertising.'

The sinister meaning of Mr Issy Bodd was clear, and Educated Evans felt himself go pale.

'Get out a real classy circular,' Issy went on, 'with pictures. There's nothing like pictures to pull in the punter. Get a picture of a horse talking. It's an idea I had a long time ago. Have the words "Straight from the Horse's Mouth!" Silly? Don't you believe it!

Half the people who back horses haven't seen one. Me and Harry Jolbing have got most of the street business in Camden Town and Harry's had a bad time too.'

'Do you mean that I'm to send out losers?' asked Evans in a hollow voice.

'One or two,' said the other calmly. 'Anyway, you'll send losers. It's worth money to you. If you do the thing well, and with your education you ought, we ought to get a big win.'

Evans shook his head.

'I tried to give losers to a fellow once,' he said, 'and they all won.'

'You couldn't give a winner if you tried,' said Mr Bodd, decidedly. 'I know what luck is.'

That evening Educated Evans sat in his library, preparing the circular. He was the tenant of one room over a garage. When he slept, it was a bedroom; when he ate, it was a dining-room; but when he wrote, it was library and study.

And thus he wrote:

STRAIGHT FROM THE HORSE'S MOUTH
That sounds ridiculous to anybody who doesn't know
EDUCATED EVANS
(*The World's Premier Turf Prophet*)
But with Educated Evans that phrase has a meaning of
the highest importance and intelligence!
It means that he's got the goods!
It means that he's in touch with secret information!
It means that his touts and army of investigators have
unravelled a great Turf Mystery!

What a beauty!
What a beauty!
What a Beauty!

THE BIGGEST JOB OF THE YEAR!
Get back all your losses! Double your winnings!
Put down your maximum!

There was more in similar strain.

Mr Issy Bodd helped. He got a friend of his to draw a horse's head. It was a noble head. The mouth of the fiery steed was opened and from its interior came the words:

'I shall win at 10 to 1!'

The misgivings of Educated Evans were allayed at the sight of this masterpiece.

To some two thousand five hundred people this circular was despatched. Most of the names were supplied by Messrs. Bodd and Jolbing, and the words 'Put down your maximum' were heavily underlined.

Despite the exceptionally low price at which the peerless information was offered, the response was not encouraging.

'It doesn't matter,' said Mr Bodd. 'You can send them the horse whether they pay or not.'

The race chosen was the Stockwell Selling Plate at Sandown, and the selection of the horse occupied the greater part of the day before the race. A committee of three, consisting of Educated Evans, Mr Bodd, and Jolbing, a prosperous young man who wore diamond rings everywhere except on his thumbs.

'Polecat?' suggested Evans. 'That horse couldn't win a race if all the others died.' Mr Bodd shook his head.

'He was a job at Pontefract last month,' he said. 'I wouldn't be surprised if he popped up. What about Coal Tar?'

'Not *him*!' said Mr Jolbing firmly. 'He's just the kind of horse that might do it. He's being kept for something. What about Daffodil? He finished last at Windsor.'

Educated Evans dissented.

'He got left,' he said. 'Daffodil's in a clever stable, and Mahon rides, and they like winning at Sandown.'

'What about Harebell?' suggested Mr Jolbing. 'She's never finished in the first three.'

'She's been leading Mopo in his work, and Mopo won at Newcastle,' said Mr Bodd. 'That horse could win if they'd let her. No, I think the best one for you, Evans, is Grizzle. He's been coughing.'

Evans smiled cynically.

'The boy that does him told me that Grizzle is fit and fancied. In fact, Grizzle is the very horse I should have tipped for the race.'

The entry was not a large one, and there remained only five possibles, and two of those were certain to start first or second favourites.

'What about Beady Eye?' asked Mr Bodd.

'It doesn't run,' said Evans, 'and there's no sense in sending a non-runner.'

'Gardener?' suggested Mr Jolbing, laying a glittering finger on the entry. 'That's your horse, Evans.'

But both Educated Evans and Mr Bodd protested simultaneously.

'Gardener belongs to Yardley and you know what he is,' said Evans reproachfully. 'I wouldn't be surprised to see Gardener win. The only horse that I can give is Henroost. He *couldn't* win!'

Here they were in complete agreement, and the committee broke up, leaving Evans to do the dirty.

That evening, with all the envelopes stamped and addressed and ready for despatch, Educated Evans strolled out for a little fresh air and exercise. At the corner of Bayham Street he met Mr Hackett, the eminent greengrocer. Mr Hackett was in wine, for it was early-closing day and he had spent the afternoon playing an unprofitable game of nap at his club.

'Oh! there you are, you perishing robber!' he sneered, planting himself in Evans's path. 'You ruiner of businesses! Educated! Why, you haven't got the education of a rabbit!'

Had his insults taken any other form, Educated Evans might have passed him by in contempt. But this slur upon his erudition roused all that was most violent in his usually amiable character.

'You're a nice one to talk about education!' he sneered in return. 'I could talk you blind on any subject – history, geography, or mathematical arithmetic!'

'A man who sells lies—' began Mr Hackett insolently.

'It's better than selling caterpillars disguised as cabbages and rotten apples,' said Evans heatedly. 'It's better than selling short-weight potatoes to the poor and suffering—'

And then, before he could realize what was happening, Mr Hackett, all his professional sentiments outraged, hit him violently on the nose.

In three minutes the most interesting fight that had been seen in

Camden Town for many years was in progress. And then a strong hand gripped Evans by the collar, and through his damaged optic he saw the silver buttons of London's constabulary.

The Miller was in the station when Evans and Mr Hackett were charged with disorderly conduct, to which, in Mr Hackett's case, was added the stigma of intoxication; and, in his friendly way, the detective went forth in search of bail. It was impossible, however, to discover the necessary guarantee for Evans's good behaviour. He could neither approach Jolbing nor Bodd; and when The Miller returned with the information Evans was frantic.

'I've got some work to do tonight, Mr Challoner,' he wailed. 'Three thousand tips to send out!'

The Miller hesitated. He was going off duty and he had a genuine affection for the little tipster.

'What are you sending out, Evans?'

'Henroost for that seller tomorrow. It ought to go before eleven o'clock,' moaned Evans. 'Couldn't you find anybody? Couldn't you stand bail for me, Mr Challoner? I'd never let you down.'

The Miller shook his head.

'An official is not allowed to go bail,' he said. 'But I'll see what I can do for you, Evans. I suppose they've not taken the key of your expensive flat from you?'

'The key's under the mat, just outside the door,' said Evans, eagerly. 'Henroost – don't forget, Mr Challoner. If you get somebody to do it for me, I'll never be grateful enough.'

At half-past eleven the following morning Educated Evans addressed a special plea from the dock with such good effect that the magistrate instantly discharged him. He did not see The Miller who was engaged in investigating a petty larceny; but, hurrying home, he was overjoyed to discover that the table, which he had left littered with envelopes, was now tidy.

He had spent a very restless night, for the occupant of the adjoining cell was an elderly Italian with a passion for opera, who had sung the score of *La Bohème* from opening chorus to finale throughout the night.

Educated Evans lay down on his bed and was asleep instantly. The sun was setting when he rose, and after a hasty toilet, realizing his reponsibility, he went out to discover the result of the great race.

A glance at the result column in the *News* filled him with satisfaction and pride, though he had at the back of his mind an uneasy feeling of disloyalty to his clientèle. The race had been won by Coal Tar, which had started at ten to one, and Henroost was unplaced. Thus fortified, he strolled forth to meet Mr Bodd, and came upon him in Great College Street, and the face of Mr Bodd was darkened with passion.

'You dirty little twister!' he hissed. 'Didn't you say you'd send out Henroost? You cheap little blighter! Didn't I put up the money for your something so-and-so circulars? Didn't I pay for the unprintable stamps that you put upon the unmentionable envelopes that I bought with my own money?'

'Here, what's the idea?' began Evans.

'What's the idea!' roared Mr Bodd, growing purple in the face. 'You sent them out Coal Tar! It won at ten to one, and every one of your so-and-so clients had his so-and-so maximum – don't let Jolbing see you, he'll murder you!'

Dazed and confounded, Evans bent his steps to the police station and met The Miller as he descended the steps.

'Excuse me, Mr Challoner,' he faltered. 'Didn't you send Henroost?'

The Miller shook his head.

'No, I sent Coal Tar. Just after I left the station I met one of our inspectors from Scotland Yard, who'd had the tip from the owner. Evans, your luck's turned!'

'As a tipster – yes,' said Evans, and weeks passed before The Miller quite understood what he meant.

A Story Goes With It

DAMON RUNYON

If Educated Evans was England's best-known shady tipster, then Damon Runyon's Hot Horse Herbie enjoyed the same notoriety in America. Nobody ever claimed to be closer to a certain winner or about to stake a bigger gamble than Herbie – as one of his greatest admirers, the English humorist E. C. Bentley wrote in a Runyonese introduction to a 1942 collection of Runyon's stories: 'Hot Horse Herbie is such a guy as never thinks of anything else in this world but betting on horses.' The anonymous narrator of Herbie's exploits also has a strongly developed taste for betting, says Mr Bentley, 'a taste which he shares with practically every guy mentioned in the stories – in fact the only guys I can think of at the moment who do not back horses are two guys who happen to be bookmakers.' Even the most violent gangsters who inhabit Runyon's New York study the horses when they are not involved in committing crimes.

Herbie also shared with Educated Evans a real-life model in the shape of a Broadway tipster whom Runyon met while building his reputation on the *New York American* as a journalist who could cover any event from the Kentucky Derby to the city's latest murder mystery. His fascination with the turf was evident even then in often repeated phrases like 'Gimme a handy guy like Sande (the famous jockey Earl Sande) bootin' those winners home!' and by part-owning a horse that was named after him.

The twenties and thirties, when Runyon was at the height of his powers, was a time when New York was ruled by gangsters, as Julian Symons has written: 'They owned many of the politicians, the popular mayor Jimmy Walker took every bribe offered him, and the city's most famous detective, Johnny Broderick, was ready to lose any vital bit of criminal evidence at a price . . .

Runyon soon realised the best way of writing about good-guy gangsters was to live with them and found that no trouble because he greatly preferred crooks and gamblers to dull, honest citizens.' From this underworld he fashioned the famous Harry the Horse, Milk Ear Willie, Nicely-Nicely Johnson, Bookie Bob and Hot Horse Herbie . . .

Damon Runyon (1880–1946) is, of course, best remembered today for the musical and film *Guys and Dolls*, based on his stories, which opened in 1948 and has been a worldwide favourite ever since. Although Runyon saw himself primarily as a journalist, when he turned to short story writing to supplement his income which had been dissipated on drink and gambling, he soon proved to be a raconteur in the great tradition of that other New Yorker, O. Henry. Yet despite his fame, Runyon had a wretched private life – he had little to do with his children and, after the death of his wife in 1931, married a girl half his age simply because she brought him luck at a race meeting – and then died after an extremely painful battle with cancer. Nonetheless, the anonymous, semi-literate villain who tells all his stories was a truly unique creation and the spur to generations of later writers, not least of them Roald Dahl, who admitted shortly before his own death that Runyon's work had been the reason why he left his desk in the London office of a petroleum company to become a writer. Tipster Herbie actually features in several of Damon Runyon's stories, including 'The Snatching of Bookie Bob', 'Pick The Winner' and 'A Story Goes With It', which I have chosen to include here because it so well illustrates Runyon's fascination with the shady side of race betting and offers the sort of mixture of violent criminals and outlandish humour that was the hallmark of his very finest work.

*

One night I am in a gambling joint in Miami watching the crap game and thinking what a nice thing it is, indeed, to be able to shoot craps without having to worry about losing your potatoes.

Many of the high shots from New York and Detroit and St.

Louis and other cities are around the table, and there is quite some action in spite of the hard times. In fact, there is so much action that a guy with only a few bobs on him, such as me, will be considered very impolite to be pushing into this game, because they are packed in very tight around the table.

I am maybe three guys back from the table, and I am watching the game by standing on tiptoe peeking over their shoulders, and all I can hear is Goldie, the stick man, hollering money-money-money every time some guy makes a number, so I can see the dice are very warm indeed, and that the right betters are doing first-rate.

By and by a guy by the name of Guinea Joe, out of Trenton, picks up the dice and starts making numbers right and left, and I know enough about this Guinea Joe to know that when he starts making numbers anybody will be very foolish indeed not to follow his hand, although personally I am generally a wrong better against the dice, if I bet at all.

Now all I have in my pocket is a sawbuck, and the hotel stakes are coming up on me the next day, and I need this saw, but with Guinea Joe hotter than a forty-five it will be over-looking a big opportunity not to go along with him, so when he comes out on an eight, which is a very easy number for Joe to make when he is hot, I dig up my sawbuck, and slide it past the three guys in front of me to the table, and I say to Lefty Park, who is laying against the dice, as follows:

'I will take the odds, Lefty.'

Well, Lefty looks at my sawbuck and nods his head, for Lefty is not such a guy as will refuse any bet, even though it is as modest as mine, and right away Goldie yells money-money-money, so there I am with twenty-two dollars.

Next Guinea Joe comes out on a nine, and naturally I take thirty to twenty for my sugar, because nine is nothing for Joe to make when he is hot. He makes the nine just as I figure, and I take two to one for my half a yard when he starts looking for a ten, and when he makes the ten I am right up against the table, because I am now a guy with means.

Well, the upshot of the whole business is that I finally find myself with three hundred bucks, and when it looks as if the dice are cooling off, I take out and back off from the table, and while I am backing off I am trying to look like a guy who loses all his potatoes, because there are always many wolves waiting around crap games and one thing and another in Miami this season, and what they are waiting for is to put the bite on anybody who happens to make a little scratch.

In fact, nobody can remember when the bite is as painful as it is in Miami this season, what with the unemployment situation among many citizens who come to Miami expecting to find work in the gambling joints, or around the race track. But almost as soon as these citizens arrive, the gambling joints are all turned off, except in spots, and the bookmakers are chased off the track and the mutuels put in, and the consequences are the suffering is most intense. It is not only intense among the visiting citizens, but it is quite intense among the Miami landlords, because naturally if a citizen is not working, nobody can expect him to pay any room rent, but the Miami landlords do not seem to understand this situation, and are very unreasonable about their room rent.

Anyway, I back through quite a crowd without anybody biting me, and I am commencing to figure I may escape altogether and get to my hotel and hide my dough before the news gets around that I win about five *G's*, which is what my winning is sure to amount to by the time the rumor reaches all quarters of the city.

Then, just as I am thinking I am safe, I find I am looking a guy by the name of Hot Horse Herbie in the face, and I can tell from Hot Horse Herbie's expression that he is standing there watching me for some time, so there is no use in telling him I am washed out in the game. In fact, I cannot think of much of anything to tell Hot Horse Herbie that may keep him from putting the bite on me for at least a few bobs, and I am greatly astonished when he does not offer to bite me at all, but says to me like this:

'Well,' he says, 'I am certainly glad to see you make such a nice score. I will be looking for you tomorrow at the track, and will have some big news for you.'

Then he walks away from me and I stand there with my mouth open looking at him, as it is certainly a most unusual way for Herbie to act. It is the first time I ever knew Herbie to walk away from a chance to bite somebody, and I can scarcely understand such actions, for Herbie is such a guy as will not miss a bite, even if he does not need it.

He is a tall, thin guy, with a sad face and a long chin, and he is called Hot Horse Herbie because he nearly always has a very hot horse to tell you about. He nearly always has a horse that is so hot it is fairly smoking, a hot horse being a horse that cannot possibly lose a race unless it falls down dead, and while Herbie's hot horses often lose without falling down dead, this does not keep Herbie from coming up with others just as hot.

In fact, Hot Horse Herbie is what is called a hustler around the race tracks, and his business is to learn about these hot horses, or even just suspect about them, and then get somebody to bet on them, which is a very legitimate business indeed, as Herbie only collects a commission if the hot horses win, and if they do not win Herbie just keeps out of sight awhile from whoever he gets to bet on the hot horses. There are very few guys in this world who can keep out of sight better than Hot Horse Herbie, and especially from old Cap Duhaine, of the Pinkertons, who is always around pouring cold water on hot horses.

In fact, Cap Duhaine, of the Pinkertons, claims that guys such as Hot Horse Herbie are nothing but touts, and sometimes he heaves them off the race track altogether, but of course Cap Duhaine is a very unsentimental old guy and cannot see how such characters as Hot Horse Herbie add to the romance of the turf.

Anyway, I escape from the gambling joint with all my scratch on me, and hurry to my room and lock myself in for the night, and I do not show up in public until along about noon the next day, when it is time to go over to the coffee shop for my java. And of course by this time the news of my score is all over town, and many guys are taking dead aim at me.

But naturally I am now able to explain to them that I have to wire most of the three yards I win to Nebraska to save my father's farm from being seized by the sheriff, and while everybody knows I do not have a father, and that if I do have a father I will not be sending him money for such a thing as saving his farm, with times what they are in Miami, nobody is impolite enough to doubt my word except a guy by the name of Pottsville Legs, who wishes to see my receipts from the telegraph office when I explain to him why I cannot stake him to a double sawbuck.

I do not see Hot Horse Herbie until I get to the track, and he is waiting for me right inside the grand-stand gate, and as soon as I show up he motions me off to one side and says to me like this:

'Now,' Herbie says, 'I am very smart indeed about a certain race to-day. In fact,' he says, 'if any guy knowing what I know does not bet all he can rake and scrape together on a certain horse, such a guy ought to cut his own throat and get himself out of the way forever. What I know,' Herbie says, 'is enough to shake the foundations of this country if it gets out. Do not ask any questions,' he says, 'but get ready to bet all the sugar you win last night on this horse I am going to mention to you, and all I ask you in return is to bet fifty on me. And,' Herbie says, 'kindly do not tell me you leave your money in your other pants, because I know you do not have any other pants.'

'Now, Herbie,' I says, 'I do not doubt your information, because I know you will not give out information unless it is well founded. But,' I say, 'I seldom stand for a tip, and as for betting fifty for you, you know I will not bet fifty even for myself if somebody guarantees me a winner. So I thank you, Herbie, just the same,' I say, 'but I must do without your tip,' and with this I start walking away.

'Now,' Herbie says, 'wait a minute. A story goes with it,' he says.

Well, of course this is a different matter entirely. I am such a guy as will always listen to a tip on a horse if a story goes with the tip. In fact, I will not give you a nickel for a tip without a story, but it must be a first-class story, and most horse players are the same way. In fact, there are very few horse players who will not listen to a tip if a story goes with it, for this is the way human nature is. So I turn and walk back to Hot Horse Herbie, and say to him like this:

'Well,' I say, 'let me hear the story, Herbie.'

'Now,' Herbie says, dropping his voice away down low, in case old Cap Duhaine may be around somewhere listening, 'it is the third race, and the horse is a horse by the name of Never Despair. It is a boat race,' Herbie says. 'They are going to shoo in Never Despair. Everything else in the race is a cooler,' he says.

'Well,' I say, 'this is just an idea, Herbie, and not a story.'

'Wait a minute,' Herbie says. 'The story that goes with it is a very strange story indeed. In fact,' he says, 'it is such a story as I can scarcely believe myself, and I will generally believe almost any story, including,' he says, 'the ones I make up out of my own head. Anyway, the story is as follows:

'Never Despair is owned by an old guy by the name of Seed Mercer,' Herbie says. 'Maybe you remember seeing him around. He always wears a black slouch hat and gray whiskers,' Herbie says, 'and he is maybe a hundred years old, and his horses are very terrible horses indeed. In fact,' Herbie says, 'I do not remember seeing any more terrible horses in all the years I am around the track, and,' Herbie says, 'I wish to say I see some very terrible horses indeed.

'Now,' Herbie says, 'old Mercer has a granddaughter who is maybe sixteen years old, come next grass, by the name of Lame Louise, and she is called Lame Louise because she is all crippled up from childhood by infantile what-is-this, and can scarcely navigate, and,' Herbie says, 'her being crippled up in such a way makes old Mercer feel very sad, for she is all he has in the world, except these terrible horses.'

'It is a very long story, Herbie,' I say, 'and I wish to see Moe Shapoff about a very good thing in the first race.'

'Never mind Moe Shapoff,' Herbie says. 'He will only tell you about a bum by the name of Zachary in the first race, and Zachary has no chance whatever. I make Your John a stand-out in the first,' he says.

'Well,' I say, 'let us forget the first and go on with your story, although it is commencing to sound all mixed up to me.'

'Now,' Herbie says, 'it not only makes old man Mercer very sad because Lame Louise is all crippled up, but,' he says, 'it makes many of the jockeys and other guys around the race track very sad, because,' he says, 'they know Lame Louise since she is so high and she always has a smile for them, and especially for Jockey Scroon. In fact,' Herbie says, 'Jockey Scroon is even more sad about Lame Louise than old man Mercer, because Jockey Scroon loves Lame Louise.'

'Why,' I say, very indignant, 'Jockey Scroon is nothing but a little burglar. Why,' I say, 'I see Jockey Scroon do things to horses I bet on that he will have to answer for on the Judgment Day, if there is any justice at such a time. Why,' I say, 'Jockey Scroon is nothing but a Gerald Chapman in his heart, and so are all other jockeys.'

'Yes,' Hot Horse Herbie says, 'what you say is very, very true, and I am personally in favor of the electric chair for all jockeys, but,' he says, 'Jockey Scroon loves Lame Louise just the same, and is figuring on making her his ever-loving wife when he gets a few bobs together, which,' Herbie says, 'makes Louise eight to five in my line to be an old maid. Jockey Scroon rooms with me downtown,' Herbie says, 'and he speaks freely to me about his love for Louise. Furthermore,' Herbie says, 'Jockey Scroon is personally not a bad little guy, at that, although of course being a jockey he is sometimes greatly misunderstood by the public.

'Anyway,' Hot Horse Herbie says, 'I happen to go home early last night before I see you at the gambling joint, and I hear voices coming out of my room, and naturally I pause outside the door to listen, because for all I know it may be the landlord, speaking about the room rent, although,' Herbie says, 'I do not figure my landlord to be much worried at this time because I see him sneak into my room a few days before and take a lift at my trunk to make sure I have belongings in the same, and it happens I nail the trunk to the floor beforehand, so not being able to lift it, the landlord is bound to figure me a guy with property.

'These voices,' Herbie says, 'are mainly soprano voices, and at first I think Jockey Scroon is in there with some dolls, which is by no means permissible in my hotel, but, after listening awhile, I discover they are the voices of young boys, and I make out that these boys are nothing but jockeys, and they are the six jockeys who are riding in the third race, and they are fixing up this race to be a boat race, and to shoo in Never Despair, which Jockey Scroon is riding.

'And,' Hot Horse Herbie says, 'the reason they are fixing up this boat race is the strangest part of the story. It seems,' he says, 'that Jockey Scroon hears old man Mercer talking about a great surgeon from Europe who is a shark on patching up cripples such as Lame Louise, and who just arrives at Palm Beach to spend the winter, and old man Mercer is saying how he wishes he has dough enough to take Lame Louise to this guy so he can operate on her, and maybe make her walk good again.

'But of course,' Herbie says, 'it is well known to one and all that old man Mercer does not have a quarter, and that he has no way of getting a quarter unless one of his terrible horses accidentally wins a purse. So,' Herbie says, 'it seems these jockeys get to talking it over among themselves, and they figure it will be a nice thing to let old man Mercer win a purse such as the thousand bucks that goes with the third race to-day, so he can take Lame Louise to Palm Beach, and now you have a rough idea of what is coming off.

'Furthermore,' Herbie says, 'these jockeys wind up their meeting by taking a big oath among themselves that they will not tell a living soul what is doing so nobody will bet on Never Despair, because,' he says, 'these little guys are smart enough to see if there is any betting on such a horse there may be a very large squawk afterwards. And,' he says, 'I judge they keep their oath because Never Despair is twenty to one in the morning line, and I do not hear a whisper about him, and you have the tip all to yourself.'

'Well,' I say, 'so what?' For this story is now commencing to make me a little tired, especially as I hear the bell for the first race, and I must see Moe Shapoff.

'Why,' Hot Horse Herbie says, 'so you bet every nickel you can rake and scrape together on Never Despair, including the twenty you are to bet for me for giving you this tip and the story that goes with it.'

'Herbie,' I say, 'it is a very interesting story indeed, and also very sad, but,' I say, 'I am sorry it is about a horse Jockey Scroon is to ride, because I do not think I will ever bet on anything Jockey Scroon rides if they pay off in advance. And,' I say, 'I am certainly not going to bet twenty for you or anybody else.'

'Well,' Hot Horse Herbie says, 'I will compromise with you for a pound note, because I must have something going for me on this boat race.'

So I give Herbie a fiver, and the chances are this is about as strong as he figures from the start, and I forget all about his tip and the story that goes with it, because while I enjoy a story with a tip, I feel that Herbie overdoes this one.

Anyway, no handicapper alive can make Never Despair win the third race off the form, because this race is at six furlongs, and there is a barrel of speed in it, and anybody can see that old man Mercer's horse is away over his head. In fact, The Dancer tells me that any one of the other five horses in this race can beat Never Despair doing anything from playing hockey to putting the shot, and everybody else must think the same thing because Never Despair goes to forty to one.

Personally, I like a horse by the name of Loose Living, which is a horse owned by a guy by the name of Bill Howard, and I hear Bill Howard is betting plenty away on his horse, and any time Bill Howard is betting away on his horse a guy will be out of his mind not to bet on this horse, too, as Bill Howard is very smart indeed. Loose Living is two to one in the first line, but by and by I judge the money Bill Howard bets away commences to come back to the track, and Loose Living winds up seven to ten, and while I am generally not a seven-to-ten guy, I can see that here is a proposition I cannot overlook.

So, naturally, I step up to the mutuel window and invest in Loose Living. In fact, I invest everything I have on me in the way of scratch, amounting to a hundred and ten bucks, which is all I have left after taking myself out of the hotel stakes and giving Hot Horse Herbie the finnif, and listening to what Moe Shapoff has to say about the first race, and also getting beat a snoot in the second.

When I first step up to the window, I have no idea of betting all my scratch on Loose Living, but while waiting in line there I get to thinking what a cinch Loose Living is, and how seldom such an opportunity comes into a guy's life, so I just naturally set it all in.

Well, this is a race which will be remembered by one and all to their dying day, as Loose Living beats the barrier a step, and is two lengths in front before you can say Jack Robinson, with a thing by the name of Callipers second by maybe half a length, and with the others bunched except Never Despair, and where is Never Despair but last, where he figures.

Now any time Loose Living busts on top there is no need worrying any more about him, and I am thinking I better get in line at the pay-off window right away, so I will not have to wait long to collect my sugar. But I figure I may as well stay and watch the race, although personally I am never much interested in watching races. I am interested only in how a race comes out.

As the horses hit the turn into the stretch, Loose Living is just breezing, and anybody can see that he is going to laugh his way home from there. Callipers is still second, and a thing called Goose Pimples is third, and I am surprised to see that Never Despair now struggles up to fourth with Jockey Scroon belting away at him with his bat quite earnestly. Furthermore, Never Despair seems to be running very fast, though afterwards I figure this may be because the others are commencing to run very slow.

Anyway, a very strange spectacle now takes place in the stretch, as all of a sudden Loose Living seems to be stopping, as if he is waiting for a street car, and what is all the more remarkable Callipers and Goose Pimples also seem to be hanging back, and the next thing anybody knows, here comes Jockey Scroon on Never Despair sneaking through on the rail, and personally it looks to me as if the jock on Callipers moves over to give Jockey Scroon plenty of elbow room, but of course the jock on Callipers may figure Jockey Scroon has diphtheria, and does not wish to catch it.

Loose Living is out in the middle of the track, anyway, so he does not have to move over. All Loose Living has to do is to keep on running backwards as he seems to be doing from the top of the stretch, to let Jockey Scroon go past on Never Despair to win the heat by a length.

Well, the race is practically supernatural in many respects, and the judges are all upset over it, and they haul all the jocks up in the stand and ask them many questions, and not being altogether satisfied with the answers, they ask these questions over several times. But all the jocks will say is that Never Despair sneaks past them very unexpectedly indeed, while Jockey Scroon, who is a pretty fresh duck at that, wishes to know if he is supposed to blow a horn when he is slipping through a lot of guys sound asleep.

But the judges are still not satisfied, so they go prowling around investigating the betting, because naturally when a boat race comes up there is apt to be some reason for it, such as the betting, but it seems that all the judges find is that one five-dollar win ticket is sold on Never Despair in the mutuels, and they cannot learn of a dime being bet away on the horse. So there is nothing much the judges can do about the proposition, except give the jocks many hard looks, and the jocks are accustomed to hard looks from the judges, anyway.

Personally, I am greatly upset by this business, especially when I see that Never Despair pays $86.34, and for two cents I will go right up in the stand and start hollering copper on these little Jesse Jameses for putting on such a boat race and taking all my hard-earned potatoes away from me, but before I have time to do this, I run into The Dancer, and he tells me that Dedicate in the next race is the surest thing that ever goes to the post, and at five to one, at that. So I have to forget everything while I bustle about to dig up a few bobs to bet on Dedicate, and when Dedicate is beat a whisker, I have to do some more bustling to dig up a few bobs to bet on Vesta in the fifth, and by this time the third race is such ancient history that nobody cares what happens in it.

It is nearly a week before I see Hot Horse Herbie again, and I figure he is hiding out on everybody because he has this dough he wins off the fiver I give him, and personally I consider him a guy with no manners not to be kicking back the fin, at least. But before I can mention the fin, Herbie gives me a big hello, and says to me like this:

'Well,' he says, 'I just see Jockey Scroon, and Jockey Scroon just comes back from Palm Beach, and the operation is a big success, and Lame Louise will walk as good as anybody again, and old Mercer is tickled silly. But,' Herbie says, 'do not say anything out loud, because the judges may still be trying to find out what comes off in the race.'

'Herbie,' I say, very serious, 'do you mean to say the story you tell me about Lame Louise, and all this and that, the other day is on the level?'

'Why,' Herbie says, 'certainly it is on the level, and I am sorry to hear you do not take advantage of my information. But,' he says, 'I do not blame you for not believing my story, because it is a very long story for anybody to believe. It is not such a story,' Herbie says, 'as I will tell to any one if I expect them to believe it. In fact,' he says, 'it is so long a story that I do not have the heart to tell it to anybody else but you, or maybe I will have something running for me on the race.

'But,' Herbie says, 'never mind all this. I will be plenty smart about a race to-morrow. Yes,' Herbie says, 'I will be wiser than a treeful of owls, so be sure and see me if you happen to have any coconuts.'

'There is no danger of me seeing you,' I say, very sad, because I am all sorrowed up to think that the story he tells me is really true. 'Things are very terrible with me at this time,' I say, 'and I am thinking maybe you can hand me back my finnif, because you must do all right for yourself with the fiver you have on Never Despair at such a price.'

Now a very strange look comes over Hot Horse Herbie's face, and he raises his right hand, and says to me like this:

'I hope and trust I drop down dead right here in front of you,' Herbie says, 'if I bet a quarter on the horse. It is true,' he says, 'I am up at the window to buy a ticket on Never Despair, but the guy who is selling the tickets is a friend of mine by the name of Heeby Rosenbloom, and Heeby whispers to me that Big Joe Gompers, the guy who owns Callipers, just bets half a hundred on his horse, and,' Herbie says, 'I know Joe Gompers is such a guy as will not bet half a hundred on anything he does not get a Federal Reserve guarantee with it.

'Anyway,' Herbie says, 'I get to thinking about what a bad jockey this Jockey Scroon is, which is very bad indeed, and,' he says, 'I figure that even if it is a boat race it is no even-money race they can shoo him in, so I buy a ticket on Callipers.'

'Well,' I say, 'somebody buys one five-dollar ticket on Never Despair, and I figure it can be nobody but you.'

'Why,' Hot Horse Herbie says, 'do you not hear about this? Why,' he says, 'Cap Duhaine, of the Pinkertons, traces this ticket and finds it is bought by a guy by the name of Steve Harter, and the way this guy Harter comes to buy it is very astonishing. It seems,' Herbie says, 'that this Harter is a tourist out of Indiana who comes to Miami for the sunshine, and who loses all his dough but six bucks against the faro bank at Hollywood.

'At the same time,' Herbie says, 'the poor guy gets a telegram

373

from his ever-loving doll back in Indiana saying she no longer wishes any part of him.

'Well,' Herbie says, 'between losing his dough and his doll, the poor guy is practically out of his mind, and he figures there is nothing left for him to do but knock himself off.

'So,' Herbie says, 'this Harter spends one of his six bucks to get to the track, figuring to throw himself under the feet of the horses in the first race and let them kick him to a jelly. But he does not get there until just as the third race is coming up and,' Herbie says, 'he sees this name "Never Despair," and he figures it may be a hunch, so he buys himself a ticket with his last fiver. Well, naturally,' Herbie says, 'when Never Despair pops down, the guy forgets about letting the horses kick him to a jelly, and he keeps sending his dough along until he runs nothing but a nubbin into six *G's* on the day.

'Then,' Herbie says, 'Cap Duhaine finds out that the guy, still thinking of Never Despair, calls his ever-loving doll on the phone, and finds she is very sorry she sends him the wire and that she really loves him more than somewhat, especially,' Herbie says, 'when she finds out about the six *G's*. And the last anybody hears of the matter, this Harter is on his way home to get married, so Never Despair does quite some good in this wicked old world, after all.

'But,' Herbie says, 'let us forget all this, because to-morrow is another day. To-morrow,' he says, 'I will tell you about a thing that goes in the fourth which is just the same as wheat in the bin. In fact,' Hot Horse Herbie says, 'if it does not win, you can never speak to me again.'

'Well,' I say, as I start to walk away, 'I am not interested in any tip at this time.'

'Now,' Herbie says, 'wait a minute. A story goes with it.'

'Well,' I say, coming back to him, 'let me hear the story.'

Had a Horse

JOHN GALSWORTHY

The bookmaker is an essential and integral part of the Turf, whether providing on-course betting or running a high street shop. These next two stories are both about such men and have been selected as being typical of a whole lot more. 'Had a Horse' is certainly a classic of its kind, describing as it does the life of the sort of small-time bookie who once flourished in every town and city of the land. What makes it remarkable is that it should have been written by John Galsworthy (1867–1933) an author more associated with stories about the possessive and entrenched world of the English middle classes during the first quarter of this century. Yet on closer study, his work actually opened up much wider areas of English life in a realistic and humanitarian way that had not been done before. Notwithstanding this, Galsworthy is probably destined to be remembered as the author of that great sequence of novels collectively known as *The Forsyte Saga* (1906–29), which were expensively and very popularly filmed by the BBC in 1967 starring Eric Porter, Kenneth More and Nyree Dawn Porter.

Born into a well-off Devonshire family and educated at Harrow and Oxford, Galsworthy was evidently interested in horse racing all his life; indeed the subject is featured in several of his books, not least *The Forsyte Saga* (1921), which contains a graphic description of the nobbling of a two-year-old favourite at Ascot. The theme also surfaced from time to time in his short stories, a genre that he practised all through his career and in which he demonstrated his maxim that such fictions 'require a sting in the tale'. (The late Roald Dahl admitted to admiring this trait in Galsworthy's work and used the concept in his own series, *Tales of the Unexpected*, which were also successfully adapted for television.) 'Had a Horse' is, for my money, the best of Galesworthy's tales with a racing background, and the collection in which it first appeared, *Captures* (1932), caused him to be hailed by the *Times Literary Supplement* as, 'Our best living and producing writer'. E. V. Lucas, the essayist and biographer who was associated with *Punch* for many years, also had a great admiration for this account of a bookie who takes a horse in payment for some unpaid bets and then decides to use the animal in a fraudulent betting scheme. Indeed, the tale so impressed Lucas that he wrote a letter to Galsworthy which serves as the perfect introduction to what follows: ' "Had a Horse" is splendid – but what a murky curtain that is of which you lift a corner! I shall never bet again except on the "Classics" . . .'

*

I

Some quarter of a century ago, there abode in Oxford a small bookmaker called James Shrewin – or more usually 'Jimmy' – a run-about and damped-down little man, who made a precarious living out of the effect of horses on undergraduates. He had a so-called office just off the 'Corn,' where he was always open to the patronage of the young bloods of Bullingdon, and other horse-loving coteries, who bestowed on him sufficient money to enable him to live. It was through the conspicuous smash of one of them – young Gardon Colquhoun – that he became the owner of a horse. He had been far from wanting what was in the nature of a white elephant to one of his underground habits, but had taken it in discharge of betting debts, to which, of course, in the event of bankruptcy, he would have no legal claim. She was a three-year-old chestnut filly, by Lopez out of Calendar, bore the name of Calliŏpe, and was trained out on the Downs near Wantage. On a Sunday afternoon, then, in late July, 'Jimmy' got his friend, George Pulcher, the publican, to drive him out there in his sort of dog-cart.

'Must 'ave a look at the bilkin' mare,' he had said; 'that young "Cocoon" told me she was a corker; but what's third to Referee at Sandown, and never ran as a two-year-old? All I know is, she's eatin' 'er 'ead off!'

Beside the plethoric bulk of Pulcher, clad in a light-coloured box-cloth coat with enormous whitish buttons and a full-blown rose in the lapel, 'Jimmy's' little, thin, dark-clothed form, withered by anxiety and gin, was, as it were, invisible; and compared with Pulcher's setting sun, his face, with shaven cheeks sucked in, and smudged-in eyes, was like a ghost's under a grey bowler. He spoke off-handedly about his animal, but he was impressed, in a sense abashed, by his ownership. 'What the 'ell?' was his constant thought. Was he going to race her, sell her – what? How, indeed, to get back out of her the sum he had been fool enough to let young 'Cocoon' owe him, to say nothing of her trainer's bill? The notion, too, of having to confront that trainer with his ownership was oppressive to one whose whole life was passed in keeping out of the foreground of the picture. Owner! He had never owned even a white mouse, let alone a white elephant. And an 'orse would ruin him in no time if he didn't look alive about it!

The son of a small London baker, devoted to errandry at the age of fourteen, 'Jimmy' Shrewin owed his profession to a certain smartness at sums, a dislike of baking, and an early habit of hanging about street corners with other boys, who had their daily pennies on an 'orse. He had a narrow, calculating head, which pushed him towards street corner books before he was eighteen. From that time on he had been a surreptitious nomad, till he had silted up at Oxford, where, owing to Vice-Chancellors, an expert in underground life had greater scope than elsewhere. When he sat solitary at his narrow table in the back room near the 'Corn' – for he had no clerk or associate – eyeing the door, with his lists in a drawer before him, and his black shiny betting-book ready for young 'bloods,' he had a sharp, cold, furtive air, and but for a certain imitated tightness of trouser, and a collar standing up all round, gave no impression of ever having heard of the quadruped called horse. Indeed, for 'Jimmy' 'horse' was a newspaper quantity with figures against its various names. Even when, for a short spell, hanger-on to a firm of Cheap Ring bookmakers, he had seen almost nothing of horse; his racecourse hours were spent ferreting among a bawling, perspiring crowd, or hanging round within earshot of tight-lipped nobs, trainers, jockeys, anyone who looked like having 'information'. Nowadays he never went near a race-meeting – his business, of betting on races, giving him no chance – yet his conversation seldom deviated for more than a minute at a time from that physically unknown animal, the horse. The ways of making money out of it, infinite, intricate, variegated, occupied the mind in all his haunts, to the accompaniment of liquid and tobacco. Gin and bitters was 'Jimmy's' drink; for choice he smoked cheroots; and he would cherish in his mouth the cold stump of one long after it had gone out, for the homely feeling it gave him, while he talked, or listened to talk on horses. He was of that vast number, town bred, who, like crows round a carcase, feed on that which to them is not alive. And now he had a horse!

The dog-cart travelled at a clinking pace behind Pulcher's bobtail. 'Jimmy's' cheroot burned well in the warm July air; the dust powdered his dark clothes and pinched, sallow face. He thought with malicious pleasure of that young spark 'Cocoon's' collapse – 'igh-'anded lot of young fools, thinking themselves so knowing; many were the grins, and not few the grittings of his blackened teeth he had to smother at their swagger. 'Jimmy, you robber!' 'Jimmy, you little blackguard!' Young sparks – gay and languid – well, one of 'em had gone out!

He looked round with his screwed-up eyes at his friend George Pulcher, who, man and licensed victualler, had his bally independence; lived remote from 'the Quality' in his paradise, the Green Dragon; had not to kowtow to anyone; went to Newbury, Gatwick, Stockbridge, here and there, at will. Ah! George Pulcher had the ideal life – and looked it: crimson, square, full-bodied. Judge of a horse, too, in his own estimation; a leery bird – for whose judgment 'Jimmy' had respect – who got 'the office' of any clever work as quick as most men! And he said:

'What am I going to do with this blinkin' 'orse, George?'

Without moving its head the oracle spoke in a voice rich and raw: 'Let's 'ave a look at her first, Jimmy! Don't like her name – Calliope; but you can't change what's in the Stud-book. This Jenning that trains 'er is a crusty chap.'

'Jimmy' nervously sucked-in his lips. The cart was mounting through the hedgeless fields which fringed the Downs; larks were singing, the wheat was very green, the patches of charlock brightened everything; it was lonely, few trees, few houses, no people, extreme peace, just a few rooks crossing under a blue sky.

'Wonder if he'll offer us a drink?' said 'Jimmy.'

'Not he; but help yourself, my son.'

'Jimmy' helped himself from a large wicker-covered flask.

'Good for you, George – here's how!'

The large man shifted the reins and drank, in turn, tilting up a face whose jaw still struggled to assert itself against chins and neck.

'Well, here's to your bloomin' horse,' he said. 'She can't win the Derby now, but she may do us a bit of good yet.'

II

The trainer, Jenning, coming from his Sunday afternoon round of the boxes, heard the sound of wheels. He was a thin man, neat in clothes and boots, medium in height, with a slight limp, narrow grey whiskers, thin shaven lips, eyes sharp and grey.

A dog-cart stopping at his yard-gate; and a rum-looking couple of customers!

'Well, gentlemen?'

'Mr Jenning? My name's Pulcher – George Pulcher. Brought a client of yours over to see his new mare. Mr James Shrewin, Oxford city.'

'Jimmy' got down and stood before his trainer's uncompromising stare.

'What mare's that?' said Jenning.

'Callïōpe.'

'Callïōpe – Mr Colquhoun's?'

'Jimmy' held out a letter.

'Dear Jenning,

'I have sold Callïōpe to Jimmy Shrewin, the Oxford bookie. He takes her with all engagements and liabilities, including your training bill. I'm frightfully sick at having to part with her, but needs must when the devil drives.

'Gardon Colquhoun.'

The trainer folded the letter.

'Got proof of registration?'

'Jimmy' drew out another paper.

The trainer inspected it, and called out: 'Ben, bring out Callīōpe. Excuse me a minute,' and he walked into his house.

'Jimmy' stood, shifting from leg to leg. Mortification had set in; the dry abruptness of the trainer had injured even a self-esteem starved from youth.

The voice of Pulcher boomed. 'Told you he was a crusty devil. 'And 'im a bit of his own.'

The trainer was coming back.

'My bill,' he said. 'When you've paid it you can have the mare. I train for gentlemen.'

'The hell you do!' said Pulcher.

'Jimmy' said nothing, staring at the bill. Seventy-eight pounds three shillings! A buzzing fly settled in the hollow of his cheek, and he did not even brush it off. Seventy-eight pound!

The sound of hoofs roused him. Here came his horse, throwing up her head as if enquiring why she was being disturbed a second time on Sunday! In the movement of that small head and satin neck was something free and beyond present company.

'There she is,' said the trainer. 'That'll do, Ben. Stand, girl!'

Answering to a jerk or two of the halter, the mare stood kicking slightly with a white hind foot and whisking her tail. Her bright coat shone in the sunlight, and little shivers and wrinklings passed up and down its satin because of the flies. Then, for a moment, she stood still, ears pricked, eyes on the distance.

'Jimmy' approached her. She had resumed her twitchings, swishings, and slight kicking, and at a respectful distance he circled, bending as if looking at crucial points. He knew what her sire and dam had done, and all the horses that had beaten or been beaten by them; could have retailed by the half-hour the peculiar hearsay of their careers; and here was their offspring in flesh and blood, and he was dumb! He didn't know a thing about what she ought to look like, and he knew it; but he felt obscurely moved. She seemed to him 'a picture'.

Completing his circle, he approached her head, white-blazed, thrown up again in listening, or scenting, and gingerly he laid his hand on her neck, warm and smooth as a woman's shoulder. She paid no attention to his touch, and he took his hand away. Ought he to look at her teeth or feel her legs? No, he was not buying her, she was his already; but he must say something. He looked round. The trainer was watching him with a little smile. For almost the first time in his life the worm turned in 'Jimmy' Shrewin; he spoke no word and walked back to the cart.

'Take her in,' said Jenning.

From his seat beside Pulcher, 'Jimmy' watched the mare returning to her box.

'When I've cashed your cheque,' said the trainer, 'you can send for her;' and, turning on his heel, he went towards his house. The voice of Pulcher followed him.

'Blast your impudence! Git on, bobtail, we'll shake the dust off 'ere.'

Among the fringing fields the dog-cart hurried away. The sun slanted, the heat grew less, the colour of young wheat and of the charlock brightened.

'The tyke! By Gawd, Jimmy, I'd 'ave hit him on the mug! But you've got one there. She's a bit o' blood, my boy; and I know the trainer for her, Polman – no blasted airs about 'im.'

'Jimmy' sucked at his cheroot.

'I ain't had your advantages, George, and that's a fact. I got into it too young, and I'm a little chap. But I'll send the —— my cheque tomorrow. I got my pride, I 'ope.' It was the first time that thought had ever come to him.

III

Though not quite the centre of the Turf, the Green Dragon had nursed a coup in its day, nor was it without a sense of veneration. The ownership of Calliope invested 'Jimmy' Shrewin with the importance of those out of whom something can be had. It took time for one so long accustomed to beck and call, to mole-like procedure, and the demeanour of young bloods, to realise that he had it. But slowly, with the marked increase of his unpaid-for cheroots, with the way in which glasses hung suspended when he came in, with the edgings up to him, and a certain tendency to accompany him along the street, it dawned on him that he was not only an out-of-bounds bookie, but a man. So long as he had remained unconscious of his double nature he had been content with laying the odds, as best he might, and getting what he could out of every situation, straight or crooked. Now that he was also a man, his complacency was ruffled. He suffered from a growing headiness connected with his horse. She was trained, now, by Polman, further along the Downs, too far for Pulcher's bobtail; and though her public life was carried on at the Green Dragon, her private life required a train journey over night. 'Jimmy' took it twice a week – touting his own horse in the August mornings up on the Downs, without drink or talk, or even cheroots. Early morning, larks singing, and the sound of galloping hoofs! In a moment of expansion he confided to Pulcher that it was 'bally 'olesome.'

There had been the slight difficulty of being mistaken for a tout by his new trainer, Polman, a stoutish man with the look of one of those large sandy Cornish cats, not precisely furtive because reticence and craft are their nature. But, that once over, his personality swelled slowly. This month of August was one of those interludes, in fact, when nothing happens, but which shape the future by secret ripening.

An error to suppose that men conduct finance, high or low, from greed, or love of gambling; they do it out of self-esteem, out of an itch to prove their judgment superior to their neighbours', out of a longing for importance. George Pulcher did not despise the turning of a penny, but he valued much more the conscious-ness that men were saying: 'Old George, what 'e says goes – knows a thing or two – George Pulcher!'

To pull the strings of 'Jimmy' Shrewin's horse was a rich and subtle opportunity absorbingly improvable. But first one had to study the animal's engagements, and, secondly, to gauge that unknown quantity, her 'form.' To make anything of her this year they must 'get about it.' That young 'toff,' her previous owner, had, of course, flown high, entering her for classic races, high-class handicaps, neglecting the rich chances of lesser occasions.

Third to Referee in the three-year-old race at Sandown Spring – two heads – was all that was known of her, and now they had given her seven two in the Cambridgeshire. She might have a chance, and again she might not. He sat two long evenings with 'Jimmy' in the little private room off the bar, deliberating this grave question.

'Jimmy' inclined to the bold course. He kept saying: 'The mare's a flyer, George – she's the 'ell of a flyer!'

'Wait till she's been tried,' said the oracle.

Had Polman anything that would give them a line?

Yes, he had The Shirker (named with that irony which appeals to the English), one of the most honest four-year-olds that ever looked through bridle, who had run up against almost every animal of mark – the one horse that Polman never interfered with, or interrupted in his training lest he should run all the better; who seldom won, but was almost always placed – the sort of horse that handicappers pivot on.

'But,' said Pulcher, 'try her with The Shirker, and the first stable money will send her up to tens. That 'orse is so darned regular. We've got to throw a bit of dust first, "Jimmy." I'll go over and see Polman.'

In 'Jimmy's' withered chest a faint resentment rose – it wasn't George's horse; but it sank again beneath his friend's bulk and reputation.

The 'bit of dust' was thrown at the ordinary hour of exercise over the Long Mile on the last day of August – the five-year-old Hangman carrying eight stone seven, the three-year-old Parrot seven stone five; what Callïope was carrying nobody but Polman knew. The forethought of George Pulcher had secured the unofficial presence of the Press. The instructions to the boy on Callïope were to be there at the finish if he could, but on no account to win. 'Jimmy' and George Pulcher had come out over night. They sat together in the dog-cart by the clump of bushes which marked the winning-post, with Polman on his cob on the far side.

By a fine, warm light the three horses were visible to the naked eye in the slight dip down by the start. And, through the glasses, invested in now that he had a horse, 'Jimmy' could see every movement of his mare with her blazed face – rather on her toes, like the bright chestnut and 'bit o' blood' she was. He had a pit-patting in his heart, and his lips were tight-pressed. Suppose she was no good after all, and that young 'Cocoon' had palmed him off a pup! But mixed in with his financial fear was an anxiety more intimate, as if his own value were at stake.

From George Pulcher came an almost excited gurgle.

'See the tout! See 'im behind that bush. Thinks we don't know 'e's there, wot oh!'

'Jimmy' bit into his cheroot. 'They're running,' he said.

Rather wide, the black Hangman on the far side, Calliōpe in the middle, they came sweeping up the Long Mile. 'Jimmy' held his tobaccoed breath. The mare was going freely – a length or two behind – making up her ground! Now for it!

Ah! she 'ad The 'Angman beat, and ding-dong with this Parrot! It was all he could do to keep from calling out. With a rush and a cludding of hoofs they passed – the blazed nose just behind The Parrot's bay nose – dead heat all but, with The Hangman beaten a good length!

'There 'e goes, Jimmy! See the blank scuttlin' down the 'ill like a blinkin' rabbit. That'll be in to-morrow's paper, that trial will. Ah! but 'ow to read it – that's the point.'

The horses had been wheeled and were sidling back; Polman was going forward on his cob.

'Jimmy' jumped down. Whatever that fellow had to say, he meant to hear. It was his horse! Narrowly avoiding the hoofs of his hot, fidgeting mare, he said sharply:

'What about it?'

Polman never looked you in the face; his speech came as if not intended to be heard by anyone:

'Tell Mr Shrewin how she went.'

'Had a bit up my sleeve. If I'd hit her a smart one, I could ha' landed by a length or more.'

'That so?' said 'Jimmy' with a hiss. 'Well, *don't* you hit her; she don't want hittin'. You remember that.'

The boy said sulkily: 'All right!'

'Take her home,' said Polman. Then, with that reflective averted air of his, he added: 'She was carrying eight stone, Mr Shrewin; you've got a good one there. She's The Hangman at level weights.'

Something wild leaped up in 'Jimmy' – The Hangman's form unrolled itself before him in the air – he had a horse – he dam' well had a horse!

IV

But how delicate is the process of backing your fancy! The planting of a commission – what tender and efficient work before it will flower! That sixth sense of the racing man, which, like the senses of savages in great forests, seizes telepathically on what is not there, must be dulled, duped, deluded.

George Pulcher had the thing in hand. One might have thought the gross man incapable of such a fairy touch, such power of sowing with one hand and reaping with the other. He intimated rather than asserted that Callǐ͞ope and The Parrot were one and the same thing. 'The Parrot,' he said, 'couldn't win with seven stone – no use thinkin' of this Callǐ͞ope.'

Local opinion was the rock on which, like a great tactician, he built. So long as local opinion was adverse, he could dribble money on in London; the natural jump-up from every long shot taken was dragged back by the careful radiation of disparagement from the seat of knowledge.

'Jimmy' was the fly in his ointment of those balmy early weeks while snapping up every penny of long odds, before suspicion could begin to work from the persistence of enquiry. Half-a-dozen times he found the 'little cuss within an ace of blowing the gaff on his own blinkin' mare'; seemed unable to run his horse down; the little beggar's head was swellin'! Once 'Jimmy' had even got up and gone out, leaving a gin and bitters untasted on the bar. Pulcher improved on his absence in the presence of a London tout.

'Saw the trial meself! Jimmy don't like to think he's got a stiff 'un.'

And next morning his London agent snapped up some thirty-threes again.

According to the trial the mare was The Hangman at seven stone two, and really hot stuff – a seven to one chance. It was none the less with a sense of outrage that, opening the *Sporting Life* on the last day of September, he found her quoted at 100–8. Whose work was this ?

He reviewed the altered situation in disgust. He had invested about half the stable commission of three hundred pounds at an average of thirty to one, but, now that she had 'come' in the betting, he would hardly average tens with the rest. What fool had put his oar in?

He learned the explanation two days later. The rash, the unknown backer, was 'Jimmy'! He had acted, it appeared, from jealousy; a bookmaker – it took one's breath away!

'Backed her on your own just because that young 'Cocoon' told you he fancied her!'

'Jimmy' looked up from the table in his 'office,' where he was sitting in wait for the scanty custom of the Long Vacation.

'She's not his horse,' he said sullenly. 'I wasn't going to have *him* get the cream.'

'What did you put on?' growled Pulcher.

'Took five hundred to thirty and fifteen twenties.'

'An' see what it's done – knocked the bottom out of the commission. Am I to take that fifty as part of it?'

'Jimmy' nodded.

'That leaves an 'undred to invest,' said Pulcher, somewhat mollified. He stood, with his mind twisting in his thick, still body. 'It's no good waitin' now,' he said; 'I'll work the rest of the money on to-day. If I can average tens on the balance, we'll 'ave six thousand three hundred to play with and the stakes. They tell me Jenning fancies this Diamond Stud of his. He ought to know the form with Calliŏpe, blast him! We got to watch that.'

They had! Diamond Stud, a four-year-old with eight stone two, was being backed as if the Cambridgeshire were over. From fifteens he advanced to sevens, thence to favouritism at fives. Pulcher bit on it. Jenning *must* know where he stood with Calliŏpe! It meant – it meant she couldn't win! The tactician wasted no time in vain regret. Establish Calliŏpe in the betting and lay off! The time had come to utilise The Shirker.

It was misty on the Downs – fine weather mist of a bright October. The three horses became spectral on their way to the starting-point. Polman had thrown The Parrot in again, but this time he made no secret of the weights. The Shirker was carrying eight seven, Calliope eight, The Parrot seven stone.

Once more, in the cart, with his glasses sweeping the bright mist, 'Jimmy' had that pit-patting in his heart. Here they came! His mare leading – all riding hard – a genuine finish! They passed – The Shirker beaten a clear length, with the Parrot at his girth. Beside him in the cart, George Pulcher mumbled:

'She's The Shirker at eight stone four, Jimmy!'

A silent drive back to the river inn, big with thought; a silent breakfast. Over a tankard at the close the oracle spoke.

'The Shirker, at eight stone four, is a good 'ot chance, but no cert, Jimmy. We'll let 'em know this trial quite open, weights and all. That'll bring her in the betting. And we'll watch Diamond Stud. If he drops back we'll know Jenning thinks he can't beat us now. If Diamond Stud stands up we'll know Jenning thinks he's still got our mare safe. Then our line'll be clear: we lay off the lot, pick up a thousand or so, and 'ave the mare in at a nice weight at Liverpool.'

'Jimmy's' smudged-in eyes stared hungrily.

'How's that?' he said. 'Suppose she wins?'

'Wins! If we lay off the lot, she *won't* win.'

'Pull her!'

George Pulcher's voice sank half an octave with disgust.

'Pull her! Who talked of pullin'? She'll run a bye, that's all. We shan't ever know whether she could 'a won or not.'

'Jimmy' sat silent; the situation was such as his life during sixteen years had waited for. They stood to win both ways with a bit of handling.

'Who's to ride?' he said.

'Polman's got a call on Docker. He can just ride the weight. Either way he's good for us – strong finisher and a rare judge of distance; knows how to time things to a T. Win or not, he's our man.'

'Jimmy' was deep in figures. Laying-off at sevens, they would still win four thousand and the stakes.

'I'd like a win,' he said.

'Ah!' said Pulcher. 'But there'll be twenty in the field, my son; no more uncertain race than that bally Cambridgeshire. We could pick up a thou. as easy as I pick up this pot. Bird in the 'and, Jimmy, and a good 'andicap in the bush. If she wins, she's finished. Well, we'll put this trial about and see 'ow Jenning pops.'

Jenning popped amazingly. Diamond Stud receded a point, then re-established himself at nine to two. Jenning was clearly not dismayed.

George Pulcher shook his head and waited, uncertain still which way to jump. Ironical circumstance decided him.

Term had begun; 'Jimmy' was busy at his seat of custom. By some miracle of guardianly intervention, young Colquhoun had not gone broke. He was 'up' again, eager to retrieve his reputation, and that little brute 'Jimmy' would not lay against his horse! He merely sucked-in his cheeks, and answered: 'I'm not layin' my own 'orse.' It was felt that he was not the man he had been; assertion had come into his manner, he was better dressed. Someone had seen him at the station looking quite a 'toff' in a blue box-cloth coat standing well out from his wisp of a figure, and with a pair of brown race-glasses slung over the shoulder. Altogether the 'little brute was getting too big for his boots.'

And this strange improvement hardened the feeling that his horse was a real good thing. Patriotism began to burn in Oxford. Here was a 'snip' that belonged to them, as it were, and the money in support of it, finding no outlet, began to ball.

A week before the race – with Calliŏpe at nine to one, and very little doing – young Colquhoun went up to town, taking with him the accumulated support of betting Oxford. That evening she stood at sixes. Next day the public followed on.

George Pulcher took advantage. In this crisis of the proceedings he acted on his own initiative. The mare went back to eights, but the deed was done. He had laid off the whole bally lot, including the stake money. He put it to 'Jimmy' that evening in a nutshell.

'We pick up a thousand, and the Liverpool as good as in our pocket. I've done worse.'

'Jimmy' grunted out: 'She could 'a won.'

'Not she. Jenning knows – and there's others in the race. This Wasp is goin' to take a lot of catchin', and Deerstalker's not out of it. He's a hell of a horse, even with that weight.'

Again 'Jimmy' grunted, slowly sucking down his gin and bitters. Sullenly he said:

'Well, I don' want to put money in the pocket of young 'Cocoon' and his crowd. Like his impudence, backin' my horse as if it was his own.'

'We'll 'ave to go and see her run, Jimmy.'

'Not me,' said 'Jimmy.'

'What! First time she runs! It won't look natural.'

'No,' repeated 'Jimmy.' 'I don't want to see 'er beat.'

George Pulcher laid his hand on a skinny shoulder.

'Nonsense, Jimmy. You've got to, for the sake of your reputation. You'll enjoy seein' your mare saddled. We'll go up over night. I shall 'ave a few pound on Deerstalker. I believe he can beat this Diamond Stud. And you leave Docker to me; I'll 'ave a word with him at Gatwick tomorrow. I've known 'im since he was that 'igh; an' 'e ain't much more now.'

'All right!' growled 'Jimmy.'

V

The longer you can bet on a race the greater its fascination. Handicappers can properly enjoy the beauty of their work; clubmen and oracles of the course have due scope for reminiscence and prophecy; bookmakers in lovely leisure can indulge a little their own calculated preferences, instead of being hurried to soulless conclusions by a half-hour's market on the course; the professional backer has the longer in which to dream of his fortune made at last by some hell of a horse – spotted somewhere as interfered with, left at the post, running green, too fat, not fancied, backward – now bound to win this hell of a race. And the general public has the chance to read the horses' names in the betting news for days and days; and what a comfort that is!

'Jimmy' Shrewin was not one of those philosophers who justify the great and growing game of betting on the ground that it improves the breed of an animal less and less in use. He justified it much more simply – he lived by it. And in the whole of his career of nearly twenty years since he made hole-and-corner books among the boys of London, he had never stood so utterly on velvet as that morning when his horse must win him five hundred pounds by merely losing. He had spent the night in London anticipating a fraction of his gains with George Pulcher at a music-hall. And, in a first-class carriage, as became an owner, he travelled down to Newmarket by an early special. An early special key turned in the lock of the carriage door, preserved their numbers at six, all professionals, with blank, rather rolling eyes, mouths shut or slightly fishy, ears to the ground; and the only natural talker a red-faced man, who had 'been at it thirty years.' Intoning the pasts and futures of this hell of a horse or that, even he was silent on the race in hand; and the journey was half over before the beauty of their own judgments loosened tongues thereon. George Pulcher started it.

'I fancy Deerstalker,' he said; 'he's a hell of a horse.'

'Too much weight,' said the red-faced man. 'What about this Callïŏpe?'

'Ah!' said Pulcher. 'D'you fancy your mare, Jimmy?'

With all eyes turned on him, lost in his blue box-cloth coat, brown bowler, and cheroot smoke, 'Jimmy' experienced a subtle thrill. Addressing the space between the red-faced man and Pulcher, he said:

'If she runs up to 'er looks.'

'Ah!' said Pulcher, 'she's dark-nice mare, but a bit light and shelly.'

'Lopez out o' Calendar,' muttered the red-faced man. 'Lopez didn't stay, but he was the hell of a horse over seven furlongs, The Shirker ought to 'ave told you a bit.'

'Jimmy' did not answer. It gave him pleasure to see the red-faced man's eye trying to get past, and failing.

'Nice race to pick up. Don't fancy the favourite meself; he'd nothin' to beat at Ascot.'

'Jenning knows what he's about,' said Pulcher.

Jenning! Before 'Jimmy's' mind passed again that first sight of his horse, and the trainer's smile, as if he – 'Jimmy' Shrewin, who owned her – had been dirt. Tyke! To have the mare beaten by one of his! A deep, subtle vexation had oppressed him at times all these last days since George Pulcher had decided in favour of the mare's running a bye. D—n George Pulcher! He took too much on himself! Thought he had 'Jimmy' Shrewin in his pocket! He looked at the block of crimson opposite. Aunt Sally! If George Pulcher could tell what was passing in his mind!

But driving up to the course he was not above sharing a sandwich and a flask. In fact, his feelings were unstable and gusty – sometimes resentment, sometimes the old respect for his friend's independent bulk. The dignity of ownership takes long to establish itself in those who have been kicked about.

'All right with Docker,' murmured Pulcher, sucking at the wicker flask. 'I gave him the office at Gatwick.'

'She could 'a won,' muttered 'Jimmy.'

'Not she, my boy; there's two at least can beat 'er'

Like all oracles, George Pulcher could believe what he wanted to.

Arriving, they entered the grand-stand enclosure, and over the dividing railings 'Jimmy' gazed at the Cheap Ring, already filling-up with its usual customers. Faces, and umbrellas – the same old crowd. How often had he been in that Cheap Ring, with hardly room to move, seeing nothing, hearing nothing but 'Two to one on the field!' 'Two to one on the field!' 'Threes Swordfish!' 'Fives Alabaster!' 'Two to one on the field!' Nothing but a sea of men like himself, and a sky overhead. He was not exactly conscious of criticism, only of a dull 'Glad I'm shut of that lot' feeling.

Leaving George Pulcher deep in conversation with a crony, he lighted a cheroot, and slipped out on to the course. He passed the Jockey Club enclosure. Some early 'toffs' were there in twos and threes, exchanging wisdom. He looked at them without envy or malice. He was an owner himself now, almost one of them in a manner of thinking. With a sort of relish he thought of how his past life had circled round those 'toffs,' slippery, shadowlike, kicked about; and now he could get up on the Downs away from 'toffs,' George Pulcher, all that crowd, and smell the grass, and hear the bally larks, and watch his own mare gallop!

They were putting the numbers up for the first race. Queer not to be betting, not to be touting round; queer to be giving it a rest! Utterly familiar with those names on the board, he was utterly unfamiliar with the shapes they stood for.

'I'll go and see 'em come out of the paddock,' he thought, and moved on, skimpy in his bell-shaped coat and billycock with flattened brim. The clamour of the Rings rose behind him while he was entering the paddock.

Very green, very peaceful, there; not many people, yet! Three horses in the second race were being led slowly in a sort of winding ring; and men were clustering round the further gate where the horses would come out. 'Jimmy' joined them, sucking at his cheroot. They were a picture! Damn it! he didn't know but that 'orses laid over men! Pretty creatures!

One by one they passed out of the gate, a round dozen. Selling platers, but pictures for all that!

He turned back towards the horses being led about; and the old instinct to listen took him close to little groups. Talk was all of the big race. From a tall 'toff' he caught the word Calliope.

'Belongs to a bookie, they say.'

Bookie! Why not? Wasn't a bookie as good as any other? Ah! and sometimes better than these young snobs with everything to their hand! A bookie – well, what chance had he ever had?

A big brown horse came by.

'That's Deerstalker,' he heard the 'toff' say.

'Jimmy' gazed at George Pulcher's fancy with a sort of hostility. Here came another – Wasp, six stone ten, and Deerstalker nine stone – top and bottom of the race!

'My 'orse'd beat either o' them,' he thought stubbornly. 'Don't like that Wasp.'

The distant roar was hushed. They were running in the first race! He moved back to the gate. The quick clamour rose and dropped, and here they came – back into the paddock, darkened with sweat, flanks heaving a little!

'Jimmy' followed the winner, saw the jockey weigh in.

'What jockey's that?' he asked.

'That? Why, Docker!'

'Jimmy' stared. A short, square, bow-legged figure, with a hardwood face! Waiting his chance, he went up to him and said:

'Docker, you ride my 'orse in the big race.'

'Mr Shrewin?'

'The same,' said 'Jimmy.' The jockey's left eyelid drooped a little. Nothing responded in 'Jimmy's' face. 'I'll see you before the race,' he said.

Again the jockey's eyelid wavered, he nodded and passed on.

'Jimmy' stared at his own boots – they struck him suddenly as too yellow and not at the right angle. But why, he couldn't say.

More horses now – those of the first race being unsaddled, clothed, and led away. More men – three familiar figures: young 'Cocoon' and two others of his Oxford customers.

'Jimmy' turned sharply from them. Stand their airs? – not he! He had a sudden sickish feeling. With a win, he'd have been a made man – on his own! Blast George Pulcher and his caution! To think of being back in Oxford with those young bloods jeering at his beaten horse! He bit deep into the stump of his cheroot, and suddenly came on Jenning standing by a horse with a star on its bay forehead. The trainer gave him no sign of recognition, but signed to the boy to lead the horse into a stall, and followed, shutting the door. It was exactly as if he had said: 'Vermin about!'

An evil little smile curled 'Jimmy's' lips. The tyke!

The horses for the second race passed out of the paddock gate, and he turned to find his own. His ferreting eyes soon sighted Polman. What the cat-faced fellow knew, or was thinking, 'Jimmy' could not tell. Nobody could tell.

'Where's the mare?' he said.

'Just coming round.'

No mistaking her; fine as a star; shiny-coated, sinuous, her blazed face held rather high! Who said she was 'shelly'? She was a picture! He walked a few paces close to the boy.

'That's Callíŏpe. . . . H'm! . . . Nice filly! . . . Looks fit. . . . Who's this James Shrewin? . . . What's she at? . . . I like her looks.' His horse! Not a prettier filly in the world! He followed Polman into her stall to see her saddled. In the twilight there he watched her toilet; the rub-over; the exact adjustments; the bottle of water to the mouth; the buckling of the bridle – watched her head high above the boy keeping her steady with gentle pulls of a rein in each hand held out a little wide, and now and then stroking her blazed nose; watched her pretence of nipping at his hand: he watched the beauty of her exaggerated in this half-lit isolation away from the others, the life and litheness in her satin body, the wilful expectancy in her bright soft eyes.

Run a bye! This bit o' blood – this bit o' fire! This horse of his! Deep within that shell of blue box-cloth against the stall partition a thought declared itself: 'I'm —— if she shall! She can beat the lot! And she's —— well going to!'

The door was thrown open, and she led out. He moved alongside. They were staring at her, following her. No wonder! She was a picture, his horse – his! She had gone to 'Jimmy's' head.

They passed Jenning with Diamond Stud waiting to be mounted. 'Jimmy' shot him a look. Let the —— wait!

His mare reached the palings and was halted. 'Jimmy' saw the short square figure of her jockey, in the new magenta cap and jacket – *his* cap, *his* jacket! Beautiful they looked, and no mistake!

'A word with you,' he said.

The jockey halted, looked quickly round.

'All right, Mr Shrewin. No need.'

'Jimmy's' eyes smouldered at him; hardly moving his lips, he said, intently: 'You —— well don't! You'll —— well ride her to win. Never mind *him*! If you don't I'll have you off the Turf. Understand me! You'll —— well ride 'er to win.'

The jockey's jaw dropped.

'All right, Mr Shrewin.'

'See it is,' said 'Jimmy' with a hiss. . . .

'Mount jockeys!'

He saw magenta swing into the saddle. And suddenly, as if smitten with the plague, he scuttled away.

VI

He scuttled to where he could see them going down – seventeen. No need to search for his colours; they blazed, like George Pulcher's countenance, or a rhododendron bush in sunlight, above that bright chestnut with the white nose, curvetting a little as she was led past.

Now they came cantering – Deerstalker in the lead. 'He's a hell of a horse, Deerstalker!' said someone behind.

'Jimmy' cast a nervous glance around. No sign of George Pulcher!

One by one they cantered past, and he watched them with a cold feeling in his stomach. Still unused to sight of the creatures out of which he made his living, they *all* seemed to him hells of horses!

The same voice said:

'New colours! Well, you can see 'em, and the mare too. She's a showy one. Callǐōpe? She's goin' back in the bettin', though.'

'Jimmy' moved up through the Ring.

'Four to one on the field!' 'Six Deerstalker!' 'Sevens Magistrate!' 'Ten to one Wasp!' 'Ten to one Callǐōpe!' 'Four to one Diamond Stud – Four to one on the field!'

Steady as a rock, that horse of Jenning, and his own going back!

'Twelves Callǐōpe!' he heard, just as he reached the stand. The telepathic genius of the Ring missed nothing – almost!

A cold shiver went through him. What had he done by his words to Docker? Spoiled the golden egg laid so carefully? But perhaps she couldn't win even if they let her! He began to mount the stand, his mind in the most acute confusion.

A voice said: 'Hullo, Jimmy! Is she going to win?'

One of his young Oxford sparks was jammed against him on the stairway!

He raised his lip in a sort of snarl, and, huddling himself, slipped through and up ahead. He came out and edged in close to the stairs where he could get play for his glasses. Behind him one of those who improve the shining hour among backers cut off from opportunity was intoning the odds a point shorter than below. 'Three to one on the field!' 'Fives Deerstalker!' 'Eight to one Wasp!'

'What price Callǐōpe?' said 'Jimmy' sharply.

'Hundred to eight.'

'Done!' Handing him the eight, he took the ticket. Behind him the man's eyes moved fishily, and he resumed his incantation.

'Three to one on the field! . . . Three to one on the field! Six to one Magistrate!'

On the wheeling bunch of colours at the start 'Jimmy' trained his glasses. Something had broken clean away and come half the course – something in yellow.

'Eights Magistrate. Nine to one Magistrate,' drifted up.

So they had spotted that! Precious little they didn't spot!

Magistrate was round again, and being ridden back. 'Jimmy' rested his glasses a moment, and looked down. Swarms in the Cheap Ring, Tattersalls, the stands – a crowd so great you could lose George Pulcher in it. Just below a little man was making silent, frantic signals with his arms to someone across in the Cheap Ring. 'Jimmy' raised his glasses. In line now – magenta third from the rails!

'They're off!' The hush, you could cut it with a knife! Something in green away on the right – Wasp! What a bat they were going ! And a sort of numbness in 'Jimmy's' mind cracked suddenly; his glasses shook; his thin, weasley face became suffused and quivered. Magenta – magenta – two from the rails! He could make no story of the race such as he would read in to-morrow's paper – he could see nothing but magenta.

Out of the dip now, and coming fast – green still leading – something in violet, something in tartan, closing.

'Wasp's beat!' 'The favourite – the favourite wins!' 'Deer-stalker – Deerstalker wins! What's that in pink on the rails?'

It was *his* in pink on the rails! Behind him a man went suddenly mad.

'Deerstalker! Come on with 'im, Stee! Deerstalker 'll win – Deerstalker 'll win!'

'Jimmy' sputtered venomously: 'Will 'e? Will 'e?'

Deerstalker and his own out from the rest – opposite the Cheap Ring – neck and neck – Docker riding like a demon.

'Deerstalker! Deerstalker!' 'Calliope wins! She wins!'

Gawd! His horse! They flashed past – fifty yards to go, and not a head between 'em!

'Deerstalker! Deerstalker!' 'Calliope!' He saw his mare shoot out – she'd won!

With a little queer sound he squirmed and wriggled on to the stairs. No thoughts while he squeezed, and slid, and hurried – only emotion – out of the Ring, away to the paddock. His horse!

Docker had weighed in when he reached the mare. All right! He passed with a grin. 'Jimmy' turned almost into the body of Polman standing like an image.

'Well, Mr Shrewin,' he said to nobody, 'she's won.'

'Damn you!' thought 'Jimmy.' 'Damn the lot of you!' And he went up to his mare. Quivering, streaked with sweat, impatient of the gathering crowd, she showed the whites of her eyes when he put his hand up to her nose.

'Good girl!' he said, and watched her led away.

'Gawd! I want a drink!' he thought.

Gingerly, keeping a sharp lookout for Pulcher, he returned to the stand to get it, and to draw his hundred. But up there by the stairs the discreet fellow was no more. On the ticket was the name O. H. Jones, and nothing else. 'Jimmy' Shrewin had been welshed! He went down at last in a bad temper. At the bottom of the staircase stood George Pulcher. The big man's face was crimson, his eyes ominous. He blocked 'Jimmy' into a corner.

'Ah!' he said. 'You little crow! What the 'ell made you speak to Docker?'

'Jimmy' grinned. Some new body within him stood there defiant. 'She's my 'orse,' he said.

'You —— Gawd-forsaken rat! If I 'ad you in a quiet spot, I'd shake the life out of you!'

'Jimmy' stared up, his little spindle legs apart, like a cock-sparrow confronting an offended pigeon.

'Go 'ome,' he said, 'George Pulcher; and get your mother to mend your socks. You don't know 'ow! Thought I wasn't a man, did you? Well, now you —— well know I am. Keep off my 'orse in future.'

Crimson rushed up on crimson in Pulcher's face; he raised his heavy fists. 'Jimmy' stood, unmoving, his little hands in his bell-coat pockets, his withered face upraised. The big man gulped as if swallowing back the tide of blood; his fists edged forward and then – dropped.

'That's better,' said 'Jimmy,' 'hit one of your own size.'

Emitting a deep growl, George Pulcher walked away.

'Two to one on the field – I'll back the field – Two to one on the field.' 'Threes Snowdrift – Fours Iron Dook.'

'Jimmy' stood a moment mechanically listening to the music of his life; then, edging out, he took a fly and was driven to the station.

All the way up to town he sat chewing his cheroot with the glow of drink inside him, thinking of that finish, and of how he had stood up to George Pulcher. For a whole day he was lost in London, but Friday saw him once more at his seat of custom in the 'Corn.' Not having laid against his horse, he had had a good race in spite of everything; yet, the following week, uncertain into what further quagmires of quixotry she might lead him, he sold Callïōpe.

But for years betting upon horses that he never saw, underground like a rat, yet never again so accessible to the kicks of fortune, or so prone before the shafts of superiority, he would think of the Downs with the blinkin' larks singin', and talk of how once he – had a horse.

Morning in the High Street

BARRÉ LYNDON

This next story features a man of the turf with a seemingly irresistible guarantee to refund the money of any client when his tips fail to pay off. Bert, 'The Money-Back Tipster', is an intriguing character in a world famous for its characters – and especially intriguing to a disgruntled ex-employee who is determined to find out just how he can make such a claim and stay in business.

Like John Galsworthy, the author of 'Morning in the High Street', Barré Lyndon is today better remembered for his other work as a Hollywood scriptwriter rather than for his novels of suburban English life written between the two world wars. It was, in fact, a play by Lyndon that made his reputation: *The Amazing Dr Clitterhouse*, a psychological melodrama which was premiered in London in 1936 and caught the eye of the Warner Brothers studios, who bought it as a starring vehicle for Edward G. Robinson in 1938. Barré followed this success with a number of original screenplays, including *They Came By Night* (1940) and *The Man in Half-Moon Street* (1944), a terrifying drama about a chemist who retains his youth by regular gland transplants taken from the bodies of his murder victims. The latter was remade in 1959 by Hammer Films in England, retitled *The Man Who Could Cheat Death*, starring the sinister Anton Diffring as the serial killer.

Among the other mystery films which Lyndon scripted while living in Hollywood, the best were undoubtedly *The Lodger* (1944), adapted from Marie Belloc Lowndes' novel about Jack the Ripper; and *Hangover Square* (1945), the record of a murderous schizophrenic at loose in the London underworld which he also based on a book by Patrick Hamilton. Both of these pictures starred one of Hollywood's most memorable heavies of the period, Laird Cregar, and have since become recognised as minor classics of the American cinema.

Barré Lyndon, whose real name was Alfred Edgar (1896–1972), began his working life as a sporting journalist in London. He regularly wrote about horse racing, which he later admitted turned him into a keen racegoer and often heavy gambler. For a time he was a familiar figure at several of the courses around London, before transferring his interest to the racetracks in Los Angeles when his career took him to Hollywood. Curiously, he did not put this hard-won knowledge of the turf to use in either a play or film, but merely this one short story which appeared in *Pearson's Magazine* in May 1941 and has not been reprinted since.

*

It was very, very peculiar.

Joe could see him at the window of his one-room office, sucking an orange and working like a beaver. A grey bowler hat was pushed to the back of his head, and he was wearing a new suit of delicate check.

Joe, leaning against a yellow poster on the long wall of a theatre, scowled while he stared across the High-street to the narrow buildings opposite. In imagination, he could hear Bert sucking the orange; the constant noise that he made had always annoyed Joe, and he had sacked Bert for it in the end.

Joe had found it too much when, shouting the odds on the course, he paused for breath always to hear his clerk hissing and gurgling at his elbow. That was in the days before Joe had gone broke, and before Bert's peculiar prosperity had come to him. Thirty pounds a week, Bert was making up in that little office. He did two hours of mysterious work every morning, and spent the rest of the day at leisure, spending lavishly, but never talking. He called himself a 'Turf Adviser,' and had his name on a board at pavement level.

'Turf Adviser,' Joe muttered, and shifted his sixteen stones on brown-shod feet, while the poster-frame creaked behind him. 'He wouldn't know the difference if they ran camels in the Derby!'

Anything that Bert knew about horses had been learned while he worked with Joe – squirting orange juice, and sucking like a steam engine, and providing his employer with an inhibition about oranges. Yet, in spite of his lack of knowledge, Bert was now selling tips to punters and prospering rapidly. His methods were surprising and original.

'The Money-Back Tipster,' he called himself.

'You can't lose,' he announced in the literature that he had printed. 'Win on my tip, or I return your money.'

He was as good as his word. If a man failed to win on the tip that he gave, then he did return his client's money. No tipster had ever been known to guarantee winners on the money-back principle, yet Bert was making a fortune.

' 'Ow the 'ell does he do it?' Joe asked himself, not for the first time. 'It ain't natural.'

It was not natural, and, in an anxious endeavour to learn the secret, Joe had tried to break into Bert's office two days earlier, only to find three padlocks on the door. Short of using an axe, ingress was impossible.

So Joe had formed another plan. Where the islanded shape of an old church stood like a drab grey rock, splitting the traffic, a car waited. The man behind the wheel shot constant glances from Joe to the entrance of the building where Bert sat, making money. When, at eleven o'clock, Bert walked to the post office to dispatch a sheaf of telegrams containing his selections for the day's races, the car and Joe would come into action.

Joe remained watchful, looking across the street. It was past eleven o'clock, and the road was heavy with the traffic of a populous and thriving town, when Bert straightened his bowler hat, ejected an orange pip and relaxed in his chair. His day's work done.

As Bert vanished from the window, Joe eased himself off the theatre wall and began to pick his way neatly through the vehicles which thundered past the old church. He turned towards the waiting car, nodded meaningly to the man at the wheel, then walked slowly on until he reached the tunnel-like entrance of Abbey-lane.

He paused here, pretending to read the notice which gave directions for reaching the Roman Baths, then he turned his attention to the corner of Abbeygate-street, where a point-duty policeman was controlling traffic which, screaming in gear, came up from the river. The constable was very busy, and Joe observed this with satisfaction before he surveyed the traffic rushing past the building that split the High-street.

There was nothing about Joe to suggest what was now in his mind: he seemed to be just a heavy, shabby man, florid and big-fisted, standing idly.

Actually he was marking how the driver of the waiting car had started up his engine, with the front wheels now turned outward, ready for a dash across to the theatre, round a hairpin turn, then across the traffic again into Market-street. Beyond this lay thoroughfares muddled by the congestion about the market itself; here the car was to be abandoned, while the occupants lost themselves in the streets around. They would, Joe calculated, have left the car by the time that anyone in the High-street realized what had happened.

He looked along the pavement. The street was crowded, people flocking in either direction, and soon he saw Bert. He was walking quickly and carrying a leather dispatch case; it was a recent investment, and it looked important. It contained the telegrams he was sending out.

As he came he removed a freshly lighted cigar from his lips and inspected it to make sure that it was burning properly. When he clamped his teeth on the cigar again he slipped his hand back into his trouser pocket, carefully drawing his coat-front open, so that morning sunshine caught the silver chain which stretched across his narrow waistcoat like the cable of a tug.

He came down the High-street with his new suit, his grey bowler, his cigar, his imposing dispatch case, and he came with his chin in the air, looking down his nose at the toilers who passed, while his coat pockets wobbled, bulged by a supply of oranges. He nodded patronisingly to a newspaper seller who had his stand by a fire-alarm, and the man touched his hat deferentially.

Bert was ten yards away when Joe jerked down the peak of his cap and stepped purposefully to meet him. Bert saw him coming and slowed, staring uncertainly, forcing a smile.

'Fancy meetin' you, Joe,' he said hesitantly.

One last stride brought Joe close. His right fist lashed out in a short-arm jolt that had sixteen stones behind it. Quick as a sparrow, Bert ducked and dodged, but bunched knuckles caught him above one ear. His grey bowler pitched away and he staggered, off his balance.

Joe snatched at the dispatch case, while his left foot kicked neatly forward, swinging Bert's legs from under him. He dropped full length to the pavement and Joe turned, jumping at the car.

The machine went away from the kerb with worn gears shrieking, a taxi driver shouting as he stood on his brake-pedal to avoid them. They skimmed his radiator, darted across the traffic stream and made for the turn by the theatre portico.

Behind, Bert was yelling weakly, the policeman was running irresolutely forward from Abbeygate-street, and pedestrians were standing stock-still, staring like surprised sheep.

The car took the hairpin with tyres squealing and the inside wheels lifting. A huge bus loomed in front like a red cliff, and they missed its back steps by inches as they shot towards the mouth of Market-street, boring headlong into a muddle of horse-vans, cabs, barrows, parked vehicles, and bowed figures laden with market produce.

As the car plunged into this, a vehicle came roaring from behind, bringing with it the strident note of a gong that clanged furiously. It swept alongside, and Joe saw a flat-capped figure leaning from beside the driver, reaching out, arm extended.

'Cops!' Joe's companion gasped, and wrenched over the steering wheel in an attempt to cut away at right angles into a side street.

The car skidded, slithered viciously, then hit a barrow laden with crates, which lifted at the impact and burst. As he saw the contents, Joe yelled like a man struck heavily by the hand of fate; the broken crates spouted yellow oranges as the car ground its way into their wreckage, and the police machine leaped along-side.

Joe's driver wriggled up in his seat, flung himself backwards, found the ground and bolted. Joe floundered out, clinging to the stolen dispatch case and jumping wildly to clear the debris. He covered half a dozen strides, then something squelched under one foot and he slipped. He went down, to find himself yanked upright by a hand which caught one arm.

'We want you,' a voice said harshly.

A crowd was still hovering about the smashed barrow and the car when Joe and Bert found themselves in the charge room of the police station, a little distance away. Two members of the mobile police guarded them, and two constables were at the door.

'And what's in here?' the sergeant asked, as he surveyed the dispatch case.

'Only the telegrams I was sending out,' Bert answered off-handedly. 'To-day's tips.'

The sergeant looked at him, at his new suit and silver watch-chain and lemon-coloured shoes with suede tops.

' "The Money-Back Tipster – you *can't lose*," ' quoted the sergeant softly. 'We were beginning to get curious about you.'

'You never mind about me – he's the one what's been pinched,' Bert answered defiantly.

'Yes, he knocked you down and stole this bag,' the sergeant said, snapping open the flap of the dispatch case.

Bert started forward, but a hand jerked him back.

'Them telegrams is private!' he protested. 'They're a secret – a trade secret! You're exceedin' your dooty!'

'Shut up,' a policeman said coldly.

Bert gulped as the sergeant drew out a wad of telegraph forms.

' "Golden Girl, two thirty," ' he read aloud. 'Golden Girl – Golden Girl – six wires giving Golden Girl.' He paused a moment, then went on. 'Six more giving Escapina, and six more for Winalot! All tipped to win the same race.'

Bert shuffled uneasily. He saw Joe looking at him. The sergeant silently surveyed the remainder of the telegrams. He pushed them aside, and leaned forward.

'What a brain you must have, Bert,' he commented admiringly.

'How's he been doing it?' Joe asked hoarsely.

'He's been tipping every runner to win – in each race,' the sergeant answered.

'Yes, but only one 'orse can win!' Joe protested.

'He sends the rest o' the money back!'

'But he tips each horse six times over,' the sergeant replied. 'So he gets at least six half-crowns for every winner – and there are ten races a day.'

'Gaw, blimey,' said Joe slowly.

'The winners are satisfied – they don't know about the rest,' the sergeant added.

'Them what don't win, get their money back – and come again!' Joe exclaimed. Amazed, and suddenly understanding, he turned to Bert and spoke bitterly: 'You can't lose – *you* can't!'

'Sixty half-crowns – seven pound ten a day,' the station sergeant observed. 'It must have been like sitting on top of a gold mine.'

At his words, Joe's manner changed. He heaved his bulk forward and faced Bert, his voice pleading and urgent.

'If you don't press the charges against me, Bert,' he said, 'We can work this together. I'll come in with you!'

'You are going in with him,' the station sergeant said gently. 'You for bag-snatching, him for defrauding the public – and, no doubt, you will work together.'

'I almost wish you'd got away now, Joe,' Bert said, regretfully, as they were conducted along the grey corridor to the cells.

'I would have made it, only I slipped,' Joe answered.

'Slipped?'

'Yes, on a ruddy orange.'

The Crackler

AGATHA CHRISTIE

Race courses are ideal places for passing counterfeit money, either to the punter by crooked bookies or by big money gamblers as bets. Nat Gould and Frank Johnston, in particular, used this theme in several of their novels, while the subject was also exploited in America by the prolific Barcley Northcote and S. S. Van Dine, whose dilettante detective Philo Vance became involved in a dirty money fraud on the steeplechase circuit in *The Garden Murder Case*, which was filmed in 1937 with Edmund Lowe and Virginia Bruce. Among short stories, however, 'The Crackler' is unique, being a parody which involves the passing of dud notes in England and France by a clever counterfeiter using a fashionable racing crowd as his means of disposal. The authoress Agatha Christie (1890–1976) needs little introduction, for her eighty-four mysteries featuring Hercule Poirot, Miss Marple and various other amateur detectives and policemen are believed to have sold over two billion copies in forty-four languages around the world. Yet the details about her interest in horse racing are little known.

Agatha Christie learned to ride as a child and then in later life enjoyed going horse racing regularly in the southwest of England where she made her home. Indeed, a race at the Devon and Exeter Racecourse was named after her famous play, *The Mousetrap*, while another commemorated her husband, the archaeologist and photographer, Max Mallowan. Despite these facts, she wrote very little about the sport, which gives the next story an especial interest.

'The Crackler' features her detective couple, Tommy and Tuppence Beresford, who were the heroes of her second book, *The Secret Adversary* (1922), and like Poirot and Miss Marple have subsequently been featured on the screen a number of times, initially by Carlo Aldini and Eve Gray in 1929; later by Richard Attenborough and Sheila Sim (in 1953); and most recently by James Warwick and Francesca Annis in London Weekend Television's 1983 TV series.

The story is one of a series with the generic title *Partners in Crime*, which Agatha Christie wrote in 1929 as a deliberate parody of contemporary crime fiction. As she explained in her *Autobiography*, published the year after her death: 'Each story was written in the manner of some particular detective of the time and it is interesting to see who of the writers I chose are still well known.' Among those who *have* stood the test of time are Sir Arthur Conan Doyle, G. K. Chesterton and Edgar Wallace. 'The Crackler' in fact parodies Wallace's addiction to gambling as well as his string of thrillers, with titles such as *The Ringer, The Squeaker, The Twister* and so on. Indeed, the tone of the story is set right at the beginning when Tuppence Beresford exclaims to her husband: 'We need several hundreds of yards of extra book-shelf if Edgar Wallace is to be properly represented!'

'The Crackler' is, nonetheless, an action-packed mystery solved in the best Wallace style with some intriguing references to the kind of big money gambling that so often lured him. So enjoy the meeting of 'The Queen of Crime' and the 'King of Thriller Writers', all made possible by their mutual love of the Turf!

*

I

'Tuppence,' said Tommy. 'We shall have to move into a much larger office.'

'Nonsense,' said Tuppence. 'You mustn't get swollen-headed and think you are a millionaire just because you solved two or three twopenny halfpenny cases with the aid of the most amazing luck.'

'What some call luck, others call skill.'

'Of course, if you really think you are Sherlock Holmes, Thorndyke, M'Carty and the Brothers Okewood all rolled into one, there is no more to be said. Personally I would much rather have luck on my side than all the skill in the world.'

'Perhaps there is something in that,' conceded Tommy. 'All the same, Tuppence, we do need a larger office.'

'Why?'

'The classics,' said Tommy. 'We need several hundreds of yards of extra book-shelf if Edgar Wallace is to be properly represented.'

'We haven't had an Edgar Wallace case yet.'

'I am afraid we never shall,' said Tommy. 'If you notice he never does give the amateur sleuth much of a chance. It is all stern Scotland Yard kind of stuff – the real thing and no base counterfeit.'

Albert, the office boy, appeared at the door.

'Inspector Marriot to see you,' he announced.

'The mystery man of Scotland Yard,' murmured Tommy.

'The busiest of the Busies,' said Tuppence. 'Or is it "Noses?" I always get mixed between Busies and Noses.'

The Inspector advanced upon them with a beaming smile of welcome.

'Well, and how are things?' he asked breezily. 'None the worse for our little adventure the other day?'

'Oh, rather not,' said Tuppence. 'Too, too marvellous, wasn't it?'

'Well, I don't know that I would describe it exactly that way myself,' said Marriot cautiously.

'What has brought you here to-day, Marriot?' asked Tommy. 'Not just solicitude for our nervous systems, is it?'

'No,' said the Inspector. 'It is work for the brilliant Mr Blunt.'

'Ha!' said Tommy. 'Let me put my brilliant expression on.'

'I have come to make you a proposition, Mr Beresford. What would you say to rounding up a really big gang?'

'Is there such a thing?' asked Tommy.

'What do you mean, is there such a thing?'

'I always thought that gangs were confined to fiction – like master crooks and super criminals.'

'The master crook isn't very common,' agreed the Inspector. 'But Lord bless you, sir, there's any amount of gangs knocking about.'

'I don't know that I should be at my best dealing with a gang,' said Tommy. 'The amateur crime, the crime of quiet family life – that is where I flatter myself that I shine. Drama of strong domestic interest. That's the thing – with Tuppence at hand to supply all those little feminine details which are so important, and so apt to be ignored by the denser male.'

His eloquence was arrested abruptly as Tuppence threw a cushion at him and requested him not to talk nonsense.

'Will have your little bit of fun, won't you, sir?' said Inspector Marriot, smiling paternally at them both. 'If you'll not take offence at my saying so, it's a pleasure to see two young people enjoying life as much as you two do.'

'Do we enjoy life?' said Tuppence, opening her eyes very wide. 'I suppose we do. I've never thought about it before.'

'To return to that gang you were talking about,' said Tommy. 'In spite of my extensive private practice – duchesses, million-aires, and all the best char-women – I might, perhaps, condescend to look into the matter for you. I don't like to see Scotland Yard at fault. You'll have the *Daily Mail* after you before you know where you are.'

'As I said before, you must have your bit of fun. Well, it's like this.' Again he hitched his chair forward. 'There's any amount of forged notes going about just now – hundreds of 'em! The amount of counterfeit Treasury notes in circulation would surprise you. Most artistic bit of work it is. Here's one of 'em.'

He took a one pound note from his pocket and handed it to Tommy.

'Looks all right, doesn't it?'

Tommy examined the note with great interest.

'By Jove, I'd never spot there was anything wrong with that.'

'No more would most people. Now here's a genuine one. I'll show you the differences – very slight they are, but you'll soon learn to tell them apart. Take this magnifying glass.'

At the end of five minutes' coaching both Tommy and Tuppence were fairly expert.

'What do you want us to do, Inspector Marriot?' asked Tuppence. 'Just keep our eyes open for these things?'

'A great deal more than that, Mrs Beresford. I'm pinning my

faith on you to get to the bottom of the matter. You see, we've discovered that the notes are being circulated from the West End. Somebody pretty high up in the social scale is doing the distributing. They're passing them the other side of the Channel as well. Now there's a certain person who is interesting us very much. A Major Laidlaw – perhaps you've heard the name?'

'I think I have,' said Tommy. 'Connected with racing, isn't that it?'

'Yes. Major Laidlaw is pretty well known in connection with the Turf. There's nothing actually against him, but there's a general impression that he's been a bit too smart over one or two rather shady transactions. Men in the know look queer when he's mentioned. Nobody knows much of his past or where he came from. He's got a very attractive French wife who's seen about everywhere with a train of admirers. They must spend a lot of money, the Laidlaws, and I'd like to know where it comes from.'

'Possibly from the train of admirers,' suggested Tommy.

'That's the general idea. But I'm not so sure. It may be coincidence, but a lot of notes have been forthcoming from a certain very smart little gambling club which is much frequented by the Laidlaws and their set. This racing, gambling set get rid of a lot of loose money in notes. There couldn't be a better way of getting it into circulation.'

'And where do we come in?'

'This way. Young St. Vincent and his wife are friends of yours, I understand? They're pretty thick with the Laidlaw set – though not as thick as they were. Through them it will be easy for you to get a footing in the same set in a way that none of our people could attempt. There's no likelihood of their spotting you. You'll have an ideal opportunity.'

'What have we got to find out exactly?'

'Where they get the stuff from, if they *are* passing it.'

'Quite so,' said Tommy. 'Major Laidlaw goes out with an empty suit-case. When he returns it is crammed to the bursting point with Treasury notes. How is it done? I sleuth him and find out. Is that the idea?'

'More or less. But don't neglect the lady, and her father, M.

Heroulade. Remember the notes are being passed on both sides of the Channel.'

'My dear Marriot,' exclaimed Tommy reproachfully, 'Blunt's Brilliant Detectives do not know the meaning of the word neglect.'

The Inspector rose.

'Well, good luck to you,' he said, and departed.

'Slush,' said Tuppence enthusiastically.

'Eh?' said Tommy, perplexed.

'Counterfeit money,' explained Tuppence. 'It is always called slush. I know I'm right. Oh, Tommy, we have got an Edgar Wallace case. At last we are busies.'

'We are,' said Tommy. 'And we are out to get the Crackler, and we will get him good.'

'Did you say the Cackler or the Crackler?'

'The Crackler.'

'Oh, what is a Crackler?'

'A new word that I have coined,' said Tommy. 'Descriptive of one who passes false notes into circulation. Bank-notes crackle, therefore he is called a crackler. Nothing could be more simple.'

'That is rather a good idea,' said Tuppence. 'It makes it seem more real. I like the Rustler myself. Much more descriptive and sinister.'

'No,' said Tommy, 'I said the Crackler first, and I stick to it.'

'I shall enjoy this case,' said Tuppence. 'Lots of night clubs and cocktails in it. I shall buy some eyelash black to-morrow.'

'Your eyelashes are black already,' objected her husband.

'I could make them blacker,' said Tuppence. 'And cherry lip stick would be useful too. That ultra-bright kind.'

'Tuppence,' said Tommy, 'you're a real rake at heart. What a good thing it is that you are married to a sober steady middle-aged man like myself.'

'You wait,' said Tuppence. 'When you have been to the Python Club a bit, you mayn't be so sober yourself.'

Tommy produced from a cupboard various bottles, two glasses, and a cocktail shaker.

'Let's start now,' he said. 'We are after you, Crackler, and we mean to get you.'

*

II

Making the acquaintance of the Laidlaws proved an easy affair. Tommy and Tuppence, young, well-dressed, eager for life, and with apparently money to burn, were soon made free of that particular coterie in which the Laidlaws had their being.

Major Laidlaw was a tall, fair man, typically English in appearance, with a hearty sportsmanlike manner, slightly belied by the hard lines round his eyes and the occasional quick sideways glance that assorted oddly with his supposed character.

He was a very dexterous card player, and Tommy noticed that when the stakes were high he seldom rose from the table a loser.

Marguerite Laidlaw was quite a different proposition. She was a charming creature, with the slenderness of a wood nymph and the face of a Greuze picture. Her dainty broken English was fascinating, and Tommy felt that it was no wonder most men were her slaves. She seemed to take a great fancy to Tommy from the first, and playing his part, he allowed himself to be swept into her train.

'My Tommee,' she would say; 'but positively I cannot go without my Tommee. His 'air, eet ees the colour of the sunset, ees eet not?'

Her father was a more sinister figure. Very correct, very upright, with his little black beard and his watchful eyes.

Tuppence was the first to report progress. She came to Tommy with ten one pound notes.

'Have a look at these. They're wrong 'uns, aren't they?'

Tommy examined them and confirmed Tuppence's diagnosis.

'Where did you get them from?'

'That boy, Jimmy Faulkener. Marguerite Laidlaw gave them to him to put on a horse for her. I said I wanted small notes and gave him a tenner in exchange.'

'All new and crisp,' said Tommy thoughtfully.

'They can't have passed through many hands. I suppose young Faulkener is all right?'

'Jimmy? Oh, he's a dear. He and I are becoming great friends.'

'So I have noticed,' said Tommy coldly. 'Do you really think it is necessary?'

'Oh, it isn't business,' said Tuppence cheerily. 'It's pleasure. He's such a nice boy. I'm glad to get him out of that woman's clutches. You've no idea of the amount of money she's cost him.'

'It looks to me as though he were getting rather a pash for you, Tuppence.'

'I've thought the same myself sometimes. It's nice to know one's still young and attractive, isn't it?'

'Your moral tone, Tuppence, is deplorably low. You look at these things from the wrong point of view.'

'I haven't enjoyed myself so much for years,' declared Tuppence shamelessly. 'And anyway, what about you? Do I ever see you nowadays? Aren't you always living in Marguerite Laidlaw's pocket?'

'Business,' said Tommy crisply.

'But she is attractive, isn't she?'

'Not my type,' said Tommy. 'I don't admire her.'

'Liar,' laughed Tuppence. 'But I always did think I'd rather marry a liar than a fool.'

'I suppose,' said Tommy, 'that there's no absolute necessity for a husband to be either?'

But Tuppence merely threw him a pitying glance and withdrew.

Amongst Mrs Laidlaw's train of admirers was a simple but extremely wealthy gentleman of the name of Hank Ryder.

Mr Ryder came from Alabama, and from the first he was disposed to make a friend and confidant of Tommy.

'That's a wonderful woman, sir,' said Mr Ryder, following the lovely Marguerite with reverential eyes. 'Plumb full of civilisation. Can't beat *la gaie France*, can you? When I'm near her, I feel as though I was one of the Almighty's earliest experiments. I guess he'd got to get his hand in before he attempted anything so lovely as that perfectly lovely woman.'

Tommy agreeing politely with these sentiments, Mr Ryder unburdened himself still further.

'Seems kind of a shame a lovely creature like that should have money worries.'

'Has she?' asked Tommy.

'You betcha life she has. Queer fish, Laidlaw. She's skeered of him. Told me so. Daren't tell him about her little bills.'

'Are they *little* bills?' asked Tommy.

'Well – when I say little! After all, a woman's got to wear clothes, and the less there are of them the more they cost, the way I figure it out. And a pretty woman like that doesn't want to go about in last season's goods. Cards too, the poor little thing's been mighty unlucky at cards. Why, she lost fifty to me last night.'

'She won two hundred from Jimmy Faulkener the night before,' said Tommy dryly.

'Did she indeed? That relieves my mind some. By the way, there seems to be a lot of dud notes floating around in your country just now. I paid in a bunch at my bank this morning, and twenty-five of them were down and outers, so the polite gentleman behind the counter informed me.'

'That's rather a large proportion. Were they new looking?'

'New and crisp as they make 'em. Why, they were the ones Mrs Laidlaw paid over to me, I reckon. Wonder where she got 'em from. One of these toughs on the race course as likely as not.'

'Yes,' said Tommy. 'Very likely.'

'You know, Mr Beresford, I'm new to this sort of high life. All these swell dames and the rest of the outfit. Only made my pile a short while back. Came right over to Yurrop to see life.'

Tommy nodded. He made a mental note to the effect that with the aid of Marguerite Laidlaw Mr Ryder would probably see a good deal of life and that the price charged would be heavy.

Meantime, for the second time, he had evidence that the forged notes were being distributed pretty near at hand, and that in all probability Marguerite Laidlaw had a hand in their distribution.

On the following night he himself was given a proof.

It was at that small select meeting place mentioned by Inspector Marriot. There was dancing there, but the real attraction of the place lay behind a pair of imposing folding doors. There were two rooms there with green baize-covered tables, where vast sums changed hands nightly.

Marguerite Laidlaw, rising at last to go, thrust a quantity of small notes into Tommy's hands.

'They are so bulkee, Tommee – you will change them, yes? A beeg note. See my so sweet leetle bag, it bulges him to distraction.'

Tommy brought her the hundred pound note she asked for. Then in a quiet corner he examined the notes she had given him. At least a quarter of them were counterfeit.

But where did she get her supplies from? To that he had as yet no answer. By means of Albert's cooperation, he was almost sure that Laidlaw was not the man. His movements had been watched closely and had yielded no result.

Tommy suspected her father, the saturnine M. Heroulade. He went to and fro to France fairly often. What could be simpler than to bring the notes across with him? A false bottom to a trunk – something of that kind.

Tommy strolled slowly out of the Club, absorbed in these thoughts, but was suddenly recalled to immediate necessities. Outside in the street was Mr Hank P. Ryder, and it was clear at once that Mr Ryder was not strictly sober. At the moment he was trying to hang his hat on the radiator of a car, and missing it by some inches every time.

'This goddarned hatshtand, this goddarned hatshtand,' said Mr Ryder tearfully. 'Not like that in the Shtates. Man can hang up his hat every night – every night, sir. You're wearing two hatshs. Never sheen a man wearing two hatsh before. Must be effect – climate.'

'Perhaps I've got two heads,' said Tommy gravely.

'Sho you have,' said Mr Ryder. 'Thatsh odd. Thatsh remarkable fac'. Letsh have a cocktail. Prohibition – probishun – thatsh whatsh done me in. I guess I'm drunk – constootionally drunk. Cocktailsh – mixed 'em – Angel's Kiss – that's Marguerite – lovely creature, fon' o' me too. Horshes Neck, two Martinis – three Road to Ruinsh – no, roadsh to roon – mixed 'em all – in a beer tankard. Bet me I wouldn't – I shaid – to hell, I shaid—'

Tommy interrupted.

'That's all right,' he said soothingly. 'Now what about getting home?'

'No home to go to,' said Mr Ryder sadly, and wept.

'What hotel are you staying at?' asked Tommy.

'Can't go home,' said Mr Ryder. 'Treasure hunt. Swell thing to do. She did it. Whitechapel – white heartsh, white headsn shorrow to the grave—'

But Mr Ryder became suddenly dignified. He drew himself erect and attained a sudden miraculous command over his speech.

'Young man, I'm telling you. Margee took me. In her car. Treasure hunting. English aristocrashy all do it. Under the cobblestones. Five hundred poundsh. Solemn thought, 'tis solemn thought. I'm *telling* you, young man. You've been kind to me. I've got your welfare at heart, sir, at heart. We Americans—'

Tommy interrupted him this time with even less ceremony.

'What's that you say? Mrs Laidlaw took you in a car?'

The American nodded with a kind of owlish solemnity.

'To Whitechapel?' Again that owlish nod.

'And you found five hundred pounds there?'

Mr Ryder struggled for words.

'S-she did,' he corrected his questioner. 'Left me outside. Outside the door. Always left outside. It's kinder sad. Outside – always outside.'

'Would you know your way there?'

'I guess so. Hank Ryder doesn't lose his bearings—'

Tommy hauled him along unceremoniously. He found his own car where it was waiting, and presently they were bowling eastward. The cool air revived Mr Ryder. After slumping against Tommy's shoulder in a kind of stupor, he awoke clear headed and refreshed.

'Say, boy, where are we?' he demanded.

'Whitechapel,' said Tommy crisply. 'Is this where you came with Mrs Laidlaw to-night?'

'It looks kinder familiar,' admitted Mr Ryder, looking round. 'Seems to me we turned off to the left somewhere down here. That's it – that street there.'

Tommy turned off obediently. Mr Ryder issued directions.

'That's it. Sure. And round to the right. Say, aren't the smells awful? Yes, past that pub at the corner – sharp round, and stop at the mouth of that little alley. But what's the big idea? Hand it to me. Some of the oof left behind? Are we going to put one over on them?'

'That's exactly it,' said Tommy. 'We're going to put one over on them. Rather a joke, isn't it?'

'I'll tell the world,' assented Mr Ryder. 'Though I'm just a mite hazed about it all,' he ended wistfully.

Tommy got out and assisted Mr Ryder to alight also. They advanced into the alley way. On the left were the backs of a row of dilapidated houses, most of which had doors opening into the alley. Mr Ryder came to a stop before one of these doors.

'In here she went,' he declared. 'It was this door – I'm plumb certain of it.'

'They all look very alike,' said Tommy. 'Reminds me of the story of the soldier and the Princess. You remember, they made a cross on the door to show which one it was. Shall we do the same?'

Laughing, he drew a piece of white chalk from his pocket and made a rough cross low down on the door. Then he looked up at various dim shapes that prowled high on the walls of the alley, one of which was uttering a blood-curdling yawl.

'Lots of cats about,' he remarked cheerfully.

'What is the procedure?' asked Mr Ryder. 'Do we step inside?'

'Adopting due precautions, we do,' said Tommy.

He glanced up and down the alley way, then softly tried the door. It yielded. He pushed it open and peered into a dim yard.

Noiselessly he passed through, Mr Ryder on his heels.

'Gee,' said the latter, 'there's some one coming down the alley.'

He slipped outside again. Tommy stood still for a minute, then hearing nothing went on. He took a torch from his pocket and switched on the light for a brief second. That momentary flash enabled him to see his way ahead. He pushed forward and tried the closed door ahead of him. That too gave, and very softly he pushed it open and went in.

After standing still a second and listening, he again switched on the torch, and at that flash, as though at a given signal, the place seemed to rise round him. Two men were in front of him, two men were behind him. They closed in on him and bore him down.

'Lights,' growled a voice.

An incandescent gas burner was lit. By its light Tommy saw a circle of unpleasing faces. His eyes wandered gently round the room and noted some of the objects in it.

'Ah!' he said pleasantly. 'The headquarters of the counterfeiting industry, if I am not mistaken.'

'Shut your jaw,' growled one of the men.

The door opened and shut behind Tommy, and a genial and well-known voice spoke.

'Got him, boys. That's right. Now, Mr Busy, let me tell you you're up against it.'

'That dear old word,' said Tommy. 'How it thrills me. Yes. I am the Mystery Man of Scotland Yard. Why, it's Mr Hank Ryder. This *is* a surprise.'

'I guess you mean that too. I've been laughing fit to bust all this evening – leading you here like a little child. And you so pleased with your cleverness. Why, sonny, I was on to you from the start. You weren't in with that crowd for your health. I let you play about for a while, and when you got real suspicious of the lovely Marguerite, I said to myself: "Now's the time to lead him to it." I guess your friends won't be hearing of you for some time.'

'Going to do me in? That's the correct expression, I believe. You have got it in for me.'

'You've got a nerve all right. No, we shan't attempt violence. Just keep you under restraint, so to speak.'

'I'm afraid you're backing the wrong horse,' said Tommy. 'I've no intention of being "kept under restraint," as you call it.'

Mr Ryder smiled genially. From outside a cat uttered a melancholy cry to the moon.

'Banking on that cross you put on the door, eh, sonny?' said Mr Ryder. 'I shouldn't if I were you. Because I know that story you mentioned. Heard it when I was a little boy. I stepped back into the alley way to enact the part of the dog with eyes as big as cart wheels. If you were in that alley now, you would observe that every door in the alley is marked with an identical cross.'

Tommy drooped his head despondently.

'Thought you were mighty clever, didn't you?' said Ryder.

As the words left his lips a sharp rapping sounded on the door.

'What's that?' he cried, starting.

At the same time an assault began on the front of the house. The door at the back was a flimsy affair. The lock gave almost immediately and Inspector Marriot showed in the doorway.

'Well done, Marriot,' said Tommy. 'You were quite right as to the district. I'd like you to make the acquaintance of Mr Hank Ryder, who knows all the best fairy tales.'

'You see, Mr Ryder,' he added gently, 'I've had my suspicions of you. Albert (that important looking boy with the big ears is Albert) had orders to follow on his motor-cycle if you and I went off joy-riding at any time. And whilst I was ostentatiously marking a chalk cross on the door to engage your attention, I also emptied a little bottle of valerian on the ground. Nasty smell, but cats love it. All the cats in the neighbourhood were assembled outside to mark the right house when Albert and the police arrived.'

He looked at the dumbfounded Mr Ryder with a smile, then rose to his feet.

'I said I would get you, Crackler, and I have got you,' he observed.

'What the hell are you talking about?' asked Mr Ryder. 'What do you mean – Crackler?'

'You will find it in the glossary of the next criminal dictionary,' said Tommy. 'Etymology doubtful.'

He looked round him with a happy smile.

'And all done without a nose,' he murmured brightly. 'Goodnight, Marriot. I must go now to where the happy ending of the story awaits me. No reward like the love of a good woman – and the love of a good woman awaits me at home – that is, I hope it does, but one never knows nowadays. This has been a very dangerous job, Marriot. Do you know Captain Jimmy Faulkener? His dancing is simply too marvellous, and as for his taste in cocktails—! Yes, Marriot, it has been a very dangerous job.'

Something Short of Murder!

HENRY SLESAR

The following pair of stories are about compulsive gamblers, though they are of opposite sexes and find themselves in very different situations as a result of their addiction to betting. Fran Holland, the heroine of Henry Slesar's compelling story, has reached the point of no return and now has only a few hours left to pay off her debts to a bookmaker before he makes known her guilty secret to her husband. What, though, might at first seem like a traditional enough situation is skilfully turned into something quite unexpected in the hands of a writer whose prolific career brought him a long-standing association with the late Alfred Hitchcock – for whose TV series he provided many stories – and who has been crowned with numerous prestigious awards.

Henry Slesar (1927–) was born in Brooklyn, New York and attended his first race meeting at Aqueduct in his early teens. He began writing crime and mystery tales while employed in an advertising agency, and at the last count had written over 500 short stories as well as novels and scripts for radio, television and films. Slesar was one of the most regular contributors to the long-running *Alfred Hitchcock Presents* TV show (1955–61); has won an Emmy award for the series *The Edge of Night* (1968–79); and twice been given the Poe award from the Mystery Writers of America for his fiction. Of him, Alfred Hitchcock wrote in 1963, 'He is a soft-spoken man with an excellent criminal record (in fiction, of course) who has produced some engaging characters: charming people all – scoundrels, murderers and victims alike.'

Among Slesar's stories which feature horse racing can be listed 'The Horse That Wasn't For Sale' (written for *Ellery Queen's Magazine* in 1964), 'The Horseplayer' (which Alfred Hitchcock directed himself for his TV series, starring Claude Rains and Ed Gardner) and 'Something Short of Murder!' which first appeared in *Alfred Hitchcock's Mystery Magazine* in 1963. But despite his love of the Turf and the fact that gamblers have featured in a number of his tales, Henry Slesar maintains he would never dream of betting himself. Perhaps one reason for this attitude lies in the ingenious story which follows.

*

Fran came out of Lila's apartment, shoving the green-printed racing sheets into her apron pocket. Lila, that lucky so-and-so! Three winners in a week! Fran shook her head as she went up the sagging stairs to her apartment on the next floor, displeased with her own luck and envying Lila's.

When the door slammed behind her, she hurried over to the kitchen table and shoved the remains of her husband's breakfast to one side. She took out the racing form, her eyes moving up and down the small print to find the listing of tomorrow's fourth race.

'Sonny Boy, County Judge, Chicago Flyer, Marzipan, Golden-rod . . .'

She read the names aloud running her fingers through the dry brown hair on her forehead. Then she shut her eyes and looked upwards in a gesture. They had to mean something, or it was no good. That was her system. It wasn't much, but that was it.

'Sonny Boy,' she whispered. Her husband, Ed, was an admirer of Jolson. 'Sonny Boy,' she said aloud.

She headed for the telephone and dialled quickly.

'Vito's,' the man said.

'Hello, is Mr Cooney there?'

'Hey, Phil,' the man said. 'For you.'

'Hello?' Cooney said.

'Mr Cooney? This is Fran Holland. Would you put five dollars for me on the fourth race tomorrow? I like—'

'Hold it, Mrs Holland. I'm glad you called. You see, I was comin' to see you anyway, Mrs Holland. After I got my hair cut.'

'Coming to see me?' She looked at the instrument strangely.

'Yeah, Mrs Holland. It's like this, Mrs Holland. First of all, I ain't allowed to take no more bets from you, not until you settle up. Second of all, I'm supposed to come over and see maybe if I can collect the money you owe us. That's twenty-five dollars now.'

'Twenty-five dollars? But that's not so much. I mean, is it?'

'Yeah, sure, Mrs Holland. Only you don't understand, Mrs Holland. This is front office. It wasn't my idea. Too much of this nickel-and-dime stuff around, you know what I mean.'

'No! I don't know!' She was honestly indignant, as if the butcher had overcharged her.

'Well, I'll be over to explain it, Mrs Holland. See you soon.'

'No! Wait a minute—'

But the man named Cooney wasn't waiting. The click at his end of the wire was final.

She stared stupidly at the buzzing receiver before putting it back where it belonged. Then the thought of company – any company – sent her into a series of automatic actions. She cleared the breakfast dishes and piled them in the sink. She swept the crumbs from the table into the hollow of her palm and dropped them into the paper bag that was leaning against the stove. Then she untied her apron, and flung it into a closet.

In the bedroom, she stopped to see her face in the vanity mirror. It was a young face still, with all the marks of the years concentrated around her eyes. Her hair was jutting in too many directions, so she ran a comb through it with painful yanks.

She thought of calling Lila, but the idea of seeing that cheery gloating face again was too much. No, she'd talk this over some other time, when they were both commiserating over a tardy horse.

She sat at the kitchen table and smoked a cigarette. In another ten minutes, the doorbell sounded. She walked calmly to the door.

Cooney took his hat off. The band was tight, and left a circular dent in the shiny surface of his fresh-trimmed hair. He looked like an ageing insurance salesman, eager to make good.

'Morning, Mrs Holland. All right to come in?'

'You know it's all right,' Fran said.

He stepped inside, his small eyes probing the three rooms of the apartment. He sat down at the table and began jiggling the small pile of ashes in the tray.

'Now what's this all about?' Fran said, like a scolding parent.

'It's nothing personal, Mrs Holland. You know that, I like doin' business with you people. Only the management is gettin' a little edgy about the accounts receivable.'

She almost smiled. 'That's a laugh.'

'No, seriously.' He looked hurt. 'How much dough you think we make with this kind of trade? Look, the two-dollar guy is the heart of the business. But when you start raidin' the cookie jar, Mrs Holland—'

'I use my own money! You can't accuse me of—'

'Who's accusin'? Look, Mrs Holland, you've owed us this twenty-five bucks since—' He dipped into his jacket and produced a little black ledger. 'May 20,' he said. 'This is almost two months. Now how do you suppose a big store or somebody would feel about that?'

'Listen, Mr Cooney. You know I always pay you, sooner or later. Ever since I started—'

'You're a friend of Mrs Shank, aren't you?' The question was sudden.

'You know I am. It was Lila who told me about—'

'Yeah. Well, she's not much better, Mrs Holland. If it makes you feel any better.'

'But she just won—'

'Very good for her. And when Mrs Shank wins, we gotta ante up fast, or she's screamin' bloody murder. But when she's on the short end. . . .' He scowled, and Fran no longer felt sure of herself.

'All right,' she said bitingly. 'If you're going to act that way, I'll just find somebody else.'

'Sure. You do that, Mrs Holland.' He slipped the ledger back into his pocket. 'Only there's still a matter of twenty-five bucks.'

'I'll pay you next week.'

'No, Mrs Holland.'

'What do you mean, no? I'll give you the money next week. My husband doesn't get paid until next week.'

'Uh-uh, Mrs Holland.'

She stared at him: 'What's the matter with you? I can't give you something I haven't got. What do you expect?'

'Twenty-five bucks, Mrs Holland. That's my orders. You can borrow the money, can't you? From Mrs Shank, maybe?'

'Not her,' Fran said bitterly.

'You must have the dough in the house. Food money.'

'No! I have a dollar and fifty cents. That's all! I've been charging everything—'

The man stood up, and either the light in the room had changed, or he had. The meekness was out of his face, and he looked anything but harmless.

'I gotta have that money today, Mrs Holland. If I don't get it today—'

'You'll what?' She couldn't believe his attitude; he'd always been a gentleman.

'I'll come back at six o'clock, Mrs Holland.'

'Come back?'

'To see your husband.'

It was a word Cooney had never mentioned, not once. He'd been dropping by two mornings a week for the past three months. There were always evidences of Eddie's presence around. There were his breakfast dishes, scraped clean by his sizable appetite. His crusty old pipe might be lying on the drainboard. There might be a shirt in need of mending, draped over a kitchen chair. But Cooney had never used the word before.

'Why?' Fran said. 'Why do you have to do that? I told you I'd get the money. He doesn't have to know about this thing, does he?'

'Sure he don't, Mrs Holland. All you gotta do is pay me what you owe – nothin' more. And he don't have to know a thing.'

'It's not that I'm so ashamed of it!' she said loudly. 'I haven't lost a fortune or anything!'

'Sure, Mrs Holland.'

'You can't do that to me, Mr Cooney—'

The hat was being squeezed down over the oil-shiny hair. 'I really gotta go, Mrs Holland. You know where you can find me. At Vito's. If you come down any time before six, we can forget the whole thing.'

'But I told you!' Fran's fingers were undoing the work of her comb. 'I haven't got it! I can't get it! There isn't any way—'

'You know about hock shops?'

'I've already—' She stopped, and her fingers found their way to her mouth. If Eddie knew!

'So long, Mrs Holland.'

He went out, shutting the door quietly.

She listened to the man's retreating footsteps until the hallway was silent again, and then she thought about Eddie. She looked across the kitchen table as if she could almost see her husband sitting at the opposite end, looking hurt and baffled as he had so many times before, shaking his head and saying: 'Why do you do it, Fran? What for?'

How could she face that scene again? After all the promises, the tearful scenes of recrimination and forgiveness? The first time hadn't been so bad; they had been honeymooners still, and anything Eddie's bride did was cute and cockeyed and wonderful – even betting house money on the horses. They had laughed over it, then, and made up, before the argument had gone very far, in that special tender way reserved for newly weds. But there had been a second time, and a third, and at each discovery, Eddie had looked more hurt and bewildered, until the bewilderment became anger. And then there had been the terrible scene last October, the day when he'd detected the white circle round her finger where Fran's engagement ring should have been . . .

She shivered at the memory. There had been no forgiveness in Eddie that time. She had sworn to him that the habit was broken; she had tried every way possible to convince him that she had learned her lesson. But still Eddie hadn't forgotten; he had merely warned.

'One more time, Fran, so help me. One more time and I walk outa here. . . .'

She got up from the kitchen table and ran into the bedroom. She attacked the drawers of her bureau, scattering clothes and department boxes filled with buttons and hatpins and scraps of fabric. She foraged through all her purses, her fingers digging into their linings in search of stray coins. She slapped at the pockets of her husband's two suits which hung in the closet, listening for the

,sound of jingling metal. She flipped open the plastic jewellery box Ed had given her the Christmas before, and was shocked at the scarcity of everything with more than dime-store value.

Even as Fran hurried into the living-room, she had the feeling of having done all that she had just done before.

Beneath the pillows of the love seat she found a dime and a black penny. In a small porcelain vase on a bookshelf she found a folded dollar bill.

She brought all the money she had found to the kitchen table, and counted it.

'Two dollars and seventy-eight cents,' she whispered.

She put her head between her elbows.

'Oh, God, God,' she said.

Twenty-five dollars wasn't so much, she thought. But where would she get it? She had no friends, except Lila. Her family lived miles away. Where would she get it? And before six o'clock. She glanced at her wrist, but the watch she expected to see there she remembered was ticking in a pawnshop on Broadway. She glanced up at the electric clock on the kitchen wall, and gasped when she realized that it was almost eleven-thirty.

Less than seven hours! she thought. Twenty-five dollars! Nickels and dimes. Cooney had called it . . .

Then she had her idea. It was born of a painful memory, of an unpleasant scene on a windy street corner only two weeks before. She had just concluded a day of shopping, and there was an overpriced dress in a fancy striped box beneath her arm. She had been standing on the corner, her feet aching, praying that the Number Five bus would be empty. Then she had clicked open her purse, *this* purse, the one on the table looking for nickels and dimes. . . .

She stood up so fast that the chair scraped the linoleum. She went into the bedroom and did further repairs on her makeup. She put on her best pair of black suedes, and then took the silken thing she called her 'evening stole' out of a drawer. The effect in the mirror didn't please her, so she changed her dress too.

When she was through, she looked a lot like the girl Ed used to show off at parties.

Then she went out.

*

The bus stop was four blocks from her apartment building. The good bus stop, that is, the one where Number Five, and Number Fifteen, and Number Twenty-Three nuzzled one another against the curb during the rush hours. Number Five was just lumbering off, only half-filled at midday. But there were still people around, waiting for transportation to God-knows-what errand.

They were old people mostly. Old people weren't so good for what she had in mind. But Fran stepped determinedly up to the arrow-shaped stanchion and looked like a woman with a purpose.

Out of the corner of her eyes, she selected her first subject. She knew the first would be the hardest, so this one had to be good. He wasn't too old, really, maybe a little over fifty. His eyes were puffy, and his shoulders were hunched up as if the July sun, strangely enough, had made him cold. Both hands were in his pockets, and coins within them were making noises.

She sidled up to him, peering down the street for signs of the approaching bus. He looked at her with only mild interest.

Then she saw Number Fifteen heading in. She opened her purse and began to rummage inside it.

'Oh, my God!' she said loudly.

The man's eyes widened at her exclamation.

She looked at him helplessly, and the half-humorous, half-worried expression on her face was a skilful blend.

'How do you like that?' she said. 'I haven't got a *red cent.*'

He smiled uncertainly, not knowing what to do. And his hands stopped jiggling the coins.

'What in the world should I *do*? I *must* get downtown—'

'I – uh—' The man cleared his throat. 'Look, why don't I – uh—'

'Oh, would you? Could you lend me fifteen cents? I feel like such a fool—'

He was smiling now; this was anecdotal material for him. Fran didn't feel badly; she was the one doing the favour.

His hand came out of his pocket filled with silver. He plucked out a nickel and dime and handed it to her.

'Think nothing of it,' he said. The bus braked to a halt in front of them. 'You can mail it to me,' he said. 'Hah-hah. Well . . .

here's the bus—'

'Not mine,' she smiled. 'I take the Number Five. Thank you *very* much.'

'You've very welcome!' he said cheerfully, and clambered aboard his bus.

That makes your day, Pops, she thought.

A young man, who had just stepped off the departing bus, was folding a newspaper in front of her.

'Pardon me—'

'Huh?' He looked up, his pale eyes bewildered.

'I feel like such a fool, but . . .' She batted her lashes prettily. He was a very young man; he blushed. 'But I left the house without a cent. And I simply must take the next bus downtown—'

'Gosh,' he said, grinning with embarrassment. 'I know just how you feel. Here. . . .' He dug into his coat pocket. 'Only got a quarter—'

'Oh, really—'

'No no. Keep the whole thing. Happens to me all the time.' He looked at her face more closely, and seemed to realize she was older than her smile. He nodded and smiled and moved on.

'Pardon me,' she said to the elderly lady, who was peering myopically down the street. 'I feel simply terrible about this, but an awful thing has happened to me—'

'Eyah?' the old lady said.

Fran smiled tightly. 'Nothing,' she said wryly.

A slim gentleman with glasses, carrying a book under his arm, was walking slowly towards the bus stop. He blinked as she approached.

'Pardon me,' she said.

An hour later, she could have sworn that there was a blister on her right heel. Funny how simply standing at a bus stop could have done that to her foot. Why, she could walk for miles through a department store, and never . . .

Then she thought of the coins in her purse, and walked rapidly across the street. There was a drug store on the corner, and she entered one of the telephone booths and folded the doors closed.

She counted carefully.

The total was three dollars and fifteen cents. Added to the amount she had started out with, made it five-ninety-three. She sighed. She had a long way to go . . .

A man was standing outside the booth as she opened the doors.

'Pardon me,' she said automatically. 'I feel like such a fool, but I came out without a *penny*, and I have to get downto— I have to make a call.'

The man grinned feebly. 'Yeah?' he said. Then he realized what was expected of him, and his hand dove into his change pocket. 'Oh, yeah, sure,' he said. 'I gotta dime.'

'Thank you,' she said. 'Thank you very much.'

She folded the doors again, and dialled a number without depositing the coin. She talked cheerfully into the dead instrument for a moment, hung up after a musical good-bye, and smiled winningly at the man who succeeded her in the booth.

Then she went back to the bus stop.

By three o'clock, she had collected almost ten dollars more. At a quarter of four, she returned to the telephone booth for another accounting.

'Fourteen dollars and nine cents,' she said aloud.

Her finger poked into the coin-return aperture at the bottom of the telephone, and came out with a dime.

'This is my lucky day!' she laughed.

But four o'clock found her more discouraged. The crowd was growing thicker round the bus stanchion, but the increase in traffic didn't help her collect her nickels and dimes.

At four-thirty, she was still far short of her twenty-five dollar goal.

'Pardon me,' she said to a fat man with a vacant face. 'I feel like such a fool, but I seem to have left my house without any money at all. I wonder if I could impose on you to—'

'Go away,' the fat man said, regarding her balefully.

'But you don't understand,' she said. 'I was simply going to ask if you had—'

'Madam, please go away,' the fat man said.

It was her first refusal. She knew better than to argue; it wasn't worth it. But she suddenly felt stubborn.

'Look,' Fran said hotly. 'It's only fifteen cents. I mean, it's only *bus fare*—'

She felt a hand on her arm and whirled angrily.

'Pardon me, lady—'

She looked indignantly at the man whose fingers were lying so firmly on the sleeve of her dress. He was in his early thirties, and his clothes were cut with angular accents. The fat man moved away from them, and that made her even angrier.

'What do *you* want?'

The man smiled. His teeth were long, and his narrow eyes had no part in the smile.

'I think you better come with me, lady.'

'What?'

'Please. Do us both a favour and don't make a scene. What do you say?'

'I don't know what you're talking about!'

'Look, lady. I've been watching you for the past half hour. Does that make it any plainer? Now come quietly before I have to get nasty.'

A whirlpool began to churn in her empty stomach.

'Why should I come with you? Who do you think you are?'

'If you want to see the badge, I'll flash it. Only we got enough people starin' at us already. So what do you say?'

She swallowed hard. 'Yes. Of course.'

They walked away from the bus stop, his hand still on her arm, smiling like an old friend who had made a chance meeting. He didn't speak until they reached a grey sedan, parked some thirty yards from the stanchion.

He opened the door for her.

'Inside, please.'

'Look, mister, if you'll only let me explain—'

'You'll get your chance. Inside, lady.'

She climbed in. He went around to the other door and slid in beside her. They drove off, making a left at the corner.

'You don't understand,' she said pleadingly. 'I wasn't doing anything wrong. I wasn't *stealing* or anything. I was just asking, you know what I mean? You see, I'm in trouble—'

'You're in trouble all right.' He sneaked through a changing traffic light, and made another left.

She put her face in her hands and started to cry. But the well was dry; the tears wouldn't come.

'No use pullin' that one,' the man said. 'I've seen your type lots of times, lady. But I'll have to admit – I never seen that particular dodge before. How much money did you think you could make?'

'But I don't *need* much. Only a few dollars! I have to have twenty-five dollars before six o'clock. I *have* to!'

'How much did you get?'

'Not much. Honest. Only a few dollars! You wouldn't arrest me for a few dollars?'

'How much, lady?'

She opened her purse, and stared at the mound of coins at the bottom.

'I don't know exactly,' she said dully. 'Fifteen or sixteen dollars maybe. But it's not enough . . .'

The car was wheeling down a side street now, away from the busy thoroughfare, towards the warehouse section near the river.

'Please!' Fran cried. 'Don't turn me in! I'll never do it again! I was just desperate for that money—'

'How much more do you need, doll-face?'

'What?'

'To make the twenty-five?'

She looked down at her purse again. 'I don't know for sure. Another ten would do it. Maybe not even that.'

'Is that all?' he grinned.

His foot was pressing harder on the accelerator, as if he were suddenly more anxious to reach his destination. He whipped the car round corners, the wheels squealing in protest, and Fran became alarmed.

'Hey!' She looked out of the window at the strange, deserted neighbourhood. 'What is this? Are you a cop or aren't you?'

'What do you think?'

She stared at him. 'Why, you're no cop! You're not arresting me at all. . . .' She edged over to the door, one hand on the handle.

'Uh-uh,' he said. 'Don't do anything foolish; you'll just hurt yourself. Besides, doll-face, I could still call a cop. I could still tell 'em about your racket—'

'They wouldn't believe you!'

'Maybe. But why take the chance?' He took his right hand off the wheel and reached to put it round her shoulders.

'Be careful!' Fran said shrilly.

'You're not being smart, honey. You gotta have the twenty-five before six. It's almost five now. Where do you think it'll come from?'

'Let me out of here!'

'Maybe I can help, doll-face.' He pulled her to him, his eyes still on the road, his grin widening. 'If you let me—'

'No,' Fran said. 'No!'

He slowed to turn another corner, and she saw her opportunity. Her hand hit the door handle upwards, and it swung open. The man cursed and grabbed for her arm.

'Leave me alone!' she screamed, swinging the heavy, coin-laden purse at his head. It thudded against his temple. He cried out in rage, and in grabbing for her, his hand caught the sleeve of her dress ripping it. Then his other hand, heedlessly, left the steering wheel, and the car bucked like a wild horse suddenly untethered, throwing Fran against the open door and into the street.

She fell on all fours, sobbing but unhurt, and watched without horror or regret as the car hurtled over the side-walk and ploughed its nose into the stubborn red bricks of a warehouse building.

Her first thought was to run, for there was nobody on the street to see her flight. Then she remembered that her purse was still in the car, and she staggered to the wreckage to recover it.

The door was still open, and the purse was propped up against the side of the unconscious man. She didn't know if he was alive or dead, nor was the difference important to her at the moment. He was folded over the steering wheel, his arms dangling limply. Gasping she reached for her purse.

Then, the idea occurred so naturally that she went about the business of locating the man's wallet without her fingers showing any sign of nervousness. She found the billfold in the inner breast pocket of his suit. There were many bills inside, but – with an odd sense of justice – she took only ten dollars.

Fran reached Vito's barber shop at ten minutes to six. Vito started a grin, but his face changed when he saw her drawn features and soiled clothing.

'Cooney, huh? Yeah, he's in the back. Hey, Phil! A lady!'

Cooney looked at her curiously when he came out of the back room. He was in shirtsleeves, and holding a poor poker hand. He brightened when he saw her reach for the purse, and laughed at the sight of it full of coins.

'What'd you do, Mrs Holland, rob a piggy bank?'

'Count it,' she said distantly. 'Count it for me, Mr Cooney.'

They overturned the bag on the manicure table. Vito helped. When the addition was done, Cooney looked up.

'Thirty dollars and forty-six cents, Mrs Holland,' he said, smiling with satisfaction. 'You got change comin'. I'm sorry I had to go lay down the law to you the way I did. But you see, you done okay.'

She went up the apartment house stairs slowly. On the third floor, a door opened and a blonde woman, her hair heavy with curlers, looked out.

'Fran! For God's sake, where you been?'

'Shopping,' she said wearily.

'You look beat. Buy somethin' nice?'

'No. Nothing much, Lila.'

'Well, I got a hot scoop for you, kid. You won't have to make dinner tonight. You can come down and have pot luck with me if you don't feel like cookin' for yourself—'

'What do you mean?'

'You're on the town tonight, kiddo.' The blonde woman laughed. 'Ed musta called nine times this afternoon. Finally, he calls me up, thinkin' we were in here boozin' or something.'

'Ed?' She blinked at the woman.

'Yeah. He called from the office. Wanted to tell you that he wouldn't be coming home, not 'til tomorrow. He had some kind of emergency with a client, or something. Said he had to fly out to Chicago on the five o'clock plane.'

'Not coming home?' Fran said stupidly.

'Hey, snap out of it. You heard what I said. He went to Chicago. You can relax tonight, honey.'

Fran sighed, and started up the next flight. 'Thanks, Lila.'

'That's okay,' the blonde shrugged. 'Hey, you sure you're okay?'

'Yeah, I'm all right. I'm just fine.'

Upstairs, Fran unlocked her front door and went inside. The breakfast dishes in the sink looked grey in the fading light. She flung her purse on the table, and kicked off her shoes.

In the living-room, she flopped heavily into a chair and lit a cigarette. She sat in an attitude of exhaustion, staring at the hazy light outside, smoking silently.

She pulled the evening stole round her shoulders, as if the room had grown cold.

'Chicago,' she said bitterly.

Then the name meant something. It *meant* something. She stood up quickly. That was the whole secret of it, she thought. The name had to *mean* something.

She went over to the telephone and dialled the familiar number.

'Hello, is Mr Cooney there?'

Her stockinged foot tapped impatiently on the linoleum.

'Hello, Mr Cooney? Listen, this is Fran Holland. On that fourth race tomorrow. I'd like five dollars on Chicago Flyer. That's right. In the fourth race. . . .'

Born Gambler

THOMAS WALSH

Gambling fever affects people in all walks of life: Jack Haggerty, the central character in Thomas Walsh's story, is a dedicated cop – but a cop who finds himself in a quandry when he saves the life of a famous race horse trainer, Happy Ned O'Brien. For despite dire threats against gambling by his long-suffering wife, Kitty, he is unable to pass up the tips the veteran trainer gives him. And when these horses come up trumps and he starts to amass a fortune, Jack finds that his problems are only just beginning.

Thomas Walsh (1908–) is one of the most widely admired writers of this type of story in America, according to critic Dorothy B. Hughes. 'There has been no better writer of the police story than Walsh,' she said recently, 'and there has never been a better writer of the streets of New York.' (He has, in fact, already twice won the prestigious Poe award from the Mystery Writers of America.)

Irish-American Thomas Walsh began his writing career on the *Baltimore Sun*, covering police incidents. But he had always wanted to write fiction, he says, and hoped the experience would give him the authentic background for his work as well as speeding up his word-rate. 'My fiction always came out slow as molasses,' he once remarked. The assignment worked and soon he was contributing 'hard boiled' crime fiction to the legendary pulp magazine *Black Mask*, followed by more traditional crime stories for the *Saturday Evening Post*. His reputation was confirmed in 1950 when his novel, *Nightmare in Manhattan*, was filmed as *Union Station* by Rudolf Maté with William Holden and Nancy Olsen. The movie generated quite a controversy in the press for its increased use of brutality and in particular a lengthy scene where a reluctant criminal was dangled by lawmen in front of an oncoming railway train in order to extract the information they wanted from him. Notwithstanding this, Dorothy Hughes believes Thomas Walsh's book is 'still considered one of the most successful of mysteries transferred to the screen.' To date, he has written over 200 short stories and a dozen novels. As a writer, Thomas Walsh is also capable of creating good and sympathetic characters who unexpectedly find themselves in impossible situations where the law is concerned. Such is the dilemma that faces Jack Haggerty in the following story, which deserves to earn Walsh another accolade for having created a tale about a compulsive gambler that has few equals.

*

Jack Haggerty was a born gambler. He started as a small boy by shooting craps in a tenement cellar, and by playing penny-ante stud poker on a tenement rooftop. But at the age of 19, on his first visit to Belmont Park Race Track, something very bad happened to him. He played his two lucky numbers, nine and seven, and hit the daily double, both long shots, for $574.

From then on he was incurable. He loved Kitty Farrell very much, but twice their engagement was broken off. First he gambled away the money he had been saving to buy the engagement ring, and second, much more serious, he lost the $4,000, half of it hers, which had been intended as down payment for a house out on Long Island.

It took him three months to get back with Kitty that time. When aroused, she had more than her share of Irish temper, and Jack Haggerty, in true shameful fact, had to sit up and beg.

'But you just remember one thing,' Kitty warned, holding him a few moments longer at arm's length. 'The next time you place so much as a two-dollar show bet even on Spectacular Bid, it's going to be all over for you and me, Jack, and all over for good. I don't intend to live the rest of my life with a man I can't trust – and I won't do it. So will you swear to me now – never again, not as long as you live, no matter what? Just make up your mind. That's the promise you have to give me right here and right now. Will you?'

So Jack Haggerty put his hand on his heart, lifted his eyes

piously and honestly, and sincerely swore it to heaven. For two years then, promise kept, marriage accomplished, they were very happy. Kitty was a schoolteacher, and every morning after dropping her off at P. S. something-or-other, Haggerty drove on to a downtown precinct, where he was a second-grade detective under Inspector Iron Mike Birmingham. In the department there were two vastly different schools of thought concerning Iron Mike. The pro school believed he was the best police officer in the whole country, bar none. The con school believed he was the worst-tempered and most miserable human skunk that had ever drawn breath.

'But there's one thing you have to admit, anyway,' Jerry Wilson argued one day after Haggerty had been given the full treatment by Iron Mike. 'When he jumps on you, you deserve it, Haggerty, and you know damned well you do. But get in a jam, as we're all apt to sometimes, and Iron Mike will go to bat for you like he's your own father, and against anybody at all. I've seen him do it, too. So stop your complaining.'

'If he was my own father, I'd change my name,' Haggerty gritted. 'I'm going to smack him one day, and I swear it to God, Jerry, I'm going to put him flat on his back. That miserable old buzzard. That stinking, no-good—'

'All right,' Jerry said. 'But I have an idea that if you ever try anything like that, he'll put you flat on yours. He's quite a man, Iron Mike is. You'd just better watch your step.'

Which did not, of course, change Jack Haggerty's opinion. And it was even reinforced not long afterward, during a breathlessly humid July hot spell, when Haggerty gave the kiss of life to a pudgy little man who suddenly toppled over before him, on Madison Avenue and 63rd Street, with no one else but Jack Haggerty making any attempt to help out. A week or two later Haggerty was called in to Iron Mike's office and found the pudgy little man in there waiting for him, apparently sound as a dollar again. There were sincere thanks given, and a well-filled envelope extended, but Iron Mike cut that part short at once, with what Haggerty could only consider as the most vindictive and personally motivated dislike of him.

'Oh, no,' Iron Mike said. 'Nothing like that, sir. The department does not permit any monetary rewards for services performed in the line of duty, as this was. Give it back, Haggerty.'

And Haggerty froze, his lips twitching.

'Oh, it's just a little something by way of thanks,' the pudgy man said. 'And there's no one need ever find out, Inspector, but us three. Where's the harm?'

'I'm sorry, but I'm afraid not,' Iron Mike said. 'Department regulations, sir. So do what I told you, Haggerty. Pass it back.'

And Haggerty had to obey. There were more thanks and a shaking of hands all around, and then, the next morning, a phone call for Haggerty at the precinct. It was the pudgy man again.

'Still feel that there's something I ought to do for you,' he said, 'after what you did for me. I wouldn't want to get you in trouble with that sour-faced boss of yours, lad, but I still think I owe you. We might be able to do this thing another way, if you'd like. Do you ever lay a little bet on the ponies?'

'Not for quite a while,' Haggerty told him. 'Promised the wife. Besides, when I did, I never had a lot of luck, to tell you the truth.'

'Well, let's see if maybe we can't change that,' the pudgy man said. 'The next time I hear of something good going, I'll give you a ring. Jack Haggerty, isn't it?'

And later that day, talking to Jerry Wilson again, Haggerty felt the top of his head soar up like Mount Everest.

'Well, just don't forget to pass it around,' Jerry said, who also was a fancier of the sport of kings. 'You couldn't get it any straighter from the horse's mouth, Jack. You know who that guy is, don't you? Happy Ned O'Brien.'

And Happy Ned O'Brien was perhaps the leading horse trainer of his day. There was that promise to Kitty, of course – but how could she ever find out? No way in this world that Haggerty could see, and so Thursday morning, when Happy Ned called again, Haggerty went out and borrowed $300 cash at a nearby loan office, and put it all on the nose. Just this one last time, Haggerty swore to himself, and then never again. Might as well be hanged for a sheep as for a lamb, too. The hell with it! All on the nose, with Happy Ned giving the word.

And it proved to be a fairly good tip. Ramble On, Robert

almost made it. He went off at 18 to 1, led all the way around, and came in a close third, photo finish. Damn it to hell! Just another inch or two, the width of a hand – and Jack Haggerty would have had over $5,000 in cold cash to bring home to Kitty!

It was maddening. Haggerty could not forget it, and on the next Saturday, therefore, telling Kitty that he was going to take in the ball game at Yankee Stadium, for the first time in two years he drove out to Belmont Race Track. He located Happy Ned in the paddock after the second race, and while having a drink together Happy Ned marked off the rest of Haggerty's card. It was wonderful. Haggerty got four winners, one second, and one third, and floated home that night with his $300 recouped, and with $300 more ahead of the game.

After that, as Kitty saw it, he became the most devoted Yankee fan in New York City. Never missed a Saturday or Sunday at the stadium any more, and in one delirious stretch Happy Ned marked off 14 out of 17 winners for him, including one that paid $76.

On the last racing day at Belmont, all or nothing, he did even better. Happy Ned gave him a horse named Keep Foolin'! which had been Kitty's initials before he married her, Kitty Farrell, and it seemed to Haggerty that the only thing to do now, with that hunch going for him, was to keep riding the crest of the wave. So he bet the whole $6000 he was ahead by that time, putting every dollar of it on the nose. Keep Foolin' romped home in a breeze by four or five lengths, and paid off at twelve-something to two. That night, unable to believe it had really happened to him, Jack Haggerty bought an overnight bag, put more than $36,000 cash in it, and deposited the bag in his precinct locker.

He didn't know what else to do with it. He didn't dare bring it home. He knew Kitty. Even so, he had to swing her boisterously around in his arms at supper time, and smack her fanny. But he had been right about her. At once she pushed herself free, eyes flashing.

'I know that look,' she declared dangerously. 'So don't bother lying to me. You've broken your solemn promise, Jack Haggerty. You've been gambling again.'

'Me?' Haggerty said, all unjustly accused innocence, but of

course immediately discarding the story he had ready to tell about picking up an overnight bag on the subway, no identification at all, that had $36,798 inside.

Judging by the furious hot glitter in Kitty's eyes, it did not seem to be the right moment. 'No, no, hon. And when did I ever break a promise I gave you? Tell me just one time. One time, Kitty. Go ahead.'

'And I'm telling you,' Kitty said, fists on hips, eyes with a menacing dark gleam in them, 'not to bother thinking up some crazy cock-and-bull story about finding money in the street. I wouldn't care if you won eighty-six million dollars. I told you last time, and I meant it. If you won it gambling, Jack Haggerty, this marriage is over. Do you hear?'

So Haggerty, thanking his lucky stars that something had stopped him from telling her that found-on-the-subway story, kissed the lobe of her ear gently and attested his innocence to high heaven. But all that money was not a pleasure to him in the weeks that followed. It was a burden, rather, and he could not think what to do with it. At last, worried for its safety even in the precinct house, he took it home with him one night and hid it under some fishing tackle up on his closet shelf, way back, where Kitty would have no reason to go rummaging around for anything.

But even then it worried him. Every night when he got home he checked it first thing, and every morning when he got up he checked it again. What the hell could he do with it, Happy Ned being down in Florida now with his stable, and no more tips forthcoming? A bank? No. Kitty might find the bankbook. Then stocks, bonds, investments? No, again. She'd have asked questions about them, with her suspicion soon a dead certainty. And he knew Kitty, all right. If she walked out on him, as she had sworn she would . . .

Damned money, he began fretting. He had it now, more than he could ever have dreamed, but what could he do with it? He couldn't just throw it away, but if he didn't, an explanation would have to be given. What explanation? He began to sleep badly, waking up every hour with an idea that he had heard someone at the bedroom closet. One night he even got up to make sure, and Kitty stirred drowsily.

'What is it?' she said. 'What in the world are you poking around for at this time of night?'

'Oh, nothing,' Haggerty said. 'Just putting a dirty shirt in the hamper, Kit. I forgot it before. Go back to sleep.'

But he couldn't do that himself. He lay wakeful until first light, feeling a cold sweat on him. What to do? What to tell Kitty? How to get out of the thing? Nothing came to him, and soon the problem began to affect even his work.

'What's the matter with you?' Iron Mike demanded irritably one afternoon. 'What I asked you for was the Bannister report, and what you brought in to me was the file on Little Louie Boardman. What's on your mind these days? Have you trouble at home?'

'No, no,' Haggerty denied, grinning painfully. Trouble with Kitty! 'Nothing like that, Inspector. It's just – well, I'm a little confused about something.'

'Then if you get any more confused,' Iron Mike barked, 'it won't be in this office, Haggerty. I've had enough of this damned carrying on of yours. You're about as useful to me these days as a boil on the backside. You'll do your work around here, and you'll do it well and properly, or I'll get someone who can. What the hell were you thinking of? Little Louie Boardman! He's doing ten to twenty up in Sing Sing right now, you damned fool, you. Get out of my sight!'

Haggerty could have bought a diamond necklace for Kitty that Christmas, and wanted to, but he didn't dare. He could have bought a new car, or splurged on a Florida vacation for them – but how could he explain all this sudden affluence? The money became like an old man of the mountain to him. Enough for half a dozen men, and all his, but what could he do with it?

In January, not eating or sleeping right, he caught a heavy cold, and had to spend a week at home in bed. He was just getting up and around again when he read in the paper that Happy Ned had suffered another heart attack down in Florida, this time a fatal one. So Haggerty toasted his memory with a wistful nip of the Irish whiskey that was one of the presents Kitty had given him for

Christmas, and after lunch, when Jerry Wilson stopped by to see him, was well into the bottle, with nothing else to do.

Jerry had news.

'Looks like someone is watching out for you,' he said. 'This cold was the luckiest break you ever got in your life, Jack. Every Friday until now you and Ted Anderson worked as payroll guards for that department store downtown, didn't you?'

'Yeah, couple of months now,' Haggerty said. 'One of Iron Mike's big deals for me. We'd bring the paymaster around to the bank, wait till he got the payroll, and bring him back again. How's Ted?'

'No more worries,' Jerry Wilson said. 'He was shot dead today, along with Larry O'Neill, who took your place. Both of them, right through the back of the head. They didn't have a chance, even. It looks like somebody was waiting for them in that little hall closet on the eighth floor, where the offices are. Whoever it was, must have known the whole setup, time and all. He let them go by, way we figure, then eased out real quiet behind them, knocked off Ted and Larry like sitting ducks, laid the paymaster out cold, and grabbed the money. Nobody else around in the hall. Easy as pie. An inside job, of course.

'But we got one break. A girl clerk was coming up the service stairs, and right after she heard the shots this big fella comes racing down, and knocks her over. We got her at headquarters now looking at mug shots, but I don't know how much help she's going to be. You know how a witness like that is, all scared and upset.'

They were still talking it over when an Assistant Commissioner named Frank Culkin arrived, with two plainclothes detectives and a slim brown-haired girl with tear-stained dark eyes. Culkin allowed her only one step into the room, holding her arm. Then she began crying again, nodded at him, and whispered something, after which Culkin led her out. He came back alone.

Culkin was a big powerful man, with square jaws and icily cold gray eyes.

The eyes fastened on Haggerty.

'Look over the whole place here,' he ordered his men. 'And I mean all of it, remember. Smart guys like this crummy heel sometimes do the stupidest things in the world. Start with that closet.'

'Hey,' Haggerty said, a bit whiskey-befuddled. 'What's going on, Commissioner?'

Culkin walked up to the bed, bent down, and presented the icy gray eyes at a distance of three inches.

'Slimy little rat,' he grated. 'Who knew the routine better than you did? You've been on that assignment for three months. You knew the time, you knew how they went and how they came back, and you could pick your spot.'

'Hey, wait a minute,' Jerry Wilson said, getting up quickly, and looking a bit startled. 'You ain't trying to accuse Haggerty of—'

'Don't have to accuse him,' Culkin said, in a low hoarse growl. 'No need any more. The girl just identified him.'

'What?' Haggerty said, even more befuddled. 'Why, I've been in bed all week, Commissioner. Ask Dr Martin. He can tell you.'

'Don't tempt me,' Culkin said, presenting a fist, also at a distance of three inches, that was almost the size of a kitchen meatblock. 'You dirty yellow rat. Shut your mouth.'

'I will like hell,' Haggerty said, struggling up. 'You can't talk to me like that. I don't care if you are—'

'Commissioner,' one of the other men said. 'Take a look in this here bag for a minute. Packed with dough.'

And Jack Haggerty, turning his head a bit dazedly on the pillow, with Irish whiskey spilling all over his pajama top from the sudden wild start he had made, found himself gaping numbly at the overnight bag – the scrubby-looking little bag, open now, that had $36,798 cash in it . . .

They brought Haggerty downtown. They sat him in the back of a police car with one of Culkin's men on each side, and two more men up front, but during the whole trip nobody addressed so much as a word to him. There was early February dark outside, with rain falling, and Haggerty, although not usually a drinking man, would have very much liked another drop of the Irish by that time. He felt weak and even a bit dizzy after his week in bed, and he could not think straight.

It didn't seem to be really happening – Jack Haggerty not one of the hunters any more, but now one of the hunted. His world had enlarged. He kept twisting his hands in his lap, very foolishly, with the fellows on his right and left watching every move he made. The street lamps looked all blurry to him, and the people they passed, ordinary citizens going here and there on ordinary business, seemed light years distant.

Even when they got him downtown, to where the thing had happened about 11:30 that morning, they persisted with the silent treatment. They sat him on a chair in the hall outside the paymaster's office, and even the men with whom he had worked in the department avoided looking at him. He lit a cigarette, and had it slapped away by one of Culkin's assistants. After that he just sat there, head lowered miserably, fingers twisting and turning over each other just a second or two after he managed to stop them the previous time.

Culkin reappeared. Mysteriously whispered conferences with this one and that one; instructions given and obeyed; and Haggerty, wetting his lips nervously, shifting from one side to the other. He did not volunteer any information about the money. He knew how it was going to sound. Happy Ned wasn't around any more to back him up. Who was ever going to believe the thing? But what else could he tell them?

He wouldn't even have Kitty as a witness. He hadn't told Kitty. He hadn't told anyone. And he hadn't bought his $6,000 worth of win tickets from one clerk, who might possibly have remembered him even after six months, but from a lot of different ones. So his whole story had to sound ridiculous. Haggerty wouldn't have believed it himself from another man.

And of course they knew how to put the screws on. They kept him in that chair in the hall for three solid hours, and not a word spoken to him. Four o'clock, five o'clock, six o'clock – and at six Kitty would be home from work.

'Would you call the wife, Harry?' he asked one of Culkin's men at that hour. 'She's going to be worried about what happened to me. When she left this morning, I was still in bed. Let her know, will you? Just tell her I've been called down on something to Inspector Birmingham's office.'

'Yeah, sure,' Culkin's man said. 'We'll send Buffalo Bill up there with a special message by Pony Express. We're all real worried about how she'll feel, and about you. Then you want him to drop off a message to Mrs Anderson, and Mrs O'Neill? Right? Anything you say, Haggerty. Just sit there and keep your stinking mouth shut. Men you worked with!'

But at 6:20 Culkin opened the door to the paymaster's office and beckoned. Inside, a man stood grimly, arms folded, on each side of Haggerty's chair, while Culkin, sitting behind the desk, riffled through a looseleaf notebook. Haggerty knew what they were doing – building up the pressure – but it did not help him at all to know the procedure. He had to wipe sweat from his mouth, and wipe it again and again. It was at least ten minutes before Culkin finished with the notebook and put it aside.

'First, then,' Culkin began, his eyes boring into Haggerty's skull like steel drills. 'Just a little matter of $36,798 in cash, and in your bedroom closet at home, Haggerty. Where did you get that money? How do you account for it?'

'Found it in the street,' one of the men said.

'No, no,' the other one said. 'His own private little piggy bank, Walter. Drop a nickel or a dime in every so often and you'd be surprised how quick it adds up. Right, Haggerty?'

Iron Mike came in. He didn't look at Haggerty. At the desk he and Culkin murmured together, and Iron Mike studied the notebook.

He was a wiry man of perhaps 50, with hair beginning to gray and a hard solid mouth. When he had finished with the notebook, still without looking at Haggerty, he scratched his cheekbone.

'How much money was taken?' he asked Culkin.

'About $240,000,' Culkin said. 'I'd say if he did it alone, and he could have, the rest of it we just haven't found in the apartment yet, or else he's got it hidden someplace else. Maybe he had someone waiting for him in the getaway car downstairs and they split it up right there. The two possible answers, I'd say. Well, Haggerty? Where did you get all that money? Mind telling us?'

And Haggerty did exactly the wrong thing. He was still groping desperately for an answer, and unable to find one. He took too long to explain it, much too long. His hands twisted, and he felt his eyes jerk miserably from one office wall to the other.

'I won it,' he said.

'Oh?' Culkin said. 'Very interesting. Then who did you win it from? When? Where? How?'

'I can swear it to God,' Haggerty pleaded, but without convincing even himself. 'And the Inspector can back me up on that. I won it through Happy Ned O'Brien, Inspector. Remember last summer, when he wanted to give me some money for the kiss of life I brought him back with, and you told him I couldn't take it? He started passing me tips on the horses. That's how I won it. You can ask Jerry Wilson. All of us bet on it together the first time.'

So they called Jerry Wilson in. 'Well, yeah, the first time,' Jerry Wilson said. 'But it ran out. That's all I know.'

'Sure, it did,' Haggerty said, sweating even more now. 'Only I lost $300 on it, and it almost came in, so I figured if he could give me one tip as good as that, maybe he could give me some others. So I went out to Belmont every Saturday and Sunday, when I was off, and looked him up, and had him mark my card. One day he gave me seven winners out of nine. One day he gave me six out of nine. So after a couple of months—'

'How about nine out of nine?' Culkin said, lips curling. 'Or ten out of nine. Wilson's a good friend of yours. But did you ever let him in on the thing?'

'Well, no,' Haggerty had to admit. 'He was sore as hell when the first one lost and told me not to bother him again. Besides that, I used to go out alone to the track, and lay my bets alone. They were all just on that day's card, Commissioner. I didn't have no way to pass it around.'

'Of course. Didn't have time,' Culkin nodded, speaking out of the side of his mouth to Iron Mike. 'So just since this last summer, all by yourself, you beat the game for over $36,000? What did your wife think? Did you let her in on it?'

'Didn't want me to bet,' Haggerty muttered, avoiding all the eyes on him. 'Said she'd leave me if I ever did it again. That's why I had the money hidden away. I didn't know what the hell to do with it. You don't know Kit. Once she says something—'

'Are you trying to tell us that not even your wife knew?' Iron Mike put in. 'Your own wife?'

Haggerty looked down and found his two hands twining worse than ever.

'Nobody knew,' he burst out. 'I was afraid, I tell you. Afraid to put it in the bank, or buy stocks, or anything. She might have found out then. It's the truth, Inspector. I wish I'd never seen that damn money!'

'Yes,' Culkin said. 'I imagine you do – now, anyway. But let's look at the other side of the thing. One, you knew the procedure that was followed here every payday. Two, this morning you were sick in bed, or pretended to be. Three, there was no one in the apartment, so you could have got up, come down here with your friend the getaway driver, or in a cab, maybe, and been home again by twelve noon. Four, the girl identified you. Five, the $36,000 in cash you had – just a few dollars' spending money, eh? No good, Haggerty. You can save us and yourself a lot of trouble by admitting the thing here and now.'

'Who's the girl?' Iron Mike asked. So she was brought in.

'I think so,' she said. 'Yes, I'm sure. He had on a gray overcoat and a gray hat.'

'Another point,' Culkin said. 'Do you have a gray overcoat and a gray hat, Haggerty?'

'Do you?' Haggerty shot back. 'Don't about three million guys in New York City?'

'Just moderate your tone,' Iron Mike ordered. 'That does you no good at all, Haggerty. What did the paymaster see?'

They brought in the paymaster. He was a timid and edgy little man named Knowlton, and there was a white patch of bandage over his right ear.

'Everything was just the same as usual,' he told Culkin. 'Or at least until we got off the elevator up here on the eighth floor. Then we walked past the closet door, and the next thing I know I hear two shots. I was just starting to turn around when I got hit.'

'Who hit you?' Culkin said. 'This fellow?'

'Might have been,' Knowlton said. 'His build, anyway. Just got a flash of him, though – and low down, the way I was ducking. Black shoes, and dark-blue or black pants. That's all I'm sure of.'

'You were given no warning at all?' Iron Mike wanted to know. 'You heard nothing but the two shots?'

'Well, maybe I heard the closet door come open,' Knowlton said shakily. 'Kind of a creak, you know. I complained yesterday about it. But then everything happened so fast—'

'Of course,' Culkin said. 'It had to. You all knew him. So if you got even one quick look at who it was – that's why he had to kill Anderson and O'Neill, Birmingham. He was taking no chances.'

'Yes, plain enough,' Iron Mike said. 'Unfortunately. Well, that's it I guess. I think you've got everything you need, Commissioner.'

'Inspector,' Haggerty said, jumping up. Like your own father, he remembered Jerry Wilson telling him; stand right up there for any of his people who ever got in a jam, and against anybody, even as important a man as Frank Culkin. 'I'm telling you God's truth! I did win that money. And I was afraid to tell Kit about it.'

Iron Mike walked up to him, slapped him across the mouth full force, and slapped him again.

'Two men who worked with you,' he said savagely. 'Two decent men. You low cowardly scut, you. You rotten, cringing – take him in, Commissioner. He's your man.'

They handcuffed Haggerty. They brought him down in the elevator to the basement garage, and there they put him into a car. Two more of Culkin's men sat with him, one on each side.

'And just try making a break for it,' one of them suggested. 'Just try, Haggerty. Nothing I'd like better. I'd give you one step, then put three bullets into the back of your head, the way you did this morning, just to make sure. I don't think you have a chance in hell of getting away with this, but if you do you won't live long. Take my word, Haggerty. Anderson and O'Neill had a lot of friends, a hell of a lot. You wait and see.'

Haggerty sat crouched between them. Kit, Kit . . . That was all he could think of. In the dark garage figures moved, then stopped moving.

'What are we waiting for?' the other Culkin man asked.

'Don't know,' his partner said. 'Iron Mike told us to. He was talking to the maintenance man up in the hall when I came down, and he said sit in the car and wait for him. Guess we have to.'

They waited about 20 minutes. Everything dark, hushed, shadowy; square concrete pillars, empty cars, no one moving. It seemed to Haggerty that he couldn't feel anything, or even think normally. Time after time he would find himself squeezing his eyes shut or turning his head from right to left quickly, but nothing helped. Oh, Kit. Oh, Kit, Kit . . .

Then the elevator came down and yellow light splotched out into the garage. Iron Mike, Culkin, some others. After that the elevator doors closed and everything got dark again. Silence all around; deep, beating silence; not a sound, not a movement. It lasted perhaps ten minutes. Then the elevator door opened again.

The girl got off it this time carrying a gift box, and Knowlton the paymaster, and two or three other men. Good nights were said, and the other people got into a car to the left of the one in which Haggerty was sitting. Knowlton and the girl turned right, and Knowlton unlocked the door of a black sedan. The light came on, and when it did, Iron Mike and Culkin appeared out of the shadows. Other men circled in around the car.

'Just another question,' Iron Mike said, bending over on the driver's side. 'But only the one, sir. What does your lady friend have in that gift package?'

'You stupid fool,' Iron Mike said, regarding Haggerty with disdain up in the street. 'You always were, and I suppose you always will be. But two things struck me right away, since you want to know. First, if you had to shoot down Anderson and O'Neill like that, just because they'd have recognized you, there was another fellow present who'd have had to do the same thing because they'd have recognized him, too. Now who would that be, Haggerty?'

'Knowlton,' Haggerty said. 'Of course. Now I see it.'

'Yes, now,' Iron Mike said. 'How very open and shut it is to you after everything is explained. You haven't got the brains of a bat, Haggerty. Then I talked to the maintenance man, and he told me that he'd oiled the hinges on that closet door upstairs at eleven ten this morning, while they were all out at the bank getting the payroll money. And you might remember that when I pressed Knowlton upstairs, he admitted that he'd had a bit of warning, to cover himself up. He said that he'd heard the closet door squeak when it opened. But it didn't squeak any more, because I tried it myself. It had been oiled, which Knowlton didn't know. He was lying about it. Why? That's when I decided to give you those two slaps across the mouth, Haggerty. Injured your manly pride, did they?'

'I couldn't believe it,' Haggerty said. 'Turning on me like that. Acting like you were sure I was the one.'

'Didn't I have to?' Iron Mike demanded irritably. 'Where the hell are your brains? Knowlton had to be convinced, don't you see, that we all thought the case was decided and settled, and that you were the killer. Once he believed that, he might turn cocky enough to drop himself right into our hands, and he did.

'There wasn't much time this morning, you know. I'd say he got a step back of Anderson and O'Neill, shot them both, then ran over to the stairs door and threw the bag with the payroll in it down to the girl, who was all ready and waiting. Then he ran back, smashed his head into the wall to make it look good and pretended to be knocked cold when somebody ran out to see what the shots were for.

'Well, if I was right, Haggerty, if that was the answer, then neither he nor the girl had a chance to get away with the money this morning. They had to hide it somewhere, and this department store is a damned big building, remember. It would have taken us a full week to go over every nook and cranny of it, every counter and storage room, and God knows if they couldn't have got someone else to carry off the money for them, meanwhile. Probably five thousand people a day walk out of a store like this carrying packages with them. There would be just no way to check every one of them.

'But it seemed to me that there was a better chance. Convince Knowlton that we were positive it was you, and that no one had even a suspicion of him, and I hoped that he and the girl might be so crazy wild to get their hands on the money once and for all, they might decide to slip it out tonight, with nothing more to worry about from their viewpoint. Which they did – but unfortunately found us down in the garage waiting for them. And that's it, Haggerty. Any more questions from you?'

'I guess only one,' Haggerty said, moving after him to a taxicab at the curb. 'What the hell am I going to tell Kitty, Inspector?'

'Try the truth,' Iron Mike bawled back at him through the cab window. 'And she knows it already, from what Culkin's men must have put her through by now. I hear she's all by herself at home, crying her eyes out, so there'll never be a better time for you. She isn't worried any more about your broken promise, you great big idiot. The only thing she's afraid of now is that she's lost you forever. But no girl ever born could leave a fellow like you all alone and defenseless in this hard cruel world. So brace yourself, Haggerty, and let me get home to my supper, damn it. I don't know why I even bothered to come over here tonight.'

'I know,' Haggerty said, a humble and foolish grin on his lips. 'Jerry Wilson told me. I'm one of your men, Inspector.'

'Arrgh,' Iron Mike grunted, looking out at him in an altogether disgusted fashion, and then waving the driver on.

And he was right about Kitty, too. The moment Jack Haggerty unlocked his apartment door that night, she jumped up off the couch, screamed his name widly, screamed it again – and darted as true and straight into his arms as a homing pigeon.

The Later Edition

VICTOR BRIDGES

All gamblers know the temptation to go for the big win, to stake everything on one horse in a particular race. This is the theme of the next two stories, but by authors from very different backgrounds though with close affinities to the settings of the events they describe.

Victor Bridges (1887–1967), the author of the first story, was a bank clerk with little practical experience of the world of horse racing; Mark Daniel who follows him is the son of a trainer and grew up in the very heart of the world of steeplechasing. Bridges actually began to write while employed in a London bank and, after contributing to several magazines, broke into the crime and mystery genre with his first book, *The Man From Nowhere*, published in 1913. Several successes followed, including *A Rogue By Compulsion* (1915) and *Mr Lyndon at Liberty* (1915), which were reprinted in America and allowed him to give up banking and write full time. For almost fifty years thereafter Bridges published a new crime novel virtually every year, including a very popular series in the forties and fifties entitled *The Man Who . . .*

Not surprisingly, Victor Bridges drew on his experience in the world of banking for several of these thrillers, as well as a number of short stories. Notable amongst these is 'The Later Edition', in which bank clerk George Barton plots to use some of his bank's money in order to be able to back a sure-fire winner and escape from his life of drudgery. Then fate plays a hand in his fraud with the most unexpected result. The authentic tone of this story, which first appeared in the *Strand Magazine* in 1936, is such that the reader might well wonder whether the author himself didn't nurse ideas of a similar scheme. Or at least knew someone who *did . . .*

*

George Barton pushed open the swinging doors, and came into the bank. Several people were standing at the counter – a couple of tradesmen, an old lady, an errand boy – while the cashier, an elderly, harassed-looking man, was counting over a large heap of silver, which one of the former had just paid in. He looked up as Barton entered, and nodded in the direction of the other customers. Barton lifted the slab that led through into the office, and walking up to a side door with a frosted-glass panel, opened it, and hung up his hat upon a peg inside. Then he came to the counter, and began to attend to the people who were waiting. His work was characterized by a mechanical swiftness noticeably absent in the movements of his elderly *confrère*; so by the time that the latter had satisfied himself that the pile of silver in front of him corresponded with the amount on the slip, Barton had settled the requirements of the remaining customers. The cashier made an entry in his 'scroll', filled the credit slip, and then, after carefully wiping his pen and laying it on the desk, turned to Barton.

'I am going to lunch now,' he said. 'If you have time, you might put a few of these entries through' – he pointed to a twisted-up heap of cheques and credit slips under a paper-weight. 'We have been rather busy while you were out,' he added.

'All right,' answered Barton, without looking up from the book in which he was writing.

For the next quarter of an hour the bank was practically deserted; the silence only being broken by the scratching of pens, or an occasional sigh from one of the two junior clerks, who were working at a desk behind. Outside, the world was bathed in the golden sunshine of a perfect June day; but within, it was merely another hot afternoon dragging on its ordinary monotonous round. Barton soon entered up the pile of arrears bequeathed him by his companion, and added up the latter's scroll for him. One of the senior clerks came in from the manager's room with a pile of papers, threw them down on the desk, and sauntered up to where he was working.

'How goes it?' asked the newcomer, taking out a penknife and beginning to clean his nails.

'All through, up to date,' said Barton. 'Do you want to get out early?'

'Well, I do rather, if you can manage it.' He glanced over the scrolls. 'I see you have been giving Weary Willy a hand.'

Barton smiled. 'You would be here till six if I didn't. It is quite time the poor old chap got his pension.'

'They ought to make you cashier,' said the other. 'Furze wants to go at the end of the year, if they will let him. Why don't you apply for it?'

Barton glanced round to see if they were overheard, and, speaking in a lower voice answered: 'That is just what I did last week. The manager – he is a little brick, Blackmore – sent up a very strong letter urging my fitness, and all that sort of thing; but the directors wrote back and said I was too young. Rather sickening wasn't it?'

'Why don't you go in for something else?' asked his companion. 'With your brains you are wasted in a bank. Any fool can do this sort of thing.'

Barton flushed slightly. He was twenty-one, and the compliment was obviously genuine. 'It is all very well, Steele,' he said; 'but what can I do? I haven't got a halfpenny in the world, and I have had to keep myself ever since I entered this confounded hole. I shan't stay in it a minute longer than I can help, but at present—' he shrugged his shoulders.

'It is a bit off, isn't it?' agreed Steele sympathetically. 'I should leave myself, if I could do anything else. By the way, do you want a tip for the Manchester Cup?'

'Well, that's curious!' said Barton. 'You are the second today.'

'Second what?'

'Why, I have just had a letter from a man, offering to give me a tip. What's yours?'

' "Kildonen." It's a dead cert. What's yours?'

'I don't know till this evening. The whole thing is rather quaint. The other night I was coming down Shaftesbury Avenue very late, when I saw a fellow being set on by two or three rough-looking brutes, so I ran across to lend him a hand. He was very grateful, and turned out to be McFadden, the tipster – you know, the chap who is always advertising in the sporting papers. Well, he insisted on taking my name and address, and this morning I got a letter from him asking me to dine at the Troc. He said he could put me on to a good thing for the Manchester Cup.'

'You back "Kildonen",' said Steele sceptically. 'I got it straight from my brother, who is a pal of the trainer. Ten to one McFadden will put you on to some rotter.'

'We shall see,' answered Barton, getting up to attend to a customer who had just come in. 'At all events, I will let you know what he says.'

Barton lit his cigar and, leaning back in his comfortable seat, looked round the big restaurant with a quiet satisfaction born of an excellent dinner, a bottle of good champagne, and a really first-class Larranaga. Barton's companion, a big, sunburnt man, with a large moustache, twinkling black eyes, and a face heavily pitted with the remnants of smallpox, waited until the men serving liqueurs and coffee had moved on to the next table, and then resumed the conversation.

'I didn't want those chaps to get hold of what I was saying,' he explained; 'they know me, and it would be all over London to-morrow.'

Barton leaned slightly across the table towards him, and lowering his voice, McFadden continued: 'It's the chance of a lifetime. Not a soul witnessed the trial except Rainsford and Burch, and you can trust them to keep it dark. They want the money; besides, Rainsford is the sort of man who would cut his throat rather than give away a tip; and I know Burch has told no one but myself. Even Relf, the jockey, thinks that he was carrying about ten pounds less than he was; so you can take it from me that, with the exception of us four, there isn't a living soul who has an idea of what "Mountain Lady" can do. She will start at twenty to one, and unless she is left at the post or drops dead on the course, nothing will get near her. Why, just think, man, according to the trial, that would put "Night-jar" in at about eight stone four; while, as a matter of fact, he would be carrying nine stone, and then be a hot favourite. You must have something on – something worth winning. If you can beg or borrow "a

monkey" for a couple of days, you are made for life. I could get it
on for you with Cook at twenty to one, but he would want to see
the cash first, and I have none to spare at present, or I would do it
for you. It means simply picking up ten thousand. I am sticking on
every penny I can spare myself. We shall have to back to win for
there won't be more than six runners, but it's as safe as the Bank
of England.' His face was flushed with excitement as he finished.
Picking up his glass of liqueur, he drained it at a gulp.

Barton had listened intently; his eyes had never left McFadden's face, and he felt sure that the man had been telling him what
he at all events believed to be the truth. 'It is very kind of you to
have given me the tip,' he said, 'and such an excellent dinner into
the bargain.'

'Bosh!' returned the other shortly. 'Waiter! two more liqueur
brandies. Look here, youngster, you acted like a gentleman the
other night – got me out of a damned tight place – and I never
forget a pal.'

Barton was silent for a moment. 'What about "Kildonen"?' he
asked.

McFadden laughed. 'Oh, I know the stable are sweet on him,
but he hasn't a dog's chance against "Mountain Lady" at the
weights. Besides, he is a clumsy, bad-tempered brute at the best of
times. What I have told you is gospel truth, sonny; and if you like
to send me anything to my office, I'll shove it on for you. Of
course, do the business yourself if you prefer it; but, in case you
wanted a big deal, I thought you might have some trouble in
getting it on – safe?'

Barton's face was, perhaps, a little paler than usual, but,
beyond that, there was no trace of any particular emotion in his
appearance or manner to betray the sudden thought that had
flashed across his mind while McFadden was speaking. He sipped
the second liqueur which the waiter had just put down in front of
him, knocked the ash off his cigar, and then, leaning across the
table again towards his companion, answered quietly: 'I believe
what you tell me, and I am very grateful to you for letting me
know. It is just possible I might be able to borrow a few hundreds;
but I should have to spin some other yarn about it. Now, if I were

to send you something in notes first post Friday morning, could you let me have them back, if all goes well, on Friday night?'

'Why, of course! Cook will pay up Saturday. As long as he knows the cash is there, he wouldn't want it till after the race, even if we were to go down. There is nothing dead certain, but this is just as near to it as you can get. It's worth risking something, or I wouldn't put you on to it. I have been messing about with the turf for twenty years, and it's the best thing I ever struck.' He took out his watch, and looked at the time. 'I must be off,' he added; 'I have to meet a man at half-past. You think it over, and do just what you like; only don't talk about it.'

He paid the bill, tipping the waiter generously, and they walked upstairs. At the door he turned to Barton. 'I have dealt with you straight,' he said; 'you did me a good turn, and I always pay my debts when I can.'

Barton nodded, and held out his hand. 'If I can raise the money, I will ask you to put it on for me. In any case – thank you.'

Through the warm starlit night Barton walked home to his rooms in Bloomsbury. His face was pale and drawn, and he walked fast, staring straight in front of him. A fierce excitement was tingling in his blood; his brain and conscience seemed to be dancing together in a mad riot of contradictions. Through it all McFadden's words leaped out in letters of fire: 'It means simply picking up ten thousand.' He kept on repeating the sentence to himself. Ten thousand pounds! Was there anything impossible in the world with such a sum? A hundred paths, leading up the hills of power and fame, opened out suddenly before his chained ambition. He walked on quickly, unsteadily, his hands clenched, his eyes shining.

He turned into Burton Crescent, and stopped before a dark, untidy-looking house that stared forlornly on the ill-kept square in front. He had lived here for the last two years, a small bedroom on the third floor being the exact amount of luxury permitted him by his salary. The hall was in total blackness – no reckless jet of blue wasted on the hall burners in Burton Crescent – but experience had taught Barton to dispense with such facilities. He made his way upstairs, stumbling over a sleeping cat, that fled away into the darkness with a horrible scream. His room was poorly furnished, but saved from the usual deadly barrenness of such apartments by two large shelves crowded with books, a fine engraving of Burne-Jones' *King Cophetua*, and one or two cheaper reproductions of well-known pictures. He locked the door behind him, and turned up the gas.

He began to feel a little more collected. This excitement was contemptible – the wine must have gone to his head. He poured himself out a glass of water, and drank it off. The thing had to be faced here and now, in all its radiant possibilities, in all its cold reality. He sat down in the frayed arm-chair and filled his pipe with trembling fingers. McFadden had spoken the truth, of that he felt certain. The man might have been deceived, but Barton doubted it. He was no callow novice at the game to suck in an ordinary turf lie with such conviction. Besides, he had hinted that Burch had reasons for not deceiving him. Then there was the chance that the trainer himself had been mistaken; such a thing might happen, and, as McFadden himself had said, nothing was certain, the mare might be left at the post. He lit his pipe and began to smoke quickly, trying to see the thing in its right proportions. On the one hand, years of drudgery at the bank, mean sordid poverty, surroundings such as these – he looked round and shuddered – to lead to what? Who could tell? He knew that he had ability, but life was such a ghastly lottery. Handicapped as he was, without money or friends, what more likely than that he should share the fate of others, fully as able and ambitious as himself – men who had eaten out their hearts in the labour and disappointment of existence, while life floated past on golden wings mocking and out of reach? And on the other hand, a deliberate crime, a temporary theft; and then, either life itself, full-blooded, working, joyous life with success and fame to light the road, or – he paused a moment – death. There was no other alternative.

He got up and crossed the room to the battered deal dressing-table. Pulling open the drawer, he took out a small revolver, almost the sole legacy of his father, a cashiered major in the Army. Well, why not? His life was his own, there was no one dependent on him, no one who would ever regret his death, except, perhaps, the fellows at the office. If he chose to cast it into the scale against destiny, who had the right to question him?

He put back the revolver and paced slowly up and down the room. It would be so easy in his position at the bank. He had a perfectly free access to the cash, and was himself responsible for what he used at the counter. It was checked sometimes by the manager, but never on Friday or Saturday; on those days Blackmore went away early to play golf. He could take five hundred pounds on Thursday night, and, if he won, replace the same notes on Saturday morning. If he lost – well, there would be a headline for the papers, and another vacancy for a head clerk in the bank. It was stealing, of course; sophistry had no place in his mental equipment. Up till now he had never done a dishonourable action. The terrible example of his father, and an instinctive dislike to anything underhand, had kept him straight. For a moment he hesitated – then suddenly some words he had read in a book a few evenings before flashed into his mind. He repeated them with a sort of desperate mockery:

> 'He either fears his fate too much,
> Or his deserts are small,
> Who dare not put it to the touch,
> To win or lose it all.'

Yes – Yes. That was best. 'To win or lose it all.' He whispered the last line over again; and knew that he had decided.

'You have made a mistake', said Steele, 'and you will know it in another twenty minutes. Did you put much on?'

Barton smiled. 'Not enough to get excited about.'

'I stuck a quid on "Kildonen", so I shall be a bit sick if he goes down.'

'Yes that's a good deal to lose,' said Barton calmly. 'I have to go around now to see Johnstone and Driver for Blackmore. I shall be back in about half an hour, and I will bring a paper in with me. You will be sorry you did not take my tip when you see the result – "Kildonen" first, "Mountain Lady" nowhere. Lucky for you you didn't plunge.'

'It would have been rather foolish, wouldn't it?'

'You look a bit off colour to-day, somehow,' said Steele, tying up some deeds which he was taking to the lawyers.

'I didn't sleep much last night. I expect I want my holiday.'

'Like the rest of us. Two weeks in the year are no good to anyone. Well, so long! Prepare for a disappointment when you see the paper.'

'I am quite ready,' answered Barton.

His fellow clerk laughed, and picking up his parcel of deeds, passed out of the office. As the swing-door closed behind him, Barton suddenly realized that they might never meet again. Steele had been one of his few friends – a pleasant good-natured fellow, who had always treated him with a faint touch of deference; an unconscious tribute that some young men are always ready to pay to a stronger or keener intelligence than their own. Steele would be sorry if things went wrong. He was, perhaps, the only one who would think of him in future with anything but contempt.

Three o'clock! Another twenty minutes. They were in the paddock now. Relf would be examining his saddle. He could picture the scene; the crush round the favourite. No doubt 'Mountain Lady'—

Some customers came in, and he got up to attend to them mechanically, adding up the amounts, or paying out what was required, without the least hesitation or inaccuracy. He was scarcely conscious of what he was doing; it was like a strange dream. He felt as if he was looking on at the tragedy of his own life. How long had it been? Twenty-two hours! He laughed to himself. What fool invented the clock? Last night alone had been a lifetime. There had been no time to-day. It had drifted past in a dull trance. After hours of torture he had woken to a state of mental exhaustion, in which thought at last was numbed and powerless.

Five minutes more! A tradesman was talking to him about the weather, as he examined the endorsements on the cheques, and counted silver and notes into little separate heaps. 'Yes, it was beautiful: a regular summer day. It made one want to be outside, instead of being stuffed up in an office. However, business was business, of course,' A quarter-past. God – how the moments dragged! They were lining up, perhaps. They might even have started. In a quarter of an hour he might be dead. How those chattering fools would start if they knew!

There was a sudden lull in the work. Four or five customers went out almost together, and for a little while the office was empty. A strange apathy settled down like a mist over Barton's mind. It was all over now. The paper would be out in a few minutes.

He went on writing, slowly, correctly. He felt as though he were being stifled. Suddenly, in the distance, he heard the shrill cry of a paper-boy: 'Winner, paiper; Cup winner!' Something seemed to snap in his brain. A deadly calm succeeded the formless emotions that had been racking him. He laid down his pen, and getting up from his seat, walked to the cashier's desk.

'I'm going out for a moment, Mr Furze,' he said.

The cashier nodded. 'Don't be longer than you can help. We shall be busy again in a minute.'

'I shall be back almost immediately,' answered Barton.

By the time he reached the street, the boy was quite close, a ragged little urchin, darting from one side of the road to the other in pursuit of customers. Barton held up his hand, and the boy rushed across to him.

'Paiper, sir; winner, sir!' He held one out and Barton took it, giving him a shilling.

'You can keep the change,' he said

With a quick 'Thankee sir', the lad ran on. Barton stepped back to the wall and opened the paper. In the blank space reserved for stop-press news was the single word 'Kildonen'. It was in blue ink, stamped in by a local agent. Barton stared at it for a moment, and then laughed. So he had lost. He felt no particular emotion – just a vague disappointment. Remorse and fear left him untouched. He had played with fate and been beaten; all that now remained was to pay the price.

He crossed the road to a public-house opposite, and, going into the saloon bar, ordered a glass of brandy. A man who was sitting in the corner saw the newspaper in his hand.

'What's won the Cup, guv'nor?' he asked.

' "Kildonen",' answered Barton. 'You can have the paper if you like. I have done with it,' he found himself speaking in a perfectly level, disinterested voice.

Mixing a little water with the brandy, he drank it off, and walked back to the office. As he again crossed the road, a man raced past him on a motor-bicycle with a huge pile of newspapers strapped behind him. The Fleet Street edition was evidently down now; he could hear the boy's shouting higher and higher up the road. He hesitated a moment; it would be rather interesting to see if 'Mountain Lady' had been in the first three. Then he shrugged his shoulders, and walked on. After all, what did it matter?

There were no customers in the office. He passed through the side door into the small ante-room where the staff kept their coats and hats. From here a staircase led down into the strong-room. He knew that, if he shut the iron door below, the sound of the shot could scarcely reach the bank. It was more pleasant to die without being interrupted.

He walked downstairs quickly, and turned on the electric light that illuminated the big safe. Taking out his revolver, he tested the trigger before putting in a couple of cartridges.

Now everything was ready. There was no time to lose, for Furze would probably be sending down for him in a minute. He felt sorry for the clerk who would come to fetch him. He caught hold of the big, brass handle, and was just swinging the heavy metal slab into its place, when he heard the door open and someone running down the stairs. For an instant he faltered, and then slipping the revolver into his pocket, pushed back the door.

'Barton! Barton!' It was Steele's voice. He rushed into the safe with a paper in his hand. 'Isn't it too rotten?' he exclaimed, flinging it down on the slab.

'I should have thought you would have been pleased,' answered Barton wearily.

'Oh, I am glad for your sake, of course; but, under the circumstances, it's a bit tough on me, damn it all.'

'What do you mean?' Barton cried hoarsely.

'Haven't you heard?' shouted Steele. ' "Kildonen's" disqualified – look!' He thrust the paper into Barton's hands.

With a savage effort the latter choked back a deadly faintness that almost overpowered him, and through the dim mist that swam before his eyes, read the lines that Steele pointed out:

MANCHESTER CUP

KILDONEN 4.1	1
MOUNTAIN LADY 20.1	2
ROSE CROWN 7.4	3
SIR CHARLES 11.2	0

Also ran, Barcup and Flagstaff.

'Kildonen' was disqualified for bumping, and the race awarded to 'Mountain Lady'.

The paper slipped from Barton's fingers. If Steele had not caught him he would have fallen himself.

'What's the matter, old chap? Are you ill? I never thought you would take it like this. You hadn't much on, had you? Let me get you a glass of water.' The astonished clerk helped Barton to a stone slab, where he sat for a minute with his eyes shut.

Then he opened them and smiled. 'I am all right now, Steele. I – I have been feeling a bit ill this afternoon.'

Two and a Half Per Cent

MARK DANIEL

Chris Lauderdale, the central figure in this story, has a rather more intimate knowledge of the world of horse racing than George Barton, just as his need for a big win is even more critical: the VAT man is on his trail for unpaid bills. As a restaurateur by profession and steeplechaser by inclination, Chris's salvation lies in riding his horse Mirabelle to victory when heavily backed. Then by selling the horse which he bought for 9,000 guineas while business was good, he hopes to satisfy the Inland Revenue and save his restaurant. But even the best laid plans can be upset by the unforeseen where gambling is concerned.

Author Mark Daniels is the latest star to rise in the racing fiction firmament, and like Dick Francis and John Francome brings the insight of a lifetime's association with the sport to his stories. In fact, in the case of this story he offers a double helping of knowledge because for a time he worked as a chef in several restaurants in England, France and Italy before starting his career as a novelist. Now published by the same company as Dick Francis, Mark shot to public attention with his first racing thriller, *The Devil To Pay* (1992), an engrossing tale about a jockey, Nick Storr, who has his hopes of riding his father's horse to victory in the Cheltenham Gold Cup inexplicably dashed and then finds himself in a very dangerous game that implicates the parent he has worshipped all of his life.

Daniel's own father was, in fact, a leading trainer and the boy grew up in the heart of the steeplechasing world at Lambourn in Berkshire. He was educated at Ampleforth College and Peter-house, Cambridge, followed by a period as a 'guest' of Her Majesty at HM Prison, Ashwell – 'for handling stolen antiquarian books', he admits with engaging honesty in the blurbs on his books. Aside from the period as a chef, Daniel was also the private tutor to the son of an Italian cabinet minister and then began writing novels for children and teenagers which preceeded the best-selling racing thrillers that have now made him a familiar name on bookstalls everywhere. He followed *The Devil To Pay* with *Pity The Sinner* (1993), *Sleek Bodies* (1994) and *A Killing Joke* (1995). Since his success, Daniel has settled in Ireland, where he is able to pursue his love of oysters, fly-fishing and racing. 'Two and a Half Per Cent' is his first short story and is also making its first appearance in book form in this collection.

*

Chris Lauderdale leaned forward and clicked his tongue. Beneath him, Mirabelle bounded, and suddenly the cool breeze was stiff.

The sounds dropped away. The burble of the crowd became a distant scratching, like an old record. Now there was only the steady tattoo of hooves as they cleaved the turf, the clink of harness, the creak of leather, the horse's eager puffing as she cantered out into the country. She wanted to do more than canter. She had seen the horses and riders up ahead. She objected to the restraint. She struck out with her off forefoot, and her head rocked against the hold of the bit, but Chris drew the reins in taut beneath his crotch. He crooned, 'Easy girl. Not yet.'

It felt good to be out here, on his own, engaged in straight competition rather than the mucky, devious dispiriting competition of business. Oh, racing was mucky, all right. On a day like today, Chris could count on coming home well spattered, but that sort of dirt was clean.

Racing was dangerous, too. Better riders than he had broken their necks at these plain fences and open ditches, but at least it was a danger of his choosing, at least he was among friends, at least he was in the open air . . .

He would miss all this.

And he was on the horse that he loved. He would miss her too.

'Mirabelle, a grey mare, six years old, by The Parson out of Millamant . . .' He remembered the auctioneer's summation, remembered how he had had to sit on his hands to prevent himself from bidding too soon, remembered the choking sensation when at last he had raised his catalogue, the weakness in his knees when he had realised that she was his. He had just spent 9,000 guineas on a racehorse. She had been his first and his greatest indulgence, back then when the restaurant was fashionable and the tills were ringing like the telephones.

He had always loved riding, had thought that she would get him out of the kitchen, keep him fit, maybe win a point-to-point or two. She had proved better than that.

She had had to learn, of course. He remembered the early falls, caused in equal measure by her recklessness and his ineptitude. They had learned together. Three times now, Mirabelle had borne him into the winner's enclosure.

And now she must go.

It was not Sarah's fault. Damn it, he had been trying to skimp by asking her to do the accounts in the first place, and, what with the children and the restaurant, she had been too hard-pressed. She had noticed, of course, that VAT had been upped by two and a half per cent. It just slipped her mind when she was doing the books late at night, and now the Inspectors wanted blood.

When a VAT inspector wants blood, Dracula starves.

Chris reined in, turned Mirabelle back towards the stands so that she could examine the last plain fence. Beside them, four other horses stood patiently while one, a flame chestnut, danced like an apprentice firewalker. Chris ran a hand down Mirabelle's neck, just soothing. 'You'll be all right, girl. You'll be OK . . .'

And so, in a way, he supposed, she would. Terry Colburn was a mouthy, flash, slimy prat (this assessment had nothing, Chris assured himself, to do with the fact that Terry Colburn had gone out with Sarah for two years), but there was no reason to suppose that he was cruel to animals. Terry was a hard-nosed business-man, however. Mirabelle would henceforth be ridden by tough professionals, ridden to win. And Terry would crow. That was what really stuck in the craw. Terry Colburn made roosters seem modest. He would crow and chortle and brag about 'my nag' and 'how he pulled Chris's fat out of the fire'.

Chris almost wished that Sarah had never swallowed her pride and sneaked off to Terry, seeking help. Terry had had all sorts of good reasons for refusing a loan 'things being what they are,' but 'tell you what,' he had said, 'I quite fancy that nag of his. Save you training fees and all. Give you forty grand for that . . .' Sarah had not even told Chris about the offer for two months, until the VAT man had started talking bankruptcy . . .

There was just this one last chance – this race. Chris had sold a watercolour and a pair of guns, cashed in his Premium Bonds. The whole lot would ride on Mirabelle today. If Sarah could get, say, 6–1 . . . ?

'Come on, old girl,' he murmured, and he turned her head. 'It's up to you.'

'Oh, for Christ's sakes, come *on*,' Sarah Lauderdale glanced at her watch. Five minutes to the off. Her half-clenched fist beat against the steering wheel. She flung back her heavy brunette hair. 'Oh, thank you *very* much.' She flung the VW dormobile into gear. She could see no parking space on the High Street. Very well, then, the Swan Hotel's car-park would have to do, and if any officious busybody tried to challenge her, he'd regret it.

Sarah was quite exceptionally angry. She told herself that it was all Chris's fault, and at times she believed it. She was angrier still at the murmuring thought that she might share the blame.

Chris had been impossible this morning – that stupid row over a parking space when they went to pick up the fish, his cheap jibes – 'of course the thing won't fit, woman. The Beetle that just came out had millimetres to spare. God, I'd trust Samson's eye sooner than yours! Ever think of taking up blues-singing for a living?' – but then Chris had been impossible ever since she had told him of Terry's offer.

Just why were men so pompous, so insecure in their manhood? So she had had a fling with Terry before she was married. So? Chris had won the day, hadn't he? And all right, Terry was brash, but he was funny – or, at least, he had been then. It was the logical thing to approach him. He was easily the richest of their acquaintances. And he had come up with the goods, hadn't he? What had Chris expected, a free gift of more than £30,000? She understood – she shared, even – Chris's distress at losing the horse, but if the sale of the horse kept the business afloat, the horse must go. However much that fact might hurt, it was no excuse for the constant bitter jibes about Terry, the constant snarling at her.

And then the meat order had come in all wrong, so she had had to rewrite the menu at short notice, and there had been those pigs who came in at lunchtime, ate their way through the menu, stayed on forever and then only complained, and now she was held up by aggressive morons on the road.

Sarah should not have been trusted with a nuclear bomb today.

She saw the opening in the contraflow and she shot through it, into the car-park of the ivy-clad hotel. There were plenty of big, gleaming cars here, including Terry's pale blue Roller. She could have been riding in that, instead of this scruffy little dormobile which was 'ideal' for school-runs, fetching and carrying provisions for the restaurant, cramped holidays in Cornwall . . .

She parked, unclipped the seat-belt, grabbed her bag and ran. If she didn't get this bet on, she reckoned that divorce or murder were the only options on this evening's *table d'hôte*.

She clutched the bag to her side as she ran out on to the pavement, jinking to avoid passers-by, past the jewellers and the shoe-shop, and into the betting-shop on the corner. She squinted up through the smoke at the clock. Three minutes to go. She swivelled round, grabbed a fiche, pulled out her pen and scrawled 'MIRABELLE £8,127 WIN'. She had pictured writing those words, had assumed that she would do so with trepidation or with a guilty thrill. She had time for neither. She scampered towards the counter. Ahead of her, an old woman with horsehair sprouting from her chin turned away, mumbling. She had laid her bet. A man in a grey suit stood at the sheet-glass now – dear God, it was Terry – and behind him a slight man in baggy cords and a flat cap.

'No, tell you what, doll,' she heard Terry, 'better safe than sorry, eh? Make that a grand on the nose and a monkey place, will you? Cover my tracks, that's the thing, isn't it? Oh, and, hold on. Got a few for the dogs at Hackney and all. Where'd I put it . . . ?'

Sarah was shifting from foot to foot with the urgency of one with a bursting bladder. She reached forward and clasped Terry's sleeve. 'Terry?' she pleaded.

He turned. His face was fleshier than in the old days, his belly fuller, but he still had that boyish grin, those pale, roguish eyes. 'Sarah! Hello, love. Good to see you!'

'Terry, quick, please. The race'll start . . .'

'Oh, sure, sure. No problems. Want to get a bet on old Chris, do you? Same here. Her old man's riding in this one,' he announced to the girl behind the counter. 'Right. Forget the dogs. Do them later.' He stepped to one side. The man in the cap took his place. Terry laid a hand on Sarah's arm. He bent to kiss her. 'Don't worry,' he said, 'they never start on time. Big bet?'

'Huge. Terrifying. Oh, not for you, perhaps, but for us.'

The woman behind the counter was saying, 'Will you be paying tax on that?'

The tannoy said, 'And they're away at Kempton.'

And Sarah's shoulders sank. She said, 'Oh, Jesus.' It was prayer, not profanity.

And they were away – a typical, straggling, spread-out start to a three-mile 'chase, and Mirabelle wanting to win it before it had begun, wanting to skip the boring business of running and jumping and simply to fly the course. Again Chris had to tell her, 'Not yet, girl,' and he tucked her in on the inside rail. Ahead of them, Nick Storr, the current champion, crouched on a washy bay. Two other animals were upsides, including the favourite, Clontarf, a beautiful, burly brown. A horse moved up at Chris's right. The rider was in blue with a yellow cap. He hummed as he rode.

The first fence, then. The horses up ahead rose. Divots were kicked up and spun past Chris's head. There was a ragged chorus of 'Yah!' and 'Garn!', a Velcro crackle as the animals' bellies dragged through the birch, then Chris and Mirabelle were on it. Chris counted the strides. One, two, three and . . .

There was silence then, and the fence was beneath them, behind them. Chris rocked forward as Mirabelle's hooves hacked into the damp turf. He gathered up the reins, ready to urge her on, but there was no need. She was a double handful today.

This was what made Monopoly unconvincing. You started to lose and just went on losing. The game did not take into account the possibility of a win on the pools, an inheritance from a distant aunt, a good thing at the races.

That chance was here, and now. And Mirabelle told him, clear as day, that, with his help, she would take it.

'Poor old you.' Terry kissed the top of Sarah's head. He released her slowly from his arms. 'Real bad luck, that.'

'Oh, God, Terry,' she sniffed, 'You don't know the half of it. It was his last chance to . . . He'll kill me. He'll never forgive me, anyhow.'

'Silly bugger, if you ask me.' Terry pulled the green silk handkerchief from his breast pocket and dabbed at her eyes.

'Should be counting his blessings, I reckon. I know I would be. Come on, now. Come and meet the lads. They'll cheer you up.' He put his arm about her shoulders. He steered her to where two men leaned against the wall. One, the older, wore a blazer and grey flannels. His hair was slick and grey as iron. The younger man was blond. He, like Terry, sported gold at his wrist and on his fingers. He wore denim, desert-boots and leather. She was introduced to them, vaguely gathered that the older man was called Sam and the younger Jim, vaguely smiled, vaguely nodded at their expressions of sympathy, but she had eyes now only for the screen high on the wall above the strand of smoke, for that figure in green and white, crouched on the white horse, both of them giving their all for a cause which was already lost.

She leaned back against Terry's chest because his arm was still around her and because what the hell. The ragged banter and laughter of the men around her was consoling and meaningless as the rattle of a tram.

Chris felt good. Mirabelle was jumping like a stag, had her ears pricked and was full of running. Three of the opposition had already fallen. Relax, he told himself. Enjoy this. If they were destined to lose, this would be his last race. As well to make the most of it.

Mirabelle careered up to the open ditch, and suddenly, too late, he realised that she had got it wrong, all wrong. She put in an extra short stride which brought her far too close to the ditch. She leaned back and skidded almost to a halt. It was his fault, but he pretended to blame her. It was all that he could do. He raised his whip and gave her a crack down her off quarters. She rose to the fence almost vertically, scraped through the top with a jolt which slammed Chris's teeth together and rocked him forward so that he mouthed mane, and, with a deep grunt, descended as steeply.

For a moment then, as her off foreleg buckled, there was nothing between Chris and the hoof-pocked turf, and a giant, invisible hand seemed to be heaving upward at the seat of his breeches. On either side, other horses were landing. Somewhere down to their right, a thud and a puff and a rattle told of a faller. Mirabelle raised her head. Her neck hit Chris hard in the mouth. He recoiled from the blow, and suddenly he was back in the saddle, and Mirabelle was running again. Chris wiped mud or blood from his nose. His vision was smeared. He heard his voice like someone else's. 'Come on, come on, come on!'

'Come *on*!' Terry roared, 'Call that riding? Jeez, that's my chunk of horseflesh he's risking, not to mention my money. Gawd, I mean . . . !'

'Goes on a bit, doesn't it?' said Jim. 'Thought it'd be all over in a minute or two.'

'Nah. That's Flat you're thinking of.'

'Races are shorter there, are they?'

'Course they are. God, you can tell Jim here's a computer man. No. Jumping, they go up to four-and-a-half miles, like the National. Flat, well, the longest race under Jockey Club Rules is the Newmarket Town Plate. Three miles, six furlongs, and that's a one-off.'

'Oh,' said Jim.

Sarah nestled closer to Terry. She opened her eyes wide and looked up at him, admiring. 'Are you sure about that, Terry?' she said, and her voice was husky.

'Course I am! Common knowledge. Won't get me on racing. God, I should've been the rider round here. Would have been, if it hadn't been for my skiing accident. No. No question.'

'Oh, I thought there was one longer race under Jockey Club Rules.'

'Nope.'

'Oh, well. I don't know much about this sort of thing, but I'll tell you what. I've got to bet on something. Fat lot of good this money'll do me now.'

'Don't worry! I'll always look after my girl!' Terry hugged her tight.

'Yeah, but let's just have a bet, shall we? Just so as I can say I've had one. You guys game?'

They smiled indulgently. They looked from one to the other. And they shrugged.

Mirabelle swung round into the straight. There were four horses still ahead, but two of them had their ears back and were running down their fences. They were hers for the taking. Otherwise, there were just Clontarf, still bowling along like the gutsy old trouper he was, two lengths ahead, and Nick Storr on the bay at Mirabelle's right shoulder.

And if it was lese-majesty to take on such august competition, Chris decided, he and Mirabelle were about to commit high treason . . .

'The what?' had been the first reaction, then 'You have got to be joking!' A trip to the library had settled matters. Then it was a mildly resentful 'Oh, very clever, young lady,' from Sam, a 'Well, I'll be . . .' from Jim, and a hug from Terry, who, having won almost eight thousand on the race, was content to part with half of it.

'The Boat Race,' she had simply said, and the point had been established. The Newmarket Town Plate, she had falteringly and fetchingly explained, was too old to be run under Jockey Club Rules. The Oxford and Cambridge Boat Race, however, when founded, had, for want of any other adjudicators, been placed in the hands of the Jockey Club, and she was very sorry to take their money from them, but . . .

They had walked back to the Swan, where a few gins and a lot of smiles had done much to appease them. At last, and reluctantly, Sarah had announced that she must go. There were the children to be collected, and the preparation of dinner to be supervised. The three men had accompanied her to the door out to the car park. It was there that the idea had struck her. 'Why don't you guys come out to dinner tonight?' she had asked. 'We can celebrate. My treat.' There was a murmur of appreciative agreement. 'Oh, and Terry?'

'Hmm?'

'You and I can have a little word in private, OK?'

Terry had clenched his fist and made a little punching gesture which he accompanied with an exhaled 'Yes!'

Sarah had smiled.

She had a boy of her own.

When Chris returned to the restaurant, it was after midnight. Starting price had proved to be 15–2, and he had been celebrating not wisely but just a little too well. He had telephoned four times on the long journey home. On each occasion, he had been informed that Mrs Lauderdale was unavailable. On each occasion, he had taken the opportunity to have a couple of jars. Now, therefore, as he paid off the taxi-driver and surveyed the floodlit car park, he rocked slightly, heel to toe. The car park was empty. The lights and the music from the restaurant were switched off. Only one light yet burned, and that was the light in his and Sarah's room.

As the taxi drove off, he fumbled for the keys in his pocket and, lurching slightly, made his way across the deep gravel to the dark yard and the private door to their upstairs quarters.

He felt well pleased with himself. Mirabelle was his. He was going to beg Sarah's pardon for all his ill-tempered outbursts. Terry Bloody Colburn could take a running jump. It looked as though recession was on its way out. Life was going to be happy again.

He bumped into a car.

He swayed around it, but he kept bumping into it. There was an awful lot of car there. It took up half the yard. He reached for his lighter, and, at the fourth attempt, managed to obtain a flame. It showed him pale blue coachwork. He winced. He said, 'What?' He felt his way along it to the front. His hand hit something cold, something knobbly. Again he squatted down, again flicked the lighter.

The Spirit of Ecstasy.

He started to tremble.

It was too late to beg Sarah's pardon. She had taken her own revenge.

Terry Colburn was up there, now. He had tried for the girl but lost her. He had made money instead. He had tried for the horse but had lost her. He had won the girl instead.

There was enough of his ancestors in Chris to make him want to murder both of them, but there was enough of justice in him to acknowledge that, though it was cruel, it was, at least in part, his due. Sarah had had to put up with a life of hard work and relative poverty, knowing that she might have travelled first class. On top of all that, she had had to cope with a man who was bloody and resentful and unfair.

It had all proved too much.

He wanted to murder her, then, and say sorry afterwards, or murder her and hug her at the same time.

Suddenly the horse did not matter that much, nor the restaurant, nor scoring off Terry Colburn.

Had he driven home, he might simply have driven away again, but the night was cold, the taxi gone and the spirit of his ancestors curious as well as vengeful . . . He let himself in, therefore, and wearily trudged up the stairs. He was English, so he made no attempt to pad up quietly. He opened the door at the top of the stairs, switched on the hall light, hung up his coat, coughed loudly, then walked heavily into the sitting-room. 'Hello? Sarah, darling?' he called. 'Hi. It's me.'

He poured himself a whisky with shoulders, and slumped into the nearest chair. This would take a lot of working out.

There were soft, whispering sounds from next door. The Spirit of Ecstasy, Chris thought. He sipped and shuddered. He waited.

Sarah appeared in the doorway. She wore nothing but an oversize Guinness T-shirt. Her hair and skin had a whispy halo in the light. She looked very slender, very beautiful. She said, 'Hi, darling. Well done.' She gulped. 'I'm going to say this quickly or I'll never dare to say it. I'm afraid – I never got the bet on.'

'It doesn't matter,' he rasped. 'It's OK. I was planning to come home and say sorry I've been such a sod, but I suppose I've left it a bit too late. I'd better . . . Could you lend me your car?'

She cocked her head. She frowned. 'What? Why? What are you on about?'

'I'm not blind, or stupid,' he said. 'I bumped into a rather large Roller out there. It's all right. I probably deserved it. Anyhow, I'd rather not stay, if it's all the same to you.'

She walked very slowly towards him. Her eyes were amused. She was thinking. Suddenly, those eyes turned hard as marbles. 'You're right,' she said. 'Right.' She swept some keys down off the mantel and tossed them into his lap. 'Take my car.'

'That's it?' He stood and drained his drink.

'That's it.' She shrugged.

'Right . . . Well . . . OK. See you in the morning.'

'Whenever.'

He nodded. He turned back to the door, and it must have been the whisky, or perhaps the race, which had caused everything to go all smudged. He trudged slowly towards the door.

'Chris?'

He walked on.

'Chris, darling?'

'What?' he managed.

'You are blind and you are stupid. Did you really mean it, about not minding that I didn't get the bet on?'

He did not turn. 'Of course I bloody meant it.'

'So look at the keys.'

He had difficulty in looking, but he managed in the end, thanks to a speck of dust, which had got caught in his eye and which he had to rub away. He swung round, suspecting further humiliation. 'No? Stop playing games, for God's sake,' he pleaded. 'I may have been a prat, but I haven't deserved this. These are . . . these are . . . *his* keys, aren't they?'

She leaned provocatively against the wall on one elbow, which caused the T-shirt to rise above the PG level. 'No, you idiot,' she grinned. 'Believe it or not, they're yours.'

And afterwards, in bed, with £20 notes liberally sprinkled about the carpet, he murmured, 'Come on, Tell me.'

'Well, you tell me, eagle eyes. Which is longer, a VW Beetle or our dormobile?'

'The dormobile, of course.'

'Fancy a bet on that? Your car for a £100,000 Rolls?'

He pondered, then he grinned, and kissed her. She said, 'Ever think about taking up blues-singing for a living? Bumper to bumper, the Beetle is two and a half per cent longer.'

'You're kidding.'

She shook her head. 'I measured them.'

He kissed her nose, her chin, her throat. He whispered, 'Darling?'

'Mmm?'

'Why did you choose me when you could have had that canny shyster?'

She laughed from somewhere deep down within her. 'Try two and a half per cent,' she said.

En Famille

ED GORMAN

This final story of gambling and the influence it can have on those who are absorbed by it is quite unlike any other I have come across in racing fiction. It is the dramatic and moving tale of a compulsive gambler as seen through the eyes of his small son and the effects that the days they spend together at the races have on his own subsequent life. Although author Ed Gorman is not a racing man, he did ride horses as a child and has first-hand experience of overwhelming compulsions in both the life of his father as well as in his own. Born in the Midwest of America, he has spent much of his time in Cedar Rapids, Iowa, a locality that has also had a big influence on his writing. He recalls with great candour, 'I remember living on a farm where I would ride my uncle's horses every day. And I remember my mother and father, whose only real problem was my father's drinking. Years later, this became a problem for me and my first wife, too.' Gorman's subsequent fiction has often reflected his tough childhood as a boy who suffered injury in a car accident that made him very much of a loner and, equally, the dark and often dangerous Midwest countryside all around his home. Both elements will be found in 'En Famille'.

Gorman grew up in a working-class Catholic background where, he says, the uncertainty of his parent's marriage and the fact he got expelled from school for fighting, made him 'a rather pessimistic guy'. He then worked in advertising for twenty years as a writer and director of commercials, often promoting people and products he hated. In 1985 he drew on his long-standing fascination with crime and detective stories to start the now highly regarded *Mystery Scene* magazine; but it was not until he was into his forties that he seriously began writing his own fiction.

477

Success came slowly, but his reputation has now been made with the series of Jack Dwyer private eye novels inspired by the work of John D. MacDonald, and his superb thrillers, *Blood Red Moon* (1992) and *Cold Blue Midnight* (1994). Gorman is today regarded as one of the masters of the detective story genre and was praised even higher in an issue of the English magazine *Million*, which is devoted to popular fiction, as 'one of the world's best storytellers'. His story which follows, of obsessive gambling and its after-effects, will, I guarantee, leave a chill up the spine that remains long after the book itself has been closed.

*

By the time I was eight years old, I'd fallen disconsolately in love with any number of little girls who had absolutely no interest in me. These were little girls I'd met in all the usual places, school, playground, neighborhood.

Only the girl I met at the racetrack took any interest in me. Her name was Wendy and, like me, she was brought to the track three or four times a week by her father, after school in the autumn months, during working hours in the summer.

Ours was one of those impossibly romantic relationships that only a young boy can have (all those nights of kissing pillows while pretending it was her – this accompanied by one of those swelling romantic songs you hear in movies with Ingrid Bergman and Cary Grant – how vulnerable and true and beautiful she always was in my mind's perfect eye). I first saw her the spring of my ninth year, and not until I was fifteen did we even say hello to each other, even though we saw each other at least three times a week. But she was always with me, this girl I thought about constantly, and dreamed of nightly, the melancholy little blonde with the slow sad blue eyes and the quick sad smile.

I knew all about the sadness I saw in her. It was my sadness, too. Our fathers brought us to the track in order to make their gambling more palatable to our mothers. How much of a vice could it be if you took the little one along? The money lost at the track meant rent going unpaid, grocery store credit cut off, the telephone frequently disconnected. It also meant arguing. No matter how deeply I hid in the closet, no matter how many pillows I put over my head, I could still hear them shrieking at each other. Sometimes he hit her. Once he even pushed her down the stairs and she broke her leg. Despite all this, I wanted them to stay together. I was terrified they would split up. I loved them both beyond imagining. Don't ask me why I loved him so much. I have no idea.

The day we first spoke, the little girl and I, that warm May afternoon in my fifteenth year, a black eye spoiled her very pretty, very pale little face. So he'd finally gotten around to hitting her. My father had gotten around to hitting me years ago. They got so frustrated over their gambling, their inability to *stop* their gambling, that they grabbed the first person they found and visited all their despair on him.

She was coming up from the seats in the bottom tier where she and her father always sat. I saw her and stepped out into the aisle.

'Hi,' I said after more than six years of us watching each other from afar.

'Hi.'

'I'm sorry about your eye.'

'He was pretty drunk. He doesn't usually get violent. But it seems to be getting worse lately.' She looked back at her seats. Her father was glaring at us. 'I'd better hurry. He wants me to get him a hot dog.'

'I'd like to see you sometime.'

She smiled, sad and sweet with her black eye. 'Yeah, me too.'

I saw her the rest of the summer but we never again got the chance to speak. Nor did we make the opportunity. She was my narcotic. I thought of no one else, wanted no one else. The girls at school had no idea what my home life was like, how old and worn my father's gambling had made my mother, how anxious and angry it had made me. Only Wendy understood.

Wendy Wendy Wendy. By now, my needs having evolved, she was no longer just the pure dream of a forlorn boy. I wanted her carnally, too. She'd become a beautiful young woman.

Near the end of that summer an unseasonable rainy grayness filled the skies. People at the track took to wearing winter coats. A few races had to be called off. Wendy and her father suddenly vanished.

I looked for them every day, and every night trudged home feeling betrayed and bereft. 'Can't find your little girl friend?' my father said. He thought it was funny.

Then one night, while I was in my bedroom reading a science fiction magazine, he shouted: 'Hey! Get out here! Your girl friend's on TV!'

And so she was.

'Police announce an arrest in the murder of Myles Larkin, who was found stabbed to death in his car last night. They have taken Larkin's only child, sixteen-year-old Wendy, into custody and formally charged her with the murder of her father.'

I went twice to see her but they wouldn't let me in. Finally, I learned the name of her lawyer, lied that I was a shirt-tail cousin, and he took me up to the cold concrete visitors' room on the top floor of city jail.

Even in the drab uniform the prisoners wore, she looked lovely in her bruised and wan way.

'Did he start beating you up again?' I asked.

'No.'

'Did he start beating up your mother?'

'No.'

'Did he lose his job or get you evicted?'

She shook her head. 'No. It was just that I couldn't take it any more. I mean, he wasn't losing any more or any less money at the track, it was just I – I snapped. I don't know how else to explain it. It was like I saw what he'd done to our lives and I – I snapped. That's all – I just snapped.'

She served seven years in a minimum-security women's prison upstate during which time my parents were killed in an automobile accident, I finished college, got married, had a child and took up the glamorous and adventurous life of a tax consultant. My wife Donna knew about my mental and spiritual ups and downs. Her father had been an abusive alcoholic.

I didn't see Wendy until twelve years later, when I was sitting at the track with my seven-year-old son. He didn't always like going to the track with me – my wife didn't like me going to the track at all – so I'd had to fortify him with the usual comic books, candy and a pair of 'genuine' Dodgers sunglasses.

Between races, I happened to look down at the seats Wendy and her father usually took, and there she was. Something about the cock of her head told me it was her.

'Can we go, Dad?' my son Rob said. 'It's so boring here.'

Boring? I'd once tried to explain to his mother how good I felt when I was at the track. I was not the miserable, frightened, self-effacing owner of Advent Tax Systems (some system – me and my low-power Radio Shack computer and software). No. . . . when I was at the track I felt strong and purposeful and optimistic, and frightened of nothing at all. I was pure potential – potential for winning the easy cash that was the mark of men who were successful with women, and with their competitors, and with their own swaggering dreams.

'Please, Dad. It's really boring here. Honest.'

But all I could see, all I could think about, was Wendy. I hadn't seen her since my one visit to jail. Then I noticed that she, too, had a child with her, a very proper-looking little blonde girl whose head was cocked at the odd and fetching angle so favored by her mother.

We saw each other a dozen more times before we spoke.

Then: 'I knew I'd see you again someday.'

Wan smile. 'All those years I was in prison, I wasn't so sure.' Her daughter came up to her then and Wendy said: 'This is Margaret.'

'Hello, Margaret. Glad to meet you. This is my son Rob.'

With the great indifference only children can summon, they nodded hellos.

'We just moved back to the city,' Wendy explained. 'I thought I'd show Margaret where I used to come with my father.' She mentioned her father so casually, one would never have guessed that she'd murdered the man.

Ten more times we saw each other, children in tow, before our affair began.

April 6 of that year was the first time we ever made love, this in a motel where the sunset was the color of blood in the window, and a woman two rooms away wept inconsolably. I had the brief fantasy that it was my wife in that room.

'Do you know how long I've loved you?' she said.

'Oh, God, you don't know how good it is to hear that.'

'Since I was eight years old.'

'For me, since I was nine.'

'This would destroy my husband if he ever found out.'

'The same with my wife.'

'But I have to be honest.'

'I want you to be honest.'

'I don't care what it does to him. I just want to be with you.'

In December of that year, my wife Donna discovered a lump in her right breast. Two weeks later she received a double mastectomy and began chemotherapy.

She lived nine years, and my affair with Wendy extended over the entire time. Early on, both our spouses knew about our relationship. Her husband, an older and primmer man than I might have expected, stopped by my office one day in his new BMW and threatened to destroy my business. He claimed to have great influence in the financial community.

My wife threatened to leave me but she was too weak. She had one of those cancers that did not kill her but that never left her alone, either. She was weak most of the time, staying for days in the bedroom that had become hers, as the guest room had become mine. Whenever she became particularly angry about Wendy, Rob would fling himself at me, screaming how much he hated me, pounding me with fists that became more powerful with each passing year. He hated me for many of the same reasons I'd hated my own father, my ineluctable passion for the track, and the way there was never any security in our lives, the family bank account wholly subject to the whims of the horses that ran that day.

Wendy's daughter likewise blamed her mother for the alcoholism that had stricken the husband. There was constant talk of divorce but their finances were such that neither of them could quite afford it. Margaret constantly called Wendy a whore, and only lately did Wendy realize that Margaret sincerely meant it.

Two things happened the next year. My wife was finally

dragged off into the darkness, and Wendy's husband crashed his car into a retaining wall and was killed.

Even on the days of the respective funerals, we went to the track.

'He never understood.'

'Neither did she,' I said.

'I mean why I come here.'

'I know.'

'I mean how it makes me feel alive.'

'I know.'

'I mean how nothing else matters.'

'I know.'

'I should've been nicer to him, I suppose.'

'I suppose. But we can't make a life out of blaming ourselves. What's happened, happened. We have to go on from here.'

'Do you think Rob hates you as much as Margaret hates me?'

'More, probably,' I said. 'The way he looks at me sometimes, I think he'll probably kill me someday.'

But it wasn't me who was to die.

All during Wendy's funeral, I kept thinking of those words. Margaret had murdered her mother just as Wendy had killed her father. The press made a lot of this.

All the grief I should have visited upon my dead wife I visited upon my dead lover. I went through months of alcoholic stupor. Clients fell away; rent forced me to move from our nice suburban home to a small apartment in a section of the city that always seemed to be on fire. I didn't have to worry about Rob any more. He got enough loans for college and wanted nothing to do with me.

Years and more years, the track the only constant in my life. Many times I tried to contact Rob through the alumni office of his school but it was no use. He'd left word not to give his current address to his father.

There was the hospital, and, several times, the detox clinic. There was the church in which I asked for forgiveness, and the born again rally at which I proclaimed my happiness in the Lord.

And then there was the shelter. Five years I lived there, keeping the place painted and clean for the other residents. The nuns seemed to like me.

My teeth went entirely, and I had to have dentures. The arthritis in my foot got so bad that I could not wear shoes for days at a time. And my eyesight, beyond even the magic of glasses, got so bad that when I watched the horse races on TV, I couldn't tell which horse was which.

Then one night I got sick and threw up blood and in the morning one of the sisters took me to the hospital where they kept me overnight. In the morning the doctor came in and told me that I had stomach cancer. He gave me five months to live.

There were days when I was happy about my death sentence. Looking back, my life seemed so long and sad, I was glad to have it over with. Then there were days when I sobbed about my death sentence, and hated the God the nuns told me to pray to. I wanted to live to go back to the track again and have a sweet, beautiful winner.

Four months after the doctor's diagnosis, the nuns put me in bed and I knew I'd never walk on my own again. I thought of Donna, and her death, and how I'd made it all the worse with the track and Wendy.

The weaker I got, the more I thought about Rob. I talked about him to the nuns. And then one day he was there.

He wasn't alone, either. With him was a very pretty dark-haired woman and a seven-year old boy who got the best features of both his mother and father.

'Dad, this is Mae and Stephen.'

'Hello, Mae and Stephen. I'm very glad to meet you. I wish I was better company.'

'Don't worry about that,' Mae said. 'We're just happy to meet you.'

'I need to go to the bathroom,' Stephen said.

'Why don't I take him, and give you a few minutes alone with your dad?' Mae said.

And so, after all these years, we were alone and he said, 'I still can't forgive you, Dad.'

'I don't blame you.'

'I want to. But somehow I can't.'

I took his hand. 'I'm just glad you turned out so well, son. Like your mother and not your father.'

'I loved her very much.'

'I know you did.'

'And you treated her very, very badly.'

All his anger. All these years.

'That's a beautiful wife and son you've got.'

'They're my whole life, everything that matters to me.'

I started crying; I couldn't help it. Here at the end I was glad to know he'd done well for himself and his family.

'I love you, Rob.'

'I love you, too, Dad.'

And then he leaned down and kissed me on the cheek and I started crying harder and embarrassed both of us.

Mae and Stephen came back.

'My turn,' Rob said. He patted me on the shoulder. 'I'll be back soon.'

I think he wanted to cry but wanted to go somewhere alone to do it.

'So,' Mae said, 'are you comfortable?'

'Oh, very.'

'This seems like a nice place.'

'It is.'

'And the nuns seem very nice, too.'

'Very nice.' I smiled. 'I'm just so glad I got to see you two.'

'Same here. I've wanted to meet you for years.'

'Well,' I said, smiling. 'I'm glad the time finally came.'

Stephen, proper in his white shirt and blue trousers and neatly combed dark hair, said, 'I just wish you could go to the track with us sometime, Grandpa.'

She didn't have to say anything. I saw it all in the quick certain pain that appeared in her lovely gray eyes.

'The race track, you mean?' I said.

'Uh-huh. Dad takes me all the time, doesn't he, Mom?'

'Oh, yes,' she said, her voice toneless. 'All the time.'

She started to say more but then the door opened up and Rob came in and there was no time to talk.

There was no time at all.

Acknowledgements

The editor is grateful to the following authors, agents and publishers for permission to include copyright stories in this collection: William Heinemann Ltd for the extract 'Under Starter's Orders' by John Masefield from *Right Royal* and 'Had A Horse' by John Galsworthy; John Johnson Literary Agency and Michael Joseph Ltd for 'The Protection Racket' by Dick Francis; the Author's Estate for 'Won By A Neck' by Leslie Charteris; The Executors of Frank Johnson for 'The American Invasion'; Victor Gollancz Ltd for 'A Derby Horse' by Michael Innes; A. M. Heath Literary Agency for 'The Horse That Died of Shame' by Peter Tremayne; Curtis Brown Literary Agency for 'Murder on the Race Course' by Julian Symons; Hodder Headline Publishing Group for 'The Body in the Horsebox' from *Eavesdropper* by John Francome and 'The Later Edition' by Victor Bridges; Mirror Group Newspapers for 'Calling the Tune' by Steve Donoghue; The Estate of Jack Fairfax-Blakeborough for 'Nat Wedgewood Trapped'; Jon Tuska and the Golden West Literary Agency for 'Thoroughbred' by Max Brand; Random Publishing Group and Jonathan Cape Ltd for 'My Old Man' by Ernest Hemingway; Davis Publications Inc for 'Saratoga in August' by Hugh Pentecost, 'The Photographer and the Jockey' by James Holding, 'Something Short of Murder' by Henry Slesar, and 'Born Gambler' by Thomas Walsh; International Scripts for 'Ellen Keegan's Revenge' by Mary Ryan and 'En Famille' by Ed Gorman; Constable Publishers Ltd for 'A Story Goes With It' by Damon Runyon; Pearson Publishing Group for 'Morning in the High Street' by Barre Lyndon; Hughes Massie Ltd for 'The Crackler' by Agatha Christie from *Partners in Crime*; *Inside Racing* magazine and the author for 'Two and a Half Per Cent' by

Mark Daniel. While every effort has been made to contact the copyright holders of material used in this collection in the case of any accidental infringement, concerned parties are asked to contact the editor in care of the publishers.